Emily had started working for the McGillbys when she was ten. It had only been week-ends then, Friday night from five till eight, and from eight on a Saturday morning till two in the afternoon, and her wage had been sixpence a week, and she knew she was lucky. Even on washing and baking days when she was never off her feet from six in the morning till half past nine at night, and she got undressed with her eyes closed, she would still maintain that she was lucky. But whenever she stressed this point to herself she knew it wasn't only because of the good food and the fact that she was now running the house single-handed, or because of Mr. McGillby's kindness towards her, which was no small thing, but it was because she had a room to herself, a bed to herself, a chest of drawers to herself, some place in which she could be alone and where she could lie and think.

Catherine Cookson

The Tide of Life

CORGI BOOKS
A DIVISION OF TRANSWORLD PUBLISHERS LTD

THE TIDE OF LIFE

A CORGI BOOK 0 552 11202 X

Originally published in Great Britain by
William Heinemann Ltd.

PRINTING HISTORY
William Heinemann edition published 1976
Corgi edition published 1977
Corgi edition reissued 1978
Corgi edition reprinted 1978 (twice)
Corgi reissued 1979
Corgi reprinted 1979
Corgi edition reprinted 1980 (twice)

This book is set in Baskerville 10/11½ pt.

Corgi Books are published by Transworld Publishers Ltd.
Century House, 61–63 Uxbridge Road,
Ealing, London W5 5SA.

Made and printed in the United States of America
by Arcata Graphics
Buffalo, New York

To Harold Stinton, and to his son John
for whom I wrote my first boy's story.

CONTENTS

LIFE COMES IN LIKE THE TIDE
ON A ROAR FROM THE SEA BED,

And is already dying before its ebb.
Existence is the time it takes for the shingle to be wet,
And yet,
Are they deluded,
Do they lie,
Those blind with courage
Who about above the spray,
Never say die?

C. C.

PART ONE
SEP

ONE

'You nearly ready for the road, Emily?'

'Yes, Mr McGillby.'

'That's it then. And it's a nice day, so enjoy yourself. Take a walk in the park and see the ducks on the pond.'

They looked straight at each other and smiled, the thirty-five-year-old ruddy-faced man and the sixteen-year-old girl whose mass of light brown hair just missed being blonde and who, for all her youth, already wore it in the adult mode of a screwed bun on the back of her head. She was tall for sixteen and showing promise of a good figure. As yet, however, it wasn't the figure that most people noticed, but something about her face; not because it was beautiful, even though the thick rims of eyelashes lent a depth to her already dark brown eyes; nor was it her wide-lipped mouth; nor yet the warm tint of her skin; for their combination did not as yet spell beauty, but what without question, they did combine to was an overall brightness as if the face were illuminated from within.

Sep McGillby often thought about his maid of all work's face, describing it to himself as a glad face; and this he considered to be the right description because she was glad about so many things; and she would say so; and she would also say she was very lucky. 'Eeh! Mr McGillby I am lucky to be workin' here.' Or, 'Eeh! Mr McGillby, I'm glad it's a fine day for you; it's awful when you've got to work out in the wet.' There was one thing certain, you could never be dull where she was.

He had been made to wonder too, of late, what life in this house would have been like without her; she had become like a beloved daughter.

He turned away from her now, saying, 'You'll look in on the missis before you go, won't you?'

'Oh! aye, of course, Mr McGillby. Of course.'

'Away you go then.'

Emily did not immediately make for the stairs that led upwards from behind a door at the far end of the kitchen, but she watched her employer moving towards the front room, and when he had closed the door she rolled up her sleeves and went into the scullery. There, turning on the single tap, she ran some water into a tin dish that stood in the shallow brown earthenware sink, then washed her face with the blue-mottled soap, the same that she used for scrubbing the floors, and with damp hands smoothed down her hair from its middle parting in an attempt to make it conform, for it was the most unruly hair, and bits of it would keep springing out from her bun and from behind her ears. This worried her because Mrs McGillby didn't approve of hair that wouldn't stay put.

When she had come out from the scullery and was crossing the kitchen towards the staircase door she was arrested by a peculiar smell, peculiar that was to this particular house. She looked towards the sitting-room door for a moment, then bit on her lip to stop herself from grinning widely. Mr McGillby was indulging in a smoke. She hoped he had the sense to open the window, because if that smell wafted upstairs there would be skin and hair flying. Well, not skin and hair. Mrs McGillby didn't row, that was she didn't shout, but she had a way of saying things that had the same effect on the listener as if she were bawling.

She now ran on tiptoe to the end of the kitchen and

gently eased the bottom window upwards for about six inches or so. That was another thing that wouldn't have been allowed if Mrs McGillby had been on her feet; the windows were never opened because of the dust.

She paused again as she made her way to the stairs, her eyes slanted towards the sitting-room door while wondering yet again where he hid his baccy. She hadn't found a place in the room that he could use as a hidey-hole, and he wouldn't have dared carry it about on him because Mrs McGillby had a nose like a ferret.

She went quietly up the steep dark stairs now to the small landing, which had a door on each side. The right-hand door led into Mr and Mrs McGillby's bedroom, the left one into her own room. Once inside her room she squeezed past the iron bedstead and towards the chest of drawers that was wedged between the foot of the bed and the window-sill.

Opening the top drawer, she took out a clean blue print frock. Divesting herself of her bibless holland apron, striped blouse, and serge skirt, she got into the dress; then she changed her house slippers for a pair of boots, their ugliness being almost hidden by the hem of the dress.

From the second drawer she took out a straw hat and two long hatpins, and when she had secured them in the hat it sat dead straight across the top of her head. She now lifted her coat off a nail on the back of the door and put it on. Lastly, she took out a clean handkerchief from a box on the top of the chest of drawers, together with a brown worn leather purse. This she opened, looked at her week's wages of one and sixpence, which again aroused in her the thought of how lucky she was; then snapping the purse closed and holding it and the clean handkerchief in her hand, she went out of the room, took the three steps across the landing, tapped on the bedroom door before entering and saying with a smile, 'I'm ready for off, Mrs McGillby. Is there anythin' you want doin' afore I go?'

Nancy McGillby was propped up in bed. She had been propped up in bed for two years now and she took it calmly because it was God's will. God had seen fit to give her a complaint. Why, she didn't question, but believed firmly that the answer would be given to her when she entered the other life—in the mansion He had prepared for her all knowledge would be hers and the rewards for her suffering and patience would be bountiful.

In answer to Emily's enquiry Mrs McGillby said, 'Let me see if you're tidy,' and on this Emily walked towards the window and stood, her arms extended from her sides, before turning slowly about. It was when Mrs McGillby viewed her back that she said with a note in her voice that spoke of patience tried to the edge of endurance. 'That hair! You'd imagine I'd never spoken to you about it. I've told you to wet it to keep it down, haven't I?'

'Yes, Mrs McGillby, but it dries.'

'Well, there's only one thing for it, if you can't keep it under control you'll have to have it cut off.'

Each feature on Emily's face seemed to stretch; the gladness was wiped from it. She gabbled now, 'Eeh! no, Mrs McGillby, don't say that. I'll see to it, I will; an' I'll snip off all the frizzy bits that stick out, I will.'

Mrs McGillby sighed deeply, lifted the frill of her calico nightdress further up under her chin, then smoothed the sheet that covered the edge of the quilt with her two transparent looking hands before saying, 'Get along now. But be back mind in time for the prayer meeting. I don't want you running up the stairs at the last minute like last Sunday. You understand?'

'Yes, Mrs McGillby, I'll be here on time. Good-bye, Mrs McGillby.' She almost retreated backwards out of the room.

On the landing she paused for a moment and pressed

her hand across her mouth, and it was still there when she closed the staircase door and entered the kitchen, where Sep McGillby, turning from raking some coal from the back of the grate on to the open fire, paused with the rake in his hand and, straightening his back, said, 'What is it? What's up?'

'Nothing, nothing, Mr McGillby.'

'Come on. Come on.' He laid the rake down against the edge of the brass-railed high steel fender, then came towards her, saying under his breath, 'The missis? What's she been saying to you?'

'Noth ... nothing.'

'Tell me.'

'It's ... Well, it's about me hair. She said if I don't keep it down flat I'll have to have it cut off, and I can't keep it flat.'

'She said what!' He glanced up towards the ceiling, his square blunt-featured face screwed up in an unusual show of anger, which made Emily defend her mistress's threat, saying, 'Well, she's right an' all, Mr McGillby, because it does flap all over the place, the ends. Anyway, I said I'd snip it off ... I mean the ends.'

'You'll do no such thing.' He was bending towards her now, his face within inches of hers. 'Don't you snip off one single hair of your head. Do you hear me?'

She drew her chin in and pushed her head back in order to see him better, for he had never used that tone of voice to her before, and she'd never seen him look like this before.

After a moment he straightened up, and with the edge of his forefinger he wiped the spittle from his lips; then his expression changing to a more recognizable one, he nodded at her and said, 'Go on, get yourself along. But mind what I've told you, leave your hair alone.'

'Yes, Mr McGillby. Thanks, ta.' She backed from him now, nodding and smiling, until she reached the back door, when, her face lighting up, she said, 'Ta-rah, Mr McGillby,' and for answer, he said, 'Ta-rah. Emily. Enjoy yourself.'

The McGillbys' house was fortunately placed, so considered Emily, for it was in the middle of a short street facing the river, and they had only one neighbour, a Mrs Gantry, a widow woman who was stone deaf. If you were standing with your back to the river and looking at the street you wouldn't think there were any ordinary houses in it at all, for on either side of the McGillbys' and Mrs Gantry's houses there were warehouses, and below the warehouse adjoining Mrs Gantry's was a lock-up grocery shop, and below that a chapel. To the side of the warehouse flanking the McGillbys' was a cold meat store, and at the very end of the street, which was named Pilot Place, was a second-hand furniture shop, the windows of which extended around the corner into Nile Street. Nile Street was long, and by virtue of the fact alone that the houses were of the two-up and two-down variety they were of much lower class than the two select dwellings in Pilot Place, for both these houses boasted, besides a large kitchen and scullery, a sitting room and two bedrooms. Moreover, there was a cold tap inside the scullery; and that was something to be proud of.

This latter miracle had been brought about by the manipulations of Mr McGillby. The word was his. Six months ago he had said, 'I am going to have that tap brought from the bottom of the yard and put inside the scullery. A little manipulation here and there, and there'll be no more lugging buckets up in the snow.' And he had gone on to explain the word. 'People can be manipulated you know, Emily,' he had said, 'with a backhander.' He had demonstrated by scratching the palm of one hand with the middle finger of the other.

Emily had started working for the McGillbys when she was ten. It had been only week-ends then, Friday night

17

from five till eight, and from eight on a Saturday morning till two in the afternoon, and her wage had been sixpence. But the very day she left school she started full time and living in, with a wage of one and sixpence a week, and she knew she was lucky. Even on washing and baking days when she was never off her feet from half-past six in the morning till half-past nine at night, and she got undressed for bed with her eyes closed, she would still maintain she was lucky. But whenever she stressed this point to herself she knew it wasn't only because of the good food and the fact that she was now running the house single-handed, or because of Mr McGillby's kindness towards her, which was no small thing, but it was because she had a room to herself, a bed to herself, a chest of drawers to herself, some place in which she could be alone and where she could lie and think. Only she hadn't much time to lie and think. Still, that wasn't the point. It was the wonder of sleeping by herself, not having to share the bed with three others; not having toe-nails scratching your legs if you attempted to stretch them out; and not having to listen to the coughing, spluttering, snoring, and the cursing of six children who were in no way related to her, yet whom she was told almost weekly it was her duty to help support, simply because Lucy, her blood sister, was still at school. It was no use telling Alice Broughton that their father left his half-pay note to support Lucy; Alice Broughton just shouted you down and declared she was as good as the wife to John Kennedy and mistress of his house.

It was ten minutes' walk from Pilot Place to Creador Street, and it was a nice walk, Emily considered, when like today the sun was shining on the river to the left of her and a big steamer with the smoke coming out of its two funnels was making down river for the opening between the piers.

At a certain point on the road she turned sharply right

and away from the river, walked along a street of respectable houses, then into a main road, from which jutted a series of less respectable ones; then down into King Street. Here she took a short cut through a maze of small streets.

It being Sunday, the whole town seemed bereft of adults, and when she came to it, Creador Street was no exception. There were numerous children playing in the back lanes and in the front gutters. Girls were playing the summer game of bays, hopping on one leg, their bare foot pushing the clean-cut bottom of a glass bottle from one chalk-marked paving square to the next; boys, in groups according to their ages, were playing chucks in the gutters; and here and there a bare-bottomed young child crawled on the hot pavements; but nowhere was there the sign of an adult. The main meal over, they would all have retired to bed. At least that would be the pattern in most of the houses around this quarter, except for those cranks who sent their bairns out to Sunday school and took themselves for a walk in the park.

It had always puzzled Emily why when the sands and the sea were so near, only a matter of minutes away down Ocean Road, most of the children preferred to play in the streets.

When her mother had been alive she would make her take Lucy down to the sands on every possible occasion because, as she would say, the sea air was good for Lucy's cough. But even on a very hot day her mother had never accompanied them; she had, like the rest of the people in the street, lain down on a Sunday afternoon.

18 Creador Street was an upstairs house. It had three rooms, the largest twelve feet by ten. The water had to be carried from a tap in the back yard, which was shared with the people downstairs. The one luxury afforded each house was a separate lavatory, mis-termed dry. In the winter when the ashes were plentiful it tended to live

up to its name, but as on this June day, when it was warm, as it had been for the past fortnight, the lavatory was anything but dry, and the stench from it and the line of its companions on each side of the back lane was overpowering.

Every week when Emily entered the house she found herself saying, 'I'll never come back here; no matter what happens I'll never come back here,' only to realize immediately what a silly thing it was to keep telling herself, for she was set for life with Mr and Mrs McGillby.

Today was no exception to her way of thinking, but to it was added, If only our Lucy was fourteen and away from school I'd get her out of this. That there were only ten more months before this should be was of no comfort to her, for she knew ten months was a long time and anything could happen in ten months. What, particularly, she didn't put a name to. She only knew her vague fears were connected with Alice Broughton. She would never call the woman ma, as her da had asked her to.

There were a number of children in the passageway of No. 18. Two of them were the Broughton boys, Tommy aged ten, and Jack, seven; and the eldest girl, Kate, was there too. The other children she recognized as the Tanners from next door. They all stopped in their play and looked at her. It was Tommy who greeted her, saying 'Hello. You back then?' For answer, she said, 'Where's Lucy?'

'Upstairs. She's been gettin' her hammers.'

As her eyes flashed from one face to the other, Kate said, 'She set her lip up to me ma. She said she didn't take our Tommy's knife'—she pointed to her brother, who was expertly twirling a penknife round his fingers—'and she had, she had thrown it down the netty.'

Emily now hastily pushed her way through them, and Jack's voice followed her, saying, 'Have you a ha'penny, our Emily?'

She made no answer, but having reached the small landing she went towards the middle of the three doors leading off it and, opening it, she entered the kitchen.

The room was as usual, cluttered and dirty. It held a square table, a battered couch, and an assorted number of chairs, besides a pedal organ and a chest of drawers. She could remember when everything in this room had shone, but that was a long time ago. The room was empty now except for Lucy, who didn't leap up as usual and run towards her, but sat with her head hanging as if she were half dazed.

'What is it? What's happened?' Emily was sitting by her side now holding her hands.

Lucy made no reply, she just leant her body sideways and rested it against Emily's. But within a minute Emily had pushed her upright again and was pointing to her face, demanding, 'She did that? She punched you? Why? What had you done?' Although Tommy had told her what Lucy had done she couldn't accept that Alice Broughton would batter Lucy in the face simply because she had thrown away Tommy's knife; bairns were always pinching each other's things.'

'Had you cheeked her?'

Lucy blinked and the tears slowly welled into her eyes and ran down her red and swollen cheeks; then drooping her head, she muttered, 'She's got a lodger. I don't like him. He wanted me to sit on his knee an' I wouldn't. An' ... an' I told her I'd tell me da when he came home....' She now raised her wet face upwards. 'When do you think he'll be back, Emily?'

Emily shook her head. It would be a year or more before her father returned; sometimes the voyages would last eighteen months, even as long as two years, and this time he'd been gone only for three months.

'Who is the fellow?' she asked. 'Is he a sailor?'

'No; he works in the docks on the prop boats.'

'Where's he sleepin'?'

'In the back room.'

'That means you're all in the front room?'

Lucy nodded.

'An' her?'

'She says she sleeps out here.' Lucy patted the couch.

At this Emily turned her head to the side and bit on her lip, and at that moment the door opened and Alice Broughton entered.

Alice Broughton was still in her early thirties. She was big-boned, and fleshy; she must, at one time, have been attractive, and there was still some semblance of it left in her round blue eyes and full-lipped mouth. She gave no preliminary greeting to Emily but from the middle of the room she stood looking at the two girls sitting on the couch, while she unfastened another button of her blouse and wafted the collar back and forward from her sweating skin before saying, 'Well, she's filled yer ears I suppose, an' it'll be no use me saying anything, will it? She's a damn little thief. She stole our Tommy's knife and threw it down the netty. He lays great stock by that knife for his whittlin'.'

'Aye, and jabbing it into people's arms.' Emily had now risen to her feet; then bending sideways she grabbed at Lucy's arm and, pulling it up and pointing at it, said, 'That looks a fresh nick to me.'

'He wouldn't do it on purpose; it's when they're carryin' on.'

'She doesn't carry on with your Tommy.'

'Now look here, miss, we're not goin' to have another day of it; you never enter this house but there's trouble. Once your da comes back I'm gonna have somethin' to say to him.'

'And you'll not be the only one. Will the lodger be here when he arrives?' Emily didn't flinch as she saw the hand flash out towards her, but she cried, 'You do, Alice

Broughton, you do, an' I'll go straight from here over to the polis station, an' I'll put a notice in against you for cruelty. What's more, I'll tell them you've got no right here, you're not married to me da and you're gettin' his half-pay note under false pretences.'

The colour rose in Alice Broughton's face until it took on an almost purple hue and she spat out, 'You young bugger you! I'll see me day with you afore me time's up, I swear on it.'

And to this Emily answered with a cockiness she was far from feeling, 'Aye, well, in the meantime you keep your hands off our Lucy or I warn you I'll go to the polis station. If that happens your number'll be up when me da comes back, for although he likes his drink he has never got in trouble with the polis. If you remember he used to brag about it. He thought it was worth bragging about that he'd had no truck with the polis. So I'm warning you.' On this she turned and looked towards Lucy, saying, 'Get your hat on, we're going out.'

Alice Broughton made no protest but her lips compressed tightly for a moment before she said, 'You're forgettin' something, aren't you?'

'No, I haven't forgotten anything.' Emily opened her purse and took out a shilling which she banged on to the table.

There was silence for a moment in the room as Alice Broughton looked down on the shilling; then slanting her eyes sideways towards Emily, she said, 'Come on, tip it up, we're not havin' any of that. You'll get your tuppence as usual, an' you're lucky to get that.'

'I'm giving you a shilling a week from now on an' no more. I've made up me mind. And I could stop that at any time an' all, because the half-pay note is so you'll see to our Lucy. You were supposed to go out to work for your lot, like you did when you first came as housekeeper. Housekeeper ... huh!'

Alice Broughton drew in one long deep breath that pushed her breasts out to fill her open blouse, then she gulped in her throat before spluttering, 'Get out of me sight while I've got some control left. I'll see me day with you, see if I don't. I've said it an' I swear by it.'

Pushing Lucy before her, Emily went out of the room, but as they reached the landing the back bedroom door opened and a man came out. He was wearing a pair of moleskin trousers; the upper part of him was bare and he stood scratching his chest as he looked at them. Then he grinned and said, 'Well, well, so this is the big sister.'

Emily said nothing but she stared at him for a moment before again pushing Lucy before her and down the stairs, then through the children and into the street. Her legs were trembling, her whole body was trembling; she had known that one day she would stand up to Alice Broughton but she hadn't expected to do it today. And she had stood up to her. By! she had that.

She now looked down at Lucy; then taking her hand she smiled as she asked her, 'Would you rather go to the park or down to the sands?'

'Down to the sands, Emily.'

'All right.' Now she bent down to her as they walked along and whispered, 'And you know what, we'll spend the sixpence, the whole of it, we'll bust it.'

'The whole of it?'

'Aye, we'll go to that ice-cream shop near the end of the road an' we'll get some hokey-pokey an' a couple of taffy apples, eh?'

She was smiling widely now and Lucy smiled in return, and as she had done on the couch she leant her body against Emily's for a moment; and then, their hands joined, they were running along the almost deserted pavement of Ocean Road which led to the sands and the sea.

As she ran Emily thought, Eeh! if Mrs McGillby could

24

see me now, she'd check me gallop with that look of hers. By! she would that; and thinking of Mrs McGillby reminded her that she must look out for the time and be back in Pilot Place well before seven to join in the prayer meeting.

TWO

The bedroom was packed with four men and four women and Mr McGillby and herself. The four men stood at one side of the bed, the four women at the other, and Mr McGillby stood at the foot of the bed. She herself stood near the door so as to be ready to open it when the visitors left, and she wished, oh she wished it would be soon because she was tired. It had been a long day, a hot trying day, and the prayers had been going on for over half an hour and it was stifling in here.

They were now taking turns reading Jeremiah. Mrs McGillby had started it off by reading the heading of Chapter Thirteen:

'By the type of a linen girdle God prefigures his people's destruction. By the bottles filled with wine their excess in misery foretold. Exhortation to repentance.'

Then Mr Goodyear took it up:'

'Thus saith the Lord unto me, Go and get thee a linen girdle, and put it upon thy loins, and put it not in water.'

He read the first seven verses. Then it was Mrs Goodyear's turn. She started:

'Then the word of the Lord came unto me, saying. . . .'

And she read up to verse thirteen.

Now Mr Dunn took it up. His voice was deep and sonorous and seemed to shake the pictures on the walls as, with the book held well away from his face, he read:

'Then shalt thou say unto them, Thus saith the Lord, Behold, I will fill all the inhabitants of this land, even the kings that sit upon David's throne, and the priests, and the prophets, and all the inhabitants of Jerusalem, with drunkenness.

And I will dash them one against another, even the fathers and the sons together, saith the Lord: I will not pity, nor spare, nor have mercy, but destroy them.

Hear ye, and give ear; be not proud: for the Lord hath spoken.'

Eeh! The words had aroused Emily somewhat, she had never heard anything like that spoken from the Bible before. Fill them with drunkenness. Well! well!

But as the voices droned on her mind slumbered again until Mrs Hailey's voice pricked her ears awake and brought her eyes wide as that lady cried:

'I have seen thine adulteries, and thy neighings, the lewdness of thy whoredom, *and* thine abominations on the hills in the fields. Woe unto thee, O Jerusalem! wilt thou not be made clean? when *shall it* once *be*?'

Eeh! well, fancy all that in the Bible, whores an' the rest. It made you wonder, didn't it? . . .

They were saying the final prayer now, all on their knees, except Mrs McGillby, whose head was bent forward, her chin buried in her chest.

'O Lord, bringeth, if it is Thy will, health to our sister here bedridden, but if it is not Thy will we will take it that her suffering is by way of atonement for the sins of others, and the greater her pain the wider the forgiveness you will shower on us poor creatures here on the sinful earth. Look upon our prayers here tonight, O Lord, with favour, and bring us safely to the dawn of a new day which we will endeavour to spend in praise of thee. Glory be to God. Amen.'

'Amen.'
'Amen. Amen. Amen.'
Silently now one by one the visitors shook Mrs Mc-Gillby's hand, while unsmiling, she nodded at them one by one. Then they went down the stairs, preceded by Mr McGillby who stood at the front door and shook each one by the hand as he thanked them, as he did every Sunday night, for their kindness in coming to pray with his wife.

But once the door was closed Emily noted, as she also did every Sunday night, that Mr McGillby heaved a great sigh as if he were glad it was all over. Tonight was no exception, except that his sigh seemed longer drawn out and his whole body seemed to slump; but perhaps it was the heat, it was affecting everybody. . . .

Sep McGillby now came towards the table where Emily was setting the cloth for his supper and said, 'I haven't had time to ask you, but did you have a nice day?'

She paused a moment before answering, 'Yes, but I didn't go to the park, I took me sister to the sands.'

'Aw, that was nice. It would be cool down there, she would like that. Is her cough better?'

'It's just about the same, Mr McGillby, thank you.'

'You look tired, lass, leave that. Go an' make the missis's drink an' take it up and I'll see to meself later.'

'Aw no, no, Mr McGillby, the missis wouldn't like that.'

He now put his hands on the corner of the table and

28

leant over it towards her and said under his breath, 'What the eye doesn't see the heart doesn't grieve over.'

'Eeh! Mr McGillby.' She bit on her lip, then smiled widely at him; and he smiled as widely back at her, saying, 'Go on now and get a good night's rest.'

'Thanks, Mr McGillby, ta, I am tired. And ... and can I tell you something?'

'Anything you like, lass.'

'I told that woman off the day, Alice Broughton. She had been hittin' our Lucy and I told her I'd go to the polis.'

'Good for you, lass, good for you.'

'And you know something else?' She was now leaning towards him. 'I docked her money.'

'No!'

'Aye. I only tipped up a shilling.'

'An' you know something, lass?'

'No, Mr McGillby.'

'You tipped up a shilling too much. You have no need to be tipping up anything there, your dad's provided; as you said he left his half-pay note.'

'Aye, I know, but if I don't give her something she'll take it out of our Lucy.'

'Aye, that would be the way of it likely.'

They looked at each other, but seriously now, then he said, 'Well, anyway, I'm glad you've made a stand, that's a beginnin'. Go on now. Good-night to you.'

'Good-night, Mr McGillby.'

When he went into the front room she lifted the kettle from the hob, took it into the scullery and there, filling a cup with hot water, she spooned into it two teaspoonfuls of cocoa and the same of condensed milk; then placing it on a wooden tray on which was spread a crocheted tray cloth, she took it up the stairs and into the bedroom.

Nancy McGillby was lying back on her pillows, her eyes were closed and her face looked very white.

Emily, approaching on tiptoe, said softly, 'It's your cocoa, Mrs McGillby.'

Mrs McGillby opened her eyes and stared at Emily, then said, 'Sin is an abomination unto the Lord and you don't have to use your tongue or your hands to sin, you can do it with your eyes.'

They stared at each other; then Emily said, 'Yes, Mrs McGillby.'

'Those who lust after the flesh shall die by the flesh.'

Again they stared at each other, and again Emily said, 'Yes, Mrs McGillby.'

'Put it down.'

Emily put the tray on the side table, then watched Mrs McGillby press her hand to a place underneath her breast. She did not speak again but dismissed her with a slight movement of her other hand.

Emily went out, across the narrow landing and into her own room. It was just turned nine o'clock and the twilight was deepening. She wished Mrs McGillby wouldn't always keep spouting the Bible at her. And she always said it in such a funny way that she couldn't understand her. But what matter, Mr McGillby was nice and kind and thoughtful. And oh, she was so tired. Wouldn't it be lovely if she could stay in bed for a whole night and a day! Oh, lovely!

She partly undressed herself sitting on the edge of the bed, and when, within a few short minutes, she had donned her night-gown she lay down, and in less time than it takes to tell she was asleep.

She was dreaming of Sammy Blacket, who lived at the top of Creador Street. They had gone to the same school but he had left long before her to take up the glorified position of apprentice in Palmer's shipyard in Jarrow. Twice he had waited for her at the bottom of their street and set her home on a Sunday night, and all the while he had talked about the shipyard and the boat he was making. It seemed as if he was making it all by himself, and it a sort of battleship. When he was out of his time, he said, he would earn as much as twenty-five shillings a week. She didn't believe him; nobody earned twenty-five shillings a week, except perhaps Mr McGillby. But then he was a gaffer in the docks, and he had the power to set men on the boats or not set them on, just as the mood pleased him.

And now Mr McGillby came into the dream. He was pushing Sammy Blacket to one side and yelling at her, 'Come on! Come on, Emily, get up! Do you hear? Get up!'

She was sitting bolt upright in bed, staring through the candlelight at the interrupter of her dream, and she spluttered, 'What's it? What's the matter?'

'Get up, Emily. Don't wait to put your things on, just slip into your coat and go in to the missis; I've got to go for the doctor. She's bad, real bad.'

The candle disappeared, she was left in the darkness. Groping her way to the back of the door, she took down her coat and put it round her; then still groping, she opened the door and went across the landing and into the bedroom. The lamp was turned up full, the room was hot and pervading it was a smell of vomit.

Nancy McGillby lay slumped into her pillows; her head was leaning to the side, her eyes were wide open and her breath was coming in painful gasps.

Emily leant over the bed, saying softly, 'You'll be all right, Mrs McGillby, you'll be all right. Mister has gone for the doctor; he'll soon be here.'

When her hand gently touched the twitching fingers clutching at the eiderdown it was pushed away, and Emily straightened up and stood looking helplessly down on her mistress who was staring at her fixedly as if she wanted to say something. And then she did say something. Her mouth wide, she cried, 'O-o-oh no! not yet.' Then her chest seemed to drop inwards, her head fell to the side, her fingers stopped twitching, and she lay still.

For a moment Emily was rooted to the spot. She knew that Mrs McGillby was dead. She felt sick. She was going to be sick. Eeh! yes, she was going to be sick. She turned and scampered from the room and down the stairs, and reached the scullery only just in time.

She was sitting at the kitchen table when Sep McGillby returned. He stopped for a moment inside the door and looked at her; then, giving a small shake of his head, he went silently past her and up the stairs.

THREE

It rained the day of the funeral. It was the first rain for three weeks and all the mourners said it was a pity because Mrs McGillby was to be put away quite grandly. The coffin was of light oak with three sets of fine brass handles on it, and the hearse was the best to be had in the town; a resident of Westoe couldn't have had a better departure; and what was more there were five cabs.

After the cortège had left the house Emily sat down for a moment in the middle of the front room and sighed, but even as she did she warned herself this was no time to take it easy because now the house was clear the tables had to be set, the food put out, the kettles kept boiling; and she told herself as she sat in the darkened room, for the blind was still fully drawn, that by the look of things she'd better cut up the remainder of the ham that was left on the bone, and also the rest of the second piece of brisket; the tongue had already been spread out as far as it would go.

She had been cooking solidly for the past two days because, as Mr McGillby said, things must be done properly, and the members of the chapel would expect a good meal.

She couldn't quite take in at the moment the fact that Mrs McGillby was no longer with them and that in future she'd have the house to herself for most of the day, and no one to give her orders.

Just before dropping off to sleep last night she had thought about it. It was as if a miracle had happened to her. But she had chastised herself harshly for daring to think like that, and Mrs McGillby laid out below her in the front room.

But now Mrs McGillby was no longer in the house, and although the place was still in deep mourning, and would be for days ahead, she already felt an air of lightness everywhere. Even though she was dog-tired and her legs ached something awful, the feeling of lightness was seeping into her.

Eeh! She roused herself. What was she sitting here for dreaming? If things weren't right when they returned she'd get her head in her hands and her brains to play with. But would she? there was no Mrs McGillby to reprimand her now. She was, she knew, in a strange way almost her own mistress because Mr McGillby would never bully her; he had never said an unkind word to her since she had come into the house.

She almost skipped from the room and into the scullery and for the next hour she made countless journeys back and forth, and when the tables in the front room were ready to seat sixteen people, and the kitchen table so arranged to seat another eight, she gazed at her handiwork, dusted her hands one against the other, then, glancing down at her apron, she said aloud, 'By! I'd better change that afore they arrive else Mrs Goodyear's goggle eyes will say, Tut! tut! tut!'

She checked the chuckle that rose in her throat; she shouldn't show such disrespect to the chapel goers. But then, she hadn't much use for them, they were all ranters; and when she came to think of it she was very surprised that Mr McGillby was one of their company. Yes she was, very surprised.

She had changed her apron and had just reached the

foot of the stairs when there was a knock on the back door. When she opened it she saw a woman standing there. She was short and plump and looked none too clean. Although she didn't look quite the beggar type, she didn't look like anyone who would have come calling on Mrs Nancy McGillby.

'Do you want something?' she asked.

For answer the woman said, 'They've gone then?'

'You mean, the funeral?'

'Aye, that's what I mean. An' I never heard a word of it till just on an hour ago.'

As the woman now pushed past her and into the scullery, Emily, putting her hand out, closed the door leading into the kitchen saying, 'Here, hold on, wait a minute. Who are you anyway?'

'Who am I, miss? I'll tell you who I am, I'm Mrs Jessie Blackmore, Jessie McGillby as was. He's me brother.'

Aw, so this, so to speak, was the skeleton in the cupboard. Once or twice she had heard Mr and Mrs McGillby talking in the bedroom, not rowing, but talking a bit loud, and if she remembered rightly it was about Mr McGillby's relations. And she recalled now the one time she had heard Mr McGillby really raise his voice was when he said, 'Look, I don't want them any more than you do, so let that be the end of it.'

Emily could see now all right why Mr McGillby hadn't wanted to keep in with his sister, because she was certainly no class. Common, that was the word for it, common as muck. People could be poor but they needn't be common, there was a difference. She couldn't explain it but she knew all about it inside herself. And so, feeling this way, she hung on to the knob of the door that led into the kitchen and she said, 'I'm expecting them back any minute, so I can't let you in there.'

'Get out of me way, you!'

'I'll not get out of your way; I'm in charge of the house until Mr McGillby comes back. An' you can stay in the scullery here or you can get outside.'

'By God! who do you think you are? Eeh! by!'—the woman nodded at her now—'I can see it, I can see it all as plain as a pikestaff. You're playin' the mistress, aren't you?'

'I'm not playin' anything. I do just what I'm paid for and that's looking after Mr McGillby's house.'

'Aw, aye, you are.' The woman's head was nodding knowingly at Emily now. 'I never had much use for Lady Nancy but I can see she was up against something.'

Indignation rising in her, Emily was about to ask and pointedly what the woman meant, when the sound of the carriages arriving caused her to open the door slightly and look through the kitchen towards the front room and the front door. Then turning to the woman again and realizing what an embarrassment she'd be to Mr McGillby in front of the members of the chapel, she actually put her hands on her and pushed her towards the open back door, crying, 'Stay there a minute; I'll tell him you're here.'

The woman staggered back as much in surprise as from the force of the push, and before she could recover Emily had shot the bolt in the door. Then running through the kitchen and the front room, she flung open the front door just in time to allow the first mourners to enter.

Mrs Goodyear led the way; then Mrs Hailey; then Mrs Robson; then Mrs Dunn and other women whom Emily couldn't put a name to. The first of the men to enter was Mr McGillby, and with what she would, under ordinary circumstances, have considered a disrespectful approach to a recently bereaved man she gripped his arm and pulled him aside and, straining her face towards his, she whispered, 'Your sister's in the back yard, Mr McGillby. I kept her there; I thought it best.'

The look on his face told her that she had done quite right to keep his sister in the back yard, and he nodded at her twice. Then whispering back at her, 'You see to them, will you?' he sidled his way through the black-clothed groups and into the scullery....

The mourners were seated at the tables, and Mrs Dunn was helping Emily to pour out the tea when Sep McGillby re-entered the room. His face looked red and all eyes were turned on him in sympathy for a moment. They understood, he'd had to leave them because he could not give way to his sorrow in public....

If a vote could have been taken on the funeral it would have been labelled a great success. When the last mourner shook Sep's hand and he closed the front door on him he leant against it for a moment, opened his mouth wide and gulped at the stale air of the room; then he straightened his thick-set body, pressed back his shoulders and, stretching his neck first one way then another out of his stiff high collar, he walked through the front room and into the kitchen where Emily was placing the chenille cloth over the table, a sign that that room was clean and tidy.

'Well, lass, it's over.'

'Yes, Mr McGillby.'

'Sit down, get off your legs, you must be worn out.'

Pulling out a chair from under the table, she sat down and smoothed her apron over her knees before joining her hands together and laying them in her lap.

Sep, too, sat down, in the high-backed wooden chair at the side of the fireplace, and for a moment he stared into the fire; then he turned his head and looked at her and said, 'We've got to get down to business, Emily, come to terms like. You understand?'

It was a little while before she answered, 'Well not

37

quite, Mr McGillby.'

He screwed round in the chair now and, leaning his elbow on the arm, he asked, 'Do you want to stay on here and look after the house and me?'

'Oh yes, Mr McGillby.' Her voice was high. 'Aye, of course.'

'Aye, I thought you would, but you know it's ... well it's going to be awkward, there might be talk, in fact they're already chewing it over, the chapel lot.' He jerked his head backwards as if the chapel lot were behind him, and the disdain in his tone widened her eyes and brought her lips apart as he exclaimed, 'Oh aye, you can look like that an' I don't blame you. You've always been a lass who's had her wits about her, I could see that from the start, and you'll likely class me as a bit of a hypocrite, but perhaps not when you know the whole story. And I'll tell it you sometime, but in the meantime, as I said, there's going to be talk. Can you put up with it?'

She didn't come back at him and ask, 'Talk about what, Mr McGillby?' for she knew what the talk would be about, her and Mr McGillby alone in the house together at night. Although she was but sixteen and he old enough to be her father, people would likely make things out of it.

An idea coming into her head, which wasn't at all new but which she proffered as if she had just thought of it, she said, 'I could bring our Lucy to sleep with me, Mr McGillby, that would put things right.'

She watched him get abruptly to his feet, she watched his head shake definitely, she watched him pace the length of the hearthrug three times, before he stopped with his back to her and, looking into the fire, he muttered, 'No, no; that wouldn't do at all. There ... there could be trouble with that woman, and your da; she was left in her care.'

'Me da wouldn't mind, Mr McGillby.'

He turned to her now and said, 'Well, all right, but I'd have to have your da's word. When will he be back?'

Her face was unsmiling, even sad as she answered dully, 'It's hard to tell, he's only been gone a short while this trip, it could be a year or more, two.'

'Oh, well then'—he turned from her again—'we'll likely have to do something afore then. But leave it for the present, eh? Leave it for the present. In the meantime, I'm goin' to put your wage up to half a crown a week, and I'll give you twelve shillings for the housekeeping. If you want any more you've just to let me know.'

'Eeh! oh! thanks, Mr McGillby.' She was on her feet standing by his side now looking into his face. 'Oh, that's wonderful. An' I'll be careful, I won't be extravagant; I'll do the shoppin' on a Saturday in the market.'

'Aye, I know you will, lass. And I'll see to the coal and the gas and oddments like that.'

Her face had spread into a wide smile. There was on it now the glad look, her whole being seemed alight, and he turned abruptly away from her and went into the front room and closed the door behind him.

She stood, her hands clasped tightly between her breasts, looking towards the closed door for the moment; then slowly she gazed about the room as in wonder. She looked from the horse-hair couch to the delf rack; from there to the chest of drawers on which stood the old-fashioned pink china oil lamp that had at one time been used; then to the mantelshelf on which were three sets of brass candlesticks and a similar number of brass ladies' boots ranging in size from a foot to six inches in height, and behind them the large wooden-framed mirror which was tilted slightly forward so that you could see most of yourself in it.

She gazed at her reflection and saw that she looked happy, bubblingly happy. And why shouldn't she be? Was she not the partaker of a miracle, and the luckiest lass on earth?

FOUR

There was talk, and not only talk but action, particularly on the part of those members of the chapel who, out of their charity, had prayed by Nancy McGillby's bed.

They came singly at first, the ladies generally in the daytime, and they questioned Emily as to her duties and what she did in her spare time. Some asked what time she went to bed, others if she had a bolt on her door.

Although she told Sep of the visits she did not relate all that had been said. Usually he was very sparing in his comments, but one night, right in the middle of his meal, he laid his knife and fork down by the side of his plate and, dropping his chin on to his chest, he laughed as he said, 'If it wasn't in your mind they'd put it there. By God! they would.' Then looking at her, he added, 'I'm going to put a stop to this. There's a chapel meeting on Thursday night and I'll be there. Yes, I'll be there.'

And he was there. After he'd had his tea, and she had seen it was a nice tea of finny haddy baked in butter and milk in the oven, followed by a shive of bacon and egg pie and new tea cakes, he had got himself dressed in his Sunday suit, donned his hard hat, and gone out to the meeting.

And all during the time he was away she was filled with a great unease. Chapel people had power, they could get people done out of their jobs, she had heard of it happening. Not that they could do Mr McGillby out of

41

his job, but they could bring such pressure on him that he'd have to get rid of her. He had said he would put a stop to the talk, but could he? She conjured up the faces of Mr Goodyear, Mr Hailey, Mr Robson, and Mr Dunn; they all looked stern and strong but yet not half as strong as their wives.

It was funny, she thought, but at bottom it was the women who had the say; at least they made the bullets for the men to fire, and the men, being men, had to be seen to be firing them. Half the men would never think of doing the spiteful things they did if it wasn't for their womenfolk.

She didn't know quite how she came to her knowledge of people, only that, so she told herself, she could sense things. And she could sense that her master was in for a rough time the night.

She hadn't expected him to return until about nine o'clock, because that was the time he usually came back from the chapel meetings, but she was openly amazed when he marched into the house not half an hour after having left it. And when he took off his hard hat and hung it on the back of the door it made a loud sound as if he had clapped his hands.

He came into the kitchen pulling the lapels of his coat together. It was an attitude that said plainly, Well, that's seen to that. Then taking up his stand with his back to the fire, he said, 'I did it. I put a stop to their gallop, I told them what's what.'

'You did?'

'Aye, I did. You mind your business in the future I said, an' I'll mind mine, and I can do it without the assistance of prayers or nosey-parkers. An' what's more, I said, I'm answerable to no man for me actions; the only thing I'm answerable to is me conscience, and that's clear and clean.'

She was staring at him, her eyes bright, when with a

42

sweep of his arm, he pointed towards the sitting-room door, saying, 'From the night I'm startin' the way I mean to go on. I had to sneak a smoke when Nancy was alive, an' I've kept sneaking a smoke since just in case one or t'other of them should pop in. Well, now there'll be no more of that. So, lass, I'm going to smoke in the kitchen here. And——' His voice dropped to a tone just above a whisper as, thrusting his head out towards her, he added, 'And there's something else I'm going to do. Do you know what it is?'

'No, Mr McGillby.'

'I'm going to have a drink of beer in the house when I feel like it.'

Her mouth moved into an elongated O, then snapped closed, and she bit on her lip to stop herself from laughing, and he, copying her, bit on his lip too; then together their laughter exploded. They stood each side of the table leaning on it doubled up with their mirth. But like a tap being slowly turned off, it dribbled away and left them wet-eyed, looking at each other, and Emily muttered, 'Eeh! I shouldn't have laughed like that.'

'Why? Why shouldn't you? Look, sit yourself down there, lass, I want to talk to you. I've been wanting to talk to you for nights, tell you things, but I thought it was too early. But I'm no hypocrite. At least'—he moved his head slowly—'what I mean is that from now on I'll stop playin' the hypocrite.'

Emily sat down at the end of the table and, her gaze fixed on him, she waited, for he was sitting now looking straight ahead as if he were seeing himself walking back into the past; then quietly he said, 'I'm only thirty-five, Emily, I'm still a youngish man. I'd only been married to Nancy two months when you first came here to work on Friday nights and Saturdays. She was nine years older than me an' I let myself think that I married her because she converted me from drink.'

He turned now and glanced towards Emily. 'I was a pretty heavy drinker in me young days, and naturally I smoked like a chimney. Anyway, I met her one stormy night when her umbrella blew inside out an' almost lifted her across the open space at the docks. I'd just come out of The Grapes, and she practically fell into me arms. I couldn't do much with the umbrella but I took hold of her, an' asked her where she was goin'. I can see her now, hanging on to me arm and looking into me face and sniffing. I must have smelt like a hogshead, and, what was more, me men had been unloading an iron ore boat that day and there's a kind of musty smell comes from that, it sort of mingles with the sweat. Anyway, in spite of that she let me lead her home right to this very house; and then she asked me in. Looking back now I can see she had made up her mind the minute I grabbed her to stop her taking off.'

He now wetted his lips, stroked his short moustache with his forefinger, then went on, 'Well, she made me a cup of tea and she found out that I was a bachelor, and I found out that she had looked after her parents, and they had both died within the last three years an' had left her this house, signed, sealed and paid for, together with an insurance kind of thing that brought her in so much a week, not a lot, but just enough for her to live on. She didn't go out to work, she had a sort of weak heart, but nothing serious she told me. Anyway, that was the beginning. In less than two years she was Mrs Septimus Mc-Gillby, and in less than three months from the day we were married she took to her bed, not all the time at first, as you may well remember, but more than she needed to have done I'm thinkin'. She was a woman, Emily, who should have never married.... You know what I mean?'

When Emily made no answer he said, 'Well, if you do or you don't it makes no difference, you will some day. Anyway, she got me off the beer long afore we married but she didn't get me hymn singing until the very last. You know what, Emily, you know what I've found out about life? Everything in it has to be paid for an' through the teeth. I didn't want Nancy, but I wanted the comfort of a house, the cleanness of it, and the thought of coming home to a fire and decent meals. You see, I was in digs in me sister's in Dock Street, and you know what Dock Street's like. Moreover, she owned this house, lock, stock an' barrel, and all in it. Well, as I saw it then, if I married her it would in time be mine, so I married her. But God in heaven! I was made to pay for it. Oh aye, I paid for it, Emily. Mind you, I kept my part of the bargain, I was never other than decent to her. Now you can vouch for that, can't you?'

'Oh yes, Mr McGillby, oh yes.'

'Emily.'

'Yes, Mr McGillby?'

'Do you think you could drop the Mr McGillby now and call me Sep?'

'Eeh!' She shook her head. 'It would be kind of funny. I don't think I ...'

'Now, don't say you don't think you could ... go on, have a try. It's not hard to say, is it ... Sep?' He poked his face towards her, and she laughed and said, 'No. Why, no.'

'Well, go on, no what?'

'No ... Sep.' Again they were laughing together but softly now, and, his head to one side, he asked her quietly, 'Do you think me awful?'

'Oh no! no. I think you're very good. I mean you were to Mrs McGillby, you were always nice to her ... kind.'

'Aye, well, I tried to be; I felt I owed her something after all. Although mind, at times I must confess I was hard put to stick it, especially when I couldn't have a smoke.... I bet you often wondered where I kept me baccy.'

45

'Aye, I did.' Her mouth was wide now, her eyes wrinkled with amusement.

'Come on then, I'll show you.' He put his hand out and grabbed hers and pulled her into the front room, saying, 'Pull down the blind, I'll light the gas.'

When this was done he pointed to a small bureau standing in the alcove to the right of the fireplace. 'That's the only piece of furniture I ever bought. Do you remember the day I brought it in? Pushed it all the way on a borrowed barrow from Frederick Street, I did. It's funny how I came by it. I was passing a secondhand shop, like Paddy's Market it was, all full of jumble. I happened to stop and glance at the conglomeration in the window, an' beyond it I saw the fellow in the middle of the shop open a drawer like this'—he now went to the bureau and lifted the lid which fell back on the other half of itself to reveal a writing desk flanked by three drawers. He now said, 'The fellow pulled this drawer open.' He demonstrated. 'Then I watched him put his hand inside, like this.' Again he demonstrated. 'Then before me very eyes, like before yours now, the top of the desk moved slowly upwards.'

'Eeh! Mr McGillby ... I mean——' She gave a little giggle, then said, 'Sep' as she pointed to the small cupboard, with drawers on either side, which had revealed itself. Then again she said, 'Eeh! who would believe it?'

'I didn't, lass, but like a flash I was in the shop and I said to him, the man like, I said, "That's a neat piece of work", and he said, "Aye, it is. I just came across it the day. An old girl sold it to me. Been in her family for years, she said. Hard up she was. And you know something? She knew nowt about this, the secret drawer, but I recognized the type right away, I'd seen one or two afore. Nice piece, isn't it?"

'I stood there nodding at him. Then I said, "How much do you want for it?" "Oh," he said, humming and

haaing, "it's worth a bit." I pointed out then that it was all knocked about round the feet and the top was badly scarred as if there had been hot dishes put on it.

'That was easily rectified, he said, and he would take nothing less than six pounds.

'"Huh!" I said. "Six pounds!" Well, to cut a long story short I got him down to five. Believe me I wanted that desk so much, Emily, I would have given him ten. Aye, I would, I would have given him ten because me first thought was that I had some place to put me baccy.' He grinned at her now, and she grinned back at him, saying, 'I always thought there was a smoky smell in this corner, and the few times the missis was downstairs she remarked on it an' all. She even asked if I had been having a fire in the grate on the quiet.'

He nodded at her now as much to say, Aye, she would; then drawing one of the straight-backed plush chairs that formed part of the seven-piece suite up to the desk, he sat down and beckoned her closer to him; then as if he might be overheard he strained his face towards her, saying softly now, 'I'm going to show you something else, Emily, something that nobody else knows about. You see, by doing it it'll prove that I trust you. And I do, lass; I think there's not another like you. Do you know that?'

She blinked down at him as she felt the colour flooding her face, and she answered just as softly, 'That's good of you. It's good to be trusted, and ... and I'll never give anything away that you tell me.'

'I know you won't, lass. I'm not the one to take long shots; I know you won't. Well now, have a look at these.' And with this he pulled open one of the drawers and tipped it up on to the writing pad.

She was now looking down at a number of rings, two chains with pendants hanging from them, and two big gold lever watches.

'What do you think of that lot, lass?'

47

She said nothing, but shook her head.

'There's some money's worth there, eh?'

Again she made no reply, and so he said hastily, 'I didn't steal them.'

'Oh! Oh no, I know you wouldn't steal them, Mr ... Sep.' Her lips moved into a small smile, then became set again as she continued to stare down at the jewellery and watches.

'I'll tell you how I came by them. It was like this; it was after I bought the desk. You see the chaps come in from long trips, they spend up an' they're broke; and here and there one of them has picked up something abroad, cheap like. Well, to be honest I don't know how they come by the things, I only know that they want to sell them. They generally find their way to the pawnshop. Mind, I'd been offered stuff like this afore, I mean afore I got the desk, an' I refused it. Oh aye, I could have taken it to the pawnshop meself, but I used to think I might not get as much on the things as I paid the fellow for it. Do you follow me?'

She nodded at him.

'So once I had the desk and a place to put the stuff I thought well, why not. Mind, if Nancy had known, oh begod! I don't know what would have happened then. Hell on earth it would have been. But anyway, she was upstairs tied to the bed, and I had me desk, and that's how it started. Now take these rings.' He lifted up one ring after the other. 'I don't know much about jewellery but there's a stamp of eighteen carat on the gold, and I reckon they don't put paste stones in eighteen carat gold, what do you say?'

She made a little movement with her head, and he stared at her for a moment. Then picking up one of the rings he said, 'Try that on for size.'

'What, me?'

'Yes, you. Try it on.'

She took the ring and stared at it. It had five white stones in it, and the light was making them dance. Slowly she put the ring on to her first finger and stared at it for a moment; then as if it were burning her she pulled it off quickly and handed it back to him.

'What's the matter?'

'Nothing, only ... only it felt funny. I've never worn a ring.'

He held the ring between his finger and thumb as he said, 'Well, you will some day, lass.'

'Yes, yes, I suppose so.' She gave a little giggle.

'Aye, well, there's plenty of time, eh?' He nodded at her: then having replaced the jewellery, he opened the drawer at the far side of the little cupboard and pointed down to a number of sovereigns spread over the bottom, saying, 'That's me private bank,' and he stared at her for a moment before adding, 'You see, I trust you, Emily.'

Her face was red again as she answered, 'Yes, I know.'

Now he opened the door of the little cupboard and, taking out a small black book, its leather cover so old that it was cracked in places, he handed it towards her, saying in a lighter tone, 'That was all the fellow found in the drawers, and he left it there. It was no use to him, he said. Well, it was less use to me, but it must have meant something to the one that put it there, so I left it in peace. Look, it's full of odds and ends of writing. Whoever owned it must have done some thinking 'cos listen to this. It says on this page: "Thoughts in the mind should be diluted through the sieves of propriety before they are allowed to pass through the lips." Now what do you make of that, sieves of propriety? Somebody with learning could make something of it, I suppose, an' it would likely make sense.

'And listen to this one.' He turned over a page. 'It's like a bit of poetry and it's headed "Sunday":

'Chopin and gold crests
In the garden,
In the sun,
Doctor Arnold,
And philosophy,
And God,
All are one.

'Funny, isn't it?'

She nodded at him again.

'And then there was something else here that reminded me of you. You know I heard you at the back door one day trying to cheer your sister up an' you said to her, "Never say die." You often say that, don't you? Never say die.'

'Yes, yes I do'—she smiled at him now—' 'cos ... 'cos me mother used to always keep saying it. "Cheer up," she would say; "never say die." And sometimes she would say, "Buck up, and be a rabbit." I used to think that was funny.'

'Aye, it is. Buck up and be a rabbit. But listen to this; this is what put me in mind of you:

'Life comes in like the tide
On a roar from the sea bed,
And is already dying before its ebb.
Existence is the time it takes for the shingle to be wet.
And yet,
Are they deluded,
Do they lie,
Those blind with courage
Who shout above the spray,
Never say die?'

He gazed at her now, saying, 'That's what made me think of you. It's an odd piece of writing really, but it's one I can understand. Can you?'

She hesitated. 'A bit. Read it again, it sounded nice.'

So he read it again; and now she said, 'Well, I suppose it just means that life is short but you should keep your pecker up.'

He laughed outright now, crying, 'You've hit it on the head, Emily, you've just hit it on the head. Aye, that's what it means. Life's like a wave coming in and goin' out again, as short as that. So we should make the best of it, shouldn't we?'

'Aye, we should.'

They stared at each other in silence before he added, 'Perhaps your mother knew that poem, that's where she got the saying from.'

'No, I don't think she knew that one because I know the lines where she got it from.'

'You do?'

'Aye, they go like this: "While there's wood to burn and a kettle on the hob, and a fish with its eye on a fly, never say die." '

His head was back, his mouth wide, 'Well, I've never heard that one afore. But that's one I can understand. Well, lass, would you like this little book, it's no use to me?'

'Oh, thank you. Oh, ta, I'll read it right through. Ta.'

'Well, what do you think of me find?' He pressed the top of the secret drawer down and when it clicked into place he turned and looked at her, and she answered, 'Oh, I think it's marvellous to have a place to hide things where nobody can set their eyes on them.'

'Nor their fingers.'

'Aye, nor their fingers.'

'Well, lass'—he now turned the light down—'it's chilly in here, let's go into the kitchen. And by the way, thinkin' about it being chilly, we'll have this room fire on every week-end, Saturday and Sunday. What do you think about that?'

'That'll be nice and comfortable for you.'

'Comfortable for us both, lass.'

'Oh aye, yes.'

'Well now'—he was standing with his back to the fire again—'what do you think of me now?'

She looked at him straight and she answered him straight, 'The same as I did afore. I think you're a good man, and a kind one.'

He pursed his lips and wagged his head from side to side before nodding at her and saying, 'And I think you're a good lass, and a kind one an' all. We get on well together, Emily, you and me.'

After a short awkward silence during which he stared at her, she said, 'I'll get you some supper.'

'Aye, do that.'

While she was in the scullery he called to her, 'How would you like a trip up the river on Sunday?'

'Up the river?' She came to the scullery door and stretched her neck towards him.

'Aye, I said up the river. You can bring your young sister along an' all.'

'Oh, that'll be lovely. Thanks. Thanks, Mr...'—She put her hand over her mouth now, then added on an embarrassed laugh, 'Sep.' And as she withdrew her head he said, as if half to himself, 'We'll make that a start,' and she stopped for a moment, half inclined to pop her head out again and ask him what he meant. But like the sound of a far distant bell there rang through her mind just what he might mean. Even so, she closed her ears to it as if it were the distorted thinking of a dream, then continued the business of making his supper.

FIVE

Nancy McGillby had been dead for three months. It appeared much longer to Emily for at times it seemed she had been running the house on her own for years, and that she and Lucy had been going to the market on a Saturday morning to return laden with butcher meat, vegetables and groceries of all kinds for as long as she could remember.

She was worried about their Lucy, even though it would appear she had less cause now for she was seeing to it that she was well fed. She had an arrangement, with Sep's permission, that Lucy should call in each day after school and have a meal.... Sep hadn't been agreeable that Lucy should come in at dinner-time when he was having his meal. He was funny that way, Emily considered, he liked his meal on his own; well, at least just with her.

But in spite of her packing food into Lucy she didn't seem to put on any weight, and she had a worried look; all the time she had a worried look on her face. When Emily questioned her all she would say was she didn't like the lodger.

Had he touched her?

No, only slapped her across the bottom sometimes as if he were having a bit carry on. In any case, Alice Broughton nearly always sent her out when he was in the house.

When she was asked if Tommy had been at her, she

answered, no, because Jack was sticking up for her.

Emily was pleased to know that Lucy had one advocate in the house; Jack, to her mind, had always been the best of the bunch; and so she had seen to it of late that he didn't lose by it for she slipped him a penny every week.

But today, more than ever, she felt worried about Lucy, for she looked so peaky and down in the mouth, and she said to her now pointedly, as they entered the house and dumped their bass bags on the kitchen table, 'Look, our Lucy, what's up with you? You've had a face like a wet week-end all mornin'.'

'I'm just feelin' tired, Emily.'

'But you're always feelin' tired. Why do you feel so tired? Is she makin' you work?'

'Not more than usual, just the washin' up and the sweepin' an' things. . . . Emily.'

'Aye.' Emily sat down on the kitchen chair and heaved a sigh while pulling the hatpins from her hat before taking it off; then, sticking them back again, she looked at the thin girl standing silently at her knee and she said sharply, 'Well, get on with it, what do you want to say?'

'Couldn't I come here and live with you?'

'Aw, our Lucy'—Emily had now closed her eyes and was shaking her head—'how many times have I told you I've asked him, an' I keep hintin' at it times without number, but he keeps sayin' we'll have to have the consent of me da; if he takes you away from her there could be trouble. And there could be, you know, because me da left you in her care. And she has the half-pay note to prove it, she'll say. And that's what me da said it was for an' all.

'Now look'—she caught hold of Lucy's hands—'I know it seems a long time till me da gets back but you'll have to be patient. Come on, cheer up, never say die. Look, let's get these things sorted out and then we'll have a cup of cocoa.' She now hunched her shoulders upwards, adding, 'An' we'll have it in the front room afore the fire, eh? ...'

When, a short while later, they were seated on the rug in front of the fire sipping their cocoa, they smiled at one another and Emily said, 'Isn't this nice?' and Lucy, the smile sliding from her face and her eyes showing a depth of sadness that brought an ache to Emily's heart, said, 'Aye, it's like heaven.'

Silently now they looked at each other until Emily muttered softly, 'I'll do me best. I've got something up me sleeve, I'll do me best.'

After this they sat in silence, Lucy with her head down, but Emily with hers up looking round the room. It was a lovely room, wonderful to her eyes, the seven-piece plush suite, the glass-fronted china cabinet in the corner which showed off a complete tea-set, the piano against the wall opposite the fireplace. Sep said she must start to learn the piano, and she would. Oh aye, she would love to play the piano; she would feel educated if she could play the piano. And there in the corner to the right of her the desk, Sep's desk as she thought of it; and in front of the window a small polished oak table on which stood a beautiful plant pot with an aspidistra in it. Then there was the floor covering, not lino like in the kitchen and in the bedrooms, but a real carpet, with a shop rug at the fireside, on which they were sitting now, not a proggie mat like most people had in their front rooms but a bought rug; and everything everywhere was shining. Never a day went by but she dusted every article in the house, and once a week saw to it that they were polished. And every minute of her work was a joy to her. She never wanted to leave this house and ... and what was more she needn't leave it.

Now her head was bowed over the cocoa. She knew the time wasn't so very far off when he would say something to her. And what would she say back to him? She'd have to think carefully about this. But hadn't she thought carefully about it? If she didn't give him the answer he wanted somebody else would, for he was a man of position anyone would be glad to have; besides being the owner of a house he was a gaffer in the docks.... It was a pity he was old.

When she sprang to her feet she startled Lucy; then she went towards the kitchen, saying, 'Eeh! sitting here wastin' time when I've got the dinner to see to.'

Although she had been expecting it, when he did broach the subject that was in both their minds, it came as a surprise to her, for it was on that very same Saturday night when she was almost ready for bed that he said suddenly, 'Sit down, lass.'

He often said, 'Sit down, lass,' but there was a different note to his voice now. He had been out most of the evening, and when he came in she could smell beer on him. But he wasn't drunk, and no way near it. He had told her that he would never get drunk again, because it was a mug's game, but he would have his pint when he felt like it, and she had agreed with him that he should. All men except ranters liked their pint, and were no worse for it.

As was usual when she was slightly disturbed, she joined her hands together and laid them on her lap, and she sat looking at him and he at her. Her mind was telling her that he wasn't bad looking. His face was squarish, he had a kind of ruddy complexion with brown eyes, and a nice shaped mouth, and he looked better, younger, since he had shaved his moustache off. When she first saw him he'd had it waxed at the ends, but then he had cut them off and just had an ordinary tache. Then not long after Mrs McGillby died he had become clean-shaven and looked better for it.... But he was still thirty-five!

And now he was talking to her.

'You know something, Emily? I feel that the missis has been dead for three years, not three months; in fact, at times I feel she never existed. Can you understand that?'

Again, as was usual when disturbed, she merely nodded.

'Now I don't want to frighten you, an' I don't think I'm goin' to, by what I'm going to say, for you've got a head on your shoulders an' you know what's what. That being so you're bound to know I've got a feelin' for you, Emily, and it hasn't just come up the day or yesterday, it's been there a long time. She must have known about it too. Aye'—he turned his head to the side—'the way she went on at times she knew about it all right. Yet God knows by neither word nor look did I ever let on to you how I felt. Now did I? Speak fair.'

She made another small movement with her head.

'Well then, I won't beat about the bush any longer. I want to marry you, Emily. Now'—he raised his hand—'don't say you're too young, or I'm too old; I'm not an old man, I'm young in every way a man can be young, an' that's what counts. And you ... well, I know you're only sixteen but we can keep this between ourselves for the next few months until you reach seventeen, and then, what d'you say, Emily? What d'you say?'

Her eyes were wide, stretched; her lips were slightly open, drawing in a thin stream of air; she felt it going down her throat and swelling her breast.

'You don't dislike me, do you?'

'Oh no! No!' The answer shot out of her.

And it was true, she didn't dislike him, in fact she liked him very much. But to get married to him, to lie in the big bed with him, would she like that? She didn't know. She didn't think she would somehow; and yet she'd have to get married one day, wouldn't she? And who would she marry? Somebody from their street and live from hand to mouth like Peg Watson did, or Mary Nichols, or

Hannah Threadgill. Pawnshop on a Monday, getting them out again on a Friday night. And if she married a man like Hannah Threadgill did she'd be knocked black and blue at times.

'You like the house?'

'Oh aye, yes, oh aye, Sep, I like the house. I love it.'

'Well then, lass, it's yours just for the sayin'. I'd be good to you, Emily.' He was holding her joined hands now, gripping them tight. 'You need fear nothin' bad from me.' It was as if he were reading her thoughts. 'You'll have your own way in everything, I promise you that. And what's more, once it's settled you can have Lucy here with you an' welcome. Aye, you can; and I'll put up with the consequences of taking her from that woman and make it right with your da when I meet him.'

Somewhere along the line she felt he was taking an unfair advantage now; and not only now, she had glimpsed his reason for not having Lucy in the house before. He guessed that when it came to the push what she wouldn't do for herself she'd do for Lucy. Yet she didn't blame him; people went to all kinds of lengths when they wanted something, and he wanted her. His need of her was deep in his eyes. She'd seen it there for a long time. She felt a rising pity for him, an urge to please him, and a sudden overpowering desire for security, security for both herself and Lucy for the rest of their lives. To have a man who was always in work, and more than that, one who had a bit behind him, for he had confided in her that there was a tidy little sum in the bank besides the money in the drawer. But the main thing was she'd really be mistress of the house if she married him.

He had said he would wait till she was seventeen. That was more than eight months away and eight months was a long time. She'd likely not mind being married in eight months' time.

Her hands relaxed within his. She smiled at him and

moved her head once, and the next minute she was pulled to her feet and hugged to him and, his lips pressing hard on hers, she received her first kiss.

Then he was holding her at arm's length, laughing loudly while shaking his head, and crying, 'I didn't mean to be rough, lass. It won't happen again, but ... but I thought I had a fight on me hands. Somehow I thought you would say, "Thank you very much, Sep, but I just want to be your housekeeper." Aw, lass, I feel the happiest man in the world. And look'—his voice now dropped to a confidential whisper—'I'm going to tell you something. Come Monday perhaps I'm going to give you something, something bonny, beautiful.'

'You are?' She looked at his face. It was gleaming with sweat, his eyes too were gleaming; and his voice still a whisper, he went on, 'You know that lot in there, in the drawer?' He thumbed back to the front room. 'Well, I'm selling the lot, and all to get one piece. Aw'—he now slapped her on the shoulder with the flat of his hand—'wait till you see it, lass. I'll not tell you anything about it, so it'll be a surprise, but just wait till you see it; it's fantastic. When I first glimpsed it I thought to meself, by! lad, I'd like to give that to Emily as a wedding present. And now you'll have it, lass, and you won't have to wait for the weddin', I'll give it you straightaway when I get it.

'Aw, Emily'—he now took her gently by the shoulders—'I'll make you happy, I promise you. You could, I know, with your looks an' the kindness of you, and your jollity, marry anybody. But let me tell you something, Emily. Nobody in the wide world could think of you as I do, an' will take care of you as I will, and will love you like me. What do you say to that?'

'I know, Sep, I know.'

'An' something more. When we're married I'll give such a do they won't have seen anything like it since

59

Coronation night. Queen Alexandra's won't hold a candle to the one I'll give you.'

She did not doubt but that he'd give her a big do, but why didn't it make her heart glad? All she wanted to do was to cry.

He said gently now, 'Away to your bed afore I eat you.'

She went, and she did cry. Her face buried in the pillow, she cried as she had never done before, and she told herself perhaps it was with happiness.

It had been a strange week-end. Her position in the house had changed from Saturday night. It was because of Sep's manner to her she supposed. He acted towards her like a young lad might. He'd put his arms around her waist, or around her shoulders, and when he did things he rushed at them, as when he brought in the coal, or took the ashes down the yard; and he went round the house talking about the alterations he was going to have made. He said the back yard wasn't of much use, but a bigger scullery would be, a scullery big enough to be classed as a kitchen. He even talked of bringing the lavatory inside.

Yet although he acted like a lad it didn't seem to make him any younger.

On Monday morning she did the washing, and when she hung it in the back lane and saw the sheets billowing in the wind it gave her a kind of joyous feeling in her stomach.

There was a cold dinner as always on a Monday, and when it was over Sep put his arms about her and kissed her. He kissed her gently, because she had struggled last night when he had kissed her rough. She felt funny when he kissed her but she supposed she'd get used to it in time.

As soon as he had gone back to work she washed the dinner dishes; then started to clean the two bedrooms, polishing everything from the windows to the floors; and she was still at it when Lucy came at quarter past four.

After placing before her three thick slices of new bread and butter and a plate of cold meat and pickles, she herself sat down thankfully and sipped at a cup of tea, saying, 'Eeh! look at the time, the afternoon's just flown.' Then, the cup half-way to her mouth, she stared at Lucy for a moment, realizing she was even more quiet than usual, and asked, 'What's up?'

Lucy swallowed on the mouthful of bread, then the tears gushing from her eyes she said, 'I ... I don't want to go back there, our Emily, I don't want to go back there. I tell you I don't.'

'What's happened?'

'It's him, that Tim Pearsley.'

'What's he done?'

'He ... he's always trying to catch hold of me.'

Emily sat back in the chair and drummed her fingers on the table. Something would have to be done; she knew Tim Pearsley and his type, oh aye. There were a lot of them about.

Suddenly leaning across the table, she grabbed Lucy's wrist, saying, 'You go on back home. Now listen, go on back home and I'll be along later. I'll talk to Se ... Mr McGillby, and I think he'll let you come now? But I can't keep you here off me own bat, you understand. Just you eat that up, then get off back. I should be there around seven. Now don't worry, you'll be all right.'

'You're sure, Emily?'

'Aye, I'm sure this time. We'll be sleepin' together again the night.' She grinned at her now. 'Come on, buck up.' She pushed Lucy's chin upwards. 'You know what I say.'

'Aye.' Lucy blinked back her tears, then wiped them off each cheek with her forefinger and she grinned in return as she said, 'Never say die.'

'That's it, never say die.'

When Lucy had gone, Emily decided she'd finish her bedroom in the morning; now she must wash herself and do her hair and put on a clean pinny before she got his tea; he liked to see her nice, and she'd not only have to look nice, but be nice when she asked him if she could have Lucy here.... No, not ask, but stress the fact that she'd have to have Lucy here ... now.

What was it he had said when he told her about his life and marrying Mrs McGillby? That everything must be paid for. Aye, well, she would pay for Lucy living here. She had given him a promise and she would keep it.

Sep usually came in about twenty past five, but it was now quarter past six and he still hadn't put in an appearance. She went and stood at the front door.

Over the wall edging the river bank she saw the funnel of a ship passing; it was going out on the high tide. It was a nice evening, a bit chilly and the twilight fast approaching, as one would expect in early October. She had kept her gaze directed towards West Holborn, from where he would come; then she happened to glance the other way and saw him in the far distance coming from the direction of Coronation Street. She was surprised at the relief she felt at the sight of him, it was so great that she almost ran along the street to meet him.

When he eventually reached her he grinned widely at her, saying, 'Sorry, lass, did you think I'd gone out on a banana boat?'

'Eeh! I didn't know what to think; you've never been late like this afore.'

'No, I haven't, but who knows, in the future I could be late like this again.... Emily, I'm on to a good thing, the night's only the beginning. Now you can get me tea, while I get me wash 'cos I've got to get out again, and quick.'

As she hurried into the scullery he called over his shoulder, 'I'll have you decked in diamonds yet, lass.'

As she squeezed past him in the scullery, she said, 'Is it that thing you were talking about on Saturday night?'

He didn't answer her immediately for he was swishing the water around his neck and over his face and spluttering and puffing the while; but in the middle of drying himself he held the towel to the side of his face as he looked at her and said, 'Aye it is, and by! it's bonny, nearly as bonny as you. But come on, no time to waste, I've got to see this fellow at half past seven. There's got to be a bit of bargaining to and fro afore things get settled.'

She put a sizzling mixed fry before him, but when she didn't put a similar helping down for herself he stopped eating and said, 'Where's yours?'

'I don't want any the night, Sep.'

'What's the matter?'

She stood by his side looking down at him. 'Our Lucy's been, she's in a state.'

He now turned his head to the side, saying, 'Ah now, Emily, another time, the morrow, but I've got this business the night.'

She moved from him now and, taking a seat opposite him, she placed her hands in her lap and said quietly, 'This is important to me, Sep. There's a fellow there lodger, I . . . I think he's tryin' to interfere with her.'

'What! She said that?'

'As much.'

'Well, well'—he rubbed his fingers across his greasy lips—'this puts a different complexion on it.' He looked hard at her now. She was sitting straight-faced; her body, too, was straight. Like this she appeared a young woman, not a young lass of sixteen. She had a look of someone nearer twenty, and if he knew anything about it she was thinking like someone nearing twenty, for it was a kind of ultimatum she was putting to him: 'You have Lucy or

63

you're not getting me.' Well it was turning out tit for tat, for hadn't he himself used the youngster as a lever to bring this bonny bit permanently into his life?

Slowly he smiled at her. She had a head on her shoulders had his young Emily and he liked that; he liked a woman to have something up top. And by! when she became a woman she'd not only have something up top but all round. By! she would that. His smile widened into a grin; he winked at her and grabbed up his knife and fork as he said, 'Go ahead, lass, bring her when you like; the place is yours and all in it.'

'Oh, thanks, Sep. Ta, thanks. I'll go as soon as I've washed up.'

Twenty minutes later he was bidding her good-bye, saying, 'Now, I don't know when I'll be back, I could be gone an hour or two, or it might be nearer eleven when I fall in through the front door.' He laughed loudly at this, adding, 'And it's more than likely I'll have a drop on me.' He put his finger out and tickled her chin. 'But I won't be drunk, I promise you. Good-bye, lass.'

After he had kissed her she closed the front door and stood for a moment wiping the moisture from around her mouth before dashing into the kitchen and up the stairs for her hat and coat.

The last thing she did after locking the back door was to put the large iron key on the wooden shelf attached to the back of the iron mangle in the wash-house. Sep insisted that one key must always be left in the wash-house. At one time he'd only had one key, and whenever he lost it he'd break a window to get in.

There seemed to be twice as many children at play in Creador Street than anywhere else in the town. When she came to No. 18 the door, as usual, was open, and, also as usual, there were children on the stairs, but only the two girls Kate and Annie, and Jack. The girls were dressing a clouty doll; Jack was standing leaning against the staircase wall. He'd had his hands in his pockets idly watching them until Emily made her appearance; then he sprang upright, saying, 'Oh, hello, Emily.'

'Hello, Jack. Where's our Lucy?'

When he simply looked back at her without giving her an answer she bent and peered at him in the dimness of the staircase and demanded, 'Where is she?'

He merely jerked his head back on his shoulders, and she stared at him before saying, 'What's the matter, what's happened?'

He now strained his face towards her as he whispered, 'Me ma's out; there's only our Tommy up there an' ... an' Tim Pearsley. He ... he made us come out.'

'Who did, Pearsley?'

'Aye.'

'And Lucy, she's still in?'

'Aye.' He moved his head slightly as he muttered, 'He wouldn't let her come down.'

She took the stairs two at a time and, thrusting open the kitchen door, she startled Tommy who was wielding the point of his knife around the edge of the table.

'Where's our Lucy?'

When he, too, made no answer she turned her head and looked in the direction of the bedroom wall; then she almost leapt across the room, grabbed the poker from the fender, rushed out again on to the landing and, having glanced swiftly from one bedroom door to the other, she picked on the door of the smaller room and, turning the knob, she thrust it open.

She had expected the door to be bolted or at least a chair stuck under the handle, which was why she had picked up the poker in the first place. But now she stood, her hand at shoulder height holding the poker, glaring through the flickering gas jet into the startled face of Tim Pearsley.

As she had seen him before, his upper body was bare,

but his trousers, now without a belt, were hanging slackly around his hips. He was half sitting, half leaning across the bed, an elbow giving him support while his other hand was gripping Lucy's leg near the thigh. Lucy was tightly pressed against the wall at the side of the bed. She was making no sound, no whimper. Her face was the colour of fresh fallen snow and her features were like the same snow when frozen solid.

'You dirty rotten pig of a man! Lucy, come out of that!'

Startled as if from a dream, Lucy jerked herself upwards in the bed. But Tim Pearsley's hand pulled her down again; and now he turned and grinned slowly at Emily, saying, 'Nice to see you.'

'Let go of her!'

'Why should I? She likes a bit of carry-on.'

She didn't stop to think, the poker seemed to leave her hand of its own volition. When it found its target the room was filled with a great cursing roar, and she saw Tim Pearsley stagger back with the blood running from the side of his face near his ear.

When Lucy sprang from the bed she grabbed her hand; and then they were racing down the stairs, past the astonished wide-eyed children, and into the street. And they ran and ran, not stopping until they entered the back lane of Pilot Place, and there, gasping, they both leant against the wall of the warehouse.

After a time Emily pulled herself upright and Lucy with her, and they stumbled down the back lane and into the yard. Still gasping, Emily pushed open the door of the wash-house, took the key from behind the mangle, and entered the house.

As she pulled her hat and coat off she looked at Lucy standing like someone lost in the doorway between the scullery and the kitchen, and she said as if clothes were the main concern, 'Don't worry about your coat and hat,

I'll get you another. Anyway, you can have me old one.'

She continued to stare at the still dead-white face before her. All the running hadn't put any colour into it, and so taking Lucy's hand, she led her gently towards the fire and pressed her down on to a chair, she herself dropping on to her hunkers before her and looking into her face, and she asked, 'Did ... did he touch you?'

Some seconds elapsed before Lucy shook her head slowly.

'You're sure?'

'Aye.'

Emily took a deep breath as she straightened up, and smiling faintly now, she said, 'You'll be all right from now on. Never again will you have to put up with that because you're not going back.... Now, now, don't start an' cry.' She lifted Lucy's bowed head upwards and, gazing tenderly into her face, she said, 'We're set for life, you and me. I'm goin' to tell you something, secret like as yet, but I'm going to marry Mr McGillby ... Sep.'

'Mr McGillby? ... Marry him?'

Emily could see that even Lucy was a bit shocked at the prospect, and so she put in quickly, 'He's not all that old.'

'Isn't he?'

'No. And ... and he's young in his ways, like a lad at times. And he's nice, Lucy; you know he's nice.'

'Oh aye, yes, I know he's nice.' Lucy now turned her head slowly and looked round the kitchen, and as if reading her thoughts, Emily said, 'And this'll be our home, our house. And it isn't rented like others, he owns it. And you know something else?' She now bent and leant her face close to Lucy's. 'He's got a bank book, he's got money in the bank. Now that's something, isn't it?'

When Lucy made no reply Emily turned away and said aloud, as if to herself, 'Never in me life will I need to worry where the next bite's coming from.'

It was as if her mother or an older woman were expressing her thoughts; indeed at this moment she felt old, grown up. She had made a decision, a great decision, all by herself, she had made it in order to get herself and Lucy fixed for life. And she wasn't cheating on it, she told herself; she'd pay her way, for by marrying Sep she wouldn't be getting things on tick, she'd be paying her way.

As he had foretold, Sep was late in coming in, and also as he had foretold he had beer on him; but he wasn't drunk. Emily had kept Lucy up in order to meet him and when he saw her sitting by the fireside, a long coat over her nightie, he smiled at her kindly and said, 'Well, you've come home, lass.'

Lucy didn't speak, and so Emily said, 'She's shy, but I've told her everything's all right.'

'What did you find when you got there? Did you have any trouble?'

She nodded at him as she said, 'It was as she told me, he was trying to get at her. He had her in the bedroom in the corner of the bed and'—she stopped and bit on her lip.

'Well, go on.'

'He had a hold of her leg an' wouldn't let go, an' ... an' I seemed to go a bit mad ... I hit him with a poker.'

'You what!' His voice came small as if from someone of half his stature.

'I picked it up to batter on the door but the door was open, the bedroom door, and there he was lying across the bed and her in the corner'—she thumbed now towards Lucy—'screwed up against the wall. An' she's got bruises all over her backside ... bottom, the lot, where he's been nippin' at her. She's been scared out of her wits.'

Sep looked down into the small white face of Emily's

68

sister. They didn't appear like sisters. Emily was robust and bonny whereas this lass was puny. He feared she had the consumption on her. Was that why he didn't want her in the house? No, because he wasn't afraid of picking up anything; if you had to get anything, you got it was his philosophy. But what he said now was, 'You hit him with a poker? Did you hurt him?'

'Yes. Aye, I think ... I think so; I saw the blood running down his face, and he fell back against the wall. But we ran. We just ran.'

'Good God!'

She was standing straight now, stiff, as she said, 'I'm not sorry, I'm not a bit sorry. If you like I'll go to the polis the morrow and tell them what I did, 'cos look'—she now pulled the coat from around Lucy's shoulders and pushed up the wide sleeve of the calico night-dress as she cried—'Look at that!'

And he looked. The top of the girl's arm was almost black and blue.

'And that's not all. I'm ... I'm gona show you this.' With a swift movement of her hand she had pulled up the bottom of the night-dress until it was half-way up Lucy's side. 'Just look at them! He stuck his finger nails into her. And there's other places that I cannot show you.'

As Sep looked down on the bruises and small weals on the child's leg his face became grim and he said between his teeth, 'The dirty bugger!' Then bending down to Lucy, he asked, 'What d'you say his name is, lass? Tim? ... Tim?'

'Pearsley. Tim Pearsley.'

'Pearsley.... Big fellow, reddish hair?'

Lucy's nod confirmed the description.

'Pearsley? I know Pearsley, big Tim Pearsley. Oh, I know him, an' I'll have a word to say to Mr Pearsley the morrow. Now, lass, if you've had something to eat go on get up to bed, and from now on this is your home, there'll be no more Pearsleys in your life if I've got anythin' to do with it.' He patted Lucy's head and pushed her gently forward, and Emily called softly to her, 'You know where to go. Go on, I'll be up in a minute.' And then they were alone together.

Seating himself in the wooden armchair, Sep said, 'You did the right thing, lass. Yes, you did the right thing. And with a poker an' all! Though somehow I can't see you throwin' a poker.' He put his head back and laughed. 'You won't try on anything like that with me, will you?'

'No, Sep.' She smiled, but her smile was weary, and he said, 'You look tired, lass.'

'It's been a kind of busy night; I ... think I'm just feeling the effect now.'

'Yes, you would, it always sets in after. But you did right. Aye, you did right. The dirty swine. Just you wait till the morrow. But now I said I'd something to show you, didn't I?'

'Yes.'

'Well, somehow, I don't think you're wide enough awake to appreciate it at this minute.'

'You don't?'

'No, I don't, lass, so I'm gona leave it, because I want it to do you credit, an' I want you to do it credit. Do you see what I mean?'

She smiled gently at him as she said, 'Not ... not quite, Sep.'

'No, no, lass, you're too tired. Well, things'll be different this time the morrow night. You have an easy day of it the morrow; you take Lucy out and go and have a look round the shops and walk down to the sands, it'll do you good. Then put your best frock on the morrow night, and after you've sent Lucy up to bed early on I'll show you what I've got for you. It's the prettiest thing.' He shook his head slowly as if he was seeing something in his mind's eye. 'You know, Emily, I didn't realize that I had a taste for bonny things. It's come on me gradually, sort of seeped into me that I like to own things, not big things like furniture and stuff, but small things, precious things, and'—he put his arm out now and grabbed her round the waist—'an' things like you. Oh aye, you're the most precious thing I've ever seen in me life. Aw, Emily, can you guess how happy you've made me, an' how happy you're going to make me? This last few days I've realized I haven't lived, not really. I haven't had anything out of life that's really been good. Aw'—he jerked his head now as he hugged her to him—'there's good an' good. That lot of ranters, they would class themselves as being good, but that isn't the good I mean. You know what I mean, don't you?'

'Aye, Sep.'

'You know the little book I gave you out of the secret drawer? Well, the line in that bit of poetry keeps sticking in me mind, an' you know, it gets truer every day. How does it go? Existence is the time it takes for the shingle to be wet.'

Existence is the time it takes for the shingle to be wet.

He shook his head slowly.

'You know Emily there's a lot in that, a tremendous lot, in fact there's everything in it. A whole life is over in just the time it takes for a wave to wet the shingle. Whoever wrote that must have thought long an' deep. Don't you think so?'

'Yes, Sep.'

'Aw, lass, I see you're dropping on your feet. Go on, up to bed, but afore you go give us a kiss.'

He pulled her on to his knee and, his arms tightly about her now, he kissed her, and the smell of beer wafted up her nostrils. But, as she had said, she wanted

71

nothing on tick and so she kissed him back. Then she did a strange thing, she thought it strange even at the moment but it was to seem much stranger still when she thought of it later in life, for having reached the door at the bottom of the stairs she ran back to him and, flinging her arms around his neck, she pressed her lips tightly to his, even indecently, she imagined. And such was his pleasure and surprise that there was moisture in his eyes as he watched her turn and hurry towards the staircase door and disappear behind it.

SIX

It was quarter to nine the next morning when Jack knocked on the back door, and when Emily opened it he looked at her apologetically and said below his breath, 'I had to come, me ma sent me.'

'What is it?' she asked quietly.

'She says you've got to send Lucy back or she'll have the polis on you.'

'Does she? Well, you go back an' tell her to get the polis right away 'cos if she doesn't I will. Then I'll let them see what her lodger has done to our Lucy. An' you tell her from me that when she went out she knew what would happen to our Lucy. She went out on purpose, and undoubtedly was well paid for it, you tell her that from me. Now remember every word I've said, Jack.'

When he stood staring at her, she said, 'Is there anything more?'

'Aye, but ... but she didn't tell me to say this, but I think you'd better know, Emily. Tim Pearsley says he'll get you for what you did to him last night.'

She swallowed deeply before she said, 'Will he? Well, I'm goin' to tell you something, Jack. I'd do it again and more if he comes within arm's length of me.' Her voice dropping now, she asked, 'Did I cut him bad?'

He nodded at her. 'Me ma said you could have taken his eye out.'

'It's a pity I didn't.' She sounded at this moment braver

73

than she felt for she was thinking, Eeh! if I had.

'I thought I'd better tell you, Emily, 'cos ... 'cos he means it. He's a nasty piece of work, I don't like him, no more than you did.' Then he added, 'I'll have to be away else I'll be late for school.'

'Wait a minute.'

Hurrying back into the kitchen she took tuppence from the housekeeping tin that stood on the end of the mantelpiece, and when she put it into his hand, he said, 'Eeh! ta, thanks, Emily'; then backing from her, he said, 'Ta-rah then'; but paused a moment before turning to run down the back yard and said, 'You'll look out for him, won't you?'

'Don't you worry about me, Jack. An' thanks for comin'. Go on now.'

Having closed the door and returned to the kitchen she stood near the table nodding to herself. Let him try anything an' I'll go straight to the polis. Or Sep will see to him, aye, he will. He said he would this morning afore he went out. 'Don't you worry about Lucy,' he said. 'You'll have no more trouble from that dirty swine, I'll see to that. I've got a bit of power in the docks you know. At least at my end, what I say goes, and if there's anybody questions it I just go to the dock office and I see the boss. Him and me get on well together. He knows I do a good job, an' I'm a fair man, so don't you worry any more about that dirty bas ... devil.'

But she did worry about him; he stayed in her mind all the morning, putting a weight on her spirit. Her biggest worry had been Lucy, and now that should be over for hadn't she sent Lucy out to school this morning from this very house looking happier than she had seen her in her life before. So let Tim Pearsley start anything, just let him....

Sep usually came in for his dinner between ten past and quarter past twelve. She had made a pot pie for him.

74

He loved pot pie; he could eat a whole one himself with a pound of steak and kidney in it and the top crust as well.

She gave Lucy a portion of the pie together with potatoes and cabbage when she came in from school.

At half past twelve when Sep still hadn't arrived she opened the oven and placed a large basin over the plate on which lay more than half of the pudding. Then standing gazing towards the kitchen window that looked on to the yard she muttered aloud, 'It'll be as dry as sticks if he doesn't hurry up.'

At one o'clock she was sitting alone staring out of the window, her hands gripped tightly in her lap. Something was up, something had happened, in the usual way he'd be back at work now. She felt sick. She had told herself that he might be working through; sometimes when the boats had to be turned round quickly, especially the iron ore boats that came from Bilbao, they did a double shift and worked right through the night. But he would have let her know; he always did. He would send one of the dock lads with a message and a request for some bait.

She was still sitting with her eyes fixed on the window when there came a knock on the front door and she swung round so quickly that she ricked her neck.

When she opened the door and saw a man in a blue serge suit and a white shirt and high starched collar, and by his side a uniformed man whom she knew to be a dock policeman, she gasped, opened her mouth wide, then closed it, but didn't utter a word.

'Can we come in a minute?' It was the man in the blue serge suit who had spoken, and she pulled the door wider and let them into the front room, where they stood now looking at her. And again it was the man in the blue serge suit who spoke. 'I ... I take it you're Mr McGillby's housekeeper?' he said.

She moved her head once, her eyes never leaving his face.

'Well, I'm afraid we've ... we've got bad news for you, lass.'

She swallowed deeply in her throat, then gripped it with her hand, but still she didn't speak.

'There's been an accident on one of the boats. A sling of props gave way. One of them ... well, it caught Mr McGillby on the back of the neck and he went over the side. He ... he wasn't drowned, it was the blow, sort of a million to one chance. Props, well, props are falling every day, men get knocked out with them, but ... but this one, well ... it broke his neck.'

She didn't know how she had arrived in the kitchen. She was again sitting on the chair that was facing the window and it was the policeman now who was talking. He was saying, 'There now, there now, you're all right.'

She stared up at him. She wanted to say something. Her thoughts were jumping one over the other, and one, jumping higher than the rest, caused her to gasp and choke as she said, 'He ... he didn't work ... on ... on the prop boats.'

'No, lass, we know that, we haven't got to the bottom of it yet. He had gone to see somebody, I understand, on one of the boats just afore knocking off time. We've got to go into it. Nobody seemed to know what really happened. The buzzer had gone and they were all making for the dock gates. The last men to see him said he was talking to a chap called Pearsley, and they know nothing more after that but that the sling must have given way.'

She heard herself give a loud cry, then she saw the floor come up and hit her.

It was the policeman again whom she saw when she opened her eyes. She was lying full length on the mat now, but it was the man in the serge suit who said, 'Take a drink of this, lass.'

A few minutes later she was once more sitting on the

chair. Her body was trembling from head to foot, and her mind was repeating one name, Pearsley, Pearsley, Pearsley. It was right then, Jack's warning. He said he would get her, and as the saying went, there were more ways than one of killing a cat. He had killed Sep. Oh no! No! No, Sep couldn't be dead; it was impossible. She had seen him go out of that door at six o'clock this morning. She had put his breakfast bait into his hand and he had kissed her.

'Who is Mr McGillby's nearest relative?'

'What?' Her head was back on her shoulders, her mouth was open and she gazed up at the man.

'Who is his nearest relative? Do you know?'

'He ... he has a sister. She lives in Dock Street—a Mrs Blackmore. That's the only one I think.'

'She'll have to be informed. Have you anybody who can come and stay with you?'

'No, no, I don't want anybody.'

'Well, we'll have to leave you now, lass, there's things to be seen to.'

Suddenly she was gripping the policeman's arm. 'But where is he? Where have they put him?'

'They took him to hospital but ... but they couldn't do anything. He's in the mortuary there.'

She moved her head slowly. She couldn't take it in, she couldn't believe it; and what was more strange still, she wasn't crying. She couldn't cry, her whole body seemed to be frozen, numb.

'We'll have to go now, lass. Sure you'll be all right?'

She moved her head once and as they went towards the front room the man in the blue serge suit turned and said, 'We'll inform his sister. She'll come along and see you, lass.'

She didn't nod now, she just stared at them. Sep hadn't liked his sister, he had hated his sister, he had never invited her to the funeral, nor would he let her in that day to the tea. He had said that she was a no good, lying, slovenly bitch and nothing more than a dock whore; he had actually said that about her. And now she would come and take over.

An only relative.

The house, everything, everything that had been Sep's would be hers.

She stood up and supported herself against the kitchen table, her hands behind her. She pressed her buttocks tight against it as she gripped the edge. This beautiful house, this house that she loved, and every stick in it, this house that she had looked after for years. She could hardly remember a time when she had lived in Creador Street; even when she had lived there she had dreamt about this house at nights, about being able to work full time in it. And then lately she had known that it was hers. Sep in a way had already given it to her; she was to be married to Sep. *It was hers.*

No, no, it wasn't. She turned slowly now and pressed the flat of her hands on the table and bent over it. She wasn't married to Sep; as the man had said, she was his housekeeper. She couldn't claim stick or stone in it. But did it matter? Did it matter now that Sep was dead?

And why had Sep died? That's what she should be asking herself. He had died because of her really. If she hadn't hit Tim Pearsley with that poker Sep would never have gone for him.

Yes, yes, he would. It was the marks on Lucy that had made him angry ... Lucy. If it hadn't been for Lucy, Sep would be alive. If she hadn't insisted on bringing Lucy here.... But if she hadn't what would have happened to Lucy? Oh dear God! Her mind was in a whirl, what was she going to do? Oh Sep. Sep. Suddenly she had a deep overwhelming longing for him, she wanted to feel the toughness of his arms, the hardness of his chest, to put her face against his neck. She had felt a certain kind of security when she had put her face against his neck and he placed his hand on her hair.

What was she to do now? Would that woman turn her out?

Of course she would turn her out.

No, no, she wouldn't; she wouldn't be as bad as that.

'Don't be so daft: of course she'll turn you out.'

She was speaking aloud, even shouting. She put her hand over her mouth. She felt she was going funny, mad. Where would she go? What would she do? How much money had she? She had nearly twenty-five shillings of her own saved up; after giving the shilling to Alice Broughton she hadn't touched the one and sixpence since Sep had raised her wages. Then there was the odd half-crown he had slipped her now and again to go and buy herself something on a Saturday morning. She never had, she had saved it. But she had never skimped the house-keeping to save anything for herself.

The housekeeping! She took down the tin from the mantelpiece. There was six and elevenpence in it. This was the accumulated residue of weeks. She paused a moment before taking the money out and thrusting it into her apron pocket; then she went into the front room and stood in front of the bureau. There was money in there in the secret drawer, a lot of money. The rings and things had likely gone to help buy that present for her. And he had brought it last night, and she would have got it if it hadn't have been for the do over Lucy. But she was to have had it tonight. Make yourself bonny, he had said, because it's a bonny piece. What was it?

She could open the drawer now and have a look. But what if she came in, that woman, and saw the top open?

Go on, open it, now, quick!

It was as she actually obeyed the inner command and pulled open the drawer with the intention of pressing the button that she heard the latch of the back door being lifted, and she banged the little drawer closed, pulled down the lid of the desk and was at the entrance to the kitchen when Jessie Blackmore entered the room.

Emily saw immediately what she was up against, for the woman was actually bristling with triumph; it came over in her voice which was high and almost a screech, as she cried, 'Well now, well now, I can see you've heard, an' so you know your number's up, don't you, miss? An' not afore time, 'cos only death would have opened our Sep's eyes to you. And he's gone, hasn't he? I'm no hypocrite.' She now tossed her head from side to side, 'Nobody'll say that Jessie Blackmore is a hypocrite. There was never no love lost 'tween him and me, but I'm his only living relative. That's what the polis said an' the boss from the docks. "You, Mrs Blackmore, are Mr McGillby's only living relative, and the young lass has taken things badly. You'd better get yourself along there," he said, "an' take charge. There'll be papers and things to see to. Like a will perhaps." Or'—she now nodded her head deeply— 'no will. Well, in the meantime I'm takin' charge an' you know what you can do, miss.'

'Yes, I know what I can do.' Emily was choking on her words. 'I ... I don't need you to tell me.'

'No, you don't need me to tell you anything, you know everything, everything there is to know about ensnaring a man. The whole town's been talkin' about you and him.'

'We were going to be married.'

'Huh! listen to her. How old are you? Sixteen, if that, and him old enough to be your da. You were going to be married? Huh! that's a laugh....'

'We were, we were. As soon as I reached seventeen, we were. And nobody could say anything about us because there was nothing to say.'

'If you told that to the cat it would scratch your eyes out.... Who do you think you're kiddin'? Livin' here with him all these months by yourself and his wife an invalid and not being able to give him anythin' for years.... Nothin' atween you? You've got a nerve even to look me straight in the face when you're sayin' it. Well now'—she made a deep obeisance with her head, at the same time pulling her coat off and throwing it across a chair—'we'll set you on your way; we'll see you get packed and take only what's yours.'

Emily had the urge to take her hand and slap the woman across the mouth but she knew if she did what would happen. A woman such as Jessie Blackmore would tear the hair from her head in handfuls; she had seen her like fighting in the docks, women rolling in the gutter joined together, their hands entwined in each other's hair like the entangled horns of wild animals. She had seen a picture of animals like that once in a school book.

Slowly now she looked around the kitchen, not bidding it a last farewell but to see if there was anything of hers lying about. Then she went past the woman into the scullery and took her coarse apron from behind the door. It was a hessian apron she used when scrubbing the scullery and the lavatory outside. She had sewn two pieces of felt on it to act as knee-caps. Slowly she rolled it up, and as slowly returned to the kitchen, opened the staircase door and mounted the stairs; and Jessie Blackmore came close behind her.

When the woman went to follow her into her bedroom she stopped her by placing her arm against the stanchion of the door as she said, 'This is my room. What's in it belongs to me, that is except the furniture.'

'Well, if everything belongs to you then you won't mind me seeing what you put into your box. Go on!' The woman's voice now changed into a raucous growl and she pushed Emily from the door and almost on to the bed.

Bracing herself against the foot of the bed, Emily now turned on her and cried, 'You touch me again, just once, and you'll see what you'll get. Now I'm warning you. An' what's more I'll go to the dock office and I'll tell them there that Sep ... Mr McGillby hated your guts and wouldn't let you into the house, not even to his wife's funeral, and that I was going to marry him and that I have a case. Aye'—she nodded her head briskly now— 'I've got a case and you look out that I don't put it forward and fight you. And I can! I can!'

Her head was bobbing on her neck like a golliwog's, the tears were swelling her throat, aching to give vent.

She bent down swiftly and pulled from under the bed a wicker-work hamper held together by two leather straps. She threw it on the bed and took off the lid; then going to the chest of drawers, she pulled open the top drawer, gathered up her few belongings of underclothes and threw them into the case. From the next drawer she took two print dresses and four aprons; from the bottom drawer she lifted out her two best dresses, one of which was a light summer cotton that Sep had given her the money to buy shortly after she had become his housekeeper. The case now full, she crammed on the lid, fastened the straps, then almost threw it on to the floor. She next took down the two coats that were hanging on the back of the door. Putting her best one on, she flung the other one down on top of the case. Lastly, she put on her one and only hat, rammed the hatpins through it, then turned and, facing Jessie Blackmore, cried at her, 'There! I'm ready. I'm going, but you'll see, I'll be back; I'll be back in this house if it takes me all me life. I'll show you; I'll be back in this house, you'll see.'

'Huh! listen to who's talkin'. Go on, get yourself away before I spit in yer eye, you trollop.'

Emily was in the act of lifting up the hamper from the floor, but now on the woman's words she flung it aside and it bounced heavily from the wall almost to Jessie Blackmore's feet, making her jump and not a little startled now, not only by the near impact of the hamper but also by the look on the young girl's face and the sound of her voice which laid no claim to that of a sixteen-year-old, for she was yelling at her now deep from within her throat. 'You dare call me a trollop? You take that back; don't you tack your name on to me. Sep said you were a dock whore, and you are, you're stinkin', he said you were. Now get down those stairs an' out of me way else you'll get this hamper round your lugs next, I'm tellin' you.'

It wasn't only something in her voice but something in the girl's face that made Jessie Blackmore, head tossing, go quickly down the stairs, but when Emily reached the kitchen there she was with the back door held wide waiting for her departure.

Emily didn't stop to look round for she was experiencing a strange feeling of rage intermingled with injustice and bewilderment. Yet somewhere inside her a voice was whimpering; things shouldn't happen like this, she had done nothing to deserve it, she had worked hard for years in that house. She had been going to marry Sep and she would have made him a good wife. She hadn't loved him, at least she didn't think she had loved him; but then she didn't know very much about love, proper love and how it made you feel.

Out in the back lane she stopped and, putting the hamper and her coat down on the ground, she stood with her back against the warehouse wall as she had done last night when she and Lucy had stopped running....

Was it only last night that she had brought Lucy home?

Home. She had forgotten about Lucy. What would she do with her? She couldn't get into a place with Lucy; people wanted servants without attachments, and Lucy wasn't only a schoolgirl still, but she was weak. For a long time now she had realized that Lucy had a weakness on her. And she'd be coming back any time now, her face bright, as it had been at dinner-time.

What was she going to do? One thing was certain, she wasn't going to let her go back to Alice Broughton's, no no. Well then, what was she going to do? Where could they go? She had her money on her. It was in her purse in the pocket of her best dress. Jessie Blackmore hadn't seen that. And then there were the oddments in her work apron that she had rolled up. In all she had over thirty shillings, enough to get them into lodgings for a night or two and give her time to think. But in the meantime she must watch for Lucy coming. She'd better go into the front street.

Picking up the hamper again, she went out of the back lane and into the street. But there she was overcome by a feeling of humiliation. There were people going in and out of the warehouse at the far end and also customers going into the shop; if she stood here she'd be noticed, especially with the hamper.

Across the road where the wall bordered the river bank, and away to the left, there was a cut that led down to a little ship-building yard. She would stand there; she wouldn't be noticed, yet at the same time she'd be able to see Lucy coming.

Having entered the cut and put the hamper down just inside, her legs began to tremble. She felt for a moment they were going to give beneath her and just in case they did she sat down on the hamper.

There was little traffic on the road now, but at five o'clock it would be black with men from the docks and the yards. It was the time she had always looked forward to because it was a signal that Sep would soon be home.

She mustn't cry, she must try not to think about Sep. Anyway, she didn't think he was dead; he couldn't be dead not really, not as quick as that.

She was sitting with her head leaning against the end

84

post of the wooden railings when her attention was drawn to two men. One of them she thought she recognized as the man in the blue serge suit who had come to give her the news earlier on. When he and his companion stopped outside the green-painted door she knew it was him and she pulled herself slowly to her feet and stood pressed against the railings in case they should turn round and look in her direction.

She saw the door open, she saw the man in the serge suit pointing to the other man; then they went inside the house.

What had they come back for? The time seemed endless before the door opened again, but it couldn't have been more than five minutes, and then to her amazement she saw emerge into the street not only the two men but Jessie Blackmore. Then she saw something that lifted her heart, she saw Jessie Blackmore lock the door, then, with definite reluctance, hand the key, not to the man in the blue serge suit, but to the other one. And now she heard her talking. She couldn't make out what she was saying but she was talking loud and fast, and the man who had taken the key made a very expressive gesture that was understandable to Emily: he flapped his hand almost in Jessie Blackmore's face, it was as if he had said, 'Oh, shut up! woman.' Then the two men walked away, coming in her direction, while Jessie Blackmore, after staring after them for a moment, went in the opposite direction.

Had the two men looked across the road they would surely have seen her, but they were talking earnestly to each other and they passed on.

She now stood with her fingers across her mouth. What did it mean? Well, for a start it meant one thing, they weren't letting that individual have the run of the place straightaway; that other man had looked an important type, like the men who went into the offices in King Street. Anyway, they were holding a key.... The key!

'Always keep one key behind the mangle, lass, just in case.' It was as if she heard Sep's voice speaking to her.

The key behind the mangle, that was the solution for the night. When it was dark they could get inside and they'd have shelter, and she'd have time to think.

She now saw Lucy running along the road towards her. She looked happy, thinking she was coming home to a good tea.

Emily stepped from the alleyway and waved her hand, then called, 'Lucy! Our Lucy!'

The girl stopped at the corner near the chapel and looked across to the cut in amazement; then she obeyed Emily's beckoning hand.

Lucy didn't ask what was up, she just looked in amazement at Emily dressed and with a hamper and a coat at her feet, and Emily, taking her hand, said, 'Listen. Listen, our Lucy. You'll get a shock, but Sep's been killed.' Her voice broke. 'He was killed in the docks.' She didn't at this moment say, 'And Tim Pearsley had something to do with it,' because that would put a load on Lucy's shoulders as young as she was; instead, she added, 'And that woman, his sister from Dock Street, she came and took over and turned me out. But now the men from the offices have been, an' it seems they've shown her what's what, for they've taken the key from her and until things are sorted out she won't be able to take over. Listen——' She now bent down to the startled white face and said, 'We'll go down into the town and have a cup of tea and wait till it's dark, and then we'll come back and get in the back way, there's another key, so ... don't worry, we're all right for the night.'

'Oh, Emily.' The name was a tremor coming through the pale lips, but Emily admonished her harshly, saying, 'Now look, our Lucy, don't you start to bubble, I've got enough on me plate. Now be a good lass and keep a straight face and ... and things will pan out. They've got to somehow.'

'But ... but where'll we go the morrow?'

Emily bent and picked up the coat, saying, 'You carry that,' then added, 'The morrow'll take care of itself. One thing you needn't worry about, we're not going back to Creador Street. I'd rather suffer the workhouse than let you or me go back there, so I'm tellin' you don't worry. Anyway, if I've thought of nothing by the morrow we can always go to me Aunt Mary Southern in Gateshead; she'd put us up for a night or so.'

'Me Aunt Mary Southern!'

'Yes, you know in Gateshead. It's a long time since I've seen her but she wouldn't turn us away.'

'But she's got a squad, hasn't she? The last time we were there the house was full.'

'Well, you'll find, our Lucy, that it's always those with squads that can make room for another one or two. It'll be all right, I'm tellin' you, it'll be all right.'

But Lucy didn't seem to think so for now she persisted, 'What about Mrs Gantry next door?' She pointed across the road.

At this Emily tossed her head in impatience. How could she explain that Mrs Gantry hadn't spoken to her since she had taken over the post of housekeeper to Sep. Mrs Gantry, although deaf as a stone, must have heard enough to cause her to condemn the situation next door. And so she said, 'We're not going to Mrs Gantry's. She's deaf, stone deaf, and ... and not well, she can't be bothered with people. So come on, and, I've told you, everything will work out all right.'

She hadn't the courage at this moment to add, 'Never say die....'

They waited until it was quite dark, they were both stiff with cold and very hungry. Emily had afforded them a cup of tea in a cafe, but that was all, going on the assumption that Lucy had had a good dinner and could last out until they got into the house. As she remembered, Jessie Blackmore had carried no bags as she came out of the house, so the food would still be there.

They had sat in the park until the park-keeper had turned them out and locked the gates; then they had walked the streets, their steps dragging as the weight of the hamper became heavier; and now they were in the back lane and outside the back door. The back-yard door was on the latch; Sep locked it only at nights.

Within a matter of minutes she was in the wash-house and had taken the key from behind the mangle and had the back door open and they were inside the house. It was black dark and there was no thought of lighting the gas, but she knew every inch of the place and where every article was, especially in the pantry; that is if that woman hadn't moved things around.

Her gropings proved that things in the pantry had been moved around quite a bit, but eventually she found the bread and the butter and some cheese. But there was no pot pie in the bottom of the oven and her thought was, She scoffed that straightaway, I suppose.

As she sat in the dark cold kitchen, Lucy pressed close to her side, munching on the bread and cheese, she again had the urge to cry, to cry for Sep. Poor Sep. He had been so kind, she'd never meet anyone like him again. It seemed impossible to believe that he was here last night in this very room.

When Lucy whispered, 'Do you think I could have a drink, Emily?' she was silent for a moment. The fire was quite dead but she could light the gas ring in the scullery. She could pull the blind down; no one would see a small glow like that.

After groping for the matches she lit the gas ring, boiled the water and made them some cocoa; then she said to Lucy, 'You go to bed. Come on, I'll take you up. But sleep in your things. Just take your boots off because we'll have to be ready and out afore daylight.' Then she added, 'I'm going downstairs again but I won't be a minute or so. I ... I want to pack up a bit of bread and stuff for the morrow.'

Lucy made no answer, she just coughed a hard dry cough.

Emily had decided to pack the remnants of the food to take with them tomorrow but her main reason in returning downstairs now was something different.

Groping her way into the front room and to the desk, she lifted up the lid, pulled out the bottom right-hand drawer and pressed the knob. The slight click as the weights were released told her that the enclosed apartment was rising. When there was another click and the little structure had settled into place she pulled open the right-hand drawer, then gave an audible gasp as her groping fingers touched nothing but the bare wood, and her mind yelled at her, 'She's been here! She's found it!' Then reason said quietly, 'She couldn't. She couldn't.' Swiftly now she pulled open the left-hand drawer and when her fingers touched the coins she let out a long-drawn breath. Jessie Blackmore wouldn't leave sovereigns lying about, but there didn't seem as many as when Sep had shown them to her. There had been a couple of layers of sovereigns covering the bottom, but now they seemed sparse.

She pulled open the middle cupboard and when her fingers touched something strange she lifted it out and felt it, and from the shape of it she made out what appeared to be a watch with a strap attached to one end of it, and that was all, the watches and the other pieces were gone.

She now raked the coins together, and when she had cleared the drawer she pressed her hand on the top of the risen structure and pushed it downwards and so into place; then groping her way back to the scullery she lit the gas ring again and in the meagre light it afforded she looked at the solitary trinket in her hand. It was a watch. A gold watch on a gold strap, an intricate gold strap. It was like one of those watches that ladies had pinned to their bosoms. But it wasn't plain gold like you'd expect a watch to be, there were stones round the edge of the watch, white stones that glinted in the light from the gas jet; and the strap, too, had stones, a row of blue ones right up the middle, and white ones around the edge. There was a round ring at the top of the strap and this had a big stone set on the top of it. This one had a red glint. Across the back of the ring was a kind of safety pin, for pinning it to the frock, she surmised.

He had said he was getting her something bonny, worth all the stuff in the drawer, and not only that, it had seemingly cost half the money in the drawer too.

She now counted the sovereigns. There were fifteen of them. There must have been three times as many as that, and he had given all that stuff and all that money in exchange for this little watch! It didn't look worth it, well not in this light. But it just went to show what he had thought about her. And he had been so excited about getting it for her. What use would it be to her now though? She couldn't sell it. If she went to somebody and said, 'Would you buy this watch?' they would likely have her run in for stealing it. Even the man in the pawnshop would want to know where the likes of her had come by a fancy bit of jewellery like this.

Aw well, she'd keep it, 'cos by rights it was hers. She wasn't stealing it. But where would she put it? She'd pin it to her shift until she had time to make a bag for it.

She peered down at the pin in the back of the ring. It wasn't quite an ordinary safety pin, it had a movable part on the top. When she pushed the little knob towards the end and found she couldn't open the pin she nodded to herself. It was a kind of safety catch, so she could pin it anywhere underneath her skirt and there'd be no fear of it dropping off.

What was more important at the moment was the money. If she didn't get set-on anywhere within the next week or so they wouldn't starve; and they'd also have a roof over their heads at nights. And now she must get some sleep because she must be up before the lark in the morning. . . .

They didn't wake until the dock buzzer hooted over them at six o'clock. It brought her out of the bed and alert and bustling and whispering to Lucy to get up out of that.

Unlike herself, Lucy took some time to come round in the mornings and she was still blinking the sleep from her eyes as she groped her way downstairs behind Emily.

Five minutes later they were going out through the kitchen door, out into the biting air of the dark morning. Emily turned the key in the lock, then went towards the wash-house. But at the door she stopped; no, she wouldn't put the key back, she'd keep it as a keepsake, and as she dropped it gently into her coat pocket she thought of it with much deeper sentiment at that moment than she did the fancy trinket pinned to the inside of her skirt.

SEVEN

They took the early train to Gateshead. It was black with workmen and some of them had looked curiously at the tall young lass with the rosy complexion, clear blue eyes, and great mass of brown hair with the straw hat set on top of it, and whose appearance was in sharp contrast to that of the smaller girl who looked thin and puny, even enveloped in the coat that was much too big for her.

Emily had forgotten the name of the street where their Aunt Mary lived, but she remembered her way to it, and the fact that the house was the third from the top end.

When she reached the street she couldn't help but be appalled by the sight of it. It must be three years since she had been here. Then she had only been able to compare it with Creador Street, now she was comparing it with Pilot Place, which although on the river front and amidst the working area, she had considered select in comparison with other parts of the town. The street was strewn with paper, the gutters were dirty; she thought that the scavengers must have closed their eyes and passed it by for weeks on end.

When they stopped outside the third door from the top end of the street and looked at the scarred paint and the battered footboard, and the step that hadn't seen bathbrick for years by her counting, then listened to the racket that was coming from beyond the door, they looked at each other and the apprehension in Lucy's eyes was reflected in her own.

She had to knock three times before the door was opened and a girl of about Lucy's age confronted them and demanded, 'What is it? What you after?'

'I ... we've come to see Aunt Mary. The Southerns do live here, don't they?'

'Aye, they do.' The girl stared from one to the other for a moment; then, her mouth dropping into a big gape, she turned her head on her shoulder and yelled, 'Ma! Ma! here a minute.'

And it was almost a minute before Mrs Southern appeared at the door, and when Emily looked at the enormous body almost filling the little passageway she couldn't believe that she was looking at her Aunt Mary, for she hadn't remembered her being this size.

'Hello, Aunt Mary.'

'Emily and Lucy!' The woman was bending towards them, her huge breasts almost bursting out from her faded blue blouse. 'What's up, an' at this time in the mornin'? In the name of God! what's brought you? Somethin' happened your da?'

'No, no, Aunt Mary; he's still at sea. Can ... can we come in?'

'Come in. Come in. Of course, come in, lass.' She now almost hauled them one after the other, together with the hamper, over the step, along a passage, and into the room that appeared thronged with children.

'Shut up! Quiet! the lot of you or I'll swipe the hunger off you.' The bawl Mary Southern gave silenced her brood for a moment and they all looked towards Emily and Lucy. And now their mother, who was still yelling, said, 'This is your cousin, Emily. Don't you remember? Sit yourself down.... Huh! lass I said sit yourself down. That's easier said than done. Get your backside off that form!' With a sweep of a large none too clean hand she pushed two small boys and a girl on to the floor, then turning to Emily and Lucy, she said, 'Sit your-selves down and I'll get you a sup tea. Now tell us all about it. What's brought you out at this hour an' with your baggage?' She nodded towards the hamper and bass bag. 'The last I heard of you you were well set up in a good place, that's when your da called in last.'

'Yes, yes, I was, Aunt Mary, but ... but the lady died and me ... me boss, well ... well he was killed yesterday and his sister come and turfed me out.'

'The bugger, she did! What for did she do that?'

'Because she thinks that the house is hers, she's the only livin' relative. But he hated her guts; he wouldn't let her in to his wife's funeral.'

'And she turfed you out?'

'Yes, Aunt Mary.'

'The grasping swine. By! I wish I'd been there, I'd have put me foot in her backside.... Leave that milk alone else I'll stick your nose in the tin!' This last remark was fired at a boy of about seven who was now sucking his finger free of the condensed milk, and as Emily watched him grinning back at his mother and took in the con-dition of the room, its overcrowdedness, its dirt, its smell, its overall pattern of poverty, she couldn't help but be amazed by the cheerfulness of them all. There were nine children in the room, but not one of them looked like those back in Creador Street, particularly in No. 18; and she noticed that only two of them wore boots, the rest were in their bare feet. The fortunate ones were a boy of about six and a girl, whom she remembered faintly from when she was last here as being the eldest girl called Maria.

Mary Southern, seeing Emily's eyes on her daughter, said, 'You remember her; that's Maria. Grown, hasn't she? ... How long is it since you were here? Over three years? Well, I've had three additions since then. There they are.' She pointed to three children sitting near the fender. 'Betty, she's nearly a year, Mike there, he's on two ... an' Geordie ... Oh, him! He's a bloody rip if ever there was one. Just look at his eyes, can't you see it! He's only three by years but he's thirty-three by wits and wiliness, aren't you?' She bent down to him. 'Aren't you, you little bugger? Aren't you wily?' Her hand went out and she clipped her offspring none too gently but with seeming affection across the side of the head; then continuing her conversation, she said, 'Well, drink up your tea and I'll do you a fry in a minute when I get rid of some of these. I've got two in work now, you know, full time, and two part time. And by! isn't it a godsend. Pat's with his da in the steelworks; Jimmy, he's the eldest, he's in the shipyard at Hebburn. And there's two in the blackin' factory, a couple of hours afore school, an' as many as they like to get in after. If they'd only attend school as quick as they go to the factory there'd be less trouble. The school board man's never off the door. Aye, you'd think they would know when they're well off, wouldn't you? By! if only I'd had the chance. Me, no schoolin' at all, here I am at thirty-eight years old and can't write me own bloody name. The only thing I can do is bring another pair of bare feet into the kitchen every year. I've told Frank it's got to stop, I'm sick of being bloody churched. Me, purified!' Now she let out a great bellow of a laugh, pushed her hand in the direction of Emily and ended, 'And I will when water flows uphill.'

Emily was smiling. Since yesterday she had thought she'd never smile again in her life, but here she was smiling. Her Aunt Mary was a card; and she was nice was her Aunt Mary. She mightn't be over clean, and the house was like a padden can, but everybody in it seemed happy, and that's all that mattered, wasn't it? It was funny but she had always thought that you couldn't be happy unless you were clean; but her Aunt Mary and her family certainly gave the lie to that.

She was learning things, and fast, but what she didn't need to learn was the fact that they couldn't stay here; this house consisted of two rooms and when the family were altogether they would count up to thirteen. Anyway, for the next hour or so they could rest here and she could talk to her Aunt Mary; in spite of her aunt not being able to read or write she was, in a way, understanding.

At ten o'clock the breakfast mugs and greasy plates were still on the table, and Mary Southern, the youngest child on her knee, the others crawling round her feet, was still talking and Emily and Lucy were listening; Lucy with a weary expression on her face, and her dry cough piercing the conversation at regular intervals. At one point Mary stopped and, nodding towards her, said, 'That cough, it's just like our Maria's. It portends no good that, it should be seen to. The school doctor is looking after Maria's. He says she's got to keep out in the fresh air, there's nothing like fresh air for clearin' a cough like that. An' you're quiet, aren't you, hinny?'

When the big woman bent towards her, Lucy smiled weakly and nodded, but what Emily said was, and returning to the former line of conversation, 'About these hirings, Aunt Mary.'

'Oh, the hirings. Well now, lass, there's some in the Bigg Market in Newcastle just across the water, and if I'm right about the time it's the first Monday in November. That's about three weeks or so ahead; it's a long time to wait. There's one in Hexham an' all, but I think that one is further away still, around the middle of November. Anyway, I know they're twice a year, May and November. But you wouldn't want to go as far as Hexham, all those miles away. But listen, I tell you what, lass. Not a kick in the backside from here is Fellburn. You know Fellburn, now they have a market the day, an' every Wednesday. It's nothin' like the Bigg Market in Newcastle or the Shields market. By! it's a nice market, the Shields market, isn't it? Homely.'

'Yes, Aunt Mary, it is a nice market . . . an' homely.'

'But they don't do any hirin's there, do they?'

'No, Aunt Mary.'

'Well now, in Fellburn on a Wednesday afternoon they used to do quite a bit of hirin', at least in the summer. It was a weekly affair, not on a big scale mind, it was just for people who wanted part-time work, like tattie pickin' or extra hands for haymaking, or to replace some lass on a farm, say she had died an' of course broken her bond, so they'd take another on temporary until the end of the year, you see. Now as far as I know they might be still doing a hiring or two on the side even this late in the year. Haven't you ever been to Fellburn?'

'No, Aunt Mary.'

'Well now'—she considered for a moment—'as I said, it's not a kick in the backside away, two or three miles or so I'd say, an' you can take the tram. But don't get on the wrong one an' land up in Low Fell or Birtley. Once there anybody 'll show you where the market square is. Now there's a clock in the middle of the square, an' there's fruit and vegetables on one side, stalls I mean, not hanging on the clock!' She put her head back and let out a great gaffaw of a laugh; then baring her breast and pushing the discoloured teat into the child's mouth, she hitched it closer to her before continuing, 'As I was sayin', t'other side is fish mostly, but to my mind it's never fresh, not in Fellburn. Anyway, there's a pub at the end of the fish stalls. It's known all over as Paddy's pub, but it's got a name on the sign that says, The Kicking Donkey. Well now, it's just to the side of that, this stand for those who's wantin' a job, and those who's wantin' to hire them come along and look them over an' have a natter. Now why don't you go along and try your luck, eh? It'll be for some place out in the country mind at this time of the year, likely out in the wilds. But beggars can't be choosers, can they?'

'No, Aunt Mary. An' I wouldn't mind going out into the country where it's quiet like.'

'Oh, lass, don't get any delusions about the country being quiet. I once stayed in a cottage in me young days. Two nights I was there, an' I couldn't sleep a wink, what with the cock and the hens and the pigs, not forgettin' the birds; some of them were on the roof. I couldn't get back home quick enough.'

Again she laughed, and her head went back taking her breast with it, and the child, denied for a moment of its feed, yelled and she cried at it, 'Oh! There you are. There you are, stuff your kite.' Then without a pause she went on, 'Leave your things here, nobody'll touch them. But I think you'd better take Lucy along of you, you want to let them see what they're in for. By the way, did you inform the school that she was leavin'?'

'No, Aunt Mary, there wasn't time.'

'Oh well, don't wonder if you have trouble from that quarter.'

'She's only got seven months to go.'

'Even so they're funny. Still, they might let it pass. Well now, what are you going to do?'

'I'll do as you say, Aunt Mary, and go along there.'

'You might have to stand all day waitin', you know that?'

'Yes, yes, Aunt Mary, but I don't mind how long I stand as long as I get a place, somewhere where we can both be together. I won't take it unless.'

'Well, go on, lass, and good luck to you. And by the way, if you don't get set on straight away you can always come back. But I've got to tell you I can't put you up here; I'll have a word with Mrs Pritchard across the street, she's got a spare bed she often lets. Anyway, don't worry about where you're going to kip, we'll fix somethin' up. An' look, take a shive of bread with you, you'll be hungry afore the day's out.'

'Thanks, Aunt Mary, but I've got cheese and bread in the bass bag, I'll take that.'

'All right, lass.' Mary Southern now lumbered to her feet, the child still clinging to her, and she threaded her way between her family, out into the passage and opened the front door, and again she said as she called at Emily, 'Good luck, lass.' Then she added, 'By! you've grown into a bonny piece. In another year or so when you get a bust on you an' fill out all round with some pads on your backside you'll have a job to keep the lads off you with a pitchfork.'

'Oh, Aunt Mary!' Emily bowed her head, but not in laughter, she had a great desire at this moment to cry, just to lay her head on her arms and cry.

Taking Emily's action for smothered mirth, Mary pushed her on the shoulder and over the step, and then called after her, 'And if there's more than one about, lass, you pick and choose.'

They had been standing to the side of Paddy's pub for almost three hours. Her Aunt Mary had said if there's more than one about pick and choose, but nobody had even spoken to them, either man or woman. Some men on their way into the bar looked at them curiously, and some woman would check her step and turn her head towards them when Lucy coughed.

Emily's legs were aching, her feet seemed to have swollen inside her boots; they were also dead cold. She looked down anxiously at Lucy, and when she coughed again she said, 'Look along there, there's a herbalist shop, they'll likely sell sarsaparilla. Here's a penny. Go and get a glass, it'll likely ease your cough. But if they sell other drinks ask the man what he advises to take best for a tickly cough, he'll tell you.'

'Yes, Emily. Can ... can I bring you something?'

'No, no, I'm all right. You go on; but don't stay too long, mind.'

Left alone, she looked about her again. She felt she knew every fish on every stall in the row to the side of her. She certainly knew every fishmonger, even if she had been blindfolded she could have made each one out by his particular call. Business had been brisk at all the stalls over the last two hours but now it had slackened off and she wasn't surprised when the man from the end stall came towards her and spoke to her. 'Hoping to be set-on, lass?' he said.

'Yes.'

'I doubt you'll have no luck the day. It's service you want, I suppose?'

'Yes.'

'For you and the little lass?'

'Yes.'

'Aye'—he shook his head—'I doubt you'll be lucky, it's the wrong time of the year. An' then there's never much doin' in that line here now, anyway.'

'I know, but ... but I thought I'd try.'

'Well, there's no harm in tryin', lass, but you've been here since this morning, you must be froze to the bone?'

'Yes, I am a bit cold.'

'I'd get meself away home, lass, if I was you.'

'I'll ... I'll stay a little longer.'

'Well, please yersel, please yersel.' He nodded at her, smiled, then went back to his stall, where he slapped a fish back and forth on his slab and cried his wares to an almost empty market.

It was as she made up her mind to return to her Aunt Mary's as soon as Lucy came back from that shop—and she seemed to be taking her time—that she saw the high trap being driven into the market square from the far end. At first, she took no notice of it, not even when it passed her and the driver looked down on her; not until the gentleman, for she judged him to be so by his clothes and the fine turn-out he was driving, pulled the horse to a halt almost opposite the herbal shop, dismounted, then tied the horse to an iron post, one of many that ringed the market square; after which he walked back towards her.

She knew he was going to speak to her because he kept his eyes on her all the way along the pavement. Then he was standing in front of her. 'You're out for hire,' he asked.

'Yes, sir.'

He didn't speak for a moment but looked her over; then said, 'Have you been in service before?'

'Yes, sir, over two years full time, an' for part time long afore that.'

'In the town, I suppose?'

'Yes, sir. In South Shields.'

'You know nothing about farm work then?'

She shook her head slowly and her voice had a dull note to it as she said, 'No, sir, I know nothing about farmin' work.'

'Can you cook?'

'Oh yes, sir. I'm ... I'm told I'm a good cook, and good at housework an' washin' an' bakin', and the rest; anything to do with the house.'

He pursed his lips, half turned from her, looked towards the ground; then swinging round to her again, he said, 'Would you object to seeing to an invalid?'

'An invalid? ... Someone in bed, kind of bedridden?' Her voice was rising to a squeak.

'Yes, you could say that.'

Now her smile was wide as she answered, 'Oh no, sir, I wouldn't mind at all. That's what I've been doin' for most of the last two years. Mrs McGillby, that was my missis, she ... she was ill in bed nearly all the time an' I saw to her. She died three months gone.'

'Why are you out of work?'

She swallowed deeply, 'Mr McGillby, he ... he died an' all, just ... just recently.' The thought of how recently caused a lump to come into her throat again, but she swallowed on it when the gentleman said, 'I'll take you on. Three shillings a week to start, and all found. Your hours are six to six and later if needed; half a day off a week. You'll have to learn how to do outside work too, at odd times in case you're needed, such as dairy work and milking. My name is Birch. My house is Croft Dene House; it lies a mile or so outside the village of Farley Dene. Do you know it?'

'Farley Dene? No, sir.'

Her face was wearing the glad look that Sep had admired so much, and she stared at him speechless for a moment until she saw Lucy emerging from the herbalist's doorway; then the gladness seeped from her face and her body as she said, 'I think I'd better tell you, sir, there's not only me, there's me sister.' She pointed, and at that he turned round and looked at the puny young girl hurrying towards them and almost tripping over her long coat, and without looking back at Emily, he asked, 'Why ... why have you to bring her along?'

'My father's at sea, my mother's dead, there's no one; she was with me in me last place.' That wasn't a lie, not really. 'I've got to take care of her. And ... and I'd better tell you, she's not all that strong. But she can run about, do errands and light work. I'll keep her busy, she'll be a help, and ... and she only needs her food; I wouldn't expect anything for her.'

Lucy was standing to Emily's side now staring at the strange man.

'Hello there,' he said. 'What's your name?'

'Lucy.'

A slight nudge from Emily and she added, 'Sir,' then repeated, 'Lucy, sir.'

'And yours?'

'Emily Kennedy, sir.'

He half turned from them again, shaking his head as he looked down the street towards the trap, and he muttered something that Emily didn't quite catch.

'All right, you're on. Where's your things?' he said.

'They're ... they're at me aunt's in Gateshead.'

'How long will it take you to get them?'

She reckoned up quickly. 'Just under an hour, sir. We could be back within an hour, sir.'

He pulled a heavy watch from his waistcoat pocket, considered it for a moment, and said, 'That'll be all right. I have things to do; I'll meet you back here in an hour.' He nodded at her, then turned abruptly from them and walked away.

Neither of them moved, but watched him until he reached the trap; then, as if they had been shot into action, they both ran from the pavement and only paused a moment as they passed the first fish stall, when the man shouted cheerily to them, 'You made it then? Good, good. You made it, surprisin'.'

Yes, it was surprising. She kept telling herself that as the tram rumbled along the road, and it was the first word she said to her Aunt Mary. Almost bursting into the house, she said, 'Surprisin', Aunt Mary, surprisin', right out of the blue. I've got a job. It's ... it's on a farm. Croft Dene House it's called, in Farley Dene. And his name's Birch. I've got to do housework, but learn about outside, dairy and milkin' an' things. And he's takin' Lucy. He made no bones about her, he just took her on. Didn't he?' She turned to Lucy, who nodded, saying, 'Yes, Aunt Mary. And he seemed nice.'

'Well, I'll be damned! When you went out of that door I thought you had as much chance of getting into a job at this time of the year as I have into a convent. But you've landed one. Well, wonders 'll never cease. What's he like? I mean to look at.'

What was he like? She screwed up her face, then said, 'Well, Aunt Mary, it's funny but he's hard to describe. He's gentlemanly like except ... well....'

'Except what?' Mary Southern was leaning towards her. 'Go on, except what?'

'Well, his voice sounded a bit rough, ordinary like. But he was turned out like a gentleman, an' his trap was smart....'

'He had nice brown leather gaiters on, Aunt Mary, and brown eyes. And he had a fine long coat and ... and a tall hat.'

Mary let out a great bellow of a laugh as she pointed at Lucy, crying, 'There now, there now, she beats you at it, Emily; she even noticed his eyes matched his gaiters. You'll go far, lass, you'll go far.... Is he fat or lean? Tall or short?' She was now looking at Emily again.

'Oh, he's tallish; but not really tall; bigger than me da. An' well built, sturdy like.'

'Did he give you any details, how many in the house and such?'

'No, only that I'd have to learn about outside work.' She did not mention that she'd have to see to another invalid for that would set her Aunt Mary off talking again and she had to get away. And she said so. 'We'll have to be going, Aunt Mary, but ... but I want to say thank you. If it hadn't been for you I'd never have gone there the day. And you've been kind.' She choked now and bowed her head, and Mary said gently, 'Aw, come on, lass, come on, you're not goin' to start bubblin' because you've got a new place. An' if I hadn't sent you there somebody else would have. God has a way of providin', He makes the back to bear the burden. What for do we have donkeys?' She now let out another laugh and pushed first Emily and then Lucy on the shoulders, ending, 'Well, get yourselves away. But mind, don't go and forget us. You're welcome here on your days off, or at any other time. Yet God knows, when the next one comes'— she patted her stomach—'I'll have to entertain you on the roof.... What's this?' She was looking at Emily's extended hand and when she saw the three shillings in the palm she let out a high scream of protest, saying, 'Oh no! Aw now, fair's fair. Three shillings! Aw, be buggered! What have I done for that? No, lass, no, I wouldn't take that off you.'

'Go on, Aunt Mary, I can spare it. Really I can. I've ... I've got a bit saved up.'

'You're sure, lass?'

'Yes, Aunt Mary.'

'All of that?'

'Yes.'

'Well, thanks, lass.' Her voice was low now. 'I won't say I don't need it an' I can't do with it, but I still feel it awful takin' it from you. Aye, lass.' She now took Emily's face between her hands and squeezed it gently, adding, 'You were welcome afore, but this has set the seal on you. I'll never forget it, lass. A bit of a bairn like you givin' me three bob, an' the day of all days when, believe it or not, hinny, I haven't got a penny for the gas.' She nodded her head now. 'It's a fact, I haven't got a penny for the gas. Well, as I was sayin', God's good an' He provides for his own. But go along now, go on, else that fellow 'll be off in his trap an' away without you.'

Once more she was ushering them towards the door, and when they reached the bottom of the street and turned round she was still standing there waving to them. They waved back, and Lucy said, 'I like me Aunt Mary. She's mucky lookin' and her house isn't clean but ... but I like her. Don't you?'

'Oh aye.' Emily nodded at Lucy. 'You can't judge

people by the way they keep their houses or the clothes they wear. I've learned that much this day.'

'Do you think we'll like it there, I mean this place where we're goin'?'

Emily smiled tolerantly down on her sister who wasn't in the habit of talking, but the excitement that was filling her was loosening her tongue, and she said, 'Well ... well, we'll have to make ourselves like it, won't we? And you'll have to do all you can to help me.'

'Oh, I will, Emily! I will. An' perhaps I won't cough so much if I'm in the country.'

'No, you've got somethin' there, perhaps you won't....'

The man was standing by the trap as if waiting for them and Emily had the idea that he looked relieved to see them, for he didn't say, 'I've been waiting for you,' or, 'Where have you been all this time?' but he smiled at them and said, 'Well, here you are then.' Then taking the bass bag and hamper from her he pushed them along the floor of the trap, saying, 'Come on, up you get.'

Emily helped Lucy up the high step and when she herself lifted her long skirt and put her foot on the step he put a hand on her elbow and hoisted her up. Then mounting himself, he gathered up the reins and said, 'Get up there! boy.'

When the horse began to move and the trap swayed and Lucy fell against Emily they both looked at each other and smiled.

'Do you know Fellburn?'

'No, sir.'

'Ah well now, you'll likely come to know it in the future if you stay with us long enough.' He made a little moue with his lips. 'We're going up the High Street now, behind us is a place called Bog's End. That's the low quarter of the town, so called.' He again made the same gesture with his lips, indicating that his description was questionable.

A few minutes later, when they had turned out of the main street and were passing a park, he flicked his whip to the side, saying, 'That's the local park, and that road up there to the left leads to Brampton Hill. That's the fashionable part of the town.'

As he talked Emily nodded at him but made no comment. She wasn't as much interested in the places they were passing through and his description of them as she was bewildered by all that had transpired since yesterday. Her mind seemed to be grabbing at yesterday, which seemed to be falling away into endless time. It couldn't be just a day since she had seen and spoken to Sep. It wasn't just yesterday she had been turned out of the house. Things didn't happen as quickly as that. But they had.

Her attention was recalled to her new master. He was saying, 'Now we're leaving the town and there's only Farley Dene Hall between here and the village. The house is about a mile and a half beyond the village.'

Following this he became silent. The horse trotted briskly, the trap swayed. Emily looked about her. She had never seen country like this. The only time she had been in the country was when she had gone with a school treat up Simonside, and they had sat on a bank above a stream near a pub called The Robin Hood. Some of the children had plodged but she hadn't, she hadn't liked to take her boots off as her stockings were all holes. This country was flat, but there were hills stretching away into the distance; the fields were mostly ploughed but there were a few with cows in them, and in others, sheep.

The road ran now between hedges and quite suddenly it began to twist and turn. The flat land disappeared. They went through a steep tunnel of trees and when they came out on the other side she knew a moment of fear for the road was now skirting a deep quarry. From where she sat it looked as if the trap, should it veer the slightest, would topple over the edge and roll down to where the water lay black and green at the bottom.

Lawrence Birch must have noticed her look of alarm for he laughed and said, 'It's all right, we're not going over the edge. I usually come this way in the daylight for it cuts off quite a bit from the journey.... We come into the village from the bottom end this way.'

As the trap swayed and rumbled over the narrow uneven road Emily thought it was a dangerous place even in the daylight. But then it was what you were used to, she supposed, and he was apparently used to driving this way.

The village appeared to her as a long straggly street with houses on each side interspersed with a few shops. There was a grocer's shop, the window of which was high and the entrance to it, she noticed, was up five stone steps. She was intrigued by the name, John Rington, on a board above the shop window. Vans went all round Shields selling Rington's tea. They had the name in big letters on the outside of the vans.

There were four stone built houses between the grocer's shop and the butcher's shop. The latter shop amused her slightly as it was only in a house window, but through it she could see hanging a whole sheep and half a pig and a long loop of sausages, so she came to the conclusion that, small as it was, it must do a bit of business.

On the other side of the road from the butcher's was a baker's and corn chandler's. It said so above the shop window. Beyond the shops on both sides of the road were more houses made of stone, and they looked old, but old in a nice sort of way.

On the baker shop side of the street was a public house called The Running Fox; then more houses, separate ones these with gardens in front and lying some way back from the road. Then at the end of the village stood a church. It was a real church like St Mary's off Eldon

Street in Shields or the one in the market; it wasn't a ranter's place. There was a graveyard next to the church, then fields, and almost opposite the graveyard was a blacksmith's shop. This was right at the end of the village and, outside it, her master drew the horse to a halt.

Emily had noted that the village was very quiet, likely because it wasn't yet knocking off time for the men. Yet the bairns should be out of school by now. But she hadn't seen any bairns; perhaps they had a long trek to school from here; perhaps they had to go right back into Fellburn. She also noted that the four adults they had already passed on the village street, three women and an old man, had looked at her new master but hadn't nodded at him or given him the time of day, nor he them. Now she watched him dismount, then tie the reins to a wooden post that acted as a support to a lean-to beside the blacksmith's shop.

Both she and Lucy turned in their seats and looked at the blacksmith's shop. The front was wide open and the singey smell of hot iron wafted to them. Emily recognized the smell; there was a blacksmith's on the Jarrow road. She had never seen inside it though because it was set high up behind a wall, but she had often smelt that odd aroma that she associated with a hot iron.

She could see the blacksmith standing near the anvil, and she noted something very odd. He didn't straighten his back when her master spoke to him but went on with his hammering. When he did finally stop his hammering she heard her master say 'When shall I bring him?' and the answer he got was, 'Please yersel.'

She now saw Mr Birch stretch upwards like a man does before he throws out his fist, and his voice was like a growl now as he cried, 'There's other places you know, Goodyear.'

'Aye, twice the distance and twice the money.'

'Now look here, you're wrong. I tell you you're wrong.'

'You have your opinion an' I have mine. Her belly's there to prove that somebody's in the wrong, an' not only me but the whole village knows who it is.'

Emily now saw Mr Birch clench his fist tightly and beat it against his own chest like someone does when they're choking, and his voice sounded as if he was choking as his words came to her, saying, 'Con would never have done it, he's not that way inclined. I tell you I know, he's not capable of it.'

'Aw, don't act so bloody gullible, 'cos you're not.' It was the blacksmith now who was roaring. 'He could never keep his hands off anythin' with a skirt on, pawing at them. I've seen him with me own eyes.'

'Yes, yes, he might, but it's just a kind of affection. I tell you Con isn't capable....'

'Shut up! and get on your way. I know what I know, an' so does everybody else. But I'll ask you this afore you go. If it isn't him, can you put a name to who it's likely to be?'

'Yes, yes, I can, and you'd be surprised. But it's for you to find out. I can tell you this though, and I can swear on it, it wasn't Con. Anyway, have you asked her who it is?'

'Asked her! I've tried to knock it out of her.'

'Does she say it's him ... Con?'

'She doesn't say yes or nay.'

'No, she wouldn't, she wouldn't dare name him.'

'They were seen together over near Bamford's Farm. He was at his stroking business.'

'She's been seen a number of places besides Bamford's Farm.'

'What the hell do you mean by that?'

'Just what I say; she's a little trollop. And you won't get her entry into my house through her belly, so don't think you will. And ... and put that down; you don't frighten me, Goodyear.'

Emily, holding her breath, had half risen in her seat

and she watched the blacksmith slowly lower the iron hammer, then Mr Birch turn away and march towards the entrance. But there he stopped and, looking back at the blacksmith, he cried. 'You've begrudged me me good fortune, the lot of you. You can't bear to see anybody get on, can you? But there's one thing I'll swear on, you won't share in it through your Bella.'

There followed a moment of silence during which the two men glared at each other; then Emily sank slowly back on to the seat when she saw her master turn and walk towards the post, and, having torn the reins from it, mount the trap. Then they were off again.

She did not look at him for some time but when she did his face was still black with anger. From what she gauged from the heated conversation she guessed that the blacksmith's daughter was going to have a bairn, and someone connected with her master called Con was supposed to have given it to her.

The thought now entered her mind that in a very short while she'd meet this Con.... Well, if he started any of his pawing on her she'd make him look out....

It was in the last rays of the dying sun that she saw the house. It was like nothing she had expected. She had seen two or three farmhouses in her time, one at Marsden, one up Simonside, and another the day they had gone on the school trip, but they hadn't looked like this house. This was a big house, made of big blocks of stone, not unlike the stone used for the houses in the village, but it looked more yellow in the fading light. It was plain-fronted and had three very large windows on each side of the front door; the second-floor windows were smaller than those on the ground floor, but even these looked enormous. The third row of windows were smaller still and she guessed these to be the attic windows. The roof was slate with four ornate chimneys rearing up from it like little turrets.

Her master drove the trap past the front of the house and round the corner, and here the side of the house looked almost as broad as the front for it flanked a big yard with a wall along two sides of it. In one wall was an archway.

She saw immediately that the flagstones that made up the yard were clean and not like a farmyard at all. Then her master drove the trap across the yard and through the archway. And here, she recognized, was the farmyard. But immediately she saw that it still wasn't like any farm she had seen before because everything looked so spruce and clean. One side of it was flanked by byres, another by two big open barns, and on the third side opposite the byres were stables with what looked like little houses above them, four in all.

It was as her master drew the trap to a stop that he looked towards one of the stables and called out, 'Abbie!'

Both she and Lucy had alighted from the trap before the door of one of the stables opened and she saw, standing there, an old man with a white stubble of beard around his chin and up his cheeks. She half smiled to herself at the sight of him, thinking that he looked more like a sailor than a farm worker.

Slowly he walked towards the horse's head, whilst keeping his eyes on her and Lucy, until her master, addressing him, said, 'Well now, what about "Corn in Egypt", what did I answer you to that? "Seek and ye shall find", I said, and I found.'

She watched the two men looking at each other. They could have been father and son, but there was no liking in their glances. And they were quoting the Bible. Funny, but she always seemed to land among people who quoted the Bible.... Sep hadn't quoted the Bible. Oh Sep. Poor Sep. If only she was with Sep....

'Come along, this way.'

At the sharp command she picked up the hamper,

beckoned Lucy with a lift of her chin, then followed Mr Birch across the farmyard, through the arch, across the paved court and to a door almost opposite the arch, and so into the kitchen of the house.

Her first impression of it was its size. It seemed half as big again as the whole of the ground floor in Pilot Place. She took in quickly a bread oven to the side of a big open fire, but what looked odd to her was the absence of a fender before the fire. It was fronted only by a long raised stone slab. The whole of the floor too was made up of stone slabs. The walls were made of stone, not slabs but rough-faced stone like the outside of the house.

'Put your things down.' He was pointing to the hamper that she was still gripping in both hands. He now took off his hat and his long coat, which he laid over his arm, then saying, 'I won't be a minute, sit yourselves down,' he made towards a door at the far end of the room. But before he reached it it opened, and there entered the kitchen a tall young man. Or was he a boy?

In the dimness at the far end of the room Emily couldn't quite make out how old he might be. But they were both now coming towards her again, her master saying, 'This is my brother-in-law, Mr Conrad Fullwell. You'll be seeing a lot of each other.' He half smiled, then looked at the young man, adding, 'Con works both inside and outside the house. He's a very handy young fellow, is Con. Aren't you, Con?'

'Yes ... yes, Larry, I ... I can turn me hand to ... to most things.'

Both Emily and Lucy were staring at the boy now, because that's all he looked, for all his tallness, a mere boy. His face was long and pale, his eyes large, his nose straight. But his mouth seemed too small for his overall features, and the words that issued from it came as if they were being spoken by a small child. Yet they sounded sensible.

'Hello ... what's ... your name?'

'Emily, sir. And this is my sister Lucy.'

Now the young fellow laughed and his face became bright as if he were deriving great pleasure from something, and he turned to his brother-in-law, saying, 'She called ... me sir. That's funny, Larry ... isn't it? She called ... me sir. Chrissey never called ... me sir, did she? Just Con.' He now turned his head towards Emily again and ended, 'Everybody ... calls me Con.'

Emily was about to smile in return but she reminded herself not to be too free. Anyway, this was the young fellow the blacksmith was talking about who did the pawing with his hands. Well, she'd call him more than Con if he started any of that jiggery-pokery with her ... or Lucy.

He was looking at Mr Birch again now, saying, 'I took Rona up ... a cup of tea. She wanted to know ... what about supper. I ... I told her I had been over to Chrissey's and asked her if she'd ... she'd come back. But she wouldn't. She said they were going ... to move. Her da was seeing about a job....'

'All right, all right.' Mr Birch's voice was curt now. 'We'll talk about that later. Be a good fellow now and give the girls a cup of tea. I'll be back shortly.' And with this he turned once more and went from the kitchen.

Left alone now with the young boy, as she already thought of him, she watched him going busily between the long narrow wooden table that ran down the middle of the room and the delf rack that flanked the wall opposite the fireplace, bringing from it cups and saucers and milk and sugar; then scurrying to the fireplace and taking up from the hob the big brown teapot. He might talk slow but his movements were quick, bustling, as if he were in a great hurry.

The tea in the pot must have been boiling for it spluttered out of the spout when he poured it into the cups.

114

He pushed the cups to the edge of the table in front of where they were sitting, then handed them the sugar basin, saying, 'Put as many in ... as you want. Some people ... like it sweet. Chrissey and ... and Betty used to take five ... spoonfuls each.'

'Oh!' She nodded at him, then said, 'Thanks, I'll take two, and Lucy the same.'

After spooning the sugar into the cups they sipped at the tea, but with some embarrassment, for the young fellow stood with his hip against the side of the table watching them, but not speaking now, just staring at them.

In the silence she thought she heard voices coming from overhead, raised voices, but decided they couldn't be angry because they ended on a laugh. Then a minute or so later the kitchen door opened and her master entered once more and, looking directly at Con, he said, 'Go and give Abbie a hand. I'll be with you shortly, but first I must get'—he paused—'Emily settled and show her the ropes.'

'Yes, Larry. Yes, I'll go ... and help Abbie.'

As obedient as a well trained child, the tall young fellow left the room, and Larry Birch turned to Emily, who had risen to her feet, and Lucy too, and said with some hesitation, 'My ... my brother-in-law ... well, he might seem a little strange to you at first, he's somewhat retarded in his speech, you've likely noticed, but he's quite all right otherwise. You understand?'

That had yet to be proved, but she said, 'Yes, yes, I understand.'

'Well now, I think I'd better show you round. This, of course, as you've gathered is the kitchen. Through here is the cold store, meat store and larder.' He led her through a doorless aperture in the stonework and into a small corridor from which opened three rooms. He went into the first one, saying, 'This is the larder. Most of the dry goods are kept in here; flour, tea, sugar, the like. In this one'—he came out of the larder into the corridor again and pointed—'This is where we keep the milk and cheese and butter and such. For some reason I've never found out it seems to be the coolest spot in the house. Some say there's a well below or a stream runs underneath. But the floor looks solid enough and I've never bothered to investigate.' He smiled thinly; then pointing to the third room, he said, 'This is the meat store.'

She stood for a moment looking into the small room and at the hams hanging by hooks from the ceiling, and the two halves of a pig suspended from the wall on one side, and the carcass of a sheep at the other. On a marble slab at the end of the room lay a long cut of bacon from the back to the streaky, and as she noted the slices of gammon lying near a thin-bladed knife she said to herself, Well, it'll be a good meat house anyway.

He was leading the way through the kitchen again and through a door and into a hall. And now she actually gaped. Here again everything was stone, but it was the size of the place that astounded her.

To her eyes it looked very bare. There were rugs on the stone floor, but they seemed thin to her feet and their colours appeared dull in the fading light. The windows on either side of the front door looked enormous from the inside too, and the door itself looked jet black. Right opposite the door was the staircase, but half-way up it she saw that it divided, one part branching to the right the other to the left.

Her eyes were drawn back to the hall and to her master, saying as he opened a door, 'This is the drawing-room.'

Slowly she followed him into the room, and her breath seemed to catch in her throat. It was a beautiful room. She had never seen anything like it. The wooden furniture was a gold colour, mostly upholstered in blue. And

116

this room had a wooden floor, covered by a grey carpet, and she could feel the thickness of it through her boots. There were long windows in this room too and they looked out on to the side of the house and a lawn with a sun dial in the middle of it. One thing about the room appeared strange to her. The fireplace hadn't had a fire in it for some time for there was not a sign of soot at the back of the grate, it had been brushed clean.

They were in the hall again and he was opening another door. Here there wasn't so much colour, it was rather a dark dull room. 'This is the library,' he said. There was a desk at the far end of the room and it was strewn with papers, but she noted that this room was used, for there was dead ash in the fireplace. He had called it the library but there weren't all that many books in it. She had thought a library would be all books but the walls were mostly covered with pictures, and nearly all of horses.

They were crossing the hall now back towards the kitchen again and he led the way through a door to the side of the staircase and into a dining-room. This, too, was a lovely room. It also had a wooden floor and a thick carpet on it. The table was long and shining and there were ten chairs around it, four single ones at each side and a big armchair at the top and bottom ends. There was silver on the sideboard and china in the two glass cases at each end of the room.

One thing was already very evident to her. Whoever had worked here before had kept the place spotless; all the furniture had been polished regularly. Well, it would be up to her to keep it like that, wouldn't it? And that was something Lucy could help with.

'That's the butler's pantry.' He pushed open a door to disclose a room that went off the hall between the dining-room and the kitchen door in which the walls were mostly lined with racks to hold bottles, and at the far end was a wooden sink with a bench attached. He smiled wryly now as he said, 'Only we no longer have a butler.' Then turning and pointing to the end of a short dim passage, he said casually, 'The back stairs go off there, but they only come out on the first landing.'

He next led them back into the hall and up the main staircase, and she saw that both sets of stairs opened on to a long gallery with an ornamental balustrade around it, the same as skirted the stairs, part of it extending into a wide landing. Before going on to the landing, however, he stopped and, his voice low, he said, 'As I've already told you my wife is an invalid. It will be part of your duty to see to her. You know that?'

'Yes, sir. Oh yes, sir.'

He paused, his mouth half open as if he were about to explain further, then said, 'Come along then.'

They crossed the landing and they paused, as he paused, outside the second door on the right. Then with a quick movement he pushed open the door, went into the room and, turning to them, said briskly, 'Come, come.' And they both entered and stood within the doorway and looked towards the bed and the woman sitting in it.

The bedhead was against the same wall as the door, and when the door was opened it almost touched the side of the bed. This position of the bed immediately struck Emily as strange for the room was large and there was space to spare. She would have thought that the invalid would have wanted to be near the windows so she could look out.

She was held now almost as if she were in a trance, or dreaming, by the two eyes that were fixed on her. They were large eyes, but pale; grey, she supposed they were, yet they seemed colourless. But Emily saw immediately there was no difficulty in recognizing that the boy downstairs was the brother of her new mistress because their faces were almost identical, except that the woman's face was much older. In a way, she could be his mother, not his sister; she had the same straight nose, the small mouth, and the long, pale face; only her face was much paler than the boy's. She noticed, too, that her arms were long, her hands also.

'This is Emily ... Emily Kennedy and her sister, Lucy.' Larry Birch was standing at the far side of the bed, his face looking stiff, and it was matched by his voice as he went on to explain, and as if she weren't there, 'She says she's a good cook and used to running a house; also she can attend an——' he swallowed slightly before finishing, 'invalid.'

'How old are you?' The voice in its thinness matched the face; it was also slightly nasal. It was as if the words had come down the nostrils and not through the lips.

'Sixteen, missis.'

'You will address me as madam.'

... 'Yes ... madam.'

'And she?' The hand didn't lift from the coverlet but the index finger was pointing at Lucy. 'What use is she to be put to? She looks puny.'

'She'll help me in light work. I'm ... I'm not expectin' any wage for her ... madam.'

As Emily said the word her lower lip trembled just the slightest. She had thought Mrs McGillby to be difficult, but this one, she saw, was going to be worse. But her judgment was then sent topsy-turvy when the woman in the bed smiled and said quite nicely, 'Well now, we know where we stand, don't we? But the future will prove the reference my husband has given you.' She glanced towards her husband, who was looking at her, his expression still stiff; then turning her attention to Emily again, she said, 'We have supper at six; I have my breakfast at nine o'clock and my dinner at two. There are certain things I require doing for me and certain things I don't require being done for me, but of these my husband will inform you.'

She stopped speaking but continued to stare at them now, and Larry Birch, coming round the bed, said in the same brusque way in which he had ushered them into the room, 'Come, I'll show you where you sleep.'

Out on the landing they moved some way from the door before he stopped and, turning to her said, 'My wife suffers a great deal. It ... it is her spine; she can't walk at all. There are times when she may prove a little difficult; you'll have to show patience.' He now went before them to the far end of the landing and, pushing open a door to disclose another large bedroom, he said, 'This is my room. The others on the landing are guest rooms.'

He continued along a short passage before mounting another flight of stairs; steeper these and narrower, more like those in Pilot Place, Emily thought. But the attic room he showed them into was larger than the front room in Pilot Place, and comfortable. It held a double bed and had woollen rugs on the floor; also there was a real wardrobe standing in the corner, besides a chest of drawers and two chairs, one a basket rocker.

When he said, 'I hope you'll find it comfortable,' she turned to him and smiled, saying, 'Oh yes, sir. Yes, sir. It looks lovely. Doesn't it, Lucy?'

'Yes, it does.' Lucy was gazing round the room in admiration.

'Well then——' He was smiling now as he said, 'Go down and get your hamper and when you've changed make us something for supper. It doesn't matter what it is tonight, as long as it's something hot; my wife is partial to savouries.'

'Yes, sir, I'll do that right away. You stay here, Lucy.' She almost ran past him now on to the landing and down the stairs.

Lucy, standing in the middle of the room, began to cough, and he turned from the door and looked at her and asked, 'Does that cough hurt you?' and she answered, 'No, sir. No, sir. Well, not much.'

He stared at her for a moment longer before going out of the room, but at the top of the steep stairs he paused and with his first finger and thumb he pressed tight down on his eyeballs as if to relieve some kind of strain; then letting out a breath that was an audible hiss, he went slowly down the stairs and towards his wife's room.

PART TWO

THE MASTER

ONE

It took Emily a week to get into the swing of things and each day she learnt something fresh from the minute she rose in the morning until she dropped into bed at night. One thing she learned quickly; there wouldn't be much time for either her or Lucy to enjoy their attic bedroom. Six to six, he had said; it was more like six to eight or nine, or, as last night, nearly ten. But that didn't matter; they had a roof over their heads, she was earning money, and there was plenty to eat. Oh aye; you couldn't fault the table, and she had the best of everything to cook with.

It would, she decided, be a wonderful job, she would feel she had fallen on her feet if it weren't just for one or two things, the main one being she didn't think she would ever come to like her mistress. Not that she hadn't been civil to her; this morning she had even thanked her when she had combed her hair. But that was one of the snags; every morning she seemed to find more things for her to do. The first morning she went to attend her she had carried up a can of hot water, which she poured into the dish and placed on the side table, and her mistress had washed herself. By the time she had emptied the slops, made the bed, under and around her, which was a difficult job, and tidied the room a good half-hour was gone. But the second morning, it was nearly an hour before she could get downstairs because on that morning her mistress said that she must be washed down for the doctor was coming; yet the following morning, when no doctor was expected, she still demanded to be washed all over. And that arrangement had gone on for the rest of the week. Then this morning she had asked her to comb her hair again, and it was well over an hour before she could leave her.

But one good thing was, once the morning session in the bedroom was over, Con then did most of the running up and downstairs during the day.

It was strange but she found she liked Con. Although he would stand staring at her at times with that odd smile on his face, she wasn't afraid of him; and she didn't think she would be even if he put his hand on her and, as the blacksmith said, got up to his patting games, because she could soon put a stop to that. She had discovered she just had to speak to him sharply and he would obey her. Moreover, he liked Lucy, and she him; they were like two children together. Lucy had talked more to him than to anyone ever before, even herself. Last night they had sat here in the kitchen cleaning the silver, he putting the polish on and Lucy rubbing it off, and she had been amazed at the chatting and mingled laughter that went on between them. Already, too, Lucy seemed to be putting on weight.

But as to her master, she was in two minds how she regarded him. Sometimes she liked him and other times she didn't; it was the way he spoke to people. She considered he treated Abbie like dirt. But then perhaps there was something to be said for that because Abbie didn't give him his place; he never addressed him as sir or master. He was a grumpy old man was Abbie. Yet he seemed a hard worker, and he had been civil enough to her and had gone out of his way to show her how to go about things in the dairy, and so he had surprised her by saying, 'Remember, I'm not doin' it because he said I was to show you the ropes.'

There were a number of things she found puzzling about the house and its occupants. True, she had only been here a week but nobody as yet had called, except the doctor, and the miller bringing the flour. You would have thought the mistress, bedridden as she was, would have had some personal friends to call and see her, but she supposed it was early days yet....

Then someone did call. The back door opened abruptly and a small plump woman entered. Her face spoke of her age as being in the mid-fifties, but her hair was already snow white. She wore a felt hat that apparently had seen much weather for its once fawn colour was now green in parts. Her long black coat had a fur collar and this, too, showed years of wear. But her voice and smile were bright and she said immediately, 'Oh, there you are then. I heard Larry had got somebody. Where is he?'

Emily clapped her hands together to get the flour off them, then wiped them on her apron as she said, 'The master? Oh, he's out an' about; on the farm I think.'

'Yes, yes, of course. How are you liking it?'

'Very well, thank you, ma'am.'

The short woman now came slowly towards the table and, looking straight into Emily's face, she remained quiet for a moment before saying, 'You look strong and healthy, you'll cope I should think. How old are you?'

'Sixteen, ma'am.'

'Aw, don't call me ma'am, I'm Mrs Rowan, Hannah Rowan from a couple of miles over yonder.' She jerked her head backwards. 'I'm known to most by my christian name. I've known Larry since he was a bairn.... How is she?' Her head was now bobbing towards the ceiling, and Emily answered, 'Oh, the mistress. Oh, she seems about the same as when I first met her a week gone.'

'Aye, she'll be worse before she's better will Rona.... Are you troubled with your nerves, girl?'

'No, I ... I don't think so, ma'am, I mean Mrs Rowan.'

126

The woman laughed and said, 'You're a highly respectful piece, I can see that, and a bonny one into the bargain. Has anybody told you you're bonny?' She now poked her face forward and Emily blushed and suppressed her laughter with tightened lips, and the little woman said, 'Oh aye, I can see it's no news to you. But as long as your nerves are all right you'll last out. Sixteen, you say? Chrissey Dyer, the one before you, was coming up eighteen and a bundle of nerves she was, and her mother not much better. And then you would have thought she'd have had more sense at her time of life. Still, there's nothin' like a change, and as Larry said there never was a good one but there's a better. And it's up to you to prove it to him, girl. You prove it to him. . . . What are you making there?'

'A rabbit pie.'

'And what you using in your crust, lard or dripping?'

'Dripping.'

'That's it, that's it; there's nothing like dripping for savoury pastry. Well, I suppose I'd better go upstairs; but if Larry pops in you tell him where I am, will you?'

'Yes, yes, I will.'

When the little woman had marched across the kitchen and out into the hall Emily let a slow smile spread over her face. Now there was someone she understood. It was like being back home in Shields, no hoity-toity about her.

She went on with the preparation of the meal until about ten minutes later when through the kitchen window she saw her master. He had entered the courtyard from the farm, but he wasn't making for the house, and so she ran to the door and called, 'Mr Birch! Sir!'

When he met her half-way across the yard she said, 'A Mrs Rowan has called; she's gone up to see the mistress.'

She watched his face show his pleasure, and he nodded to her, saying, 'I'll be in in a minute,' and was about to move away, but paused and asked, 'Are you very busy inside?'

'I've just finished the pie for dinner, sir; and then there's the vegetables.'

'Can't Lucy see to them? What's she doing?'

'She's polishing in the drawing-room, sir.'

'Well, she can leave that. Put her on the vegetables; I'd like you in the dairy as much as possible today, there's too much milk going sour.'

'I'll slip over as soon as I get the pie in the oven, sir. As you say, I'll put Lucy on the rest.'

He still did not turn from her, but stared at her as he said, 'You were a long time upstairs this morning. I was in the kitchen twice. What was the matter? Anything wrong?'

'No, no, sir.' She shook her head emphatically. 'Only I had to wash the mistress down an' . . . an' do her hair.'

'Do her hair!' He screwed up his face at her. 'Since when have you been doing her hair?'

She was hesitant now as she said, 'Well . . . well she asked me to do it this mornin'.'

'And this washing down . . . you mean bathing her?'

'Yes, sir.'

'Every day?'

'Well . . . this last day or so, sir.'

He hesitated, then said, 'Later on tonight, I must have a talk with you.'

'Yes, sir.'

He turned away now towards the kitchen gardens, and she, hurrying into the house, went through the kitchen and the hall, and into the drawing-room, there to catch Lucy sitting in one of the French chairs gazing out of the window. Her reaction was to bark at her sister, crying, 'Get out of that, our Lucy, and on your feet!' only immediately to put her hand over her mouth and glance upwards as she whispered harshly, 'This is a nice kettle of fish, isn't it? I thought you were polishin'.'

'I've done it, Emily.'

'Everything?'

'Yes; well, nearly.'

'I told you you had to polish everything.'

'I get tired, Emily. I can't help it, I just get tired. I was only sittin' down for a minute.'

Emily sighed. 'All right, but what if anybody else caught you. I'm just warnin' you. Now come on, I want you to do the vegetables. I've got to go into the dairy; there's a lot of milk spoilin'.'

On her way out of the room she stopped and, turning to Lucy, she said, 'That's another thing: drink as much milk as you can. There's piles of it here; stuff yourself with it; it's bound to do you good.'

'Yes, Emily, but ... but I don't feel hungry. And Emily.'

'What is it?'

'I've had a bit of diarrhoea.'

'Well, what do you expect coming off starvation meals on to rich food, it's bound to affect your stomach. Now come on. And do the tatties properly mind; get all the eyes out; and scrape the carrots away from you so you won't muck up your apron.'

Back in the kitchen, she hurriedly put the pie in the oven, sorted out the vegetables for Lucy to prepare, threw another bucket of coal on the fire; then telling herself, since she was going to the farm she might as well kill two birds with one stone, she filled a tin can full of tea from the ever stewing teapot on the hob, cut off a two-inch-thick shive of currant loaf, placed a square of cheese on the middle of it, then, admonishing Lucy for the last time, 'Do them properly mind,' she hurried from the kitchen, across the yard, through the arch, and into the farmyard.

Abbie Reading was coming out of the barn and she called to him, saying, 'I've brought your bait, Mr Reading,' and when she handed it to him she said, 'I've got to go into the dairy, the master says there's a lot of milk souring. Will you show me what to do?'

He did not smile, nevertheless his voice was bright as he answered, 'I showed you t'other day; but go on, I'll come and watch you at it while I eat.'

They passed the byres from which a thick warm smell wafted at them, which caused her to sniff as if at a perfume. The dairy was the last in the line of buildings, one wall of it being that which separated the farmyard from the courtyard. It consisted of two rooms, both spotlessly clean. In the middle of one was a stone table with a rim round it, which was intended to hold water in the warm weather. Against one wall was a long slate slab. On this was an array of milk dishes, and under it a line of wooden pails. On another slab, there stood three shallow glazed earthenware dishes and a similar number of hair sieves. In the other room stood a wooden churn, and in the corner of the room was fixed a boiler and to the right of it a long wooden bench with a cold tap at the end.

'Well now'—the old man seated himself on an upturned wooden keg, then said, 'What did I tell you t'other day?'

'Strain the milk through the hair-sieve and then leave it for twenty-four hours.'

'Well, that lot's been left for twenty-four hours and more. Then what do you do?'

'You skin the cream off with the slicer and pour it into the earthenware dishes to turn.'

'Then what?'

'Well, when it's ready you put it in the churn and start turnin'.'

He laughed here and said, 'Aye, you start turnin'. An' that's where the knack comes in. That's what you've got to do now. But it's how you turn, lass, it's how you turn. And you know somethin'? This is no time to start turnin', twelve o'clock in the day; early morning's the time, twixt five and six.' He was nodding at her. 'And how did I tell you to turn?'

'Steady like.'

'Aye, steady like. Well, go on, make a start with that lot there.' He pointed. 'It's ready.'

She carried one dish of cream after another to the churn and tipped it in; then putting on the lid, she gripped the handle and started to turn, while Abbie sat drinking his tea and chewing on the bread as he watched her in silence.

Of a sudden he startled her by crying, 'That's too fast! Every time you get tired you go fast, thinkin' the quicker you turn it the quicker it'll be done. Steady does it, else you'll have it so blown up with air it'll come out soft as pap, and as likely come out without a vestige of colour in it. I should've told you about the carrot.'

She was gasping slightly as she repeated, 'The carrot?'

'Aye, the carrot. You get a nice bit of colour in your butter by scraping a nice deep coloured carrot into a piece of linen cloth, then squeezing it into the cream. Give it a dip in water first then a squeeze. It makes all the difference. Or you can use arnatto. But I like the carrot, an' to do things really properly every bit of that milk should be scalded. You do that when you want thick cream for your fruit, like in the summer, you know?'

She nodded while her body swung up and down as she turned the handle.

'But what's just as important as scalding the cream is scalding your buckets and dishes after. I've seen more ruined butter come from a mucky bucket than enough. It's hard work, girl, isn't it? But nothin's easy in this life.' He pushed the last of the currant bread into his mouth, then mumbled, 'No, nothin's easy; 'cos livin' itself ain't easy.'

He now wiped the crumbs from his bristly beard and,

leaning towards Emily's sweating face, said, 'I've been on this farm since it was first made thirty years ago. Do you know that? There wasn't any farm here thirty years ago, but the old master—and he was a master, a proper master, not like some I could mention—the old master created this farm when they sold the other two an' most of the land. There used to be a lot of land to the house, acres and acres of it. It isn't a farmhouse that, you know.' He thumbed over his shoulder. 'But I was reared on a farm, one belongin' to the house.'

'Oh.' At the moment this was the only response she was capable of making. She was used to wielding the poss stick and turning the mangle, scrubbing floors and white-washing ceilings, but this continuous movement, which had to go on for at least twenty minutes, was breaking her back. Either she was too tall or the handle of the butter tub was too low, one or t'other.

'No; never was a farmhouse.' The old man was still going on. 'Gentleman's residence Croft Dene House was, a gentleman's residence, a manor. The colonel kept one farm for his own use, rented t'other out. The Rowans rented it for years, then they bought it. God only knows where they got the money from, for they were like the one that plays master now, hadn't one penny to rub against t'other. But the master, the real master, the colonel, her father'—he now jerked his head back in the direction of the house—'Miss Rona's father, he was a gentleman. He'd turn in his grave if he knew the plight she was in now. Adored her he did, thought the sun shone out of her. That was her trouble, she had got everything she wanted in life. But why in the name of God she wanted him, I'll never know.'

Emily kept on turning. The sweat was running off the end of her chin, the ache in her back had reached her finger tips and her knees. She looked at the old man. His head was slightly bent as if he was no longer aware of her, but he was still talking. 'Scum he was beneath her feet. All right, all right, they can say he had a farm, or his father had, but what was it? A few shippons attached to the house. And no loss I said when the land enclosure swallowed his bit land up. He looked upon it as a comedown when they went to live in the little but an' ben up in the hills. But as I've said afore, an' I'll say it again, it was their rightful habitation. Drovers they were at one time, his grandfather and his father afore him, nothin' but drovers. An' then he comes here.' He now lifted his head. 'Do you know that? Do you know what that fellow, that one you call your master was when he first came here? An odd job man, a farm hand. That's what he was. . . . Well, that's surprised you, hasn't it?'

It had surprised her. She had stopped turning the handle and was staring open-mouthed at the old man as she repeated, 'A farm hand? The master? Just a farm hand?'

'You've said it, lass, just a farm hand. But an upstart one right from the beginnin'. Thought he was somebody; put on the act of a gentleman what was in reduced circumstances, so to speak. And I'll tell you something else, lass, and that's atween you and me.' He was now leaning well towards her and his voice was just above a whisper. 'He knew what he was after from the minute she came dashing back from America. She went on a long holiday to see a cousin, and then she got word that her da had died. Just nine years ago this month it was. There she was, a high-spirited lass, alone in the world you could say, although she had friends all around who stood by her then. But not the day they don't. Oh no; there's not one of them shows their face here the day. An' can you wonder at it? Anyway, he saw his chance. I'm tellin' you, he played her like a salmon, an' she, like a salmon battling against the tide, gave in. What else could she do? Two years he had been here when he marries her.

An' he didn't marry only her, he married the farm an' the house. Oh, he wanted that house. I used to watch him at nights standing on the drive there, staring, staring at it. He coveted it, he did, and the whole place, more'n he did her. Oh, I know what I know. An' you know something else, lass? The day they married I stood in this very dairy, and I leant against that very wall, and I cried the first tears of me life. And I'm not tellin' you a word of a lie.'

She shook her head at him.

And he shook his head back at her as he ended, 'And I'd like to bet you I wasn't the only one crying that day. I bet you young Lizzie Rowan had a wet face an' all. She's the daughter of them that bought the other farm I was tellin' you of, and afore that upstart came here him and her were as thick as thieves an' would have been wed if it hadn't been for her old man. But Dave Rowan knew a thing or two; he kicked his backside out of his gate.'

Her mouth was agape. She was amazed at all the old man had said. She had thought her master was a gentleman ... well, except for his voice, which at times she thought was a bit ordinary. Yet at other times he spoke like a gentleman; when he was giving orders he spoke like a gentleman.

She asked softly now, 'But ... but the mistress's accident?'

'Oh, that. Well that was the strangest thing, and it happened quite simply. She came downstairs for something in the middle of the night once, slipped on one of the slabs in the kitchen and put her back out. They found her there the next morning. They thought she was going to die.'

'As simple as that?'

'Aye, as simple as that, lass. The doctor said she must have come a toss. At first she could move about a bit, then it got worse, and now ... well, she's there till they carry her downstairs.'

Again they were staring at each other until Emily, turning towards the churn, said, 'Eeh! I've forgotten; did I do the time?'

'We'll soon see.' He lifted off the lid; then nodding at her and giving her a thin smile, he said, 'It'll do, not bad. It's almost the colour of lint but it's not soft.'

'Oh, thank goodness. About the water from it, I mean the buttermilk.'

'Oh, Con likes that. I should make your sister drink it an' all, it's good for the disease, the rest 'll go to the pigs.'

She swung round from the churn. 'Disease? What disease?'

'The consumption. The youngster's got it, hasn't she?'

'Lucy? Consumption? No, no.'

'Well, if that cough doesn't spell consumption I've never heard one that does.'

'You think so?' The question was a frightened whisper now.

'Aye, yes. Didn't you know?'

'No. Well, I knew ... I mean I felt she was sick with something, but I thought it was just being sort of bloodless like, not consumption, not that.'

'Well, you ask the doctor to have a look at her next time he's round. It'll cost you a couple of bob but it'll be worth it.'

'Aye, yes, I will. An' thanks.' Then of a sudden she exclaimed, 'Eeh! the pie. I've forgot it. I left it in the oven. I'll have to come back and finish.' She stopped on the point of a run, and he said kindly, 'Don't rush yourself, I'll see to it. And I'll stoke up for you. You can wash the pans when you've time.'

'Thanks. Thanks.'

She was now running across the farmyard, through the arch and towards the kitchen, her mind a maze of conflicting impressions: Her master not being a gentleman; her mistress being enticed into marriage with a farm hand; and her father being a colonel. Then her master again being thick with Mrs Rowan's daughter. And then the rabbit pie! Eeh! if the crust was burnt. And Lucy, their Lucy, having the consumption.

As she burst open the kitchen door she nearly knocked Hannah Rowan on to her back, only Larry Birch's outstretched arm saving her.

'My! my! somebody's in a hurry.'

'Oh, I'm sorry. Oh I am, Mrs Rowan, I am. But it's the rabbit pie.' She was retreating across the kitchen now pointing to the oven.

She lifted up the heavy iron sneck and opened the oven door; then heaved a big sigh as she turned her face towards them. 'It's all right,' she said, 'it isn't quite done.'

Both Larry Birch and Hannah Rowan looked at her for some seconds, then at each other, and simultaneously they burst out laughing. Putting her hand over her eyes and bowing her head, Emily joined them; but she didn't give her laughter rein, not as Lucy was doing.

'Well, there's one thing that can be said for her,' Hannah Rowan said, looking at Larry Birch, 'she's quick at least at opening doors, and she's concerned for her pastry.... Good-bye, girl.'

'Good-bye, Mrs Rowan.'

'And good-bye to you.' Hannah was now nodding towards Lucy, who was at the sink, and she added, 'And don't leave one eye in them taties or they'll wink at you out of the pan.'

Again Lucy was laughing, her head back.

The little woman went out into the yard now, saying over her shoulder, 'You say Con's working on the bottoms, what's he doing there? Them fields are full of boulders and bracken.'

The closing of the door cut off their voices, and Emily, turning now to Lucy, exclaimed, 'You're not still on with those vegetables, are you?'

'I'm nearly finished, Emily.'

She was about to add, 'Well, put a move on', but she checked herself and looked at her sister's back, the fair hair tied with a piece of faded ribbon, the narrow shoulders, the thin body. She herself was thin, but Lucy's was a different thinness, she was skinny. Yet only this morning she had told herself that Lucy was putting on weight. Her face seemed to be fuller. Had she the disease? Eeh! people died with that like flies. But when they coughed they spat blood. Lucy had never spat blood. Ena Blake up the street died when she was seventeen, and John Purley from around the corner, he had died an' all, and just when he had started work. But they had both spat blood, she had seen it. Her mother had always said Lucy's was a kind of tickly cough caused by nerves and thin blood.

She went slowly towards her now and putting her arm around her sister's shoulders she brought her face down to hers, saying, 'You feelin' all right?'

'Oh yes. Oh yes, Emily, I'm feelin' fine now, I'm not tired anymore.... Are you all right?'

'Oh me, I always feel all right.'

They looked at each other and smiled.

She didn't know what she would do if anything happened to Lucy. Lucy wasn't just like a sister, she was more like ... well, a child; she had looked after her since she was a baby.

Back at the table preparing the pudding, she began to pray, using the prayers she had heard the ranters pray in Mrs McGillby's bedroom, for they seemed much stronger, more in touch with God than the prayers she had learnt at school.

It had turned eight o'clock; she had cleared up the kitchen and was setting the table for breakfast the following morning. She set only two places. These were for the master and Con, as she had come to think of him. Abbie Reading didn't eat with the family at all; he didn't even come and collect his meals from the door, she had to take them to his place above the coach house. She and Lucy had their breakfast after the others were finished. At dinner-time she laid the table in the dining-room for the master and Con, and for their evening meal too.

She had finished setting the table when, looking towards Lucy who was sitting near the fire, her head nodding with sleep, she said, 'You go on up and get into bed; I'll be there shortly.'

'I don't like to go up on me own, Emily.'

'You're not frightened, are you?'

'No, not really, but it's a long way.'

'Aw, don't be silly.' She went to her and pulled her playfully from the chair, saying, 'Go on; you'll be asleep afore your head touches the pillow.'

As Lucy went out of the kitchen Larry Birch entered, saying, 'Good-night, Lucy,' and she answered, 'Good-night, sir.'

Emily was now throwing a bucket of coal on to the fire and she did not stop in her work. Afterwards, taking the big teapot, she emptied the contents over the top of the coal, then stood back and coughed as the steam rose hissing from the black mass.

She was at the sink washing her hands when he said, 'Come and sit down a minute, Emily, I want to talk to you.'

She turned swiftly, grabbed a hessian towel that was hanging to the side of the sink, then went obediently to the table and sat down, and for a moment she was reminded of the kitchen in Pilot Place, with Sep sitting at one side of the table and she at the other. But Mr Birch didn't look a bit like Sep. He was better looking, taller and not so bulky in the body, and he held himself very straight. She sometimes thought his back looked too

138

straight, and his neck always seemed to be stretching out of his collar, yet now as she stared at him she was even more reminded of Sep because his shoulders were sloping downwards and his head was slightly forward, his chin almost touching his chest. He looked a bit weary, in fact he looked as tired as she felt.

He did not lift his eyes towards her as he said, 'Emily, you must not spend time combing your mistress's hair, or bathing her.'

'No, sir?' There was a high note of surprise in her voice. She watched him lift his head, and now he was looking straight at her as he repeated, 'No, Emily.' Then moving his body round in the chair, he placed his fore-arms on the table, joined his hands together, and, his head to one side, said, 'There are one or two things I must tell you. The first is that your mistress is quite capable of doing her own hair and washing herself down. Admitted she cannot use her legs, but there is nothing wrong with her arms or her upper body. Up till now she has always attended to that part of her toilet herself; all you are required to do for her is to provide her with the water and towels, make the bed, and keep the room tidy.'

She was now sitting with her hands tightly clasped on her lap, and her face was straight as she said, 'But what if she demands I do it, sir?'

'Tell her I've said that you can only spend half an hour up there, except when you're through cleaning the room, and that only requires doing once a week. Just do as I've told you and then come away.'

'But if she should get angry?'

'Let her!'

She started, for he had almost shouted. And now she watched his hands gripping each other until the knuckles showed white.

His head was bent again and there was silence in the kitchen except for the slight hissing still coming from the banked down fire.

When he raised his head he looked hard at her and began to speak. His voice was calm and his words came slow but with quiet emphasis as he said, 'There are a number of things you have yet to learn about us, Emily. For a start I have no doubt that Abbie has already put you in the picture with regard to myself and my position here.'

She could not help the flush sweeping over her face, nor her eyes from blinking, and he went on, 'I thought as much. Well, believe what you like, but I will say this, Abbie is an embittered old man, a frustrated embittered old man, who imagines I've usurped his place here. What is more, he has always been very fond of my wife, having seen her grow up from a baby. But what Abbie Reading says or anyone else for that matter doesn't worry me.' On the last words his tone had suddenly become defiant and from it Emily deduced he wasn't being quite truthful on this point; people didn't get mad about something that didn't annoy them, and what people said about him evidently did annoy him. And, of course, it was natural.

Her hands on her lap moved apart, her body sank against the back of the chair. It was odd, but she had the strong feeling that she was once again in Pilot Place and that it was Sep sitting opposite her, for she was now experiencing the same feeling towards this man as she had done towards Sep. She felt sorry for him, and because she felt sorry for him she liked him. He might be an upstart as old Abbie said, but she was beginning to see that he had quite a lot to put up with.

'Anyway'—his head jerked to the side now—'I'm not concerned about Abbie. I just want you to know where you stand; you will take your orders from me.... And there's something else I must warn you ... tell you about. Because of her illness my wife suffers from nervous bouts. She is just as likely, when frustrated, to pick up something and throw it. Now should this happen you mustn't show her you're afraid, or run from the room. You know what you must do?' He leant further across the table now and, his voice low and with a quirk of a smile to his lips, he said, 'Should she try that on, threaten to throw something back at her, and make a good act of the threat. You understand me?'

Yes, she understood him. He was telling her she must throw things at her mistress should she get upperty. Why, surely her number would be up if she as much as lifted her hand to her.

As if reading her mind, he said, 'Don't worry about her reactions, but if she thinks she's got you cowed, you're finished, I mean as regard your ability to cope with her. That's where Chrissey went wrong ... the other girl. She gave in to her, she showed her she was afraid.' He again paused, and now his smile widened as he said, 'But somehow, Emily, I don't think you'll be afraid, not of her or anyone else. Am I right?'

Her lips were compressed; she was blinking now; then, her face breaking into a broad smile, she replied, 'Well, I wouldn't let anybody trample on me, sir. Yet at the same time I cannot see meself'—again she pressed her lips together—'throwing something at the mistress.'

He was laughing quietly now, his mouth wide, his eyes crinkled at the corners. She noted that he had all his teeth and that they looked good.

As his laughter died away he shook his head, saying softly, 'I'm glad you came, Emily. One more thing. Don't be surprised if you should find her door barred and she won't allow you into the room.'

'Barred!' Her eyes stretched slightly. 'But how can she bar the door, sir? She can't get at the lock.'

'She doesn't need to. I suppose you've noticed the wooden loops at each side of the door.'

'Yes, sir, I have.'

'And the wooden post resting against the stanchion?'

Her eyes widened still further; then she said, 'I knew it was a bar for droppin' into the slots, but I couldn't see what use it was there.'

'Oh, it has a use, Emily. My wife likes privacy, especially when her nerves are at fever pitch. It is then that she pushes the bar across the door. It's quite easy from where she's sitting.' He smiled cynically now. 'She thought it up herself when she first took to her bed.' Now he sighed and ended, 'I suppose it's understandable; she hadn't been used to people entering her room unless they were bidden. Sometimes her door can be closed for a full day. When this happens just go about your work in the usual way. There'll come a time when the bar is removed.'

Well, well! She made the remark to herself. There were some queer people in the world. Yet in a way, if somebody had been brought up private like, that bar was one way to ensure that they could still be private when they wanted. That was to be understood, she supposed.

And that was the word he used to her now. 'You understand, Emily?' he asked.

'Yes, sir.'

'Good. Well now, get yourself off to bed, I'm sure you are ready for it. Good-night.' He rose from the table and without more ado left the kitchen.

She stared along the room towards the door that had just closed. You imagined that people only had to have money and a big house and they'd be happy. Well he'd got both, but there was one thing certain, he wasn't happy. He was paying a high price for his coveting so to speak. Another thing Abbie had said, and this, inside herself, she knew to be true: her master wasn't a real gentleman, for a gentleman would never under any circumstances advise his servant to throw things back at his wife; a gentleman was more likely to tell you to put up with it and if you didn't like it you could go. No, Abbie was right, he wasn't a gentleman. And there was one more thing that went to prove this. While he sat at the table his way of talking had been ordinary. But then he was no worse in her eyes for that.

TWO

Emily had been at Croft Dene House for a month when she asked her master if it would be possible to take her half-day every Monday instead of every Sunday for she would like to go into Gateshead and visit her aunt.

She could not remind him of what he had said when he was driving her from Fellburn market and through the town on that first day, that she would often see the town. But over the past four weeks on the numerous occasions he had driven the trap or the waggon into the town he had never suggested that she should change her half-day off and he would give her a lift into the town. Yet when she did put the suggestion to him, he agreed without any demur.

And now this Monday morning she was scrambling round to get everything done before eleven o'clock, at which time the waggon was to leave the yard.

She was running up the stairs now towards her mistress's room when she met Lucy, her arms stretched wide carrying a laden breakfast tray.

Emily stopped on the first landing and watched her for a moment as she came down the right hand set of stairs; then exclaiming, 'Oh, be careful!' she grabbed at the tray and held it while Lucy leant against the banister.

'What is it?'

'She's been goin' on at me.'

'What about?'

'Everything. She called me stupid and ... and a nitwit.'

'Did she indeed!'

'And she kept talkin' at me.'

'What did she say?'

'Well, things like, we won't reign long. Then she said, who stole the pie and hid it in her room?'

Emily, putting one foot on the next step, balanced the tray on her knee as she said, 'She didn't!'

'She did, Emily.'

'She knows it was Con.'

'She said it wasn't, it was me.'

'Oh!' Emily now shook her head. There had been high jinks last week when the whole bacon and egg pie that she had made for supper disappeared overnight from the pantry and she herself straightaway accused Con of taking it. 'What have you done with the pie?' she had demanded, and he had answered quite innocently, 'What pie?' And she had come back at him, 'You know what pie, the bacon and egg pie that I made last night.'

He was swearing blind that he hadn't taken it when the master came into the kitchen and when she told him about the pie disappearing he looked at Con and said, 'Not again, Con. For God's sake! don't start that again.' And Con had started to cry, and there followed an awful scene when the master yelled at him, saying, 'Stop denying it, Con. Just own up. Why do you have to steal food? You may go and stuff yourself until you burst——' He had waved his arms wildly indicating the whole kitchen, then had pointed to the store cupboard and yelled at him, 'Go in there and slice up a whole side of bacon and stick it in the pan, but do it openly.'

She herself had been very upset, mostly by witnessing the helpless crying of the tall young fellow, for he had cried like a child, and when the master had left the kitchen she had gone to him and put her arm around his shoulder and, just like a child or their Lucy, he had turned and buried his head against her neck, and put his arms around her waist; and strangely she had felt no embarrassment because it wasn't like a man holding her.

When he had calmed down and dried his eyes he said to her, 'I didn't ... take it, Emily. They say I take ... things just because I used to take a bit of cake up to bed. I like eating, Emily, I like eating ... I do ... like eating, Emily.' And she had said, 'Yes, I know you do, Con. And take what you like out of the pantry, only let me know.'

At this he had stared at her, then had slowly turned from her and walked out, leaving her with a bewildered feeling.

Now she was handing the tray back to Lucy, saying, 'Go on; carry it steady now and don't take any notice of her. I told you what the master said, didn't I?'

'Emily.'

'What is it now?'

'I'd better tell you, 'cos if I don't she will. I was in the linen closet and I felt sick, and I brought a bit up on to a towel. She heard me and called me names and things.'

Emily closed her eyes for a moment, then said, 'You didn't touch your breakfast, are you eating on the sly?'

'No, Emily; but I'm feelin' sick now and again.'

'I'll give you some bicarb when I come down. Go on.'

Emily now walked slowly up the remainder of the stairs. With one thing and another life was very harassing; she looked back to the days in Pilot Place as to a dream holiday. She hadn't realized how happy she had been, especially when she was running the house on her own. Oh, if only Sep hadn't died.... She wished she could stop thinking about Sep.

She straightened her back as she tapped on the door and entered her mistress's room, but before she had time to close the door, Rona Birch was crying at her, 'That sister of yours, she's a clumsy idiot. Look what she's done; she's spilt the water all over the bed.'

146

Emily stood looking from the wet bedclothes down to the large glass jug that held the drinking water; then she lifted her eyes and stared at her mistress. She knew that Lucy hadn't spilt the water because Lucy would have told her, just as she had told her about being sick; the woman herself had done this on purpose because she knew that they were rushing through the work this morning in order to be ready to go on the cart at eleven o'clock.

'Well! strip the bed. Get fresh linen. Pick that rug up.'

'My sister didn't upset the jug, madam.' She was trembling as she made the statement.

'What! What are you saying?'

'You heard what I said, madam. My sister never tipped that water on to your bed.'

'How dare you! How dare you! Change this bed immediately and bring me a fresh nightdress.'

'I'll do it after you've been washed, madam, just in case there's another ... accident.'

'You insolent slut you!' As the hand shot out and picked up a thick bound book from the table Emily reared and cried, 'You throw that at me, madam, and you'll get it back. An' me aim is likely to be better than yours.'

She stood gasping as Rona Birch dropped back on her pillows, her face a picture of suppressed fury, while at the same time showing incredible astonishment. Her mouth opened and shut like a fish, her rage was choking her and checking for a moment the spate of words fighting for release. And then they came: foul words, blasphemous words, swear words, filthy words, words that Emily had closed her ears to when she had heard them uttered in Creador Street or by drunken women fighting in the gutter, or by men rolling up the street late on a Friday night.

Now her mouth was open, she was aghast, she couldn't

believe her ears. This was a lady! There might be doubt about her master being a gentleman, but there was no doubt that her mistress was a lady born and bred. But she was a lady with a filthy mouth. She was mad, she must be. The master had told her to make a stand against her, well, she could make a stand against her throwing anything but not against such talk.

Rona Birch's voice had reached a pitch of intensity that was causing Emily to screw up her face against it as she backed from the bed when the door was thrust open and Larry Birch entered, crying, 'Shut up! Stop it this minute, woman!'

Emily watched him grip his wife by the shoulders and shake her roughly until her head wobbled and her voice was lost in a gasping breath.

Quite suddenly he let go of her and she slumped into the pillows, her eyes, which at times appeared colourless, now showing a dark depth from which hate seemed to rise like a vapour. Then seeming to forget the presence of Emily, she now said slowly and quietly, but in the same venom-filled tone, 'You! you low down muck-raker. You dung-bespattered drover! You would, wouldn't you, you would engage the lowest of the low. She attacked me; she threatened me; and you put her up to it, didn't you? You stopped her doing my hair and attending to me and when she tells her sister to spill water over me and I ask her to clear it up, what do I get? Threats. She threatened me. But you won't let this affect your judgment, will you, dear Larry? Such a good worker, you said she was. We mustn't do anything to upset her, you said. ... And does she work well in bed, Larry?'

Her lips had hardly closed on his name when his hand caught her with a resounding whack full across the side of her face.

As Emily gasped he turned and yelled at her, 'Get out! Get out!' and she got out.

But once on the landing, she stood there, her hands cupping her face. He had hit her. Well, she deserved to be hit, didn't she? She had seen women hammered black and blue for less, oh much less. But then they were common people, not like ladies and gentlemen.

She had the urge to run up into the attic, throw their things into the hamper, and leave this place. There was something not quite right about it, she didn't know what, but it was something that she could feel, and not only just now, and the feeling made her uneasy. She could hear her mistress's voice now, saying in a perfectly steady tone and with no sound of tears in it, 'You'll regret that, Mr Birch, for the rest of your life. I promise you, you'll regret that.'

'I'll regret nothing, only having taken you on. And I should have done that afore. You're filthy! Do you know that? Rotten right through, and filthy.'

'Well, you've changed your opinion since you took me on, haven't you? But then it wasn't me you wanted, was it? It was the farm, the house. Oh you wanted this house, didn't you? "It's a lovely house, Miss Fullwell," you used to say; "a beautiful house. It has a charm about it." '

'Yes'—and now his voice came harsh and clear from the room, crying, 'and you invited me in, didn't you? You broke your neck to get me inside, and up into your room.'

'Yes, yes, I did, Larry; but you weren't to be tempted, were you? No. You know I've often thought it's a pity that you couldn't have become pregnant and so trapped me into marrying you. But you did the next best thing, didn't you, you kept me at arms' length and whetted my appetite by going off on a Sunday to meet your dear Lizzie. But dear Lizzie didn't stand a chance against Croft Dene House, did she? And now you are master of all you survey, from the kitchen to the attic. . . .'

'Stop it! stop it! Rona, I'm warning you. But you're right. As you say, I'm master of the house, and you can't

149

do anything about it now, not a blasted thing, can you?'

Emily waited to hear her mistress answer, and when none came her fingers began to beat against her lips. Was he choking her? Then she actually started as she heard the high-pitched hysterical laugh and the voice breaking through it, crying, 'Master! Master! Oh, it's funny. If you could only see yourself as I see you, you'd die at this moment, and not with laughing. Master, you say? Oh, you've got a surprise coming to you, Larry. One of these days you'll get such a shock you'll wish they would bury you alive.'

'You're mad. You're mad, woman.'

'You'd like to think I was, wouldn't you, Larry? But I'm as sane as you are.' There was no laughter in the tone now, only a deep bitterness, a grinding bitterness. 'It's a wonder I haven't gone mad lying here all these years, but I determined that I wouldn't. I don't know how long I've got left but I hope to live long enough to see you brought low, right down to where you were at the beginning.'

'Well, you'll have to wait a long time for that, Rona, I'm afraid.'

'Not as long as you think, Larry.'

Emily shook her head. They were now talking in ordinary voices but the substance of what they were saying was more awful than when they were screaming at each other. Lucy wasn't the only one who was feeling sick.

She turned quietly away and went down the stairs and into the kitchen, to find Con standing in front of the fire. He was looking down into the burning glow, and he showed no sign that he knew she was in the kitchen; but when she sat down by the table he said quietly, 'You won't go, Emily, will you?' When she didn't answer he turned about and came and stood before her, and she looked up at him. There was that expression on his face that always made her think of a young child, and he said softly in his slow way, 'Don't ... go, Emily. She's sick, she

150

doesn't ... mean it, not what she says. And ... and we need you. Larry needs you. He says you're better than ... Chrissey and Betty ... put together; you've got ... a head on your shoulders ... he says. And Abbie likes you. And Abbie ... doesn't like everybody. But Abbie ... likes you. And Hannah likes you, Hannah Rowan. She told Larry he ... was lucky and we had to keep you. And then ... there's Lucy.' He turned now and looked towards Lucy where she was sitting on a cracket with her hands pinched tightly between her knees. 'The air's good for ... Lucy's cough. Don't go, you won't will you, Emily?'

The tears were spilling from her eyes now and she blinked them away before, taking her apron, she moved it roughly round her face as she said, 'It's all right, Con, it's all right. Don't worry.'

She was still rubbing her face when the kitchen door opened and Larry entered and, speaking straightaway to Con, he said, 'Go up. Take the top covers off the bed and give her dry ones. Then stay with her. I'll be up again directly.'

'Yes, Larry.' When Con obediently went from the room, Larry looked at Emily, who was now on her knees before the hearth slab raking the ashes from under the grate on to a shovel, and he said to her, 'Well, what have you decided to do?'

She stopped raking and turned her head and looked at him. 'If you want me to stay on, I'll stay.'

He was standing to her side now and of a sudden he dropped on to his hunkers so that their faces were on a level, and he stared at her for a moment before he said, 'Want you to stay on? Of course, I want you to stay on; you've handled her better than anyone for years.'

Her mind was saying, I have? Well, mister, you could have hoodwinked me. However, she didn't voice it, but looked at him as he went on, 'You can see how things are for me. It's like walking a tight rope; you never know how you have her from one minute to another.'

'You shouldn't have hit her.'

He was staring at her, his lips slightly apart, and she was staring back at him, and she knew that from this moment things would be different between them. She didn't know in what way, but the fact that she had dared to tell him he shouldn't hit his wife had somehow broken through a barrier, and strangely she viewed him no longer as someone on another sphere, but as an ordinary man, as ordinary as Sep McGillby. In a way she thought that Sep had more about him than this fellow. Sep would never have hit Mrs McGillby. But then she must remember that Mrs McGillby hadn't a filthy mouth. Mrs McGillby wouldn't have come out with the things that that one upstairs had.

He now made a small sound like a laugh and shook his head slowly as he said, 'You know, Emily, you are the only human being I've really talked to in years; those from where I sprang, in my own class, they look upon me as an upstart, and those from higher up look down on me as an upstart, and both sides are waiting to see me topple from me perch. But inside here'—he now tapped his forehead—'are claws, Emily, and those claws are fast on my perch and I'll take some knocking off. What do you say?'

She didn't say anything for a moment. The perch, she knew, he was referring to was this house and the farm, and he was proud that he was master of them. That's what made him assume the cloak of a gentleman. But the cloak didn't quite fit him; he couldn't keep it buttoned up all the time, as it were, and when he let it slip he showed the ordinary fellow he was; and she found she liked the ordinary fellow better than the one he pretended to be.

'I'll go along with you there,' she said evenly; 'you'll take some knocking off.'

152

Still looking at each other, they both now stood up, and he said quietly, 'Go and get changed, we'll leave straightaway. I'll be better out of the place for a while. Con can see to her till we get back.'

He turned and looked towards Lucy. It wasn't that he had forgotten she was there, but as if it didn't matter what he said in front of her. Emily thought that he looked upon Lucy very much as she herself did, like part and parcel of herself.

Up in their room they changed their clothes. They had already washed in the kitchen; it was easier than carting water up all this way.

When she took off her dress she lifted up her top petticoat and from the band of the under one she unpicked a tiny bag that held a sovereign. She had already explained to Lucy about the money and the watch, and together one night they had cut up two of her three handkerchiefs and sewn each sovereign into a little bag, then diligently attached them at intervals like buttons around the band of her petticoat. The watch also she had placed in a bag but this she pinned to her shift.

Now and again she would take the watch out from its cover and they would both look at it. Only last night they had looked at it in the candlelight and she had said to Lucy, 'What am I ever going to do with it? I daren't wear it.' Lucy had giggled and said, 'You could the day you got married; you could say your husband bought it for you as a weddin' present.' At this she had pushed Lucy across the bed and fallen on it herself, and both smothered their laughter. Then she had stared at Lucy, saying, 'Fancy you thinkin' a thing like that, talkin' about me getting married! It'll be years afore I get married now, that's if ever. But what matters as long as we've a roof over our heads. Never say die, eh?' And again they had fallen on the bed and held each other for a moment.

Now holding Lucy's hand, she said, 'I'm going to get

you some woollen bloomers an' a woollen habit shirt.'

'Habit shirt?'

'Yes, camisole like.'

'Oh. . . . Oh, that'll be lovely. Woollen?'

'Aye, woollen to keep you warm. And if we can find a second-hand shop in Gateshead, we'll go and see if we can get you a coat. And meself one an' all; you can almost see the wind through this one.'

'Emily.'

'Aye, what is it?' Emily was now standing with knees bent in order that she could see in the little mirror on the low dressing-chest as she pinned on her hat.

'Are you frightened of her?'

She paused in the act of pushing the hatpin through the back of the hat, and she looked at her reflection in the mirror; then, her head drooping to the side, she said, 'No; at least I'm not going to be. If she starts any of her capers again I'll do what he says and give her as much as she sends, like I did the day.'

She continued to look at her reflection. She was filling out, her face looked plumper, her cheeks were rosy. Was she bonny? Everybody said she was. . . . Eeh! fancy asking herself such questions at this time, and on a day like this, after that do downstairs an' all. Was she bonny indeed! Huh!

She straightened up and smoothed down the front of her coat. It was a nice feeling to be told you were bonny but to be really bonny you had to have nice clothes, smart clothes, and shoes, not boots. She looked down at her feet. That's what she would do an' all the day when she was out, she'd get herself a pair of shoes. Yes, that's what she'd do the day. She needed something to take the bad taste of this morning out of her mouth, she'd spend, and be damned.

'Come on.' She caught hold of Lucy's hand; then pulled her to a stop as the younger girl made for the door, and she bounced her head down at her, saying, 'We're goin' out and we're gona enjoy ourselves. Remember that, Lucy Kennedy. Do you hear me? We're gona enjoy ourselves, and forget about this place and everything.'

Her face crinkled with laughter now, Lucy leant against her for a moment; then they looked at each other, warm from the endearment, and went out and down the stairs determined to enjoy their brief period of liberty.

They arrived in Fellburn market about twelve o'clock. It had been a beautiful drive; the sun had shone all the way; the air was nippy but bracing. Two incidents had occurred on the road that puzzled her and made her think again of Con. She recalled her first impression of him as someone who seemingly couldn't keep his hands to himself. Yet this she had proved to be wrong; anyway, in her case and in Lucy's. Though Lucy was more than fond of him, she had never seen him touch her, not in the way they were suggesting anyhow.

The first incident took place when they had been on the road about ten minutes. They were passing a drover sitting on the bank above a ditch while his herd cropped the grass behind him, when he shouted from the bank, 'Hello there, Larry, how's tricks?' She had been surprised at the man's familiarity and also at Mr Birch's response when he said, and in his ordinary voice, 'Not too bad, Joe. Could be worse.'

'I'll say, I'll say,' was the man's next response. Then when the trap was well past him, he shouted, 'How's Con? Don't see him about these days.'

Emily had looked at Mr Birch. He was staring straight ahead and he made no reply to the remark.

Then when they were passing through the village there was a girl standing beyond the blacksmith's shop. She was carrying a wooden bucket in each hand. The buckets were empty but they seemed to weigh her down and backwards, and Emily realized the reason was that her stomach was well up towards her time. She, too, called to Mr Birch. 'Hello there!' she said. But this time the only answer Larry Birch gave was to turn his head in her direction and stare at her. But when he jerked the reins to hasten the horse on, her voice came to them, shouting. 'Tell Con I'll be takin' a walk over to see him one of these days.' At this he swung round in his seat and glared at the girl, and Emily turned her head, too, and saw that the girl was laughing.

Other folk on the village street had looked towards the trap but as on the day she had first driven through the village no one gave him any sign of recognition.

They were out of the village and going round the frightening curve above the quarry when he next spoke. Looking straight ahead, he said, 'She's a liar, that girl. She's been with more men than there's days in the week. Con never touched her. I want you to believe that.' He now jerked his head towards her. 'He isn't like that. Affectionate, yes, but not in that way. It wasn't Con. But it's only her word against his.'

She could believe him but she said nothing, it wasn't her business. . . . Had more men than days in the week, he had said, and she could believe that about the girl, for she looked a low, common piece, and not one to be easily tripped up in the dark.

In the market he helped them both down on to the road, then said, 'Be back here by half-past three sharp, I want to get home before it's dark. But if I shouldn't be here when you arrive . . . well, you'll just have to wait.' He gave her a tight smile, then added, 'I'm driving over into Washington, I have some business to see to there.'

'Yes, yes, all right. We'll be back here at half-past three. Good-bye, sir.'

'Good-bye, Emily. Good-bye, Lucy.'

'Good-bye, sir.'

As they walked along the pavement she had the idea that he was still standing watching them, and when, at the top end of the street, before turning into the main road, she looked back to see if she had been right, sure enough there he was standing by the horse's head looking in their direction. And then she did a silly thing. She didn't know what possessed her, she lifted her hand and she waved. Then she wished for a hole in the ground to swallow her up for being so silly and forward when, after a pause, she saw his hand go up and move twice, and Lucy said, 'He waved to us!'

When they got into the main street she looked at Lucy and exclaimed, as she shook her head, 'I should never have done that, steppin' out of me place like that. Eeh! he'll think I'm takin' advantage, and I don't want him to think that.' Then, nodding down at Lucy, she went on to explain, 'You see you've got to be so careful, you haven't got to be your natural self with bosses and masters and such like, 'cos they're not all like Sep. Sep was different. So don't you take any liberties because he waved an' speak out of turn when you get back. Wait until you're spoken to, as always.'

'Yes, Emily.'

And as they walked on she thought, I wouldn't have waved to him this time yesterday, I wouldn't have dared.

Mary Southern greeted them with open arms, and hardly stopping to take breath, she told them that a school board man had been there enquiring about Lucy, that Alice Broughton had put him on the scent, but she had put him right off it again by saying that Lucy's big sister had taken her down to the south of the country and into service there. Finally, she poured out more tea, ladled out more potato hash, pushed the assortment of dirty dishes aside, then, spreading her forearms on the table, leant her breasts on them and demanded to be told all the news.

And Emily gave her all the news, about the house, the farm, the master, Con, Abbie, and lastly her mistress. But about her she gave the slimmest of descriptions, simply saying that she was bedridden and rather hoity-toity because she was a lady, for she knew that if she told her Aunt Mary all she had put up with from her mistress in the past few weeks that big and downright woman would have cried at her, 'Get yersels out of that; there are other jobs to be had where you don't have to put up with people like her. To my mind she sounds barmy.' Yes, that's what Aunt Mary would have said, because anyone describing Mrs Birch was bound to give the hearer the impression that the woman was barmy. Yet, Emily knew, she wasn't barmy, not that kind of barmy where you had to be put away, and so she skimmed over her mistress's character, leaving her Aunt Mary with the impression that in taking this new job she had fallen on her feet.

The history of the farm and its occupants exhausted, Emily now asked the question which was uppermost in her mind. 'Do you know of a good second-hand shop around here, Aunt Mary, 'cos we're both in need of a rig-out?'

'Second-hand shop around here, lass! There's nowt else; some good, some bad, and some worse. The clothes you get out of some of 'em, why they're walkin', you could put a rope round 'em an' lead 'em home.'

Now they were all laughing, even the children on the floor joining in.

After Emily had wiped her eyes and taken a gulp of the strong sweet tea, she said, 'I'd like one or two decent things, Aunt Mary; something different from the usual run of the mill, with a bit of colour in it, you know?'

'Well now.' Mary Southern was wagging a fat dirty finger in Emily's direction as she said, 'I know the very place over in Fellburn. Mind you, I've never been inside the shop meself, it's much too ah-la for me. Paddy's

Market over the water in Newcastle is more in my line; I can get the whole lot rigged out for ten bob, leading them home or not!' Again she let out a roar. 'Have you ever been to Newcastle, lass?'

'No, Aunt Mary.' Emily waited patiently.

'Oh, you should go, lass, it's marvellous. There's some wonderful places. I never appreciated it when I had the chance. You know I was in place over there when I was eleven. St Thomas's Square, that's where the house was, and you talk about swank, my God! Lady Golightly or the Duchess of Fife wasn't in it with that one. He managed a bank but you would have thought he managed the Mint. There were only four servants, me included, but they had us kneeling at prayers afore breakfast, eight o'clock in the morning. And mind, I'd been up since five; no six o'clock in them days. They took me from the cook when I was fifteen to train me as housemaid. The missis had what she called ladies' afternoons, and the first time I handed the tea round I spilt some into an old biddy's lap, an' that was that. The very next day when I packed me bundle I cheeked the cook an' she promised a dark end for me. "Every dog has his day," she said, "and you'll get bitten afore long." And you know what I said back to her?' Again her head went back and her laugh rang out as she spluttered, '"Aye, every dog has his day," I said, "an' a bitch has two afternoons." ' Then her chin coming forward, she thrust it towards Emily's and Lucy's laughing faces and, flinging her arms wide to encompass the children on the floor, ended, 'And I've had some afternoons, haven't I?' And all Emily could say at the moment was, 'Oh! Aunt Mary. Oh! Aunt Mary, you're as good as a dose of medicine.'

When the laughter died down, she asked, 'About that shop, Aunt Mary, the good second-hand shop.'

'Oh aye, lass. That's me, I get in a train for Shields and land up at Durham so to speak. . . . Have you ever been in

Newcastle station? By! it's as good as a treat goin' to Newcastle station. All right ... all right ... all right.' She now beat her fist against her head as she cried, 'There you go again, Mary Southern. Stick to the point for once. Well, now, Emily, about this second-hand shop. I understand the wife gets all her bits and pieces from them on Brampton Hill, an' there's some big houses up there, you know, lass, so it's bound to be good stuff. But she's pricey. They say, you'd pay as much as five shillings for a coat. ... Well now, as to where it is, it's almost at the foot of the hill itself, but across the road on the opposite side and down Bower Street. You can't miss it. She's got one or two things in the window nicely arranged like a proper shop, you know?'

'Oh, thanks, Aunt Mary. And ... and would you mind if we got off now because I've got to meet the master in the market around half-past three.'

'No, lass, no, get yourself away, but by! I've been pleased to see you both.'

When the shilling was slipped into her hand she made loud protest; then she bestowed on each of them a smacking kiss, assured them that they were as welcome as the flowers in May even if they were to bloom every day in the year, and on this she set them to the front door and waved them on.

They were still laughing when they reached Fellburn, and Emily said, 'Eeh! me Aunt Mary's as good as a magic lantern, isn't she?' and Lucy replied, 'You know, it's funny, Emily, the house is mucky an' there's bairns all over the place but I wouldn't mind livin' there.'

Emily looked at her for a moment, then asked soberly, 'More than you like livin' up at the house?' and Lucy, returning her gaze, nodded and replied, 'Aye. Aye, I would, Emily.'

As they walked on in silence now, Emily thought, She's right; I would an' all. But—she ended on an inward laugh—that would be after I'd cleaned them all up, me Aunt Mary included.

At half-past three prompt they entered Fellburn Market Square each carrying a large brown paper parcel and their faces shining bright.

But as they approached Larry Birch standing seemingly where they had left him earlier by the horse's head, their steps slowed, and when they stood before him they were silent, and so was he. He stared from one to the other in open-mouthed amazement. Then, his eyes resting on Emily, he began to laugh, and as his laughter mounted and he put his hand over his mouth to quell it the brightness slid from her face.

'I look funny?' The statement was quiet.

'Funny?' He shook his head. 'No, no, Emily, you don't look funny.' He did not add, 'No, but you look ridiculous,' for as extreme as her clothes were and so utterly out of place, either in this dirty market square or for the position that she held, she didn't look ridiculous, she looked amazing. Why had he laughed? He didn't know. Perhaps because he had seen a moth turn into a butterfly. But she had never been a moth; no moth ever glowed like she did. And now her glowing had changed into a bright light, a starkly bright light. Nevertheless, he knew that he preferred her as a moth. He looked at the hat she'd replaced, the flat straw one with its two round-headed hatpins protruding like eyes on stalks from its brim. The replacement, too, was straw, but a leghorn straw, and around the front of its brim lay a large blue feather, and at its back apparently was a similarly coloured large bow of silk ribbon, for the ends of the bow were sticking out beyond the brim, and in one place the wire that kept them in place was exposed.

But it was her coat that was most astonishing. It was green and its collar was made of fur; its sleeves were voluptuous and each fell in three cape folds to the elbow. The coat followed her slim waistline, then swung out into a gored skirt heavily trimmed with braid. It was a coat such as any lady of the city would wear for an occasion, the launching of a ship perhaps or when being the guest at a ladies' afternoon in some fashionable apartment. In certain parts of Newcastle it would have gone unnoticed. But this wasn't Newcastle, this was Fellburn, which boasted of only one select area and that on Brampton Hill.

His eyes moved down to her feet. She no longer wore her sturdy top boots which he had noticed were well down at the heels, but had on now a pair of shoes which were, he imagined, a size too small for her but were very neat, yet too pretty for everyday use. Moreover, her new attire, bought apparently from a second-hand shop, had, in the matter of an afternoon, turned her from a young girl into a young woman. She looked at this moment near twenty. And that was a pity.

But Lucy ... Lucy, dressed in a thick grey, but pretty, coat with blue cuffs and collar and a blue hood, itself lined with the coat material, looked warm and snug, and not out of place.

'You ... you think I've been silly?'

'No, no, Emily, I don't. Believe me I don't.' He was eager to reassure her now because there was no longer any gladness in her face. 'It ... it was only that you went away a short while ago like a young maid, and now you come back like a young lady. The clothes are ... beau ... beautiful. How did you come by them?'

'My Aunt Mary told me of this shop. It's a very good shop; they ... they only deal with the best.'

'Oh'—he nodded solemnly at her now—'I can see that. That coat must have cost a small fortune in the first place.'

'But you think I should have got something a little plainer; I know I should, but ... but I've never seen a coat like this afore.' Her chin drooped now while at the same time she stroked her hand lovingly over her waist.

'You weren't silly, you did right. And how you spend your wages is your business. Now come on, up you get, both of you.'

They got up, and they sat at their side of the trap and he at his, and every now and again he turned his head and looked at them, more often at Emily, and smiled, but the nearer they got towards the village he had the irrepressible urge to say, For God's sake! take that hat off before we go through there. But he had already dampened the glow in her face and he wouldn't risk putting it out altogether. Yet he knew what would happen once they drove up that street.

And it did happen.

On the two previous occasions she had driven through the village no one had taken much notice of them. True, there hadn't been many people about, but those who had been had merely glanced up at the trap then gone about their business of walking or talking. But now not only did the village people turn and stare at them, but a group of miners, about ten in all, who were on their way home from the Beulah pit outside of Fellburn and whose pit cottages were situated behind the village, stopped and gaped, and one or two of them laughed and shouted something.

Emily knew that miners were rough customers, worse than dockers when they got going, for they cared for neither God nor man and seemed to fear nobody, and when one shouted, 'Some poor cock 'll be cold the neet without its tail,' her hands went instinctively to her hat, to freeze there as Larry Birch's voice growled through lips that hardly moved, 'Leave it be!'

163

The trap joggled up the main street towards the black-smith's shop and it was the blacksmith's wife who made the last comment. She was standing at the forge door and as they passed her she shouted over her shoulder, 'Begod! Sandy, come and look at this! ... Fine feathers make fine birds, so they say, an' who said you can't make a peacock out of a partridge? Well! Well!'

Larry Birch remained silent until they were nearing the gates of the house, when, without looking at her, he said, 'You know something? The next thing you'll hear is that I bought you your rig-out, so be prepared for that, won't you?'

'But you didn't, and I'll deny ...'

'You can deny it until your heart stops for want of breath, me girl, but they won't believe you. That village is inhabited by people who want to believe what they want to believe, and in this case, they'll tell you they believe the evidence of their eyes. You pass through there at noon a serving maid, you come back at evening dressed like—' he now turned and looked her up and down then said with heavy weariness, 'like nothing they've ever seen before.'

When she felt Lucy's hand creep into hers she had a great desire to cry, but instead, her head bowed, she said, 'I could leave.'

'Don't talk nonsense!'

It was the almost scornful note in his voice that caused her to flare. 'I could! I will!' Her head was up now, and she was shouting at him. 'You can't stop me! I'm not bonded. Neither is she.' She jerked the hand within hers. 'And I'll tell you this much. I don't care what they think in the village; I don't care about them, they're nothin' to me; I don't care what anybody thinks, them or me mistress, or old Abbie, or ... or ...'

When she hesitated he put in quietly, 'Or me?'

And now she nodded at him fearlessly as she said, 'Aye, you an' all; I'm not beholden to anybody. As long as I've got two hands on me I'll get a job. An' I can always go to me Aunt Mary's until one turns up. I don't have to put up with all this. I'm not tied to that house like you....'

Her eyes were wide, her mouth was wide. The cold evening air was rushing into it down her windpipe and into her stomach, yet she was hot, sweating. What had come over her? Eeh! To talk to him like that. To tell him he was tied to the house.... Well, he was, and to that mean bitch lying in bed up there. ... Eeh! what was the matter with her? ... She was angry, that's what was the matter with her, and she was a fool. She had been a fool to spend her money on these clothes, on this damned hat, and this coat and the dress underneath it. ... But no, the dress was bonny. It was plain, but bonny.

The dress was made of a soft woollen material, pink woollen material. Never had she seen anything like it in her life before.

She'd keep the dress, but she'd burn the coat and the hat. ... No, she wouldn't. When she left she would take it and give it to her Aunt Mary. She would wear it. Aye, she would, an' the hat an' all. She'd cause a riot of laughter in the street, and she'd enjoy it, and everybody with her. ... The whole pound she had spent on herself wouldn't be wasted after all. ... But it was winter, jobs weren't two a penny in winter. Don't let her forget that.

'Yes, I am tied to the house; you have spoken the truth there.' There was no scorn in his voice now. He wasn't speaking to her as if she were a numskull.

'I'm sorry.'

'Oh, you needn't be.'

She looked at him through the fading light and again she had the impression she was sitting with Sep for again

165

she was sensing the same need in this man as she had done in Sep. But this man was playing two parts, and because of his double role he had become an upstart. Yet, strangely, she understood his need to be an upstart, which after all only meant that he wanted to be different, to get on, rise in life. She didn't know from where she drew the perceptive power to recognize the need in people, she only knew she could tell. She had known that Sep had needed something, someone; but she had also known whom Sep had needed. Herself. But she didn't know whom this man needed; she did know though that the need wasn't new in him, that she herself hadn't awakened it, but that someone else had. Was it Mrs Rowan's daughter, the one called Lizzie?

He was speaking again, quietly now as if he were very tired. 'I thought we had come to an understanding this mornin'. I told you then I needed you in the house, and I'm telling you again, so let there be no more talk of packing up.'

He jerked the reins which made a motion like waves rolling towards the horse's head. He drove through the gates, past the front of the house and into the courtyard, and as he jumped down from the trap and put out his hand to help her from the high step Con opened the kitchen door.

She saw him standing tall and straight like a faceless shadow against the light of the lamp from behind him in the kitchen, but as they approached him he moved back and the expression on his face was one of wonder. Then stepping hastily towards them again, he grabbed the parcels from both their arms and hugged them to him as he looked from one to the other, from Emily standing in her fur and braid-trimmed magnificent coat, and now holding the big hat with the bright blue feather and outsize bow between her two hands, to Lucy, appearing at this moment like some fragile child who had stepped out from an expensive story book, and he exclaimed on a high note of awe and admiration, 'Oh! you look lovely. Lovely.'

He now turned and dropped their parcels on to the table; then going to Lucy, he put out his hand and his fingers traced the bonnet around her face. Then moving his long arm, he turned it in Emily's direction and caressed the curling fronds of the feather on the hat. Now he lifted his eyes and looked at Larry standing behind them, and he said, 'You've bought ... them these, Larry? Oh, that ... was nice of you. And don't they ... look lovely?' As his eyes came to rest again on Emily, saying now, 'Beautiful, beautiful,' her face crumpled. She turned her head quickly and glanced over her shoulder, and Larry said, on a sound that held both amusement and bitterness, 'What did I tell you?'

It was too much. Almost staggering to the table, she dragged out a chair, dropped on to it and buried her face in her folded arms, and cried as she had wanted to cry for weeks now. She cried for Sep; she cried for the loss of the house in Pilot Place, the house that she would always think of as lovely; she cried because Lucy had the disease; and she cried for herself because she was ignorant and didn't know how to choose clothes.

They stood about her, Lucy close to her, her thin hands gripping her arm, and Con on the other side, with Larry behind her. They, too, had their hands on her. Con was stroking her shoulder, and Larry touching her hair, but so tentatively she never felt his hand at all. But she listened to his voice talking quietly, saying, 'There now. It's over. Come on. It's nearly the end of the day, and what a day all round. But there'll come another. ... Never say die.'

She raised her head and straightened her shoulders, gulped in her throat, then rubbed her hand over her wet face. It was funny; she wanted to laugh now, someone had said to her, 'Never say die.' Miles from Shields and the place where she imagined the saying had been born through adversity, someone had said to her, 'Never say die.' Huh! it was funny. Life was funny.

Never say die.

THREE

It was on the following Sunday, and again her half-day, when Emily decided to wear her new frock. There was no reason, she told herself, why she should do so, because she wasn't going anywhere special, just for a walk. And not in the direction of the village either. She had said to Lucy earlier they would take a tramp over those hills they could see from their bedroom window; they looked quite near and she often wondered what lay beyond them. Perhaps they'd be able to see Chester-le-Street from there; and Durham. No not Durham, that was too far away. But some day she'd go to Durham, and to Newcastle, and Sunderland, and all those places. Yes, she would some day.

As she bent her knees to look at herself once more in the mirror she admonished herself for being in 'one of those moods'. And it wasn't new; the mood had come and gone all the week; in fact, ever since she had bought the clothes. One minute she was up in the air full of defiance and telling herself what she could do, and what she was going to do, the next minute she was in the depths reminding herself that she was nothing or nobody, and she'd better be careful and not open her mouth wide and speak out of turn; she was forgetting herself, and in her position she couldn't really afford to, no matter how she felt, because after all jobs didn't grow on trees.

So, as they were only going over the hills, why did she

want to put her new frock on? It would only be covered up by her old coat. One thing was sure, she'd never wear *that* coat again . . . or the hat. That hat! Never!

Oh, get on with it. She supposed she was in a temper because he had told them to take their half-day today because he couldn't take them into the town tomorrow, and he hadn't said why. She straightened up so abruptly that she almost over-balanced Lucy.

As Lucy watched her now pulling off her workaday clothes and getting into her bonny frock she asked, 'Do you want to walk over them hills, Emily? Can't we just stay around the yard and the farm?'

'Stay around the yard an' the farm!' Emily almost barked at her. 'Our one free time in the week and you say stay around the yard! I'm sick of looking at that yard. That's all I see for nearly seven days a week; the inside of this house, that yard, and the farm. Do you know we never see a single soul from one week's end to the other but them about here, except perhaps that Mrs Rowan, and then she just flits in and flits out. By!'—she let out a long-drawn sigh—'I never thought I'd miss Shields but I'd give me eye teeth to be back there again, wouldn't you?'

They looked at each other, and Lucy nodded, saying, 'Aye, I would, Emily. I'm not taken with the country.'

Again Emily was barking, 'Well, you should be! Because it's good for your cough. That's another thing I want to have out with you: what are you eating to make you sick? You had nothin' that I saw yesterday to make you sick.'

'Perhaps it was the fat in the mutton stew.'

'I cut nearly all the fat off. . . . Anyway, you're not eating as you should.'

'I never feel hungry, Emily.'

'Well, I can tell you this, I bet you do this afternoon when we get back from our walk 'cos I'm goin' to walk you off your legs, and there's nothing better for giving people an appetite than walkin'. So get your coat and hat on and put on an extra pair of bloomers. An' that scarf round your neck. An' be quick about it, because I can't wait to get out of here.'

Lucy didn't do as she was bidden straight away but stared at her beloved sister before she complained, 'What's the matter with you, our Emily? You're always going for me, you never used to be like this.'

Of a sudden Emily flopped down on the side of the bed and she stared at Lucy for a full minute before she said, 'I don't know either what's come over me. I thought about it last night, and I've come to the conclusion I'm just now feeling the shock of Sep going. They say that you don't feel the shock of things happenin' like that until long after. Then this house, one thing happenin' on top of another. They've never stopped since we came here, have they? And look at this morning when I answered him back. Eeh!'—she shook her head at herself—'I wouldn't have dreamed of speaking to Sep like that, would I?'

'No, Emily.'

'No, I don't know what's come over me. Oh, come on, let's get out of this....'

Some minutes later they left the house and grounds and walked along the road until they came to a stile. Having crossed this, they went over an open space, entered a copse, and when they came out at the other side, there before them was a broken-down bridge with a burn running past it. They stood and looked at the water until Lucy shivered, and Emily said, 'Come on, let's get moving. Look, yonder's the first of the hills we can see from our bedroom window.'

Ten minutes later when they reached the top of the hill, Lucy's scarf was no longer around her neck, nor was Emily's coat buttoned up.

'By! that was a slope, wasn't it?' They looked back

over the way they had come down the side of the hill and across the field to the broken-down bridge; then they turned and looked ahead to where the land running downhill was covered in parts with dead rust-coloured bracken.

They stood panting and gaping, for they couldn't see any town or habitation on any side of them, only another rise in front of them, and this was across a widish valley.

'Well, I never! I thought we'd see the towns from here.' Emily wiped the sweat from her face.

'It's bare, isn't it, Emily? No houses, nothin', nothin' to see anywhere.'

'You've missed something, our Lucy. Look over there, top of the next hill, that's a cottage.'

'Aye, so it is. Do you think we'd get a drink of water if we asked, I'm as dry as a fish?'

'I see no harm in tryin'. Perhaps if there's a cow, they'd give us a sup milk.' She pushed Lucy, and Lucy pushed back at her, and now they laughed together as they ran stumbling between the bracken down the hill to the valley below.

Again the distance was deceptive for it took them a good five minutes after crossing the valley to breast the slope to the cottage. And then their approach to it became slow because, full of disappointment, they could see from a distance that it was a deserted and tumbledown place. A dry stone wall surrounded it, but it was almost obliterated by grass and bracken, and the wooden gate that had once been set in the wall was now lying buried in grass to the side of it.

'Eeh! it's empty.... But isn't it tiny, small?'

'Yes'—Emily laughed—'like a doll's house compared with that down there.'

There was a distance of more than fifty feet from the gate to the cottage door and Lucy stopped half-way, saying, 'Eeh! our Emily, you're not goin' in, are you?'

Emily had her foot on the slate step and she turned her head and laughed as she said, 'No harm in havin' a look. But I bet it's locked.'

She put out her hand towards the latch of the door and noted as she did so that it was a sturdy door, likely made to match the stone in strength when it was first built, and when she felt her fingers lifting the latch and the door swinging inwards she jumped back off the step and giggled as she looked over her shoulder at Lucy, who had now retreated to the gateless aperture in the wall, crying, 'Eeh! don't go in, our Emily.'

But Emily went in. Tentatively now, she placed her foot over the threshold and found she was standing in a little room, little compared to those she had become used to working in of late, but she gauged it was about the size of the kitchen in Pilot Place. There was no furniture in the room, but there was a stone fireplace with a rusty iron oven to the side of it. She went back to the door now, calling and beckoning to Lucy, 'Come on, come on! It's canny. Come an' see.'

When Lucy also tentatively put her foot over the threshold she stood still for a moment looking round in the dimness before smiling at Emily and nodding as if to confirm her statement.

'There's another room through there.'

They now went through into what was the bedroom and there, on the floor in the corner, was a large wooden plank bed with an old flock mattress still on it.

'It's old-fashioned, isn't it, Emily?'

'Aye, it is that. I bet that was like bricks to sleep on.' She bent down and pressed the mattress against the boards with her hand. Then looking at the little window at the foot of the bed, she said, 'They could have let more light in.'

In the kitchen again, she went towards a door opposite that by which they had entered, and opening it, she exclaimed, 'Oh look! it's a scullery,' then ended, 'of sorts. It's got no water in. This must lead out on to the back.' She now opened the door facing her; then, turning to Lucy, she cried, 'Come an' see. It's a little yard with cattle shippons.'

She was about to step down into the yard when she noticed something, and pointing, she said to Lucy, 'Look, the grass is trampled flat from that gate there; somebody comes here.'

'Eeh! we'd better get away then.'

'What for? It's empty. It's likely a tramp's hide. You know, they leave messages on gates and things tellin' other tramps if the woman is good for a penny or just bread, because me ma used to say many a time she's given beggars bread and she's seen it thrown in the back lane. ... Come on.'

They took a few steps along the side of the stone wall and entered the first shippon. This one had definitely been meant for a horse, for it had a manger stuck to the wall. But the second had evidently been for the cows, but only two at most. The third building must have been a storeroom, and at one time held a boiler, for part of an old iron flue still protruded through the wall. Pointing to it, she said, 'They must have had pigs and boiled the stuff in here.'

'Like Abbie does?'

'Yes. But Abbie's boiler house is a sight different from this.'

'Oh yes. Aye, it is. I wouldn't fancy living' up here, Emily.'

'No, nor me. But I wouldn't mind the cottage if it was in a village ... but'—they both looked at each other quickly as Emily finished—'not that one down there. They're a right sticky lot, them down in that village. Even Abbie says some of them wouldn't give you daylight if they could shut it out. And he should know, seeing as

Mr Atkins who keeps the inn is his cousin.... Well, come on; we'd better be gettin' back. But I must close the doors and leave the place as we found it....'

Some time later they were standing once again on the top of the hill looking back over the way they had come from the cottage, and they were about to turn and resume their journey when Lucy, pointing to the right of her, said, 'Look, there's a man goin' towards that place.'

'Where?'

'You'll see him in a minute, the bracken's hidin' him now. Yes, there he is!'

Emily screwed up her eyes and concentrated her gaze on the figure in the distance below them. Something about his walk was familiar. But long before he had neared the cottage and turned off to the right and made his way by the side of the stone wall and round towards the back she knew who it was. That place, that cottage, was the but an' ben Abbie had talked about; it must have been there that Mr Birch had lived, the place where he had come from to work on the farm. She couldn't believe it. It was such a lowly place.... But one thing now she could understand, and that was the villagers' attitude towards him; of course he would be classed as an upstart because the jump from that two-bedroomed little place with its shambling rotting shippons to Croft Dene House was too enormous to imagine.

Although they were supposed to have a half-day off a week it appeared to Emily that as soon as they should come back to the house he expected them to take up their duties again, and she herself had done this without questioning, until today. Returning from their walk, she passed immediately through the kitchen and was making for the back stairs just as Con entered the hall from the main stairway. He was carrving a tea tray and he stopped and smiled at them, saying, 'You got ... back then?'

'Yes, Con.'

'I've ... I've made ... some tea.'

'We don't want any yet; we'll be down presently, Con.'

'All right ... Emily ... Rona's in a bad temper.... She's asking for Larry, but Larry ... went out. I told her he said he had to go over to ... to Wrekenton.'

Wrekenton? She repeated the word to herself while her eyebrows moved slightly upwards. When she had seen him he was going in the opposite direction to Wrekenton.

'She's upset. Her ... her bed ... is dirty, but she wouldn't let me ... change it. I could have ... changed the sheets, couldn't I?'

'She'd dirtied the bed?'

'Yes, Emily.'

She sighed. She didn't like her mistress, in fact she disliked her intensely, but she told herself she wouldn't let a mangy dog lie in a dirty bed if she could help it, and so with a sigh she whipped off her coat and hat and thrusting them into Lucy's arms, said, 'Bring me down an apron, not one of me good ones, a brown holland one.'

She now followed Con back into the kitchen, saying, 'I'll have that cup of tea first'; and he answered brightly, 'Yes. Yes, Emily, I'll get it.'

As she stood drinking the tea she said, more to herself than to him, 'She should have a nurse; that's what she should have.'

'She did ... Emily ... three. But they ... all left. She doesn't like ... like nurses.'

Was there anybody she did like?

With a feeling now of exasperation, Emily put the unfinished cup of tea down on the table and went hastily from the room, across the hall and up the main staircase. She tapped once on her mistress's door, and not waiting for the command to enter she went in.

The two lamps were already lit, one at each side of the bed—she was very extravagant with oil. The room was very hot, the fire was blazing high—it was a duty shared between Lucy and Con to see that this was always kept built up—and now the heat was emphasizing the smell of human excrement.

Rona Birch had been leaning forward in the bed, her arms stretched towards her useless knees. Emily took it to be a sign of desperation and she said quietly, 'I'll change your sheets, madam.'

Rona Birch's head slowly turned towards her and when she took in Emily's overall appearance, which seemed to be transformed by the elegance yet simplicity of the pink woollen dress, her upper body shot backwards and the jerk must have been painful, for she gasped and pressed her hand tightly between her breasts for a moment before she demanded, 'Where did you get that?'

'The dress, madam?' Emily touched one of the two buttons at her waist, then said, 'I bought it, madam.'

'*You bought that!*'

'Yes, madam.'

They stared at each other before Emily turned away and went into the linen room.

As she returned with two sheets and an under blanket over one arm, and towels and a nightdress over the other, there was another tap on the door, and Lucy came in, still in her outdoor things, and silently she handed the apron to Emily, who first unbuttoned the cuffs of her dress and rolled up the sleeves as far as they would go, then put on the apron.

Now the mistress's eyes were on Lucy. Her head moved up and down a number of times before she said, 'Those aren't her usual clothes, I suppose you bought those too?'

'Yes, I did.' With a lift of her hand Emily now flung back the top coverlet, then the blankets, and her nose wrinkled with distaste when she came to the sheets. Turning now to Lucy who was still in the room, she said,

'Take your things off and bring me some hot water, quick now!'

'Where did you get the money to buy such clothes?' Rona Birch was lying back, her voice quiet as if she were relaxed.

'I had money saved up.'

The answer acted like an injection, for Rona Birch was now shouting, 'Who do you think you're talking to, girl! You never in your life would have enough money to buy a dress like you're wearing now, nor that outfit you've decked your sister in. Who gave you the money?' Once again she was sitting upright.

Emily pulled off the top sheet, and then gathered the bottom one round the inert limbs, wiped them as she gradually decreased the sheet into a ball before tugging it away and dropping it on to the floor. She now folded the top sheet in half and placed it under her mistress's buttocks before picking up the dirty sheet again and taking it into the linen room and dropping it into a wooden bucket.

When she returned to the room she stopped in the middle of it as her mistress rasped at her, 'Don't leave me exposed like this, girl!'

Emily stared hard at her mistress and swallowed deeply before she said, 'You have hands, madam, you can pull the blanket over you.' On this, she actually heard her mistress's teeth grind together.

Emily now turned to Lucy who was entering the room staggering under the weight of a can of warm water, and having taken it from her, as she poured the water into the dish she said, 'Perhaps you will wash yourself, madam, before I put the clean sheets on.'

'You'll finish the job you started, girl!'

'Madam'—Emily backed from the bed—'the master said you could wash yourself.'

'The master said...? The master said...? Listen, girl, I

am master here. I'm both master and mistress of this house. Get that into your head.'

'The master doesn't seem to think so, madam.' Even as she chastised herself for daring to say such a thing she sprang back, her hand before her face, crying, 'I've warned you, madam. I warned you once, an' I mean it, you throw anything at me....'

Slowly Rona Birch replaced the soap dish on the bedside table; then slapping the flannel into the water, she said slowly, 'I'll see my day with you, girl, remember that, as I will with the man you call master.'

Emily made a motion for Lucy to leave the room; then she went into the linen room and leant her head against the tallboy as she told herself that she couldn't stand this, while at the same time reminding herself yet once again that it was now deep winter and her Aunt Mary's house was crowded, and if both of them went into the lodgings the sovereigns sewn to her petticoat band would soon disappear. If only she knew where she could sell the watch without questions being asked, she'd be out of here like a shot. But there was a snag. Wherever she went Lucy would have to go too, and it wasn't every house that would take a consumptive in.

A banging on the side table told her that her mistress was ready. The soiled nightdress was on the floor by the side of the bed, as were the towels. The soap and flannel had not been put back in the dish but had been placed on the polished top of the bedside table.

Silently Emily eased the clean linen sheet on to the bed and in the process it was impossible not to touch her mistress's flesh and the contact created in her a feeling of revulsion. Finally it was done, and she was drawing up the top cover over the stiff legs underneath the bedclothes when the neck of her dress was gripped and she was pulled upwards until her face was within inches of her mistress's.

'How much did he give you? Where did he take you last Monday?'

There was an unpleasant smell on the breath that wafted in her face. She tried to strain away from it as she gasped, 'The ... the master gave me nothing ... only me wages.' She was almost choking and now in desperation she gripped the wrists that were gripping the collar of her dress and stuttered into the face, 'Le ... leave go of me, madam.'

'When you tell me how much he gave you. Don't think you are the first. Oh, not by a long chalk! Why did Chrissey leave? And there's the other one, dear Lizzie, you'll find out about her too.'

'*Madam!*'

'Tell me, girl, or I'll wrench this off your back.'

'You do! madam. Just you do!' Anger was replacing her fear again, and what she would have done if her mistress had carried out her threat she didn't know for at that moment the door opened and Larry Birch stood as if struck dumb looking at them.

After thrusting them apart, he stood glaring down at his wife, where she was now lying back on the pillows, panting like a horse that had finished a race and with the froth round her lips very like that seen on such an animal, and he cried at her, 'You're insane, woman, mad!' Then jerking his head back towards Emily, where she stood supporting herself at the foot of the bed, he demanded, 'What's all this about?'

'She ... she won't believe I bought me frock meself, she ... she says....' When she stopped he said, 'No!' Then looking down on his wife again, he brought out slowly, I tell you you're going mad, woman, you're a maniac.'

Rona Birch's chest heaved a number of times before she managed to speak, and then she said, 'Well, tell me, dear husband, where our maid of all work got the money to buy a dress such as she's wearing and to deck her sister out too in a matching outfit of finery that is seldom seen in these parts, except as I myself wore when I was a child?'

He did not answer her, but turning now to Emily, he said, 'Go and bring the hat and coat down.'

'What?'

'Do as I say, bring your hat and coat down, the one you bought with the dress, and the other things you got that day.'

She did not move immediately; but then slowly she went from the room and she passed Lucy, who was standing biting hard on her thumb nail against the foot of the attic stairs, without a word.

Within a few minutes she returned to her mistress's bedroom. Across one arm was laid the coat and hat, across the other a long grey skirt sporting a mud fringe on the bottom, and on top of it a striped linen bodice.

She had scarcely entered the room before Larry whipped the coat from her and, holding it at arm's length and to the side, cried at his wife, 'Look at that! Now look at it.' Then without glancing at Emily, he said, 'Put the hat on top of it. No, better still, put it on. Put it on your head.'

Slowly she put the hat on top of her mob cap, and there she stood looking at her mistress. Then, as if waving a cloak, he swung the coat in front of her and as he held it there he shouted, 'She went to a second-hand shop and this is what she bought! And all for a few shillings. And she caused such a stir in the village that they're still laughing, I'm told.'

A deep silence now enveloped the room, which he didn't break when he told Emily to take her clothes and herself away, for he just waved his hand and she went out on to the landing and up the attic stairs to her room.

She was no longer a tall bonny young lass with her wits about her, for she was seeing herself as a low type serving maid, one of no consequence, one so ignorant that she didn't know when she was making a laughing stock of herself....

'And she caused such a stir in the village that they're still laughing, I'm told.'

FOUR

It was strange and not understandable to Emily, but from that Sunday afternoon when she had stood before her mistress's bed wearing that hat, that ridiculous hat which had brought her low inside herself and which now she couldn't imagine herself ever being persuaded to buy, things had been easier in the house.

The very next morning she had been amazed to encounter a different Mrs Birch, someone who spoke quietly to her, civilly, and even smiled. What, she had asked, had made her buy such clothes?

'Because I'd never seen anything like them before, madam,' she had answered dully. And to this her mistress had nodded as if in understanding and said, 'Yes, that is the way of it, we always want to own things and people that are the antithesis of us.'

And that morning her mistress had washed herself without demur and put the soap back in the soap dish; she had also combed out her long thin hair straightaway, taking the loose hair from the comb and rolling it into a ball between her fingers when she was finished, but she had never said she was sorry for how she had acted the previous day. But then, Emily didn't expect her to; mistresses, especially if they were ladies, couldn't be expected to apologize to maids.... But why shouldn't they? There you go again! she admonished herself; why do you keep asking yourself such stupid questions?

But from that morning until New Year's Day, 1903, comparative peace reigned, and Emily in a way would have been happy in her work now but for two things.

First, she was becoming more worried each day over Lucy. Lucy had spasms of sickness; she wasn't eating as she should, yet she was putting on weight. It showed not only in her face now but in her body. Strangely she was coughing less, even though she always coughed more in the winter, and already it was a hard winter, an early one for they'd had two falls of snow with drifts high enough for the men to have to dig out a path to the road.

Secondly, there stuck in her mind the meeting she'd had with the former maid, Chrissey Dyer. It had been on another Sunday afternoon walk, a short one this time, and not in the direction of the hills and the wee stone house up there but straight along the carriage road and to the fork where a signpost said: To Chester-le-Street and Durham. But she hadn't gone along that road, she had continued along the carriageway and taken another path off to the right.

She was alone on this walk because Lucy was complaining more and more of being cold, but she herself had felt she must get away from the house if only for an hour or so in the week. Even if the weather was no great shakes for walking, as today, for the wind was blowing up her coat, dress and petticoats and almost lifting her from the ground, she was glad she was outside.

For three weeks now he had said he couldn't take her into Fellburn on a Monday because, after delivering his produce, he would be going to Durham, and wouldn't be coming back that way, so couldn't pick her up. She had thought about the carrier cart, but the last one from Fellburn in the winter left at 2.30 and that wouldn't leave her enough time to get to her Aunt Mary's and back. She was longing to see her Aunt Mary; she was longing to have a natter and a bit of a laugh; oh yes, she needed to have a laugh.

She must have walked more than a mile along the narrow lane when it suddenly broadened out and there to the side of the road was a stone cottage similar in design to that other one up in the hills, but this one had no shippons, only small gardens to the front and back of it. The front patch, she noted as she passed the wall, was full of winter broccoli.

She continued to walk on for another five minutes or so, then she retraced her steps and as she came in sight of the cottage again she saw a young girl standing at the gate. She had a shawl over her head and her hands were muffled in it, holding it tightly up under her chin.

It was as Emily came abreast of her that she said, 'Hello, there.'

'Hello!' Emily stopped and smiled. It was the first time anyone around here had given her the time of day. 'It's bitter, isn't it? The wind would cut you in two.'

'Then why are you out?' The question was sharp, and Emily hesitated as she stared at the girl before answering, 'Well, you see, I'm in service along. . . .'

'Yes, yes, I know where you're in service at, you took my place . . . not that I mind that. Oh no, you're welcome to it. I'm Chrissey Dyer. How are you gettin' on . . . I mean back there, with her and him?'

Emily saw at once that it was no good painting a bright picture of the conditions in the house; although things had been easier of late, especially in the mistress's bedroom, yet she had to admit to herself that she couldn't get to like the woman, not even to the extent of being sorry for her.

'Has she thrown anything at you yet?'

At this Emily laughed, while grabbing at her hat and putting her head to one side to meet the wind. 'No, but she's tried it on.'

'What do you mean, tried it on?'

'She threatened it but I told her what I'd do if she did.'

'You did!' The two hands came away from the chin, the shawl fell open and the wind caught it and the young girl grabbed at it and folded it once again round her neck before she asked now, 'What did you say?'

'I told her if she threw anything at me I'd throw it back at her.'

Emily was laughing now at the expression on the girl's face. Then her laughter died as the girl said flatly, 'I don't believe you; nobody'd dare say that to her an' be able to stay on there. I don't believe you.'

'Well, I can't help it if you believe me or not, but I did. And I was goin' to leave, but he, the master, he asked me to stay on.'

'Aw aye, he would. I'd like a penny for every time he persuaded me to stay on. Three years I put up with it. It made me bad, do you know that? It made me bad. I thought I was going batty. There were things that happened in that house that scared the daylights out of me, an' things that I got the blame for when it was that Con all the time. I used to like him at one time, feel sorry for him, but not any more. He's not so green as he's cabbage lookin'; it's all pretend with him; he's not so daft that he didn't know how to put Bella Goodyear in the family way. Mind, I didn't credit him with that 'cos he never tried it on me. He knew better with me ma about. But there were other things ... her.' She now moved her hands within the cover of the shawl, and what she next said convinced Emily that the girl was indeed ill. 'There's things goes on there. Oh, just you wait, you'll see for yourself. There's a ghost there sort of.' Her head was bobbing. 'I've seen it with me own eyes, an' I screamed an' he came dashing out. And when I saw him I screamed worse 'cos he was in a long white night-shirt. The next day he went for me; he said there was no such things as ghosts, not in that house

186

anyway; and he said if he heard any more of it what he would do. But me ma'd had enough with one thing an' another, so she didn't give him time to do anything, she whipped us both out of the place an' told him what he could do with his job. She said she'd never died of winter yet, an' neither have we. An' we're movin', we're goin' into Fellburn, me da'll be nearer the pits there anyway.'

Emily moved away from the wall, but she continued to look at the girl. One thing was evident, she was a very nervous type of person.

The girl was shouting above the wind now, and Emily shouted back. 'What d'you say?'

'I said, look out for that Con an' him pinchin' stuff.'

'Yes, yes, I will. And thanks, thanks for tellin' me. Good-bye.'

The girl didn't answer, and Emily turned away, thinking, Poor soul, she is bad.

Well, she told herself, she had been in the place over two months now, and if she was going to see a ghost she would have seen it before, wouldn't she? But just as a prevention, she would, she told herself, keep Lucy with her when she went about the house late at night, because, as she understood it, ghosts never made themselves known to two people at once, they always waited until they caught you on the hop, alone. . . .

But now it was Christmas week and she was excited and, in a way, happy. Yesterday he had given them a lift into Fellburn and she had gone into Gateshead and simply staggered her Aunt Mary by giving her a whole half sovereign to spend on the bairns' stockings. Moreover, when in the town she had bought both Con and Abbie a present, paying ninepence for a tin whistle for Con, because he could play good tunes on a whistle and the one he had was, to her mind, the worse for wear because the painted design between the holes had worn off, and for Abbie, a new clay pipe and an ounce of baccy.

She hadn't bought anything for the master or mistress although she had thought about it, but had decided it would be out of place. Now if it had been Sep.

It was strange but she seemed to be missing Sep more now than when he had first died, yet strangely enough she was glad that she wasn't married to him. Now wasn't that odd, she asked herself?

For the three days before Christmas Eve she had stood at the table baking raised pies, rice loaves, bacon and egg pies and ginger bread. The Christmas cake she had baked almost three weeks ago. She had also experimented in the making of fancy cakes, such as making thin layers of light pastry and putting different mixtures such as jam and fresh churned cream from the dairy in between them.

And there was laughter in the kitchen, real laughter, when her master slyly sampled her efforts. Lucy and Con's laughter became hilarious when Larry, in passing, nipped up some of her pastries when her back was turned and swiftly gave one to each of them.

And then because she was feeling unusually happy she made a proposal to the mistress.

It was in the afternoon of Christmas Eve. She had scrambled up to her room, put on a clean apron, and she herself had taken the tray from Con and carried it up to the bedroom. On the tray was a plate holding an assortment of her latest efforts, and she pointed to them as she looked at Rona Birch and said, 'I made these special like, small, dainty. I . . . I hope you like them.'

'Thank you, Emily.'

It was the third time in the past week her mistress had called her by her name. Wonders would never cease, she told herself. Then she put forward her idea. 'Madam,' she said, 'may I say somethin'?'

Rona Birch's hand became still on the handle of the small silver teapot and she looked at Emily as she said quietly, 'Yes. What do you wish to say?'

'Well, madam'—Emily smiled and looked down— 'Con, I mean Master Con'—this was something she had always to be wary of; she had been pulled up about it before—'he ... he was saying last night that you were grand on the piano, an' you played lovely, and I thought if ... if we put a big blazing fire on in the drawing room, the master could, well'—she bounced her head now—'he could carry you downstairs and they could place that big chair with the movable back near the piano and ...'

'*No!*'

The word was spoken in a deep, sonorous tone. There was about it a finality that caused Emily to move back from the bed and nod her head. But before she turned towards the door, Rona Birch spoke again. With her eyes still on the hand that held the teapot, she said, 'It ... it was a kind thought of yours, but it ... it is very painful for me to move, and I always feel more ill after exertion.'

'Yes, yes, I understand, madam, but ... but it being Christmas, I just thought....'

Emily watched her mistress lift the teapot and fill her cup. No, not fill the cup, she never let the tea rise above the gold rim which was nearly an inch from the top of the cup; moreover, she poured the cold milk in after, which appeared backside foremost to her way of thinking; it was different if you were putting in condensed milk. Then she watched her lift the cup up almost to her lips. But she didn't drink, she looked down into it as she repeated, 'Yes, it being Christmas.' Then slowly she went on, 'Everybody should be happy at Christmas: laden tables, the giving and receiving of presents, the Christmas tree sparkling with tinsel and coloured glass baubles, and tiny candles. One Christmas, the tree caught fire.' She turned her head towards Emily. 'Every year of my childhood I had a Christmas tree. We danced around it. When Con was three years old we had a great party. The tree was in the drawing-room. There were the six Marsden children from the Hall; there were Peter and Gwen from the Priory. Peter was very boisterous; he kicked one of the Marsden boys on the shin. They began to fight and fell against the tree, and that's how it caught fire. Peter was only six, and if I remember the Marsden boy wasn't that old. Father held them at arm's length by their collars; their legs were kicking, and everybody laughed, that was after they had taken the tree out.... I always loved Christmas trees. Queen Victoria had that to her credit if nothing else. I always disliked her intensely; everybody made such a fuss of her, and what was she after all? A dumpy, plain individual. She was lucky to acquire such a Prince Consort as Albert. And, anyway, it was he who was the instigator of her having a Christmas tree in the first place.... She wasn't a queenly queen at all, she didn't act like a queen. Did you like her?'

Emily's mouth had been dropping into a gape. She had never heard her mistress talk so much at one go before, and jumping from one thing to another. Christmas trees, fires, children fighting, Queen Victoria and Prince Albert.... Yes, she had liked her; everybody had liked Queen Victoria, because she was like somebody's granny. She remembered Sep coming in as if it were yesterday— yet it seemed years and years ago, in another life. But it was only in January of last year. He had stood by the kitchen table and moved his head as he said sadly, 'Well, the old girl's gone; we'll never see another like her. This should put a stop to Eddie's gallop.'

She hadn't been able to understand the last bit, not then she hadn't, but now she did, for now she knew the King had been a bit of a lad. Yes, she had liked the Queen and she wasn't going to say she hadn't and so she said, 'Yes, I liked her. I ... I thought she was a canny body.'

'Ho! ho! ho!'

She had never heard her mistress laugh, not like this

anyway. She was leaning back against the pillows while holding on to the handles of the tea tray, and three times she repeated, 'She was a canny body. She was a canny body. She was a canny body.'

As she straightened herself up she nodded towards Emily, saying, 'She would have been pleased by your description.' Then her upper body seemed to slump, she put her head on one side and, her voice quite soft now, she added, 'Perhaps you're right, she was a canny body. I disliked her because of her power. I envied her her power. Oh yes, I envied her her power. Do you know something, Emily?'

'What, madam?'

'Women will one day rule this country. They'll be in entire charge of everything, everything that is that requires reasoning and intellect, because women are much stronger than men you know.'

Emily blinked. She didn't actually disbelieve what her mistress was saying, although at the same time she couldn't confirm the truth of it in her mind, yet from some recess there oozed the thought that women, given the chance, could beat men at lots of things. But then they would never get the chance.

'You don't believe me?'

'Well, I don't often think on such things, madam, but I don't disbelieve you, madam, 'cos I know women rule the roost in most homes. Men do a lot of talkin', but the women act. Of course, I'm talkin' of workin' class homes.'

'You are talking of the majority of homes.... Can you read?'

'Oh yes, madam.'

'And write?'

'Yes, madam, I learned at school.'

'Have you ever been with a man?'

'*What!*'

'Have you ever been with a man? You heard what I said.'

Now Emily's back was straight, her head up and slightly to the side, and her chin out. 'No, I haven't, madam! And if I had it would just be me own business.'

They stared at each other for a moment. Then again Rona Birch's head was back and she was laughing. And as Emily went out, closing the door none too gently behind her, her mistress's voice came to her clear and loud, crying, 'And his. And his.'

She was so flustered that instead of going straight downstairs she turned and ran towards the attic stairs and up into her room.

Well, did you ever! Fancy saying a thing like that! And all that talking all at once. But to ask her if she had ever been with a man. It was indecent, nasty. She had been sorry for her when she first went into the room, but she was sorry for her no longer. When she talked, as she had done over the last five minutes, it was hard to believe that she was a cripple and tied fast to that bed because everything she said implied.... Well, what did it imply? A sort of strength, a sort of wild strength. It was funny, but she put her in mind of a dog that was chained up, and if she ever got loose she'd tear you to bits.

She sat down for a moment on the side of the bed and as she allowed the air to escape from deep within her lungs she thought, And that was a funny way to describe her, for mostly she's as weak as a kitten. What was more, she seemed to be getting weaker as time went on, and she didn't think she was pretending. Sometimes she looked as if she was going to peg out that minute, but she supposed she was like many a creaking door, she would swing on one hinge for a long time yet..... And more was the pity.

Eeh! the things she thought.

FIVE

Christmas had been mainly a time of eating, there had been no real jollification. As Lucy had said to Emily, 'You would have thought that somebody would have popped in; even that Mrs Rowan didn't come.' And she had answered, 'Well, would you expect her with the roads as they are like glar with the thaw. Whoever thought it would rain on top of all that snow? Why, the master told you what a job he had to get back from Fell-burn.'

'Yes, but,' Lucy persisted, 'the master or Con didn't even go upstairs and stay with her for a bit, they just acted like it was an ordinary day, Christmas Day I mean. And I'd thought they might even have their dinner in here with us.'

'You thought they would eat it here with us!' Emily had stretched her face at Lucy, and ended, 'You're thinkin' big, aren't you?' Yet at the same time she herself had thought that they might even do that, in fact she had expected it because ... because Con had said to her, 'Wouldn't it be nice, Emily, if we had a party and a sing-song?' and she had answered, 'It would be grand, Con,' and he had hunched his shoulders up round his face like a child in glee as he said, 'I'll ask Larry. That's what I'll do, I'll ask Larry.'

Whether he had asked the master or not she didn't know, but she served their dinner in the dining-room as usual.

But here it was New Year's Eve, and she was actually running across the hall and into the kitchen up to where Lucy was sitting in a chair close to the fire, and she shook her by the arm as she cried, 'What d'you think? Go on, tell me. What d'you think?'

'Eeh! what about?'

'Well, you were complainin', weren't you, about not having any jollification? And what do you think he's just said to me?'

'Con?'

'No, the master himself. He's just said, "Emily, we're all going to see the New Year in together."'

'All of us, her an' all?'

'No, no.' Emily shook her head firmly. 'She won't budge. Yet'—She straightened up and, holding her chin in her hand, she looked upwards as she said, 'I've got the feelin' that if he went out of his way to persuade her she'd let him bring her down.'

'Why don't you ask him to ask her.'

'No.' Emily slanted her glance towards Lucy. 'I daren't put that to him.' She gave a little laugh now, adding, 'I've forgotten me place more times than enough of late, he'll be tellin' me off shortly.'

'Do you think we'll have a sing-song?'

'Oh'—Emily moved her head slowly—'I wouldn't go as far as to say that.'

'But everybody always has a sing-song when they see the New Year in.'

'Aye'—she was bending down towards Lucy again—'everybody in Creador Street, when they were all as drunk as noodles. But they didn't bring it in with singin' in Pilot Place, I can tell you that. Mrs McGillby brought it in with a prayer.' Her head went down further until her brow touched Lucy's, and then they were holding each other and laughing. And now Emily, dropping on to her hunkers and still holding Lucy's arm, said, 'You know, the way things are going, I mean in the house, everything smoothly like, I'd be over the moon if only I could get you to eat.'

'But I don't feel like eatin', Emily.'

Emily sighed. 'It's odd. Eeh! It is odd. You remember when you were with Alice Broughton an' you were always hungry 'cos you never had a square meal from one week's end to the other, you'd have eaten a horse in those days.'

'Aye, I know.' Lucy now nodded and her flushed face looked slightly sad as she said, 'I was thinkin' yesterday, if only me Aunt Mary's squad could be here for a day, they could stuff their kites until they burst.'

'You're right there.' Emily's face too took on a veil of sadness as she added, 'But me Aunt Mary's lot has something that this house could never give them. With muck, half empty bellies, bare feet, the lot, they're still happier where they are than they would be if they'd been brought up here, don't you think?'

'Yes, yes, you're right, Emily.'

'You know what?' Emily was whispering now. 'On our next leave I'm goin' to ask him if I can buy some butter and cheese and take it down to them. He'll likely let me have it for half the price I'd pay in the shops, an' wouldn't she be over the moon?'

'Oh yes, Emily, I can just see her face.'

Emily now rose from her hunkers, turned a chair round and, sitting on it, she gazed into the roaring fire as she said, as if to herself, 'You never know where you're going to land from one year's end to another. Who would have thought this time last year we'd be in a house like this? I wonder where we'll be this time next New Year's Eve?' She turned a soft smile on Lucy now. 'Everybody says that, you know. Back in Shields on New Year's Eve I remember hearing it again and again, in the market, in the streets: "I wonder where we'll be this time next New Year's Eve." They never say it at Christmas, just New

Year's Eve. Anyway'—she let out a long sigh—'perhaps it's just as well we don't know. But there's one thing we do know at this minute——' Her mood changing yet again, she thrust out her hand and pushed at Lucy, saying, 'We're going to have a bit of jollification the night, and it won't be me if I don't persuade Con to play some jigs on his penny whistle.'

And now she sent Lucy into a gasping, choking fit of laughter as, jumping up from the chair, she lifted her skirt and petticoats almost up to her knees and, stepping off the mat on to the stone slabs, she executed a jig.

It was turned eleven o'clock. They were seated around a roaring fire in the library, Larry, Con, Lucy and herself. She had asked earlier in the evening if it would be all right to invite Abbie, and Larry, after a short harsh laugh, said, 'Well, you can but try.' And she had tried, and failed. 'What! go over there and see the New Year in with him? Never!' he had said. 'Anyway, I'm off now to the inn, an' you won't see me the morrow, or perhaps the next day; they know how to bring the New Year in down there. So you can thank him for nowt. Huh! him askin' me over there to see the New Year in. Playin' the lord of the manor, is he?' Then he had added, 'Did he ask you to come? Or did you ask for me to come?'

When she made no reply he had nodded at her, saying, 'Aw well, lass, I hold nothin' against you, and I'll drink your health the minute it's in, an' of the young un' an' all. By the way, do you know she was sick again the day? What's making her sick like that?'

He had stared at her hard while she shook her head and in answer said, 'I don't know, I think it's when she eats any fat. She always feels bad when she eats fat.'

'Aye,' he had said, then with his hand on her shoulder, added, 'A happy New Year, lass,' and she had answered, 'And to you, Abbie. And many of them.'

But now she was sitting here in the warm, glowing comfort of the fire that was scorching her hands and face, and the warm glowing comfort of the two glasses of wine that were warming her stomach and whirling in her head. She had never tasted anything like this wine. He had called it a liqueur. It wouldn't hurt her, he had said, it was made from cherries.

She still had some in the bottom of her glass, it glowed a beautiful pink. It was more like a syrup the way it clung to the side of the glass.

She put her head back and finished the cherry brandy, and if she had been alone she knew she would have slaked her tongue around the glass to savour the last drops.

The round table behind the couch was laden with food. She and Lucy were sitting on the couch, her master was in a big leather chair to the right of her, and Con was sitting in the same kind of chair to the left of Lucy.

She gazed from one face to the other. They all looked happy, especially Con and Lucy. For a moment, she thought they could be brother and sister, in fact, they could all be members of the one family; she and the master being husband and wife, and Con and Lucy their children.... Oh my God! She clapped her hands across her mouth. Fancy thinking a thing like that. She must be drunk. Eeh! She started to laugh. Then looking towards Larry, where he was pulling himself up from the deep chair, she said, 'What did you say?' and he answered, 'You're not going to wait any longer for something to eat; you must always eat when you drink or you'll soon be under the table.'

'You can't start eating until the New Year comes in.'

'If you don't eat you won't see the New Year in.'

She screwed round and rested her chin on the back of the couch and looked at him. She felt happy as she had never felt happy in her life before, and he looked happy too, easy, all stiffness gone out of him. It could have been Sep.... Poor Sep. Poor Sep. For a moment her joy was dimmed. If only Sep had been alive, what a time they would have been having at this New Year. And she would have been able to wear his present. Her hand went to her waist. She was tired of hiding the watch; she had a good mind to lift up her skirt and unpin it.... What on earth was the matter with her! Fancy thinking about lifting up her skirt. An' she'd have to lift up her petticoats an' all, three of them, 'cos it was pinned to her shift. Eeh! the things she was thinking. It must be that treacly wine. She'd better do as he said and not have any more until they had something to eat, else, who knew, she really would be picking up her petticoats.

'Here! get that into you.' He was handing her a plate with a big shive of bacon and egg pie on it, and she said, 'Oh, ta.' Then as she bit into it she looked up at him and, assuming what she imagined to be a high-falutin tone, she exclaimed, 'You must have a very good cook, Mr Birch, for I've never tasted better.' The next minute she joined in the explosion of mirth that had burst from Con and Lucy. When it subsided Larry seated himself again, and now he assumed an air of pompousness, and nodding towards her, he said, 'Yes, I am very fortunate in my kitchen staff, my cook in particular is excellent at her work, but'—and now he leant forward, pursed his lips, shook his head sadly as, his voice changing, he ended gruffly, 'but she's a rotten hand at making butter, delicate as a lily it comes out....'

'I'm not! It doesn't! Aw, that isn't fair.' She shook her head at him. 'You said last week I was gettin' a dab hand at it.... You're funning', aren't you? You're funnin'.'

'Yes, yes, I'm funnin', Emily.' He leant back in the chair, lifted up his glass of whisky from the side table and drained it; then addressing the glass, he said, 'Yes, yes, I'm funnin' ... because of you I'm funnin' the night.'

'That reminds me.' She was now leaning towards him. 'When we're on about butter I was going to ask you something.'

His head was resting in the wing of the chair; he looked at her and smiled and said, 'Well, go on, ask me something. Ask me anything you like tonight.'

'Well, it's like this. I know you sell the extra butter and cheese in Fellburn, but it's to a shop and ... and when they sell it they double the price, so I was wonderin' if you'd let me have some for the same as you do them on me day off 'cos me Aunt Mary would be over the moon if she had some fresh butter and cheese; and the bairns... well, I don't think they've ever tasted fresh butter ... or butter of any kind.'

'Oh, Emily. Emily.' He was shaking his head from side to side and his mouth was wide but the sound that he was making was not like laughter, it was as if he were pretending to groan. When he did speak he didn't look at her but across at Con, and he said, 'Well, what about it, Con? Do we trade with the cook?'

Before replying, Con leant well forward from the chair and, putting his hand on Emily's knee, he stroked it gently as he said quite seriously, 'I'd give Emily ... anything she asked for ... Larry, anything.'

'Oh, Con.' Emily now placed her hand on his. It became still, and she, bending forward and without laughing now, said, 'By! you're a nice lad, Con. I've said that from the first time I saw you. Well, not exactly from the first time; but within a few days of bein' here I knew you were a nice lad, and I don't care what anybody says I'll stick to it. And our Lucy likes you an' all. Don't you, Lucy?'

'Oh, aye.' Lucy looked shyly at the lanky figure of the young man who was leaning over her knees, his hand still under Emily's. And Con gazed at her and said, 'Do you ... know something? You haven't ... coughed since you had the ... the brandy.'

'No; she hasn't.' Emily was nodding now towards Lucy. 'You haven't, our Lucy. Brandy or wine, or whatever, you'll have to take it as a medicine. If it's goin' to do your cough good, I'll get a bottle of it for you.'

They all turned their attention swiftly to the chair now where Larry was sitting doubled up, his elbows on his knees, his hands covering his face, and his words were splintered with laughter as they came through his spread fingers, saying, 'Cheese at wholesale prices, cherry brandy as a cough mixture, and love all round. There's never been a night like this, not in this room ... not in this house ... love all round.'

Slowly now his hands slipped from his face and he straightened up and, looking towards Emily, where she sat blinking at him from the couch, he said quietly, 'There may be many things I'll be sorry for in the future but I'll never be sorry for the day I picked you up from Fellburn Market Square.'

For a moment they were all silent, until a log slipped off the iron basket and fell on to the hearth, when Emily who was feeling very hot and quite speechless at the moment because, as she said to herself, now what could anybody say to that, it was so nice, sprang from the couch and, dropping on to her knees, picked up the unburnt end of the log and flung it back into the heart of the fire. Then still on her knees, she looked back at them and said, 'It must be nearly time. Will we go and stand outside? ... No, not you, our Lucy; you can look through the kitchen window. Anyway, I forgot, only the first foot has to go out.'

Larry got to his feet now, then looked down on her and laughed as he said, 'What odds! We'll all go out, dark and fair.' He doubled his fist and punched it towards Con. 'Luck is what you make it, eh?'

'Yes ... Larry. Yes, luck is what ... you make it.' Con

now held out his hand towards Lucy, and they went out of the room like two gay children. But in the hall Larry checked their laughter by pointing towards the stairs.

The library was situated under the spare bedrooms and when the door was closed the sounds from inside were muted by the thick walls, but the mistress's bedroom was situated above the kitchen and back quarters. Moreover, the first landing led directly from the gallery and all sounds in the hall were drawn upwards to it, which was another reason why he didn't open the front door but led the way quietly into the kitchen. Even there he cautioned silence, with an upward glance towards the ceiling. Then taking his farm coat from a rack near the kitchen door, he put it on, picked up a lantern from the dresser and lit the candle, and with a backward glance at Emily said, 'Wrap up well, it's biting.'

'Oh, don't worry about me, I'm as hardy as a horse.'

She had given him no title whatsoever tonight, and she didn't reckon she was forgetting herself, for everything seemed so natural and ordinary like, he most of all.

With a careless uplifting gesture of her hand she swung a grey woollen shawl down from a hook behind the door. It was her mistress's Christmas gift, and the fact that she had hung it on the back of the door spoke of what value she put on it.

On Christmas morning her mistress said she had a gift for her and told her to open the bottom drawer of the tallboy and there she would find a shawl. 'It's cashmere,' she had said. Well, cashmere or not, the moths had riddled most of it, but she didn't find that out until unfolding it in the kitchen here. But now she put the shawl over her head and pulled the ends round her waist and tied them at the back. Then saying to Lucy, 'Go on, and stand by the window and watch the lantern, we'll just go to the arch,' she followed Larry and Con out into the courtyard.

The night was black, and the cold was a damp cold, the kind that seeped through your clothes and chilled your skin. When she shivered audibly Larry said quietly, 'You haven't got enough clothes on, I told you to wrap up,' and she answered as quietly back, 'I'm all right.' But she didn't feel all right; her legs seemed wobbly, and she felt dizzy in the head, more so than when she had first drunk the second glass of wine. Eeh! was she tight?

No, of course she wasn't; nobody could get tight on two glasses of treacly wine. Her da could down ten pints and still stand straight as a rock. He always said, don't mix your drinks and your legs won't cross.

Two minutes to go. Larry was holding his watch under the light of the lantern.

'Will we hear the ships' hooters all this way from Fellburn?'

'Oh yes, it isn't all that far as the crow flies; and if the wind's in the right direction, and I think it is, you'll hear the church bells an' all.'

She stood between them, their arms touching hers. She felt strange, slightly unreal. She looked up into the sky but could see nothing but blackness. Where would she be this time next year? Only God knew that and He wouldn't split. She shouldn't joke when she was thinking about God. No, she didn't think she'd take any more of that wine when she got inside; her mind had been playing tricks with her over the past hour or so, and she didn't know what she would think next. Why, back there in the library she had thought about lifting her petticoats up and taking the watch off her shift and showing it to them. Would you believe it! thinking a thing like that. And in the library an' all. Now that was an amazing thing, wasn't it, her sitting in the library of this house as if she were a lady....

'There they go! There they go! Do you hear them?'

'Aye, yes. By! they're clear, all the hooters. Oh, I wish I

was in Shields....' She shouldn't have said that, it sounded ungrateful somehow. She added hastily. 'You can hear them clear there, that's what I mean. I lived alongside the river an' the ships' hooters would blow you off your feet.'

'Well, here we are, the beginning of a New Year, nineteen hundred and three.'

'Yes, a New Year.' She peered at him through the lantern light, and he looked steadily back at her; then she said, 'You'll have to go in first and say Happy New Year to Lucy, an' then we'll come in, me and Con, and it'll be all right then, I mean about the luck.'

He was laughing as he said, 'All right, we'll keep your luck.'

He turned from them and, going to the back door, knocked gently on it, opened it, then went inside. She next saw him standing by the window looking down on Lucy, and when he bent and kissed her on the cheek she exclaimed in a whisper, 'Now isn't that nice of him! Aye, that is nice, kissing our Lucy a happy New Year.'

'Emily.'

She swung round to Con, her face bright.

'Yes, Con?'

'A ... happy ... New ... Year, Emily.'

'And the same to you, Con.' She groped for his hand, and he gripped it and shook it up and down as he said, 'Oh, Emily ... I'm glad you're here and ... and Lucy.... It's lovely with you here, Emily.'

'Thanks, Con. Come on now. Come on.' She pulled him at a run towards the back door and as her hand went out to it, it opened and Larry stood looking at her for a moment before saying solemnly, 'A happy New Year, Emily.'

She stared back at him, the smile seeping from her face and not until he held out his hand to her did she answer him, and as solemnly, 'An' the same to you, sir.' His title seemed to be called for in this present situation when the laughter for some unknown reason had died.

When he left hold of her hand she gave a slight start for it was as if he were throwing it back at her. Then turning quickly about, he said in an undertone, but with a trace of laughter in his voice now 'Come on, let jollification begin....'

They were standing before the library fire, with glasses in their hands, and all the glasses were touching, and all said one to the other, their heads nodding, 'A happy New Year. A happy New Year.' Then Emily was drinking the sticky wine again.

When the glasses were drained, Emily, like the mistress of the household might have done, went to the table and, taking plates from it, began pressing food on to the others.

It was as she was about to sit down that she looked at Larry and asked, 'Do ... do you think the mistress might ... might like a piece of cake and a glass of wine?'

He had a mouthful of food, and he chewed on it and swallowed before he said, 'I doubt it, Emily; not when her door was barred the day. No'—he shook his head—'I doubt it.'

Her head wasn't as muzzy as all that, she now told herself, for she had noticed that he had said the day, like she did, not today, like the educated people did.

'Would I try?' she asked.

'No, no; leave things as they are.'

She sat down with a heaped plate on her knee, but she did not begin to eat immediately. It did seem a shame that she was up there alone; yet, as he said, her door had been barred the day and that meant she was in one of her bad moods. It wasn't anything out of the ordinary for her to bar the door at nights, but when she barred it during the day, it nearly always signified temper.

Emily had found the business of her mistress barring

the door hard to get used to. You'd go with a tray or some such, then push at the handle expecting the door to open, and what happened? The tray bumped into the door and you nearly upset the lot. Once, when the door was barred, she had stood outside and listened expecting to hear some sound like a moan or her crying, or even the faint sound of her scratching the silk of the eiderdown with her forefinger. This was a habit of hers and the sound although slight was of the kind that could put your teeth on edge. But there had been no sound, none whatever, and she imagined her mistress sitting staring at her reflection in the big mirror on the dressing table against the side wall.

Aw well, she wasn't going to let the thought of her mistress or anybody else mar the jollification of this particular night ... or morning. Wagging her finger towards Con now, she said, 'As soon as you've finished that plate you're goin' to start on your whistle. Do you hear me?' and Con, almost choking, bounced his head at her, then muttered, 'Yes, Emily. Yes ... I'll ... get ... on ... me ... whistle.'

And Con got on his whistle, and with no small skill he played the tunes native to the Tyne and district, some that both Emily and Lucy knew and others they had never heard before.

It was when Con changed to a tune that Emily knew but hadn't heard for years that she cried at him, 'Eeh! me ma used to sing that one; it's called "The Mother's Lament".'

She now nodded her head to the beat and began:

'Oh, me canny lad, me canny lad,
Where are ye the day?
Yesterda' ye were down the pit,
But the day, who can say?

Are ye in one of His many mansions,
With yer face washed, clean as snow?
Or are ye still lying broken, there down below?'

She stopped now and, her mouth wide and laughing,
she said, 'Aye, it's years since I heard that one.'

'Go on. Go on, finish it.' Larry leaned forward in his
chair and nodding at her clapped his hands together
gently and said again, 'Go on ... finish it.'

Her eyes were large, bright and twinkling; she hunched up her shoulders and laughed; then she began to
sing again:

'Oh me canny lad, me canny lad,
Me heart's fair torn in two.
There's another nine still left to me,
But there'll ne'er be one like you.
For you came last, when I'd forgotten
That me body still could bear.
Now, me fifteen years of joy is buried
Away, away down there.'

When the song was ended she drooped her head half in
shyness, half in pleasure, as they all clapped. But then her
head jerked up as Larry fell back in the chair and began
to laugh, but in such a way that she didn't join in, for he
wasn't laughing like a happy man laughs or even a
drunken one; she couldn't put a name to the kind of
laughter he was indulging in. Then he startled her and
them all when he sprang up from the chair and almost
dived to the table, and there filled the glasses so quickly
that the wine spilled over the rims. Holding a glass in
each hand now, his head back, he looked around the
room and, as if he were addressing a company gathered
about him, he swivelled on his heels as he cried, 'Did you
ever hear anything as natural as that in this room ... eh,

Colonel, eh? You had shares in the Beulah, hadn't you? In fact she said you owned it at one time. But did you ever think to hear of a mother lamenting her canny lad who died behind a fall down there, and in your own particular domain, Colonel, and sung by a young lass, a wise young lass?'

At this he stopped in his turning, came round the couch, handed one of the glasses to Lucy, then bowing towards Emily, repeated again, 'To a wise young lass.'

Emily's expression had been slightly apprehensive during his performance but now she giggled a little as she took the glass from his hand, then said, 'I shouldn't you know, I shouldn't, I've had enough. I'm dizzy, I think I'm drunk.'

'Don't you like it?'

'Oh yes, it's lovely, lovely an' treacly.'

He was laughing again, and as he went back to the table he muttered, 'Lovely and treacly. Oh, Colonel, I can hear you turning in your grave. The last bottles of your best liqueur being dubbed lovely and treacly. But let me tell you, Colonel, never before has it been drunk with such enjoyment.... What! you would rather see it go down the sink? Yes, yes, you old swine, I know you would.'

Looking over her shoulder at him, Emily took in the gist of part of what he was saying and she laughed to herself as she thought, He's goin' at the colonel, he mustn't have liked him.

But now her attention was brought back to Con for he had begun to play a jig. Her feet tapping in and out from under her skirt, she looked at Lucy; then, as if a message had passed between them, they put down their glasses, sprang up and, facing each other, they both held up their skirts and began to dance to the tune of 'The Devil among the Tailors' while Larry stood by Con's side clapping in step.

With no thought in her mind now of keeping her place, Emily thrust out her hand and caught at Larry's and tugged him, without much resistance on his part, on to the hearth rug to face her. And he went into the dance with an agility that matched her own, but with a knowledge of the steps that far outdid hers and Lucy's.

When at last they stopped for want of breath, Lucy fell against him, and they were all encircled in gasping mirth for a moment, before Emily, extricating herself from the arm that held her, flopped on to the couch, thrust her feet out before her, leant her head back into the velvet padded wing, and cried, 'Never afore in me life have I enjoyed meself like that ... Eeh! That was marvellous. Wasn't it Lucy?'

Lucy began to cough and Emily chastised her, crying, 'Now don't start, 'cos you haven't done it all night; you're just out of puff, that's all.'

Then of a sudden they were all brought to a stiff stillness by the sound of a crash, a jingling crash; it was in the distance, yet clear.

The next moment Larry was making for the door, swaying slightly at he went, and the others were no more steady as they followed him.

In the middle of the hall he stopped and looked upwards, then around him. The hall lamp showed that everything here was in place, no picture had dropped, the row of assorted pewter jugs standing on the brass-bound oak chest were still in their ordered line.

Again he looked upwards before making for the kitchen.

Emily had left the lamp lit in the middle of the table in the centre of the kitchen but the wick had gutted so that now its light was flickering. But it was still bright enough to show her the chaos in front of the delf rack. The top shelf had come away and all the dishes with it, and in their falling had crashed on to those on top of the cupboard that supported the racks.

Moving cautiously among the broken crockery, Larry looked up to where the shelf had been and muttered to himself, 'How in the name of God could that have happened!'

'Slipped ... Larry. Must have ... slipped, Larry.' Con was now pointing to the pegs that had supported the shelf; they were movable pegs placed so the distance between the shelves could be spaced according to need.

Larry put his hand up and felt the pegs at each side of the delf rack. They were firm. The only way the shelf could have fallen was if it had been tipped from one end. As he stood pondering his head slowly tilted back and he looked at the hole in the wall to the side of the delf rack through which at one time had passed the pipe of a speaking tube. When the room above the kitchen had been the colonel's bedroom he'd had the tube put in. He had chosen to sleep in this particular room because of the window to the side which provided a clear view over the hills.

When he himself had first come into the house, the speaking tube was still in use, until one day towards the end of the second year of their marriage she had, in a fit of rage, torn the tube from the socket, and all because he hadn't answered her when she spoke to him. She had known he was in the kitchen and she had stormed down and gone for him. The tube had never been replaced. And now he felt he knew the reason. With her ear to the hole in the floor she could hear more uninhibited talk than she ever would through the speaking tube, which in itself hadn't been built into the wall, but merely attached to a hook at mouth level, then let drop through a hole in the floor.

But now what did she use it for? She couldn't put her ear to it any longer, but she could lean over and poke her stick down it. The devil! the she devil!

A bell ringing caused his and all their eyes to lift towards the ceiling, and Emily muttered, 'The mistress! She must have heard it. Will I go up?'

'No.' His voice was grim now. 'No; I'll go.'

After he had left the room Emily turned to Lucy and said, 'Well, come on, the jollification's over, we'll have to get this cleared up afore the mornin'.'

'Must we, Emily? I'm tired, an' I'm a bit dizzy in me head.'

'You ... sit down ... Lucy.' Con was nodding at her. 'I'll ... I'll help Emily.'

Needing no further bidding, Lucy went to the chair by the fireplace and sat down, while Emily and Con started to clear up the debris; and all the while Emily kept asking herself in a dazed way, why had this to happen, because in a curious way it had put the damper on things. And she had been enjoying herself as she had never done before; she could have gone on all night.

The broken crockery had been shovelled into two wooden pails and the floor swept by the time Larry returned, and when Con asked, 'Did ... did it frighten her ... Larry?' he answered slowly, 'Yes. Yes, it frightened her. It woke her up. She ... she's disturbed.'

He looked at the delf rack again, and his jaw tightened as he said, 'We'll have to look into the whys and wherefores of this in the morning, but animals don't know it's New Year's Day, they read the clock by the light, so we'd all better get to bed, eh?'

He turned and now looked at Lucy, where she was slumped in the big chair and he said, 'She'll not walk up those stairs tonight.'

'She'll have to; I'll wake her.'

'Don't. I'll ... I'll carry her up.'

'Oh, ta, thanks. It's all that wine; it got me an' all.' She gave a little laugh, 'She'll not be the only one who'll take some wakening in the mornin'.'

When Larry stooped and gathered Lucy up in his arms, Emily said, 'I'll just bring the things out of the library, I'd better leave it tidy like,' and she gave her head a shake as if endeavouring to throw off the muzziness, then added, 'Good-night, sir, or mornin'. And ... an' thanks for ... for the jollification.'

Larry was pushing his back against the kitchen door before he answered briefly, 'Good-night, Emily.'

'Good-night, Con.'

'Good-night ... Emily. I'll ... I'll never forget this ... this New Year, never ... never.'

'Nor me, Con. Nor me. Good-night, and a happy New Year to you.'

'Same to you, Emily. Same to you.'

She now went across the hall and into the library. The fire was still burning brightly. There was a sweet tangy smell in the air. It had been a lovely night, and she had felt so happy. They could have gone on till morning if that shelf hadn't come down.

She piled the remains of the food on to two plates, gathered up the dirty glasses and crockery, then stacked them all on a tray. She was about to lift the tray from the table when she looked at the fire and said to herself, 'I'd better bank that down, or put the screen in front of it, 'cos if a spark fell on to that rug ... whoops!'

She didn't know why saying whoops! should make her laugh, but she felt like laughing all the time now. It was silly, but somehow she couldn't help it.

She flattened the top of the fire down with the poker, pushed the dry logs to one side of the hearth; then, leaning across to the stone wall that flanked the fireplace, she pulled towards her an ornamental iron screen and placed it in front of the fire. She now sat back on her knees as she thought, Lord above! but I am tired. And only a minute ago I was thinking I could go on all night. I feel too tired to make the stairs. She turned and moved on her knees to the couch, leaning her elbow on it for a moment, and as she did so the door opened and Larry entered the room.

She was pulling herself to her feet when he reached her. He put out his hand and helped her upwards; then still retaining hold of her, he bent slightly towards her and said solemnly, 'Thank you, Emily.'

'Thank me! ... What's there to thank me for?' She knew that her face must be red for it was suddenly very hot.

'For one of the nicest, and homeliest, few hours I've had in years.'

'Aw, go on with you, sir.'

'It's true ... it's true, Emily.... Have you enjoyed yourself?'

'Oh yes; I've never felt like this afore, I feel as happy as ...' She put her hand over her mouth now and started to giggle as she ended, 'I nearly said Larry, sir. You know, there's a sayin', "As happy as Larry".'

'Yes, yes, I've heard the saying, Emily, many times.... As happy as Larry. But it doesn't apply to me; I'm not happy, Emily. You know that, don't you?'

The smile slid from her face. The feeling of laughter went from her. She blinked up at him as she said, 'I've felt it at times ... your misery.'

'That's the right word for it, Emily. Oh yes, that's the right word, my misery. Do you know something? You've brought more light and laughter into this house than it's ever seen before, and you've brought me more happiness—yes'—he nodded at her—'more happiness than I've had in years. Everything in life must be paid for, Emily, but some prices are too high.... You're warm, Emily.'

His two hands were stroking hers now, his fingers moving over the rough chapped skin. The pressure of his fingers on a keen hurt her but she gave no evidence of it, she just stared at him wide-eyed unblinking. There was in her the feeling which she had experienced a number of times of late, a kind of excitement in the region of her stomach, an irritating excitement; an excitement that demanded relief, an escape. The times when she felt like this she had told herself to go to sleep and it would pass; but now she wasn't asleep, and there was no way to make it pass. Or was there?

His face was coming closer to hers, his hands were on her shoulders, and as they moved down towards the blades on her back, her breast came nearer to him until her bodice was touching his coat. Yet still she kept her face away from his. But when he said, 'Oh Emily! Emily!' she could move it back no further. Now his breath was all over her face; then his lips were all over her face; and when they stopped on her mouth she became lost. The exciting feeling was growing, leaping about in her stomach, swirling upwards and downwards at the same moment, making her legs tremble and her chest heave; but it was when his hand, moving down her spine, pressed on her buttocks that sanity returned to her; it came like a flash of lightning. This is what had happened to May Turner and Nell Blackett, who had lived in their street. And where was Nell Blackett now? She was in the workhouse, and her bairn as well, 'cos her da turned her out. And moreover this is what had happened to that lass in the village down there, that they were blaming Con for. He had said it wasn't Con, an' perhaps it wasn't Con after all.... No, by God! perhaps it wasn't.

He was no more surprised by her strength than she was herself for she felt she had thrown him on to the couch. His mouth wide open, his breath coming in gasps, he gaped at her where she was standing well back from him, her skirt actually touching the iron fire screen.

They were staring at each other like fighters who had been momentarily separated, she as stiff as a ramrod, her arms held slightly away from her sides.

Slowly he brought himself forward on to the edge of the couch and dropped his face into his hands; and after a moment he rose to his feet and, without looking at her or saying a word, went from the room. Now her body relaxed and she lifted up her hand and, pressing it across her mouth, she muttered 'Oh, my God!'

SIX

It was ten o'clock the following morning. Emily was in the kitchen and she didn't know how she was standing on her feet. For the first time in her life she was experiencing a headache, and the pain was intense, although not as bad as when she had woken up at seven o'clock.

When she had sprung from the bed realizing how late it was, she had fallen on to her knees and buried her head in the rumpled bedclothes as she imagined for a moment that hot skewers were being banged into her temples. She couldn't understand what was happening to her until she remembered her father, his face screwed up, crawling down the back stairs and holding his head under the running tap following a night of boozing.

Had she been drunk?

At first she couldn't recall anything that had happened last night. Not until she reached the kitchen and had taken the teapot from the stove and drunk the scalding black liquid did she remember that they'd had a party ... a jollification, but the full details of it did not become clear in her mind for another hour or more.

She had managed to get the mistress's breakfast on time and was relieved when the mistress did not speak to her, not even to wish her a happy New Year, but just stared at her, which meant she was in one of her bad moods.

She had set the breakfast as usual in the kitchen but

only Con came in for it. She did not ask him where the master was, nor did he offer her any explanation for, as he had already told her, his head too was fit to burst.

Nor did she press Lucy to eat her breakfast for Lucy, too, seemed dazed.

It wasn't until she paused for a moment in her scurrying and drank her third mug of black tea that the incident that had occurred at the end of the jollification sprang into her mind. She saw it as a picture suspended in air, herself within the circle of the master's arms, his lips on hers; and as the picture unfolded she actually felt the warmth again pass through her body and she recalled her desire to lie against him, lie deeply against him. But the picture faded as she saw herself thrusting him from her, then watching him walking away without a word.

How was she going to face him? What was more to the point, how was he going to face her? for in his sober senses this morning he would consider he had let himself down ... or would he? Because, let her face it, he wasn't a gentleman, for no real gentleman would have allowed them to have such a jollification in his library, no matter how lonely and miserable he was.... He had said something about being miserable, hadn't he?

Oh, she couldn't think. She didn't want to think. If only her head would ease.

She turned to Lucy, who was standing at the sink scouring a porridge pan, and said, 'You'd better go up and bring her tray down. And mind, be careful you don't drop it; there was enough crockery broken last night.' She looked towards the delf rack, adding, 'I'll never know how that happened; I've taken things off that shelf hundreds of times an' didn't feel it was loose.... Go on now.' She almost barked at Lucy, who had been slow to turn from the sink, and when she saw her walk across the room with her shoulders stooped she thought to herself, We're all in the same boat; it's the mornin' after the night afore with a vengeance. Of one thing she was certain, she'd had her first and last fill of wine. The next bit of jollification she had would be dry, if she knew anything about it. Aye, it would....

When she heard the scream she recognized it as Lucy's and as she looked upwards her head fell back on her shoulders so quickly that a bone cracked.

She had dropped the tray. Oh my God!

She was out of the kitchen, across the hall and up the stairs and to the bedroom door before another thought entered her mind, but when she went to push the door open it resisted, as it had done many times before, and as she went to knock on it she heard Lucy's scream again. It was a high, terrified scream, and she yelled at the top of her voice, 'Lucy! Lucy! let me in. What is it?' and Lucy's choked answer came back, crying, 'Emily! Oh Emily!'

'Open the door, Lucy! Open the door!' She was banging on it with her fist now.

'What's ... what's the matter?'

She turned her head to the side as Con came on to the landing, and she shouted at him, 'Go and get the master, quick! Go and get the master.' Then she banged on the door again, yelling now, 'Madam! open the door. D'you hear me! Take that bar off the door. D'you hear me!'

But the only answer that came to her was the sound of Lucy's sobbing. Then she began to bang on the door and to yell at the same time.

'Open that door this minute, Rona!' So loud had been her own yelling that she hadn't heard Larry's approach. 'Do you hear me! Open this door at once!' The answer came back sharp and clear almost immediately, 'The door is open.'

When he turned the handle the door gave and he thrust it wide and went into the room, and Emily, rushing past him, ran towards Lucy who was cowering near the fireplace holding her torn skirt with one hand and

217

her torn blouse with the other. Her face quivering with fear, she gasped out, 'Oh Emily! Emily!' and as Emily's arms went about her she looked towards the bed and cried at her mistress, 'What's the matter with you, woman! What's she done to you? Why ... why did you do this?'

'Why?' The voice sounded calm. 'You may well ask why. I told her to take off her skirt. She wouldn't, she was afraid, and she has every reason to be, she's pregnant.'

Emily's hold became limp. She stared down into the wet, terrified face of her sister, then looked towards the bed again, and even as she whispered, 'Oh no! No!' she told herself she had been a fool all these weeks. Didn't she know that you were always sick when you dropped with a bairn. And she had thought it was something Lucy had been eating.... But she had said that that Tim Pearsley hadn't touched her. Well, he must have. And she must have known he had, she wasn't all that simple; in fact, she wasn't simple in that way at all. Nobody could be that kind of simple after having lived with Alice Broughton for any length of time.

She now gripped Lucy by the shoulder and pushed her forward, past her mistress who was now sitting almost upright in the bed, her face a picture of disgust, even of loathing, and past her master, whose expression was a mixture of anger and amazement, and thrusting Lucy before her, they went out on to the landing, not towards the main staircase but up the attic stairs and into their bedroom.

Once inside, Emily pushed the shivering girl on to the bed; then thrusting her face down to Lucy's, she said bitterly, 'You've made a fool of me, a damn fool. You knew all the time you were goin' to have a bairn.'

'No! No! Emily.' Lucy was shaking her head from side to side while the tears rained down her face and she whimpered, 'I'm not. I'm not.'

'Shut up!' Emily straightened her back, her hand held upwards. 'For two pins I'd slap your face right and left. Oh!' She turned away and, folding her arms tightly across her breasts, hugged herself as she paced the room. 'All these weeks, sick in the mornings, and at all times of the day'—she now turned her head and glared at Lucy—'and it never dawned on me, 'cos you had said he hadn't touched you, and I believed you. Oh, if ever there was a fool in this world it's me. An' d'you think them down there'—she now brought her hands from underneath her oxters and pointed towards the floor—'d'you think they'll believe me? Not on your life. An' we'll be out, out on our necks, both of us.'

She now stood still and looked at the thin, white pathetic figure sitting on the bed staring at her, while the tears ran out of the eyes and nostrils and dripped on to the chapped hands where they lay in her lap, not gripping each other as hers would have done, but lying limp, and at the sight of the abject figure all the fight went out of Emily. Going towards the bed, she sat down by Lucy's side and, putting her arm around her shoulder, she said softly, 'You could have told me.'

'Emily.'

'Aye, what is it?'

'He never, Tim Pearsley never touched me, not that way.'

For a moment her pity vanished and she had the strong urge to knock the slight form flying on to the floor; then on a deep intake of breath, her anger once more vanished and she said on a sigh, 'Well, if he didn't touch you, who did then?'

The next minute it was almost as if she had been startled out of her wits by the thought that had crossed her mind, for she was gripping Lucy's shoulders and pressing her back on to the bed again as she hissed at her, 'Con? Was it Con?'

'Oh no! No!' Lucy's voice had a strength to it now and she shrugged herself away from Emily's grip. Pulling herself upright, she got off the bed and, facing Emily, she said, 'How could you think such a thing! Con? Why, he wouldn't hurt a fly. I tell you, our Emily, I'm not. I'm not!' Now she was shouting loudly. 'You won't believe me but I'm not. I tell you I'm not, I'm not goin' to have a bairn.'

At this Lucy turned and darted out of the room, and Emily made no attempt to follow her; what could you do with somebody who wouldn't believe what was staring them in the face.

She sat dejectedly on the side of the bed now asking herself where they would go from here. Well, there was only one place they wouldn't go, and that was the workhouse. She still had fourteen whole sovereigns and some small change left. And then there was the watch. If the worst came to the worst she would risk pawning it; she would go to a big pawnshop in Newcastle and say she was pawning it for her mistress. Yes, she could do that. In the meantime they would go to their Aunt Mary's; she would know how to handle a situation like this.

She rose slowly from the bed and went down the stairs. As she reached the first landing Larry was coming out of his wife's bedroom. He was a few steps behind her when she reached the main staircase. At the bottom of the stairs he was walking by her side and he didn't look at her as he said, 'It would have been better if you had brought it into the open.'

'I didn't know.' Her voice was dull, lifeless.

He stopped now and confronted her and said quietly, 'I find that hard to believe, Emily, seeing you appear so wise in so many ways.'

'That's as may be, sir.' Her face was tight now. 'But apparently I wasn't wise in that. I thought it was the food, the rich food. And anyway, as I understood it, you were only sick in the mornings, she's been sick at all times of the day, and in the night an' all. An' she had told me, sworn to me, that Tim Pearsley never touched her.'

'Tim Pearsley?' He screwed up his face at her.

'A lodger in me da's house. Me da goes to sea, and the woman that he took on as housekeeper took this lodger in.'

'Had he attempted ... to ... to molest her?'

'Something like it, but ... but I got her away in time, at least'—she paused—'I thought I had. Yet she swears that he never touched her. Well, as I said to her, if he didn't somebody else has.'

They were peering at each other now in the dim wintry light of the hall; then, as he had done last night, he turned from her and walked away without speaking further.

A short while ago she hadn't known how she was going to face him about last night's business; now that was seemingly forgotten. After all, what was it? A little incident at the end of a bit of jollification. She even thought now that, having taken so much wine, she had exaggerated it all. Things appeared different when you were drunk ... and she had been drunk; oh yes, she had been drunk. But as she said before, it would never happen again.

She went into the kitchen and, not finding Lucy there, she went in search of her. She found her in the byres, and she wasn't alone, Abbie was with her. She hadn't known he was back, he had said he never came in on a New Year's Day, and it was evident to her straightaway that Lucy had cried out her trouble to him for, straightening his bent back as far as possible, he looked at Emily as he nodded his head slowly, saying, 'Aye, aye, another nice kettle of fish. It seems the mistress tore the clothes off her back. Now why would she do that, eh?'

'Go back into the house, our Lucy.' She thrust her arm out and pointed towards the open doorway, and Lucy, her head down, and running again, went past her and across the yard. From the open doorway she watched her disappear through the archway before turning to Abbie and saying, 'I don't know why the mistress wanted to tear the clothes off her back 'cos if she is going to have a bairn it's nobody's business but hers and mine.... Nobody's!' She emphasized the last word with an upward jerk of her chin.

'No, you're right there, lass, you're right there, except you're leavin' out the one that did it. And I'll tell you this, lass. Some folks can be nice an' normal like, quite decent for nine-tenths of themselves, but the last bit, the tenth bit has only to touch a woman, or a young lass, as your sister is, an' then something happens to them. They can't help it, it's in their nature, I'm not blamin' them, but nevertheless it's a fact.'

She stared at the old man for a moment before saying grimly, 'Well, you're barkin' up the wrong tree, Abbie. Con wouldn't touch her, not that way; I'd swear me life on it. An' anyway, it would have had to have happened straightaway when we first came here, an' it couldn't have else she'd have told me.'—But would she? She was beginning to think she didn't know their Lucy.

The old man half turned away, put his head on one side, and looked towards the ground as he muttered, 'And I would have said I was barkin' up the wrong tree an' all at one time, lass, but young Bella Goodyear in the village, she swears by the Lord above it was Con. And I'm only tellin' you what's common knowledge, lass, so work it out for yourself. And it could have happened straightaway and the bairn was too scared to say anything.' On this he walked along by the row of cows, thumping one after the other on the rump, then went on into the dairy, leaving Emily standing with her hands doubled into fists and pressed between her breasts.

'Tweren't me, Emily, 'tweren't me.' Con stood before Emily, his back pressed against the kitchen table, his hands gripping the edge of it, and there was moisture in his eyes and tears in his voice as he repeated, 'Tweren't me. I ... I couldn't. And ... and Lucy. I ... like Lucy, but ... 'tweren't me.' He bowed his head now and there came over in his voice an untold sadness as he ended quietly, 'Not me, Emily ... not me.'

'All right, Con, I believe you.'

He lifted his head slowly and he looked at her like the child he was inside, and the tears filled his eyes as he muttered, 'Thank ... thank you ... Emily.' Then bringing himself from the support of the table, he said, 'You ... won't go ... away, will you?'

'I don't know, Con; we mightn't be able to stay.'

'Larry won't ... won't ... send you away, never ... never.'

No, he mightn't; but she might, her up there, that vicious woman. And she was vicious, because after all, no matter what Lucy had done, she had no right to tear the clothes off her back. There had been a battle upstairs a short while ago, in which she had even outdone the master in her yelling.

When she now saw the tears raining down the young fellow's face she went to him and, taking his hand and patting it, she said, 'There now. There now. Don't worry any more. Things 'll take their course, either one way or another. Come on, cheer up. Come on now, stop cryin'. It's still New Year's Day. Never say die....'

Why in the name of God had she to come out with that saying, never say die, when, at this minute, she wouldn't care if she were to drop down dead, because she was tired both in body and mind. This house was far too much for one to run, because Lucy understandably now, had become less of a help these past few weeks. And she was tired in her mind, tired of thinking of Sep and what might have been, tired of worrying about Lucy's complaint—well, she had two complaints to worry about now, hadn't she?—tired of the feeling that pervaded this house, the feeling that frightened her in a strange way, so much so that at times she felt she was becoming like that Chrissey and imagining things.

As she set about her work again she came to the conclusion that it wouldn't matter if she did get the push, it might be the best thing that could happen to her, to them both.

SEVEN

The following Monday morning at eleven o'clock, when the doctor called to see Rona Birch he also had a look at Larry's wrist, which he had strained while lifting a sack of grain. His whole hand and part of his forearm was swollen.

Always when the doctor had finished his visit to the bedroom he would go into the library where a tray would be set for him and the master, with coffee and sandwiches, special sandwiches, bread cut paper thin with sliced pickles on the ham, not mustard. And this morning the pattern was the same except that instead of the doctor going straight into the library when he came downstairs he came into the kitchen, accompanied by Larry, and there he spoke to Emily. 'Good-morning,' he said.

'Good-morning, doctor.' She bent her knee slightly to him because doctors were quality, like people who lived in halls and manors.

'How is your sister's cough?' he asked her, and she replied, 'About the same, doctor.'

The doctor now put his leather bag on the table and, holding the handles in both hands, he leant over it and said, 'Your master thinks that it would do no harm if I were to examine your sister, her chest, et cetera.'

She looked from one to the other. Her master was staring at her, unblinking. She knew it was he who had put this suggestion into the doctor's head because the doctor had been in the house every week since she had come here and had never before bothered about Lucy's chest. She knew what et cetera meant. Well, perhaps it was the best thing after all; it would settle the question whether she was or she wasn't, for she was still maintaining that nobody had touched her. Either she was becoming a bare-faced little liar or.... She couldn't explain the or to herself, she only knew that bairns didn't get inside you on their own, they had to be put there.

She said now, 'I'll get her.'

'Thank you, Emily. Bring her into——' The doctor now looked towards Larry who said, 'The library.'

'Yes, yes, the library.' The doctor nodded. 'There's a couch in there.'

A few minutes later she was pushing Lucy towards the library door, saying, 'It's all right, stop shakin'; he only wants to examine your chest.'

After knocking on the library door she opened it and pressed Lucy forward and the doctor said kindly, 'Ah, there you are, Lucy. Come and sit down here and we'll have a little talk.' He now turned his head to the side, saying, 'You needn't stay, you can get on with your work, Emily. I'll call you if I need you.'

Emily hesitated for a moment before turning and going slowly out of the room. But she didn't go further than the closed door, she didn't think it was right, her not being able to stay and the master in there an' all, it wasn't decent. She could hear the doctor talking but not what he was saying. For a time there was silence; then he was talking again. And now she actually jumped back from the doorway as it was pulled open and her master stood there looking at her and smiling. 'Come in,' he said. 'Come in.'

When she entered the room she saw Lucy sitting on a chair, and she, too, was smiling, a thin, watery smile, and now the doctor was speaking pointedly to her herself, saying, 'Your sister is not pregnant, Emily, she has a stomach complaint, or rather her stomach is distended because of the congestion in her duodenum.' He shook his head at the blank expression on her face, then laughed as he said, 'In a way, you know, you're to blame, for I suppose you've been packing good food into her, pork, bacon, sausages, the like.'

'Yes, sir. But she never seems hungry.'

'It's understandable; a sick person never wants food, and in her case food is her trouble. Now in future, she is to have no fat whatever, at any rate not for some weeks. All her food must be dry.' He now turned his head towards Lucy and said, 'You won't like it. I can assure you, you won't like it, but it's for your own good.'

Lucy nodded at him and said, 'Yes, sir,' and continued to smile at him as he went on, 'Dry bread or toast, not new; boiled potatoes; no roasts; a bit of chicken or rabbit; no pork or bacon; what little fat you need you get in the milk.' He turned towards Emily again, saying, 'And not too much of that either at first until her stomach is settled. She'll need a purge to scour her out, then nothing to eat for twenty-four hours; following that, dry toast or dry bread. And'—he nodded again at Lucy— 'chew it. Chew everything well.... There you are then, go along with you. And be good girls.'

They went out of the room, but even when in the hall they didn't speak, they just looked at each other. Not until they reached the kitchen did Emily turn to Lucy and, taking her gently by the shoulders, bend down to her and say, 'Eeh! I'm sorry, Lucy. I am. I am.'

'It's all right, Emily, only I knew ... I knew I hadn't been touched.'

Emily now bowed her head and bit on her lip and closed her eyes tight to press back the tears as she said again, 'Oh, I am sorry. I should have known; I should have believed you; I should have remembered years ago you were always sick when you ate fat.' Now, with an endearing gesture, she pulled Lucy tightly into her arms and said, 'I'll get you better, your stomach and your cough and everything. I will. I will, Lucy.' And Lucy, looking up at her, said, 'I know you will, Emily, I know you will.' And the burden that such trust laid on her seemed as light as a feather now.

It was some ten minutes later when Larry came into the kitchen. He was smiling broadly and he looked from one to the other as he exclaimed, 'Well then! that's all straightened out. Feel better, Lucy?'

'Yes, sir. Oh yes, sir.'

'And you, Emily?'

She bowed her head for a moment as she murmured, 'I feel a bit sick meself, but it's with relief.'

He gave her an understanding nod as he turned towards the door, but before going out he looked over his shoulder and said, 'The doctor's left a purge; she'd better take it right away. And another thing. I know it's your half-day today but would you mind going in with Con to the market? There's quite a bit of stuff needs to be delivered. I wouldn't be able to drive with my hand. Anyway, I've ... I've got to be here today, I'm expecting someone. Moreover, I think it would do Con good to have a jaunt; he's been down these past few days. I suppose you've noticed?'

'Aye, yes, I have.' And she answered his somewhat accusing glance by adding, 'Well, you can relieve his mind now, can't you?'

Eeh! she shouldn't have said it like that. She shouldn't talk to him like that. It was as if she had no respect for him.

His face was stiff as he answered, 'Yes, as you say, it will relieve his mind. I can also give the news to Abbie, but I doubt it will relieve his mind because there's very little spice in truth.'

When the door banged she gnawed at her lip. He was
right there, there was very little spice in truth, and Abbie
seemed to enjoy spice. She turned to Lucy now, saying,
'I'll go and get the medicine for you, and you'd better do
as he says and take it now. But it means you won't be
able to come with us, in case you're taken short.'

'I don't mind that, Emily; I don't mind nothin' as long
as I'm made better.'

She nodded at Lucy as she said, 'That's sensible.' Then
looking up towards the ceiling, she said, 'There's one
thing I'm going to enjoy, and it's tellin' her she was
wrong. And I'm not going to put it off either.' And with
this she rolled down her sleeves, buttoned the cuffs, pulled the bib of her apron straight, adjusted her mob-cap
and marched from the room.

Con was like a schoolboy who had been given a day's
unexpected holiday. And as he took the reins in his
hands preparatory to moving off, Larry, who was standing by the small flat cart and with his good hand finger-
ing the rope that lashed the cover over two boxes of straw-
layered eggs, a tub of butter and a similar one of cheese,
looked up at Emily and said, 'It doesn't matter if you
don't see Winters, give the stuff to his wife, and tell her
she can settle up with me next week.' Then he ended,
'You've got the list all right?'

Emily nodded, saying 'Yes ... yes.'

'Well, get going then.'

Walking beside the moving horse, Larry finally cautioned Con: 'And do what I told you, keep clear of the
quarry road. He's nervous of that part, it takes me all my
time.'

'All ... right, Larry. I ... I won't go by ... the quarry,
never ... never fear.' He gave a toss of his head as if he
were in full control of any possible emergency that the

horse might create. Then he guided the animal from the farmyard, through the arch, across the courtyard, out on to the drive and then on to the coach road, and there he cried, 'Gee-up! Gee-up! ... Lady,' and they went bowling along the road towards the village.

The sky was low and promised rain. There was a stillness in the air like that which precedes a thunderstorm, but it was a biting cold stillness and, as Emily told herself, they didn't usually have thunderstorms in January, but she hoped they reached the town before the rain came.

Looking at the distant hills she guessed there was little hope of that. But what did it matter? She felt happy, light, sort of free. And she had good right to be, hadn't she? Poor Lucy; them all thinking she was going to have a bairn when all the time it was just stomach trouble.... She'd buy her something when she was in the town. What did she like? She loved liquorice sticks and tiger nuts. Yes, she'd buy her some; and also two ribbons for her hair and perhaps a hair slide. Yes, she would love a hair slide.

Oooh! She let out a long-drawn relaxing breath. It was good to be alive and sitting here riding high up behind the horse with Con who looked so happy, as happy as she did about Lucy. And he had never come back at her with, 'I told you it wasn't me.' Poor Con. She glanced at him. Just because of some little twist in his make-up he'd never be a real man, always a young lad ... a boy. It seemed such a pity because he had a lovely face, and a lovely nature. She had a feeling for Con, a sort of love for him. Eeh! fancy her thinking that. But ... well, that was the only name she could put to it. As she stared at him she wished she was his mother and could look after him all his days. And she knew this much; whoever looked after him would keep young too, because there was a kind of light morning spirit about him.

She raised her eyebrows at herself and her head went to

one side. Fancy her thinking like that. She was getting something out of reading Sep's little black book, and it was the right description for Con, because there *was* a light morning spirit about him.

She turned her attention to the road. They were entering the village now and there in the distance, outside the blacksmith's shop, she could see a group of people, and as they drew nearer she recognized Mr Goodyear, the blacksmith. He was standing near a man who was holding a horse, but he was talking to a smaller man and wagging his finger at him as he spoke, and the smaller man was nodding at him. There were two women in the group, both wearing shawls; one woman had hers over her head, the other just round her shoulders.

Emily saw that it was the bare-headed woman who nudged the blacksmith and pointed towards them. And then all five people stood silently watching their approach. Simultaneously, Emily became aware of two things, the hostility emanating from the faces looking at them and the sudden spasm of nervousness that had attacked Con.

It was as the dray passed them that the bare-headed woman ran forward and, grabbing the side of the cart, yelled up at Con, 'She had it. She had it last night. D'you hear me? you thick-skulled idiot! And not so much of the idiot, are you? Well, you'll have to pay; an' by God! I'll see you do. Both you an' him.'

'We ... won't. I didn't.'

Even Emily was startled by Con's sudden retaliation, for his usual reaction to any accusation was tears. But now, pushing the reins into one hand, his other shot out in the direction of the woman and although his fingers weren't within two feet of her the gesture brought a roar from her and she cried at him, 'You bugger! You would, would you?' A matter of seconds later a good-sized stone scraped Con's ear and bounded off the horse's flank, setting it into a gallop, and as Emily clung on to the iron rail that edged the seat, in some panic she thought it was just as well the stone had stirred the horse for, glancing back, she could see that the men had run some way along the road after them.

They were almost a mile beyond the village when Con pulled the horse to a halt. Gasping now and his head bobbing and the tears once more in his eyes, he turned to her and said, 'I didn't, Emily. I didn't.'

Taking his hand, she pressed it tightly between her own, saying, 'I know you didn't, Con. I know you didn't. Who were they, the rest? D'you know them all?'

He nodded and, still gasping, muttered, 'The man with ... with the horse, that was John Ralston. Don't like him. Killed ... killed my badger ... pet badger, like that.' He measured a distance of about a foot between his hands. 'No bigger when ... when I found it. An' ... an' his missis. T'other man was ... Joe Brinkburn ... drover ... cattle drover.'

She nodded at him saying, 'Yes, I've seen him afore. An' the woman an' all. She's the blacksmith's wife, isn't she?'

His head drooped and he shook it from side to side and gulped before saying, 'Bella's ma. Bella used to ... just laugh, laugh with me ... at the haymaking ... she just laughed. She was ... funny. But ... but that's all, Emily; I ... I never did nothing wrong.'

She said quietly now, 'Don't worry.... Come on, drive on.'

He drove on, but there was silence between them now. To Emily the sky seemed even lower, and the gladness had gone out of the day. There came upon her a feeling of dread. She wouldn't, however, as yet, put a voice to what she dreaded, but thought, Why are there so many nasty people in the world? They seemed to be ten to one; Alice Broughton, Tim Pearsley, Mrs McGillby—aye, there was no getting away from it, she had been nasty in a religious kind of way—and that one, back there up in that room, waited on hand and foot and never a kind word out of her. And look at that trouble she caused about Lucy. But she told her straight, didn't she, when she went up this morning, and she never said a word in reply. But she bet when she returned home this afternoon her bed would be filthy; she'd do it on purpose. Oh yes, she would. She should be stuck with them lot back in that village.... Eeh! they had looked like fiends.

On the other hand, there were people like Sep, and her da, too. Her da wasn't a bad fellow. And there was her Aunt Mary. And lastly there was him ... the master. But in a way, she had her reservations about him; sometimes he was as nice as pie, while at other times, when he put his high-falutin voice on and played at the lord of the manor, she couldn't stand him, because after all he wasn't the lord of the manor type, not really.

But that night when he kissed her, what had she thought about him then? ...

What she had better think about now, she told herself harshly, was how they were going to get back through that village without any more trouble. She said to Con, 'Is there any road back without going through the village?'

He shook his head before looking at her, then said, 'No, no, Emily ... not for the cart, only ... over the stile and ... and across the field paths ... roundabout way.'

Well, she thought, if it hadn't been that one of the things on his list, and of which he was very much in need, was stuff from the mill, flour, maize and horse meal, she would leave the cart and horse at a farrier's in Fellburn and they would shank it all the way back and take the field path.... Then what would happen when they reached the house? He would likely go for them, and call them idiots for being frightened by a few black looks.

Perhaps she was an idiot, for after all there had only

been black looks; at least until Con had raised his arm. Yet she decided here and now that what she would do as soon as they returned to the village was to make Con gallop the horse through, and if things took a nasty turn she would use the whip on them.

One thing she was determined on, she wasn't going to dawdle in Fellburn; she would deliver the load on the back there, then pick up the other stock from the miller's; as for doing her personal shopping for the bits and pieces she had intended to buy Lucy, that would have to wait for another time; she wasn't going to risk driving through that village in the dusk.

It was just turned two o'clock when they left Fellburn. They crossed the bridge over the river, took a short cut which bypassed Brampton Hill and the park—Con seemed to know this way—then they were once more driving along the old coach road.

Again there was silence between them, a more nervous, more apprehensive silence now. But it lightened somewhat when, about two miles from the town, they approached a young fellow carrying a pack on his shoulders; it was weighing his head forward and when he glanced sidewards at the dray he called out, 'Oh, hello there, Con,' and Con, pulling the horse to a stop, cried, 'Hello ... Jamsie ... You ... laden?'

'Aye, Con. Any room up there?'

It was Emily who answered him now and almost merrily as she said, 'It'll be a tight fit, but you're welcome.'

And he was.

She didn't know who he might be but he was friendly and they were more likely to make a clear passage through the village with a friendly soul like him sitting up top.

'You'll have to hold your pack on your knees 'cos you see the cart's full,' she added, jerking her head backwards.

'Give it here.' She leant down and pulled the pack up towards her, then edged along the seat close to Con, while the young fellow hauled himself up and squeezed sideways into the corner of the seat. Then taking the pack from Emily, he said, 'You've got a full load on.'

'Aye, yes.' She nodded at him, and Con said, 'Haven't ... haven't seen you for a long ... time, Jamsie.'

'Been away to sea for a trip, Con.'

'Oh! Been to sea.'

'Aye, been to sea. But they can keep it for me; from now on, give me the land, even if I starve on it. Have you seen me dad, or any of them, Con?'

'No, no ... Jamsie. Never ... never been over ... your way, not ... not for long time.'

The young fellow now turned and looked closely at Emily, saying, 'You from the house?'

'Yes.'

'Chrissey still there?'

'No. No, I took her place.'

'Oh, I'd like to see Chrissey again.' He laughed as he jerked his chin upwards.

Emily smiled at the young fellow, who now smiled back at her. She thought he couldn't be more than nineteen if that.

'Me da goes to sea,' she said. 'How long have you been away?'

'Oh, just on a year.'

'Oh, me da goes away for two years at a time.'

'Well, I was lucky then.' He bent towards her now and whispered as he grinned at her, 'I jumped ship. My God! the food. The rats even turn their noses up at it. And me donkey's breakfast became so alive it used to follow me around; it only lay down when I wanted to sleep on it.'

She spluttered into laughter. He sounded just like her Aunt Mary talking about the lousy second-hand clothes.

They were about half a mile from the village when

Emily noticed, to the right of her, a boy running across the low hills. At first she thought he was keeping in time with the dray; then she saw him bound ahead and after he disappeared from view she gave him no more thought; not until they turned the curve in the road and saw the long, straggling village street ahead, and there was the boy in the distance waving his arms above his head.

The presence of the young sailor had apparently allayed Con's fears; it was as if he had forgotten what had transpired when they passed through the village on their way to the town, for he was laughing at something the young fellow had said and had his mouth open and his lips moving as he struggled to make a remark. But of a sudden the smile slid from his face; his lips fell together; he pulled the horse almost to a stop and said quietly, 'Emily!'

Emily did not answer. She was looking ahead to where at the end of the street and in the middle of the road stood the blacksmith, and as she looked towards him his wife joined him. Then, her eyes darted from one side of the road to the other. She saw three men come out of the inn. One she recognized as the drover, the man she had seen this morning, and with him the man Ralston and another man. They were making their way towards the blacksmith and his wife.

Then a door opened on the other side of the street and another man and a woman came out.

'Emily!'

'It's all right, Con. It's all right.'

'What is it?'

Emily turned to the young fellow at her side, saying haltingly, 'Them ... them up there, they're going to set about him.'

'About Con?' There was a note of incredulity in the young fellow's voice. 'What in God's name for? Why should they set about Con?'

'They ... they think he ...'

'I didn't. I didn't, Jamsie. I didn't.'

'You didn't what?'

Now Emily, not taking her eyes off the group that was slowly approaching them, said, 'He didn't give the blacksmith's daughter a bairn. That's what he's trying to say.'

'Him! Con give Bella Goodyear a bairn! Don't be daft.'

'I'm not daft; that's what they're sayin'. She's named him.'

'My God! look at them. They're comin' at us!' The note of apprehension in the young fellow's voice now threw Emily into a panic and she cried at Con, 'Get down! Get down! Go on, run through the fields ... get home.'

Needing no second bidding, Con dropped the reins and leaped from the cart and flew back down the road.

There now arose in the street a sound as if a pack of hounds had been let loose after a fox, and in much the same way the blacksmith and the rest stormed past the cart, while Emily, standing upright, yelled at them, 'Stop it! Stop it!'

One of the women looked up at her and, pulling herself to a stop, bawled, 'You're as bad as him, protecting him after what he's done to your little sister.'

Emily gaped at the woman, before screaming back, 'He did nothin' to me sister. She's not gona have a bairn; it's a stomach trouble. The doctor says so.'

'Ho! Listen to her. You're as bad as the upstart bugger over there!' The woman spat against the cart, then she, too, was running after the others.

'Oh my God! Oh my God!' Emily was gripping the young sailor's arm now, and she cried at him, 'Go on! Run to the house, please. Please go an' fetch the master. Tell him ... tell him what's happened. I'll ... I'll take the cart, I'll run them down. I will! I will! I'll take the whip to them. Go on.' She actually pushed him off the seat, and he, as if coming out of a bad dream, said, 'Aye. Yes. Aye,' then sprinted along the street and, turning up a passage in between the cottages, disappeared from her view.

The reins in her hand, she was yelling at the horse as she attempted to turn him about in the roadway, but even as she did so she was aware of faces peeping from behind curtains in the cottages on each side of the street.

'Gee up! Gee up!' She had never driven a horse in her life before, having had no desire even to try, she had not even taken the reins from Con, but she remembered how he had handled them. And now she was almost thrown from the seat as the animal, given its head, galloped down through the village, but when it came to where the road forked, because of her inexpert use of the reins it took, not the path that had brought it from Fellburn, but the narrower road which led to the quarry.

As Emily realized what was happening, she tugged and pulled at the reins, yelling now in an effort to make the animal stop or at least slow its speed. Then as abruptly as it had started it did stop, and the sudden impact almost brought her head first over its haunches.

When, gasping, she sat back in the seat and looked ahead the scene before her caused her to drop the reins and clutch her face in both hands. Con was at the far side of the quarry. He was still running but along a narrow way that was no more than a ledge, and advancing on him, one from each side, were two men.

She was again standing up in the dray but on the seat now and yelling, 'Don't! Don't! Listen!' Then in two leaps she was on the ground and running round the perimeter of the quarry, and as she ran a man, stepping from behind a boulder, shouted at her, 'Keep out of it! Mind your own business.'

Then, just as the horse had stopped abruptly, so she too pulled herself to a sudden stop; and again her hands

238

were clutching her face. She stared in horror as she watched the two men move slowly towards Con, who was standing as stiff as the rock behind him. She saw his head wag wildly just before the blacksmith's arm came out to grab him; then her heart leapt so painfully that her hands left her face and pressed themselves into her breasts.

At first he seemed to rise into the air like a bird, his arms and legs spreadeagled, it was as if he had been caught on a warm current; then he was bouncing from one pile of rock to the next until he reached the bottom of the quarry, where he lay still.

She was screaming. She heard the echo of her screams vibrating round the quarry. At her feet the ground sloped less deeply away towards the bottom; there was a churned up track where bogies had at one time been drawn up by pulleys. She was on it now, and like a crazed animal leaping from boulder to boulder, she went down it. At the bottom her feet sank into water and slime; and now there was nothing but the sound of their suction as she pulled them out one after the other, for she had stopped yelling, the moans inside her were too deep for escape.

When she sank up to her knees on the sludge she fell forward and dragged herself towards the wall of the quarry, then kept to it until she neared the place where he lay.

He was lying on his side, his head resting on one arm, the other was touching his knee which was drawn upwards; it was as if he were about to scratch it. His eyes were closed and there was a trickle of blood coming from each nostril. She knelt down by his side and, lifting his head, tried to say, 'Con. Con;' but no sound would come. When she touched his face she left traces on it of the dirty wet grey clay from her fingers.

His body was soft and warm. She gathered him to her and began to rock him while her whole being continued

239

to cry soundlessly, 'Con. Con.' She had thought this morning she could love him and now she knew that she had loved him, in a strange way she had loved this retarded lad as she would never love again. In this moment the years mounted on her, and she passed through time that gave her the experience of love in all its phases, she was a mother, a wife, a mistress, and more. She knew that never in her life again would she feel for anyone as she did at this moment. Her legs right up to her thighs were soaked in wet sludge, her body was freezing; but she wasn't aware of it, she was only aware that loving was a sorrow, that all love was pain, and that all talk of God and His goodness was just chatter created by fear of the unknown. There couldn't be a God, at least no good God, for no good God would let this evil come upon an innocent lad like Con, because he had suffered an evil. It went far beyond the wrong of an injustice ... he had suffered an evil.

She raised her head slowly now and looked for the perpetrators of the evil, but as far as her eyes could range around the whole of the quarry there wasn't a soul in sight....

What time had elapsed since she had first taken Con into her arms until Larry took him from her she didn't know; she hadn't even heard his approach, nor that of the young sailor fellow, but when he unloosened her arms from around the still body she fell towards the side. She felt so stiff she imagined that she would have snapped in two, like a piece of ice that had been trodden on, had not the sailor caught her. Supported by his arm, she looked at Larry holding Con as she had done, his head buried in the boy's neck.

When Larry and the sailor eventually lifted the limp form between them, the sailor turned to her and said softly, 'Stay there; I'll come back and help you in a minute.' But they hadn't taken half a dozen uncertain steps over the boulders before she dragged herself to her feet and followed them, but for most of the way like a crab, using her hands to assist her along.

She had just reached the path of the bogie trail when the sailor came back and, putting his arm about her, helped her up the slope, and so along to the dray. She was surprised to see the cart and horse still where she had left them. Half the sacks were lying to the side of the path and the others formed a bed on which Con was lying, partly stretched out.

The sailor still supporting her, they followed Larry who was slowly backing the horse to where the roads forked, and there he turned the animal, and, taking its head, he led it into the village street at a walking pace until they reached the inn. Here he stopped and for the first time since he had come upon the scene Emily heard his voice.

It could have been the voice of the god she knew didn't exist for it was loud and terrible, and what it said was terrible.

'He's dead! Do you hear? All of you in this hell hole of a village, do you hear? He's dead! But he'll not be the only one to go this day, I'll see to that. Listen to me, Sandy Goodyear. Con didn't give your whoring daughter a bairn because he was incapable of giving anybody a bairn, the colonel saw to that, he didn't want idiot grandchildren. You ask your slut what she was doing with John Ralston on Easter Monday night last, in Harrison's barn. And you Jim Atkins, ask your missis who she meets on a Monday on the quiet when she goes in to Fellburn, in the back room of The Bunch of Grapes. As for you, Dave Cole, why do you drop the best cuts of meat into Gladys Paine's? Her man's at sea, she can't eat all that herself, can she? He hammered her black and blue the last time he came home because if his reckoning was*

*right he had been away twelve months and there was a
bonny bairn to greet him....'*

Emily, leaning against the side of the cart but still supported by the young sailor, clutched her throat. What
they had done to Con would be nothing to what they
would do to him now. He mightn't die in a quarry, but
they would get him in some way. She wanted to go to him
and put her arms about him and plead, 'Come away.
Come away,' but now he was standing in the middle of
the road in front of the horse, his arms spread wide and
still yelling, *'You're scum! Do you hear? Every bloody
one of you is scum, the chapel goers no better than the
rest. Are you listening chapel keeper? What drove you
from Gateshead, eh? Will I tell them? No, let them find
out, and the righteous ones will burn you alive: enough
it is to whet their appetites.... And you Helen Rams-
gate....'*

She couldn't bear any more. She pulled herself from the
sailor's hold and, stumbling forward, gripped the horse's
bridle and tugged at it, and when it moved forward its
head pushed against Larry's back and just like an ani-
mated clockwork figure that had run down, his shoulders
drooped, his head drooped. He moved to the side and
waited until the back of the cart reached him, then put his
hand on to Con's dangling legs; and like this they went
from the village.

EIGHT

From the day they brought Con into the house and laid
him on the sofa in the drawing-room until the day they
carried him out again in his coffin, Larry scarcely opened
his mouth to her. It was as if he wasn't aware of her, or on
the other hand that he was so aware of her she had
become part of himself and so needed no recognition
through speech. Sometimes when passing through the
kitchen he would stand in front of her and stare at her
for a moment as if he were about to say something, then
would turn his head aside and go from her.

There had been a great deal of coming and going
during the past five days. No longer could she complain
that no one visited the house; but she wished that the
visitors could have been other than policemen. They
came out from Fellburn, and some from Newcastle, some
were in uniform and some weren't, but they were all
connected with the law or the newspapers. With the
newspaper men she had been cautious, afraid to mention
names in case of further retaliation.

She had heard that when the police went looking for
Jamsie Morgan, as a witness, his parents said he had gone
back to sea, and they didn't know from which port he
had sailed. The young fellow, she thought, was wise to
change his mind about giving up the sea, because he
could never have got work on the land around here if he
had split on them in the village.

One of the policemen who wasn't in uniform had said to the master, and in a very stiff tone, 'We understand, Mr Birch, that you weren't present at the time of the incident, but you must have an idea who the men were, and we advise you not to attempt to take matters into your own hands.' The master's reaction to this was to stare unblinking at the man.

The reactions of the mistress, old Abbie, and Lucy, to Con's death were different from what Emily would have expected. Lucy, as yet, hadn't shed a tear, and like the master she had hardly opened her mouth for days, and went about her allotted tasks like someone sleep-walking. As for Abbie, instead of showering a spate of words at Emily and telling her that he had foreseen the whole thing, and what had she expected, he, too, was strangely silent; even yesterday when she had accused him bitterly of having stirred up the feeling in the village by taking the news to the inn that Lucy was pregnant he had just hung his head. Through clenched teeth she had ground out at him, 'You're a mischief-maker, Abbie Reading, that's what you are, and you're as much to blame for what has happened as them over yonder'; even then he had not retaliated in any way, but his lips had trembled as only an old man's could and, without uttering one word in his own defence, he had walked away from her.

But the reaction of her mistress was the strangest of all. That woman, Emily thought, would go mad, if she weren't so already, for she was blaming the master for everything that had happened. After her first screaming outburst at the news she had barred the door for a whole day and a night.

And over the past four days if she had told her once what had happened on the awful day, she must have told her a dozen times; but still she didn't seem satisfied. Each time, when the telling was over, she would lie back on the pillows, clutch the quilt in both hands, and pull at it as if endeavouring to tear it in two.

But this morning, the day when Con would leave the house for the last time, she had refused to go over the scene yet again, for she felt ill inside. Her body seemed soaked in sadness, she needed comfort, someone to talk to, to put into words the feeling that had come alive in her when she had rocked Con's lifeless body in her arms, and in so talking reveal to herself the reason for such a love as she now felt.

She was leaving the bedroom when her mistress turned her blood cold by saying, as if to herself, 'He says he means to do for Goodyear; well, the sooner the better. And that will solve all problems, won't it? Two birds with one shot.'

When, her head shaking, she said, 'Oh! madam, don't say such a thing,' Rona Birch had mimicked her by repeating, 'Oh! madam, don't say such a thing'; and when, her face showing a look of fury, she cried at her, 'You are too pert, miss, much too pert. You forget yourself. Remember where you are, and what you are,' there arose in Emily a feeling of such indignation that she dared to reply, 'I don't forget what I am or where I am, and I'll tell you this, madam, I can walk out of here the day. And where would you be if I did, for there's one less now to do your biddin'? Two I'd say, for I'm not letting Lucy come into this room again.'

She saw the hand waver towards the side table, then drop on to the cover and grip it, and as they stared at each other she knew she had won a kind of victory, and one which if she intended to stay on here, she could make use of. But that was the question, did she intend to stay on?

At eleven o'clock she and Lucy stood against the wall at the end of the house and watched the undertaker's men carry the coffin out on to the drive, and push it into the black-draped glass hearse, then the hearse moved a little forward to enable the cabs, one by one, to take their place opposite the door.

The master, Mrs Rowan and her daughter, went into the first cab, followed by a number of gentlemen whom Emily hadn't seen before, who went into the second and third ones; then behind the third cab walked half a dozen men, working men by the cut of their clothes. The only one she recognized among them was Abbie Reading.

They remained by the wall until all they could see above the hedge that bordered the drive was the black-beribboned whips and the black streamers flowing from the high hats of the cab drivers.

Lucy now made a noise in her throat, then turned and buried her head against Emily, and by the time they reached the kitchen she was crying, not as she usually did, but wailing aloud and choking and coughing at the same time.

As Emily held her close, she, too, gave way to the pent up emotions inside her; but her crying was without sound, and its effect was to rack her body with a pain that stemmed from between her ribs, and flowed into her veins, and flooded her mind, washing away all thinking but that which was concerned with the agony of sorrow for Con.

Even knowing it would be heard in the room above, she did not attempt to check Lucy's wailing in any way and when eventually it subsided and the girl lay limp and exhausted against her, her own tears ceased to flow.

When at last she could see clearly, the dresser laden with plates of food reminded her of the meal that had to be set for the mourners' return. She had been cooking until late last night and also from early on this morning. She must get up and set the table in the dining-room, and she must make Lucy help her, it would take her mind off things.

Rising heavily to her feet, she held out her hand, saying, 'Come on, there's work to be done; I need you to give me a hand. But don't take the trays, I'll see to them, just take two plates at a time. I've laid the cloth.'

She did not follow Lucy immediately from the kitchen but stood looking around her. The place looked mucky, the floor needed scrubbing, the grate needed blackleading, in fact she knew that the whole house needed a good clean through, but she also knew that it was beyond her. It had been hard enough before with the excess of washing and cooking and seeing to that one up there. Con had relieved her of much of the running up and downstairs but now it would all fall on her shoulders. . . .

Con . . . Con. His name was ringing in her mind all the time. It was as if she were bemoaning the loss of a beloved child. And he had been a child; yet he had been capable of doing so many things. She was going to miss him in all ways. Yes, in all ways.

As she lifted up the heavy tray on which were plates holding large portions of roast pork and of veal and ham pie, she thought, I'll wait until he recovers a bit, then I'll have to tell him we'll have to have help both for inside and out, or else I'll go. . . . And I want to go. I do. I do.'

The funeral repast was over, the gentlemen had left, and now Mrs Rowan and her daughter were in the hall about to take their leave. She saw them standing together as she came from the kitchen and made her way to the dining-room to start clearing. She took note of the daughter. She wasn't young, nearly thirty, she'd say. She was big made and not bad looking, but the main impression Emily got was that she looked physically strong.

When she entered the dining-room she did not close the door behind her for she heard Mrs Rowan mention the blacksmith, and so she stood holding the door ajar in her hand listening.

'Now, I've told you, Larry, they've both gone, both Goodyear and Ralston; from what I can gather, John Ralston would be as much in fear of Goodyear as he would of you. What's more, the latest is that Hannah Goodyear's selling the business, likely going to join him wherever he is. But Sarah Ralston will carry on the farm regardless. Anyway, she's managed on her own for years because he's been too busy elsewhere. But, Larry, I'm telling you, forget about them now. What's done's done, you cannot bring back the dead; and their deeds will catch up on them, you'll see.'

'Just sit back and do nothing, Hannah, is that what you want me to do?'

'With regard to them two, yes, that's all you can do, because, don't forget, if you try anything else your own neck's at stake. And what'll happen to all this then?'

In her mind's eye, Emily could imagine the little woman waving her arm about the hall before going on, 'You've worked hard enough for it; and let's be honest, Larry, you've sacrificed both yourself and others for it, and now you're having to pay through the teeth in more ways than one for it. But it's your business, and it's your life, I'm not blaming you, a man must do what his urges tell him, but one thing I do say and I'll repeat it, leave Goodyear and Ralston to the police.'

'Leave it to the police? Huh! Ralston's brother Chief Constable of Fellburn, so leave it to the police you say, Hannah?'

'Aye, I still say it, for their disappearance proves their guilt, and they'll remain wanted men all their lives. We're going now, but you know where we are if you need us. It won't do for us to call on you very often here, there's been enough talk, hasn't there?'

Emily waited for an answer to this but there was none forthcoming. She heard the door open, then after some time she heard it close, but she did not hear his footsteps going across the hall immediately, and she pictured him standing with his back against the door.

When finally she heard his feet treading slowly up the stairs she went to the table and began to clear it, and as she did so it occurred to her that never once had she heard the daughter Lizzie open her mouth.

He had been over at the farm since changing his clothes in the late afternoon; now it was nearing nine o'clock and he hadn't yet come in.

She had attended to the mistress and been momentarily softened towards her by the fact that her eyes were swollen and red with crying. It was good to know that after all she possessed some ordinary human feelings, for since Con's death all she seemed to have done was to rave at the master. Tonight she was quiet, and apparently not hungry for her supper tray was hardly touched.

Now it was nearing the end of the day that had seen the last of Con, and she could not tell if it was sadness or sheer exhaustion that was weighing her down. She only knew that if she didn't sit down she would collapse. What was more, she had a cold. The sludge of the quarry bottom had soaked her to the waist, and she had shivered for days afterwards. She had tried to wash the mud off her clothes but they were so stained she'd never be able to wear her coat or skirt again. But what did it matter? What did anything matter?

She had sent Lucy up to bed over half an hour ago, for she, too, had been overcome with weariness and sadness. Slowly now she laid out the breakfast trays, filled the kettle, damped down the fire with the coal dust from the bottom of the bucket, then poured the tea leaves from the pot on top of it, after which she carried the two iron pails across the yard to the coal house, and after filling them carried them, bent almost double, back into the kitchen, setting one each side of the fireplace.

Con had always brought the coal in.

When the kitchen door opened and Larry entered she was at the sink washing her hands, and as she dried them on the hessian towel he spoke her name for the first time in days. 'Come and sit down, Emily,' he said; 'I must talk to you.'

Funny, how men always said that to her: 'Come and sit down; I want to talk to you.'

She had hung up the hessian towel on the nail, walked slowly to the table and as slowly sat down at the far end of it, and, her hands folded one on top of the other in her lap, she looked at him, where he sat opposite to her, and waited. Then something inside her gave a violent jerk as if a hammer had hit her ribs when, his two hands coming out, he gripped hers and, looking into her face and his voice low and thick with emotion, he said, 'Emily, don't leave me.'

His back was bent, his head was bowed over her knees. She was looking down into his thick hair and she noticed that he had two crowns. There was some old wives' tale about people who had two crowns but she couldn't remember what it was. He hadn't said, 'Don't leave the house,' or 'Don't leave us,' but 'Don't leave me.'

Her heart racing now, she listened to him saying, 'I know you've been worked off your feet, anybody else would have taken to their bed after what ... what you went through.' She watched his shoulders rise as he gulped in his throat, and the thick sweet smell of the cow byres wafted from him and filled her nostrils. 'I'll try to get you help inside, but I can't promise anything, not from roundabout. But I don't want to see you kill yourself with work. Leave the rooms. I'll close up both the drawing-room and dining-room and I'll take my meals here in the kitchen. I'll see to my own bed and take on what chores I can, like'—he lifted his head slightly and nodded towards the hearth—'fetching the coal and wood and such, until I can get help outside. And that, I'm afraid, is going to be as difficult as getting it inside, thanks to our dear friend, Abbie.' He now raised his head and she watched the muscles in front of his ear twitch as he added, 'If he wasn't an old man I'd horsewhip him. Do you know that? I'd horsewhip him, for if anybody's to blame for Con's going it's him. I'd send him packing tomorrow if it wasn't for....' He broke off and his eyes involuntarily flickered upwards; then he shook his head and, looking into her face, said, 'You have it in your mind to go, haven't you? But I'm not blaming you, don't think that ... only ... only——' His head drooped again.

She swallowed, blinked, shook her head in denial, then nodded as she admitted, 'Aye, yes, I ... I was in two minds, 'cos so ... so many things have happened. But now, you needn't worry any more. I won't leave, but ... but I'll have to have help of sorts, if it's only somebody to give a hand with the washin'. There's so much of it; and it's the drying of it in weather like this. I'm ... I'm sorry Lucy's not much use....'

'Oh, I don't want you to let Lucy do anything if possible; there's a chance she could get better if she has rest and the right food. I was thinking the other day, if she could be sent to a sanatorium....'

She hadn't realized that he was still holding her hands until she went to withdraw them from his as she exclaimed, 'A what! An asylum?'

'No, no.' He was gripping her hands and shaking them now, 'It's a place where the air is good for people like Lucy, those with the complaint. I know someone away down in the South of England, it's my mother's cousin, she works in one such sanatorium. I could write to her and ask her what chance there would be of getting Lucy in for a time.'

She asked softly now, 'Could they cure her?'

'Well, that's what people go for, to be cured. There's

always a chance.'

'Eeh!' Her fingers moved within his grasp as she said, 'I'd be ever grateful if she could be made better.'

'Well, we'll see.'

Their faces straight, sadness showing in their eyes, they sat staring at each other in the lamplight. Then as quickly as he had first grasped her hands, he now fell on to his knees and, his arms about her waist, he buried his head in her lap. His shoulders shook and his voice was thick and broken as he moaned, 'Oh! Emily ... Emily ... I miss Con. I ... I loved that lad. He was so good, so innocent, so trusting. I ... I used to think of him as a son.'

During the first moments of their closeness she had remained stiff, but when his words became inaudible and his crying increased she held him to her as naturally as she would have Lucy or Con himself, and she thought it was odd that she should think of herself as Con's mother and here was he saying he thought of him as his son. Con seemed to have bred love ... and hate, for he had died by hate.

When at last his crying subsided he drew himself from her arms and rose to his feet and, his head bowed deeply on to his chest, he muttered, 'I'm sorry. I'm sorry.'

She made no answer, she just sat looking up at him as, with his back to her, he dried his face and said quietly, 'I begged you to stay, but at the same time I know it's a crying sin to ask a young girl like you to bury yourself alive here, because this house had never known joy or laughter except what you've brought into it, and I doubt if it ever will again.'

She pulled herself to her feet now and addressing his back, said softly, 'I don't think I'm buryin' meself alive. In the first place, I was glad to be given a roof over our heads. I ... I think you should give yourself time for Con to rest, then perhaps things 'll change and you'll laugh again.' But had she ever seen him laugh before, really laugh except on New Year's Eve? And then, like them all, he was drunk. She ended, 'I think Con would have wanted you to laugh, for he loved a laugh and a joke.'

With the memory of Con's laughter, her throat tightened and when he turned slowly towards her now and said, 'You look tired, worn out. Go on to bed and don't get up until seven in the morning, I'll see to the fire and things,' she began to bustle around the table, saying as she went, 'I'll be down at me usual time; one hour in the mornin's worth three in the afternoon.'

He stood looking at her for a moment before saying quietly but firmly, 'Leave those trays alone and get yourself upstairs, go on now.... Good-night. Good-night, Emily.'

He had uttered her name softly, almost a whisper and she didn't look at him as she went past him to the delf rack and picked up a candlestick and a box of matches, and she was almost at the kitchen door before she said, 'Good-night, sir.'

As she went along the side of the hall and up the back stairs she knew that a new phase of her life had begun, but as to what it would hold she could give herself no inkling as yet. But whatever came of it, it was because Con had died.... Everything had to be paid for. She was coming to believe in that. Oh yes, she was coming to believe in that.

PART THREE

HOW ARE THE MIGHTY FALLEN

ONE

Emily awoke on the morning of her seventeenth birthday and stretched her legs downwards until her toes stuck out from underneath the bedclothes and she could feel the brass rails of the bed; then she stretched her arms upwards and gripped the rails behind her head. She was seventeen today, she was a woman ... well, she had felt a woman for a long time, but once you were seventeen ... well, you were really grown up then. She felt as she hadn't felt for months, happy inside, glad, gay.

A streak of yellow light across the wooden boards told her the sun was coming up and that it promised to be a fine day. She turned and looked at Lucy. In the past six months Lucy had put on inches in height and broadened a little too. She put out a tentative finger and lifted a strand of the long straight hair from off her sister's brow. She'd miss her when she went; oh, how she'd miss her, but she'd have to put up with that because it was for Lucy's own good. And Lucy herself must have faced up to it; in fact, she seemed excited about going all that way across the country. The only thing she kept saying was she wished they were both going together.

She turned on her back again. She'd never be able to repay the master for what he was doing for Lucy, for he wasn't only paying her train fare all the way down there, but had rigged her out in decent clothes. She knew, too, that he would have been prepared to pay for her stay if it had been needed, but this place where Lucy was going seemed to be a public hospital where you got in by recommendation. It was in a place called St Leonards, outside a town called Hastings. He had said it was lovely; he had been to the hospital once and he said nearly all the bedroom windows looked out to the sea.

She wished she could have gone down and seen Lucy settled in, but she knew she couldn't be spared, and so Lucy was to travel on the train in care of the guard, and the master's cousin was going to meet her in London. She could understand Lucy's feeling of excitement 'cos the very thought of it all made her feel excited too.

Well! She'd better get up out of this; birthday or no birthday the work had to be done, and Mrs Riley came the day. Oh, she thanked God for Mrs Riley, oh she did indeed. But then it wasn't God she should be thanking but her Aunt Mary. She giggled to herself as she brought her legs over the side of the bed. Eeh! the things she thought.

Mrs Riley was a widow with no family and she supported herself by going out washing. She could earn up to half a crown a day at it, at least so she had said; but that, Emily thought, was stretching it a bit, and more than a bit. However, stretching it or not, that's what she got here, together with her food. The master picked her up in Fellburn market any time between three and four on a Monday, and the minute she arrived she got down to it, putting all the washing in soak, and on the Tuesday she scrubbed, boiled, possed and mangled the entire week's wash, and if the mistress had been in one of her tantrums, or perhaps two or more of them, the bedding took on the form of a linen mountain. Then on the Wednesday she ironed, and if the weather had been good for drying and she was finished early, she scrubbed out the kitchen, blackleaded the stove, washed out the pantries and the meat store, and if time permitted scalded out the dairy.

Then on the Thursday morning she walked to the cross-roads outside the village and there caught the carrier cart back into Fellburn. And for her two days' work, and a bit, she got six and sixpence, together with her meals and a bed, though the last wasn't what she herself would have offered her, being but a straw shake-down in the barn loft. This was because the mistress wouldn't have her bedded in one of the attic rooms.

But Emily couldn't be too sorry for Mrs Riley, because whoever heard of anyone claiming a wage like that, six and sixpence for two days and a bit, and as much grub as she could push into herself; not that she begrudged her her good fortune and wasn't thankful for her assistance, but being human she couldn't but compare the wage for those two days' work with the five shillings she now got for six and a half days' work, which days began at six in the morning and if she was lucky finished at eight at night.

But this was her birthday and she felt up to moving a mountain.

She stripped off her calico nightdress and grabbed at her shift lying over the foot of the bed, then paused for a moment as she did most mornings and looked at the watch pinned to the front of it. At one time she used to keep her shift on under her nightie, but when she lay on her face the watch stuck into her. She could have un-pinned it at night and pinned it back again the next morning but she was always too tired most times to bother. It was easier to take it off altogether, even when the interval between taking off the shift and putting on the nightdress made her disturbingly aware of her body.

The light of the rising sun was glinting on the watch; it looked bonny, beautiful, and the wish returned that she could wear it just for one day, and especially today, it being her birthday. But then, if she did, she'd have to explain where she got it, and how she got it. So with a sigh she pulled on her shift and got hastily into her clothes. She no longer kept the sovereigns pinned to her petticoat band for it meant taking them off every time she washed it, and so she now kept them in the chest of drawers. She knew they were quite safe, for who was there to steal them in this house. But with the watch ... well, that was a different thing; she could never leave that lying about. . . .

Down in the kitchen, she went straight to the door and opened it to let the fresh air in, and she stood for a moment breathing deeply as she looked up into the sky. It was a beautiful day, a lovely day, a real June day, and she was seventeen. She skipped round and went to the stove, poked the fire into a blaze, then lifted the kettle off the hob where it was near boiling and set it in the heart of the fire.

When she went to the dresser to get the teapot she stopped and stared, for leaning against the teapot was an envelope, and on the envelope her name, Emily. Her face smiling, her lips apart, she tore the envelope open and took out the sheet of paper and read, 'Happy birthday, Emily. Get yourself a little present with this.' There was no signature. She peered in the envelope, then took out the sovereign.

Eeh! wasn't that kind of him. It must have been a month or more since she had mentioned the date of her birthday. Oh, he was kind. A whole sovereign! Yet while she smiled her appreciation of his gift a part of her mind was telling her that she already had a number of sovereigns upstairs and how much more delighted she would have felt if the gift had been ... well, something personal, like a little brooch, or a locket and chain, or something like that. She had seen a beautiful locket and chain for four and six in a shop in Fellburn on her last half-day, in fact she had been tempted to buy it for herself.

This same section of her mind now told her that she

was an ungrateful monkey and reminded her that the master wasn't a personal man. But what did she mean by that? Well, she told herself, the fact that he hadn't taken advantage of what had passed between them on the night that Con was buried explained it, didn't it? And he could have taken advantage. Oh yes, he could, he could have played on her feelings, but he hadn't, he had kept his place, and from that night she had kept hers. And so, she told herself that was why she could say he wasn't a personal man; and what was more, she could still go round with her chin in the air if she wanted to.

'Happy birthday, Emily.'

She actually jumped around, the letter in one hand, the sovereign and the envelope in the other, and she laughed outright now as she said, 'Oh, thanks. An' thank you for this an' all. Eeh! it's ever so kind of you. I never expected it.'

His next words belied, to some extent, the impersonal man when he said, 'I'd like to have got you some little thing, but I'm afraid I'm no hand at choosing presents. And I didn't know what you would like, anyway.'

'Oh, that's all right.' Her face was alight now, her eyes shining. 'I know what I'm going to buy with it.'

'What?'

'A locket and chain, a good one. I saw a nice one for four and six in Fellburn, but I'll get a better one.... Oh, there's the kettle boiling, I'll make the tea.'

She ran to the stove, and he stood and watched her as she laughed aloud when she went to grab the kettle forgetting that she still had the letter and the money in her hand; then putting both quickly on the mantelpiece, she lifted the kettle on to the hob and turned to him, saying, 'I don't know where I am this mornin', I'm trying to make the tea without the teapot.'

Again she was running, back to the dresser now, and after spooning the tea from the caddy into the pot she looked at him, then paused a moment. He was standing in the same place, he hadn't moved, the look in his eyes was soft, yet sad, as he said, 'Seventeen. You're going to be a beautiful woman, Emily.'

'Oh, sir!' She bit on her lip, lowered her eyes, and shook her head.

'You know you're beautiful, don't you?'

'No, sir.' Her head came up. 'Well, not ... not beautiful; I've ... I've been told I look bonny, and, as me da would say, I'd pass in a crowd, but ... but not beautiful.'

'You are beautiful, both inside and out, kind and beautiful.'

There was a mist before her eyes. It was blocking out his face and she felt an urge to push her hands through it and touch him, hold him, feel him near her.

'Eeh! the kettle. It'll ... it'll have boiled dry in a minute.'

She mashed the tea, stood the teapot on the hob, then, bending down, took the hearth brush and swept some loose ashes under the grate before turning once more to the table and him.

He was still looking at her. It was as if his eyes had never left her face, and he smiled gently at her now but with a downward pull to his lips as he said quietly, 'It's all right. It's all right, Emily, don't worry.' Then he turned away and went through the kitchen, and she heard him going up the stairs.

She was standing sipping at a cup of tea while her thoughts whirled about in her head, telling her things that were making her hot when she heard his voice raised in anger coming from above, and she closed her eyes for a moment as she said to herself, 'Oh! not again. And not the day.'

It was almost three weeks since they'd had a row, and things had been easier all round. He had looked happier and had laughed aloud on more than one occasion, he had even teased Lucy in the kitchen here.

She often wished he would take the line Sep had followed and give in to the mistress, as Sep had to Mrs McGillby, then gone his own way on the side. But, of course, she admitted to herself, there was a great difference between Mrs McGillby and Mrs Birch, because that woman up above would aggravate a saint when she got going.

As the voices rose higher she wondered what they could be on about now. She never really knew what they fought about because they would stop whenever she went into the room. The master would usually bound out, and the mistress bang her fists on the eiderdown, then mess the bed. Although her mistress had deigned to explain to her that her eviction, or some such, as she called it only happened when she was disturbed, Emily was of the opinion that there were times when it was done on purpose, just to aggravate. Well, she nodded up to the ceiling now, if that went on much longer there'd be a number of evictions this morning; of that she had no doubt.

It was at dinner-time that she found out what they had been fighting over. She was taking the dinner tray up and had reached the landing when she heard the master's voice loud and clear, which told her that the bedroom door was open, and he was barking, 'I've told you I'll pension him off; he's no good, he can't carry his weight any longer, he's too old.' Then the mistress's voice answering in slow deep tones, 'You'll not pension him off ever. As long as I'm here Abbie stays. And after. D'you hear me? And after. Listen to me, my fine fellow, and listen carefully. Abbie will be here when you're gone. Do you hear that? Abbie will be here when you're gone. Your time is running out. I've warned you, I've given you fair warning.'

'You're mad, woman. You can't do me out of this place and you know it. If you could, by God! you would. I know that too. But you can't. Women's property rights or no women's property rights, I'm your husband, and when you go I can claim this place by law.'

The laughter that now filled the landing caused Emily to screw up her face against it, for if it didn't sound like that of a mad woman, it didn't sound that of a sane person either. Then the voice, full of the same laughter now, was shouting at him, 'Oh you upstart! Listen. Listen and remember what I'm saying. You'll hear me laughing like this when I'm gone. Believe me, you will, you will.'

She didn't move from where she was when he burst out on to the landing, and when he marched past her and pounded down the stairs it was as if he hadn't seen her. She waited a few more minutes until the tray took on a leaden weight before she moved along the landing and entered the bedroom.

Her mistress was leaning back among her pillows and she was smiling, and she continued to smile as she looked at Emily and said, 'I suppose you heard all that?'

'Heard what, ma'am?'

'Don't play the gormless idiot with me, girl!' Now the smile was slipping. 'You heard what I said to him, the person you call the master.'

'I don't listen, ma'am, I mind me own business,' Emily said as she proceeded to place the bedside table across the woman's knees.

Leaning towards Emily, Rona Birch now hissed, 'You have two faces, girl, one for up here and one for down below. Down below you are the ingratiating busy, kitchen slut. Oh, I know what I know. Up here you take a stand, thinking you have the better of me because of my predicament. But you, like him, my dear, are going to get a surprise one of these days, and not so very far away either; oh no. The time is fast approaching, it is indeed; yes, it is indeed.'

'Eat your dinner, madam.' Emily put the tray on the bed table; then straightening her back, she smoothed down her apron and said quietly, 'The doctor told you a week or so ago you had to keep calm, madam, you know he did, 'cos if you didn't your tantrums would be the end of you....'

With a swiftness that belied the delicateness of the hands and the weakness of the whole frame, Rona Birch tore off the silver cover from over the dinner plate, threw it to one side, then hurled the plate of meat, gravy and vegetables into Emily's face.

The scream that Emily emitted outdid any that had as yet been heard in the room. The gravy, although not scalding, was still hot, and as she staggered back she cried, 'Oh! Oh! You ... you wicked thing you!' while her hands scraped at the pieces of vegetables and meat that were clinging to her face and the front of her bodice. She was leaning against the dressing-table gasping when Larry burst into the room.

Taking the whole situation in immediately, he stood over his wife, his hands poised as if to grip her throat as he cried at her, 'I could kill you, woman! I could cheerfully kill you at this moment. You should be locked up; you should be in an asylum; that's your rightful place, an asylum.'

Rona Birch didn't utter a word, she just stared at him, her hate of him oozing from her in sweat.

When he turned to Emily, his whole body was shaking, as was his voice as he said, 'Go on, get cleaned up ... I'll see to this. My God! yes, I'll see to this.'

He led her to the door and pressed her out on to the landing, then closed the door again; and she stood there for a moment unable to move, until she heard the crack of a hand contacting flesh. She swung round as if to open the door again, but when she heard the second slap she put her hand over her greasy face, then bowed her head and stumbled towards the stairs.

He had hit her again. He shouldn't have done that because after all, she was a sick woman. As bad as she was, he shouldn't have done that. Sep would never have hit Mrs McGillby, no matter how bad she was; but then Mrs McGillby would never have thrown a hot dinner in her face.

In the kitchen Lucy rushed at her, crying, 'Eeh! she... she never! Did she?'

'Aye, she did!' Emily went to the sink and began to pump the water, and she shook her head as she said, 'It's funny but I shouldn't have been so surprised or frightened, for I've often thought she'd throw the meal at me.'

'Eeh! she's an awful woman. Oh, you are in a mess, Emily.'

'I... I am, aren't I? Well, let's get it off. Mash a cup of tea, will you? I could do with something.'

After washing herself she sponged the grease off her dress, and Lucy, watching her, said sadly, 'An' it's your birthday an' all,' then she threw her arms around her waist, burying her head against her and muttering, 'Oh, I wish you were comin' with me, Emily. Oh, I wish you were.'

Stroking Lucy's hair, Emily silently endorsed this, thinking, 'Me too, Lucy; how I wish I was going with you,' knowing, at the same time that Lucy's going must, in a way, tie her to this house, for she was now under an obligation to its master. Nevertheless, the wish to be gone was strong in her at this moment and it wasn't only because the mistress had thrown the dinner at her; it was more in a way because of what the master had done to his wife. People in a position like the master shouldn't hit a woman; that to her mind only happened among the working class, the poor working class. Somehow he had gone down in her estimation. But then she had known right from the beginning that he wasn't a gentleman, not in the right sense of the word, not a real gentleman. So, after all she supposed it wasn't so surprising that he should hit his wife.

Only a few hours ago he had stood in the kitchen here and told her she was beautiful, and the way he had said it had put all kinds of fancies into her head.... Well, that scene up there had cleared her head.

What would she do if a man ever went to hit her? Oh, she knew what she'd do, she'd pick up the first thing to hand and let him have it, she wouldn't stand for any man hitting her; she had seen too much of it in Creador Street.... What had she just said? She'd pick up the first thing and let him have it? Funny, but that's what she up there had done, but the other way about, she had thrown the dinner first.

An odd idea struck her at this moment ... the mistress hadn't really thrown the dinner at her, she had thrown it at him.

TWO

The doctor sipped slowly at his coffee until the cup was empty; then he placed it on the table and looked to where Larry was staring fixedly at him and nodded as he said, 'I thought it only right to tell you.'

'You mean to say she suggested that I might try to do her in?'

'Yes, something along those lines. She also said she didn't wish to be buried with undue haste when she died, she would like a week to elapse before interment.'

'My God!' Larry rubbed his hand hard along the side of his jaw before saying, 'Is there any way she can do me out of the farm and ... and all this?' he made a sweeping motion with his hand.

'No, no'—the doctor shook his head—'you have a husband's rights. As far as I can see the house and farm will be yours. You are her lawful husband and, therefore, have a legal claim to what is hers. I don't really think you need worry yourself very much on that score, but I would advise you to go gently with her. She's a very sick woman; I would give her no cause for complaint against you.... She hasn't asked to see your solicitor of late, has she?'

'No. No, she hasn't mentioned him. But since you speak of it, that is another point, my solicitor does not act for her; the deeds of the house and her personal business are, as far as I know, still with Clark, Maine and Sutton. They've always attended to any legal business required.

It was she who suggested I should go for any advice I needed to Barrett and Golding.'

He rose to his feet now and started to pace the room, the doctor watching him for a moment before he, too, rose, saying, 'Well, I must be on my way.'

'I don't like it.'

The doctor turned his head to the side and looked at him and sighed before saying, 'Well, I'm afraid I can't be of any help to you on legal matters, I can only advise you that if it is at all possible you keep her happy.'

'Keep her happy!' Larry gave a huh! of a laugh now and, looking straight at the doctor, said, 'You know as well as I do, doctor, that it's not in her nature to be happy. Let's face it, she's a vindictive woman.'

The doctor now turned away and walked down the length of the drawing-room and he had reached the door before turning to say, 'Well, about that you should know best.'

The following morning a letter came from Lucy and Emily's face beamed as she read it. Lucy was settling down in that faraway place at the other end of the country. She had made a friend called Miss Rice. Wasn't that a funny name? But Miss Rice was lovely. She was twenty-two years old and her people lived nearby, and when they came to visit her they brought her lots of fruit and other things, and Miss Rice shared them with her. She ended her letter by saying that Miss Rice was a lady, if Emily knew what she meant, and she hoped Emily was as well as it left her at present.

Emily put the letter on the table, smoothed out the four corners of it, gazed down on it, and laughed aloud.

She was still laughing when George Archer, the new help, came and stood in the open doorway and, looking towards her, said, 'If you tell me what you're laughin' at I'll laugh with you, Emily.'

'Oh'—she wagged her chin up and down—'it's me sister. I've had a letter from her. She's gettin' on like a house on fire in this hospital I told you of.'

'Oh, I'm glad to hear that.'

'You want your tea? Give us your can here.' She reached out across the table and took the can from him, and as she stood at the stove filling it from the teapot he asked quietly, 'How's the missis this morning?'

'Oh, same as usual.'

'Can't she move at all?'

'Only the top half of her.'

'She can't walk about at all?'

She looked at him over her shoulder before she replied, 'No.'

'You have to do everything for her I suppose?'

'Aye, everything.' She now came back to the table and put the lid on the can, and as she thrust it down with the pad of her thumb she repeated, 'Everything.'

'Some job!'

'Yes, as you say, it's some job. But then beggars can't be choosers.'

'Huh!' He laughed now. 'I couldn't ever imagine you begging, Emily.'

'Well, I was nearly on the point of it when I got this place.... Do you like him?'

'Who?'

'The boss.'

'Aye, yes, I like him. Yes, I think he's a decent bloke, as far as I can gather. Some of them wouldn't give you the smoke that went up the chimney.'

'I'm glad you like him. You be fair to him and he'll be fair to you.'

'Well, I'm doin' me best.'

'I know you are, George. Do you want a shive?'

'I wouldn't say no.'

She now went into the pantry and returned with a

269

thick ham sandwich and a square of currant cake, and as she handed them to him he said, 'Ta, Emily.... By! you're a bonny lass.'

'Go on with you!' She flapped her hand at him. 'Go and tell that to the cows, it might work on them.'

'It does. It does.' He was laughing loudly now. 'Every time I play up to Pansy she gives me another half gallon.'

As he went out laughing she laughed too. She liked George Archer. He had been on the place only three weeks but he had already proved himself to be a good hand. He had come straight off the road, having tramped all the way from the West country doing a bit here and there without getting anything permanent, and now it appeared as if he could be set for life if he kept on working as he was doing, and he was quite young, not thirty yet, and not bad looking either.

At the end of his first week Larry had said to her, 'I think I've struck lucky with Archer.' 'Aye,' she had answered; 'I think you have. And if you could persuade Mrs Riley to come full time I'd feel I'd struck lucky an' all.'

But as yet Mrs Riley couldn't be persuaded to stay out in the wilds, as she termed it, for all of a full week. In her heart, Emily didn't blame her, for at times she got very tired of the wilds herself, when she would develop a longing like a deep homesickness to pick up her skirts and run from the place, right back to Shields and the waterfront itself. She might stop at Aunt Mary's in Gateshead but the waterfront would be her destination.

At such times she would tell herself she wasn't made for the country; this would be when she felt the urge to talk to someone, to have just a little natter. She missed Lucy. Oh, she did miss Lucy.

In any spare time she had at nights now she had taken to reading. She read the Newcastle papers that the master brought in twice a week, and now and again she would take a book from the library, but most of these she found very hard going. There was little of the love story in them; the few she had worked her way through seemed to go all round the houses before getting to the point, so she considered.

She couldn't believe that by next Tuesday she would have been in this house a year, and yet when she looked back it seemed more like ten, or a whole lifetime. Yes, a whole lifetime.... She needed a break of some kind. She'd never had a holiday in her life and she was never likely to. But apparently she wasn't the only one, for there was that funny piece of poetry in the little book Sep had given her. It went:

> John Gilpin's spouse said to her dear—
> Though wedded we have been
> These twice ten tedious years,
> Yet we
> No holiday have seen.

There were lots of funny and interesting bits in the book. She had been reading it of late by candlelight in bed. It stopped her thinking about Lucy and helped her to fall asleep.

She had come to the conclusion that whoever the person was who had written the things in the book didn't think much about women because one of the quotations, written under the heading of 'Hannah Cowley', read: 'But what is woman?—only one of nature's agreeable blunders.' And there was another which read: 'It is better to dwell in a corner of the housetop than with a bawling woman in a wide house.'

Yet of all the pieces in the book she liked the one about the tide. Somehow it brought her closer to Shields and the river running into the North Sea. And that last line, 'Never say die'; she hadn't said that for a long time, perhaps because there had been no emergency, no need to prod herself.

There was a sameness about life now. Every day in this house was a matter of routine and it all centred about the room above the kitchen ... which reminded her: it was close on eleven o'clock. She had the mid-morning tray to take upstairs, and then go across to the farm with Abbie's break tea. Oh, he was a stubborn old devil, that Abbie, for he wouldn't let George bring it across for him 'cos, naturally, he was resenting the young fellow's presence; nor would he come for it himself. One of these days she would leave his tray under the arch and yell, 'There it is, Abbie! You'll have to come to it afore it comes to you.'

The hot milk and biscuits on the tray, she whipped off the coarse apron she wore over her white one in the kitchen, smoothed out her bib, pulled her mob cap straight, lifted up the tray and went out of the room.

Outside the bedroom door, she balanced the tray on one hand, tapped on the door with the other hand, then turned the knob, and when it didn't respond to the slight push she gave it she dropped her hand from it and stepped back and stared at it as if it had personally offended her in some way.

Having placed the tray on the table to the side of the door, she took the knob in both hands and pushed at the door. But it did not even shudder.

'Well, I never!' She even said the words aloud in surprise. The door hadn't been barred for weeks; there had been tantrums and sulks, and fights with the master, and the ignoring of herself, but the door had remained open.

'Madam!'

She put her ear to the door; it was no use putting her eye to the keyhole for that was blocked.

As she listened she had the idea that she heard a shuffling movement across the room, but of course that was sheer imagination, it was likely the sound of her scratching at the bed cover, as she did with her two fore-fingers when irritated ... yet no, it wasn't like that. There it was again. What was she up to in there?

'Madam, I've brought your drink.'

She straightened her back. Oh well, she'd open the door when she got hungry enough. But then, she hadn't seemed very hungry of late. She had picked over her food; even the special tasty dishes she made for her were left, and there was never an excuse or a word of thanks such as 'I'm sorry I was unable to finish it, Emily, because it was so very nice.'

She often thought if her mistress was ever really civil to her she would faint away. It was a pity she wasn't a nice woman because she would have enjoyed looking after her, and she felt that she could have made her happy in a way. She could have made her laugh by telling her about her Aunt Mary and her squad. And what was more, she could have learned things from her. For instance, she could have asked her to explain some of the things that she read and didn't understand, especially some of the bits in the little black book. But there, the woman was made as she was and nothing would alter her now.

She picked up the tray and went down the stairs again, and when she reached the kitchen she stood for a moment by the table thinking. Should she go and tell him or wait till he came in? It wasn't half an hour ago that he had been upstairs, and there had been no row. She had heard the murmur of their voices talking, but that was all; and when he had come downstairs and passed through the kitchen he had looked quite pleasant, not grim as he sometimes did after a visit to the bedroom. Well, she had better tell him.

As she ran across the yard the wind that was fresh and cold lifted her hair from behind her ears and blew it into her eyes, so that she didn't see him until she bumped into him as he came sharply around the corner. 'Whoa! Whoa there! Where do you think you're off to?'

'Oh.' She laughed up at him now as she kept thrusting her hair back with her fingers. 'I ... I was coming to find you.' She paused now as if to let the smile slide from her face before she said, 'The door's barred again.'

He didn't answer her immediately but he screwed up his eyes and moved his head slightly; then half turning from her, he said, 'Keep going up. If it's not open by dinner-time I'll see to it.'

'Aye, all right.'

'Emily.'

She was on her way through the arch again, and she stopped and turned towards him. He had his hand half extended towards her and was about to speak, but all he said after a moment was, 'Oh, it doesn't matter.'

She watched him swing round and march back towards the byres; then she turned again and went towards the house, walking thoughtfully now.

At dinner-time the door was still locked and he banged his fist on it, calling, 'Rona! stop playing about. Come on, open up!' But there was not even the sound of her scratching the quilt now by way of an answer. ...

After three more attempts during the afternoon he was now standing at the open kitchen door looking out into the darkening twilight, and as Emily watched him biting on his thumb nail, a habit of his when he was angry or troubled, she voiced something she had often thought of before. 'Why don't you get a ladder?' she said.

He looked at her over his shoulder and answered simply, 'I promised her that I'd never attempt to get into her room by a ladder. To her way of thinking it would be breaking down the last barrier against her privacy.'

He had for a long time now when speaking of his wife to Emily referred to her as she, or her.

'Well, the way I see it, there might come a time when

you'll have to break that promise. You know, she looked poorly this mornin', whitish, and she didn't touch a bite.'

He stepped back into the kitchen and looked up towards the ceiling, then down at Emily again, saying, 'Perhaps you're right. Yes, perhaps you're right.' And on this he swung round, and from the kitchen window she watched him hurrying across the yard and through the arch; and she remained still, waiting until he returned with a ladder.

When he had placed the ladder against the wall she went out and stood at the foot of it and watched him mount upwards. She watched him place one hand over his brow and cheek and press his face against the window. He kept it there some time before turning his head slowly about and looking down at her, and even in the dim light the incredulity registered in his expression was plain to her.

'What is it?' she asked softly.

He didn't reply but again with his hand he shaded the side of his face and peered through the window. Then of a sudden he began to come down the ladder so quickly she thought for a moment he'd lose his footing and topple to the ground, and when he stood facing her he seemed unable to speak.

'What is it? What's up?'

'She's ... she's on the floor, lying on the floor near the fireplace.'

'Eeh! no!' she shook her head. 'She can't be.'

And now he repeated, 'No, she can't be.' Then he almost bawled at her, 'But she is!' At this he looked wildly around the yard; then rushed into the kitchen, to return within a second carrying a poker in his hand.

She held the foot of the ladder while he quickly mounted it, but when he broke the window-pane with the poker she sprang back to avoid the falling glass, and from a distance she watched his hand groping inside for the latch, then knock out the peg that prevented the window from being opened more than a couple of inches or so.

The moment he disappeared through the window she herself darted from the yard, through the kitchen and hall up the stairs, but when she tried the bedroom door it still held fast.

After a moment, during which she stood with her ear to the door, it was pulled open. She stared at him; his face looked colourless. Slowly she moved past him and, turning her head, looked at the bed on which her mistress lay.

There was no need to ask if she was dead, for she had the same look on her face as had been on Mrs McGillby's; but added to that there was a cut stretching from the front of her ear up to the line of her hair and it was thick with dried blood.

He was standing by her side now, and when he whispered, 'How in the name of God did she get there?' they both looked towards the fireplace. It was all of ten feet from the foot of the bed.

Emily now turned her attention back to the bed. What was puzzling her now was the fact that the quilt was on the floor. She always tucked the quilt well down at the foot of the bed in order that it wouldn't slip off, but there it was lying in a heap at yon side of the bed. Slowly now she went round the bed and picked it up, and after a moment's pause filled with reluctance to go near the still figure, she laid it gently over her mistress. When she came round the bed again to where he was standing wide-eyed and staring like someone dazed, she had to prod him with her voice. 'You'd better send for the doctor, hadn't you?' she said.

'What? Yes. Yes.' He moved his head from side to side, and looked towards the window before saying, 'Tell Archer.'

'Yes. Aye.' She backed away from the bed and him, and at the door she turned and hurried on to the landing. But when she reached the top of the stairs she stopped for a moment and gripped the ornamental wooden knob on top of the banister rail while repeating to herself, 'How did she get over there? She couldn't have done it by herself. How in the name of God did she get over there?'

When she reached the yard it was to see George standing looking up at the window, and before she could speak, he said, 'I heard the glass break; what's the matter? Something up?'

'You've got to go for the doctor, quick! Take the cart, or trap, whatever's the quickest.'

'The missis?'

'Aye.' She nodded at him, and as he hurried away she called after him, 'Bring him back with you. It's important, 'cos she's gone.'

Her last words caused him to turn fully round and face her, and he repeated her words, 'She's gone? You mean?' and when she nodded her head he put up his hand and ran his fingers over his hair before disappearing through the arch.

It was nine o'clock that night and she was tired of telling the doctor the same story and hearing him say, 'But you didn't see your master lift your mistress from the floor and put her on the bed?'

And once again she said, 'No; but I've told you that when he came down the ladder for something to break the glass he said he had seen her on the floor.'

'But you yourself didn't see her lying on the floor?'

'No, but if he said she was, then she was.'

The doctor leant his head wearily back against the top of the leather chair. He was finding himself in a quandary. It was his firm opinion that Mrs Rona Birch could never have got out of that bed by herself. It was also his firm opinion that she had died from a heart attack caused by a blow to the head. It was plausible that the corner spike of the brass and steel fender could have caused the blow, yet there was no bloodstain on the carpet at the spot where her husband had said he had found her; nor for that matter was there much blood on the wound. But this was nothing to go by, she could have bled internally.

If it wasn't for this girl here he would have let the matter rest and issued a certificate to the effect that his patient had died from heart failure; but this girl, being a maid and consequently a chatterer, had likely already told the farm hand all that had transpired. On the other hand, if she hadn't talked it wasn't his place now to warn her to silence, because in his opinion you had only to tell a woman to cease her chatter and she chattered all the more. He was sorry, but he had to protect his position; there was nothing for it but a post mortem and to bring into the open the unlikely facts that a woman whom he had attended for the past five years, and who in his professional opinion had total paralysis of the lower limbs, had walked from the bed to the fireplace, a considerable distance, and without the aid of sticks. It was all highly improbable to say the least.

He said kindly now, 'That will be all at present, Emily.'

'Yes, sir.' She went slowly from the room, closed the door behind her, and as she crossed the hall she glanced up the stairs to where Larry was descending. They looked at each other but didn't speak, and she went on into the kitchen and, going to the settle by the side of the fireplace, she sat down and, joining her hands tightly, she pressed them on to her knees and stared into the fire.

She was dead; and it was a good job in a way for her own sake, and his an' all. But she had always threatened she would get one over on him, and she had. Eeh! she had at that, for now the doctor was making out that she could never have got out of that bed by herself and that she had died by a blow on the head; and who was there to give her that blow, only her husband. Of course, there was herself too but they wouldn't tack anything on to her 'cos she stood to gain nothing, whereas him ... well, by her dying he would get everything he had married her for. At least, that would be the verdict of old Abbie and the rest.

The more the doctor had questioned her the more she saw his side of it. As he said, she hadn't seen the mistress lying on the floor; when she entered the bedroom the mistress was lying on the bed. Of course, she was lying on top of the rumpled bedclothes, but then she could have pushed them aside with her hands.... What if he had hit her when he was up there this morning, then put on an act in climbing the ladder and getting through the window? ...

... Don't be daft. She got to her feet, grabbed up the poker and thrust it into the fire. If he had knocked her cold with a hard instrument how would she have been able to slide the bar across the door?

She straightened her back and stood now with her arm upwards gripping the mantelshelf. He was in trouble, deep trouble, and there were so many people around this quarter who would like to see him drown in it, and no one more than old Abbie.

If the polis was called in and they questioned Abbie the first thing he would say was they were forever at each other's throats, and that you could hear them at yon end of the farm, especially the master's voice; oh aye, he would emphasise that, would Abbie. And then it would be in the papers, big headlines.

Why was she always getting mixed up in tragedies and the like? First, there was Sep's going, and then Con; and now the mistress. But it wasn't her going that was the tragedy here, it was what was going to happen to the master.

Suddenly she lowered her face on to her outstretched arm and the tears filled her throat and burned her eyes as she thought, I'll die if anything happens to him. I will.

THREE

The newspapers in the north-east of England were never far behind the great dailies from London in printing the latest news and the northerner was a fellow who liked his headlines big. He did not always read what was below them because the headlines spoke for themselves. In May, 1900, it needed only two words MAFEKING RELIEVED and these two words gave the go ahead for celebration. Then in January, 1901, when the old Queen died the headlines were enormous.

Of course, the headlines in December, 1901, which told of a man called Marconi who said he had received wireless signals from across the sea were no more than ordinary although they ran MARCONI SPANS THE ATLANTIC. Yet they were quite enough to start genuine arguments in pubs, clubs, and at dinner breaks in shipyards, and even in certain kitchens where the man of the house was out to impress his family with his knowledge of things up to date, even risking being derided by his doubting offspring, saying, 'By! dad, an' next week you're gonna take a tram ride to the moon, aren't you?'

And then in March of 1902 there was the death of Cecil Rhodes. FIVE MILES PROCESSION AT BURIAL OF CECIL RHODES said the headlines. Buried on top of a rock, said the headlines. But who was Cecil Rhodes? Well, said the better informed, he was born in England but became a foreigner in South Africa where he made his pile and rose to Prime Minister. There were long names associated with him in the papers: Bechuanaland and Mashonaland coupled with Matabeleland; the last two he turned into Rhodesia. Then he got himself mixed up in something shady and had to resign. But all such headlines were put into the shade with the Coronation of King Edward VII and Queen Alexandra in June of that year.

Yet no headlines, large or small, had the effect of those that appeared in the northern papers in October of 1903—especially on the population of Fellburn and the village of Farley Dene, particularly Farley Dene—concerning the scandal about that upstart who had overstepped himself; battered his wife to death in her bed he had, then made on she had fallen against a fender, and her stiff and paralysed for years. Well, they had been expecting it, hadn't they, and they hoped he swung, for he had broken the village up; it wasn't the same any more since the Goodyears had all gone, and John Ralston an' all.

Although the headlines in the papers were impressive, yet they didn't go as far as to state that Lawrence Birch had murdered his wife. But then they didn't need to; all they needed to do was to state the facts and leave the public to form its own opinion....

The post mortem on Rona Birch was held the second day after she died, and on the fourth day the coroner and jury heard all that her husband had to say; also the doctor; and finally the maid; and, as he said, the evidence seemed confused and conflicting and he would, therefore, adjourn the inquest for one week from that day.

When Emily descended from the trap at the back door her legs were still trembling as they had been since she entered the court that morning. In fact, her whole body was now trembling, for she had imbibed the feeling of the court and she knew that no one believed either her or the master, but they believed the doctor when he had said that, in his opinion, it would have been impossible for his late patient to walk the distance between the bed and the fireplace, even to crawl that distance, for when he had last seen her she was in a very weak condition.

One little gleam of hope, however, had appeared when the doctor admitted that it was some long time since he had examined his patient's legs because she had always strongly objected to any form of examination. When asked how long it was since his last examination of the deceased, he had become slightly flustered and admitted that it was some months, and then but a cursory affair. But he had been quick to add that three years ago he had brought in a second opinion, a Doctor Bilkin, who was well known in the county for his specialized work in this particular field, and he had confirmed that the late Mrs Birch was paralysed from the waist down and had even suggested that her state might be progressive.

George, who had come running through the arch and had taken the horse's head, looked at Emily and his eyes asked how things had gone, but she didn't indicate anything, even by a slight movement of her head.

Nor did Larry speak to George, he just followed her into the kitchen where Mrs Riley beamed on them both, saying, 'Now isn't that queer? I must have smelt you comin', for I've only this minute mashed a pot of tea.'

Emily took out the pins from her hat and placed them on the corner of the dresser before lifting the hat from her head; then she stood holding it in both her hands and watched the master walk silently through the kitchen and out into the hall.

'I've never expected to receive the time of day from him but he looks as if he's joined the silent order. Did things not go right for him then?'

'No, Mrs Riley.'

'Is it bad, it is?'

'It looks pretty bad.'

'Well, well.' The woman shook her head, then said, 'There's nothin' you can do about it, so don't worrit yourself. An' there's nothin' that a good strong cup of tea won't help, so sit yourself down there.'

Emily sat down and unbuttoned her coat, and as Mrs Riley poured the tea out she remarked, 'I don't suppose it's any good givin' himself one for by the looks of him it's something stronger he needs at this minute.'

'I'd pour one out in any case, Mrs Riley, and I'll take it in to him.'

'Aye well, you should know.'

Mrs Riley now poured out another cup of tea, and Emily, after merely sipping at her own, rose from the chair, put the cup and saucer on a tray and without further words went from the room.

She knew he would be in the study. He was sitting close to the fire, his body bent forward, his elbows on his knees, his hands hanging slackly between them.

'Drink this,' she said. 'Or will I get you a drop of something?' She did not add either master or sir, in times of crisis such as when Con had died, their separate states seemed to meet and communicate on the same level.

He took the cup and saucer from her hand, then shook his head and took a long drink of the scalding tea before he looked at her again. 'They all believe I did it,' he said.

She could not comfort him by denying his statement; what she said was, 'The doctor didn't help; he could have avoided all this in the first place.'

'I think he would have liked to, but he has to do his job.' He now leant back in the chair, turned his head to the side and looked up into her face as he said, 'Wouldn't it be ironic, Emily, if, becoming the real master of all this at last'—he made a waving motion with his hand—'I couldn't enjoy it because I'd be along the line?'

'It won't come to that.'

'If those wolves in that court can do anything about it, it will, Emily. Oh, it will.' His head moving against the leather made a squeaking sound that put her teeth on edge. 'My history was known to everyone in that court this morning, Major Collins, Colonel Wrighton, and the whole lot of them, and high or low they'll relish my fall. Odd isn't it, Emily, that they should take so much interest in a fellow like me just because, as they would say, I stepped out of me class.'

Looking down into his face she thought that at this moment he had stepped back into his class, for he was talking to her as an equal and in a tone of voice that she recognized as being his own natural way of speaking, and it gave her courage to put out her hand towards him by way of comfort.

When her fingers lightly touched his arm he brought his hand on to hers and, gripping it, said, 'I don't know what I would've done without you all these months, Emily. You realize you've been a comfort to me, don't you, and that I've a feeling for you?'

The heat spreading over her body brought out tiny beads of perspiration on her upper lip and she wiped them away with her forefinger as she tried to think of something to say in reply, but as his eyes held her gaze all her mind would give her were two lines from Sep's little black book:

Thy friendship oft has made me heart to ache:
Do be me enemy—for friendship's sake.

Her lips must have moved with the lines for he asked quietly, 'What is it? What were you going to say?'

She shook her head, blinked and gave a little smile. 'Nothing; it was only something daft in me mind.'

'There could never be anything daft in your mind,

Emily. Tell me, what were you going to say?'

Intuitively she realized that he hoped for something to match what he had just said to her, but how could she say anything like that to him at this time ... or at any other time, if she didn't want trouble—that particular kind of trouble that ruined girls like her? So, her head a little to one side, a slightly derisive smile on her lips, she said, 'It was a couple of lines that came into me head.'

'Yes?'

'Oh, they mean nothing, they're odd, they go:

> Thy friendship oft has made me heart to ache:
> Do be me enemy—for friendship's sake.'

'Emily! Emily!' His eyes were closed while his expression showed some slight amazement. He was shaking his head in a downward sweeping movement now as he said, 'You know you're full of surprises, you have been from the minute I clapped eyes on you. Where did you learn that?'

'Oh, I've got a little book; it's got lots of things in like that.'

'And you read them? Of course, you do. What I mean is, do you like reading lines like that?'

She considered a moment before saying, 'Aye, yes, 'cos there's bits in that book that seem to answer questions that I have in me head.'

'Where did you get it, the book?'

'Sep gave it to me.'

'Sep?'

'Yes, Mr McGillby that was; he asked me to call him Sep.' She lowered her head. 'We ... we were going to be married once I'd reached seventeen.'

There was a silence in the room now. She watched him remove his hand from hers and turn his body towards the fire again, and his voice was low in his throat as he said,

'You're the kind of girl, Emily, that men will always want, marrying or not.... You know that, don't you?'

No, she didn't know that. She knew she was a bit bonny, but she had never considered herself the kind of girl that men would break their necks over, because she had never had big ideas about herself.

He was still looking into the fire as he said, 'You want to be careful before you marry anyone, Emily, anyone, because no marriage is made in Heaven as they would have you believe. The most of them are sheer hell. And you've had some outside experience of that over the past year; which brings us back to the point where we began. What will they do to me next week?'

He now turned towards her again, adding, 'We must talk further about this, Emily, because if I ... I'm put away I'd want you to stay on here and see to things for me, because you're the only one I can trust.... But we'll talk about it later. Go on'—he pushed her gently—'get your things off and get something to eat. You look frozen.'

They exchanged a long, deep look; then she turned from him and went hurriedly out.

As she entered the kitchen she saw George leaving by the back door and heard Mrs Riley shout, 'Hold your hand a minute! Here she is,' and he turned back and came towards her, saying, 'I ... I popped over, I'd ... I'd like a word with you, Emily, because ... because things didn't look as if they had gone right.'

'No, they haven't gone right, George. What is it?'

He now cast a glance towards Mrs Riley, and she cried at him, 'Oh! if you want rid of me you've only got to say it with a look. A nod's as good as a wink to a blind donkey. Anyway, I was just upon me road out.' She turned her glance now on Emily and, jerking her head towards the ceiling, asked, 'Will I do the room up above yet?' and Emily replied, 'No, not yet, Mrs Riley. Just leave it.'

'Well, there's plenty of other things to be bottomed.' And on this she shambled from the room.

Turning now to Emily, George rasped the palms of his hands together before he said, 'I feel I should speak out about this now. I've never spoken about it afore in case I was thought to be daft or, truth to tell, that I might get the push, but ... but ... well, it's my idea that the boss is right, he did find her by the fender, 'cos if I'm to believe me eyes she could walk. Aye, yes, she could walk.'

Her mouth fell open, her eyes widened. 'What you sayin', George?'

He now leant towards her and, his voice low, he said, 'Just what I said, she could walk.' He nodded his head. 'It was like this. The first week I was here Rosie was off colour, her bags all swollen an' that. I heard her mooing, and I thought it was either Betsy going for her, 'cos they never got on those two, or she was rubbing her bag and it was giving her gip, so up I got. The moon was shining, it was a nice night, and when I got across to the byres sure enough it was her bag that was the trouble. Well, after I'd seen to her I came out into the yard an' all sleep had gone from me, and there was the moon bright and bonny and the clouds scudding across the sky. It was one of those rare nights, so I strolled to the arch, and it was in me mind to dander on into the top field when I was pulled to a stop and me breath shot up through me throat into me nose and nearly choked me 'cos as sure as I'm standing here, Emily, I was positive I was seeing a ghost in the wall above this very kitchen window. It's a fact.' He nodded at her, and she whispered, 'Well, go on, man.'

'Well, I screwed up me eyes and peered at it. I couldn't have run not to save me life, I was too stiff with fright, I'm tellin' you. All this side of the house was mostly in shadow, the door, the kitchen window, her window above it, right to the gable end, and then I realized what I was looking at. In the shadow the glass in the window appeared as black as the wall, an' I was looking at somebody standing behind the glass, in white it was, a tall figure her hair hanging over her shoulders. I stood without moving as long as the figure did, and that was all of ten to fifteen minutes or more, and that's a long time to stand still, Emily, feeling as I did.' He drew his hand around the back of his neck. 'Can you imagine how I felt? I was positive I had seen somebody standing at that window, a woman, a tallish woman, but from what I understood the only other woman in the house besides yourself was the mistress and she was paralysed and had never walked for years; so I ask you, if I had opened me mouth what would have happened? I'd have likely got the push. Anyway, I thought to meself, well, if she can walk like that he must know all about it, I mean the boss, an' for some reason he's keeping mum. I was for speakin' of it to the old man; but then I guessed what he would have said if I did.... Sit down'—he put out his hand and took Emily by the arm—'you look as white as a sheet.'

And she felt as white as a sheet, but strangely not at the moment with relief when she realized that George's evidence might help the master, but with a surge of anger that was now tearing through her. Not until this instant had she really believed that the mistress could have taken a step out of that bed; now she did believe it, and what was making her rage inwardly was the thought of the times that the dirty bitch—for that's all she was—had done her business in the bed pretending she had no power to hold it, while all the time she had been able to move those legs. How many times had her stomach heaved during the past year, and she'd had to fly along to the day closet and retch the smell out of her being! ... Oh, she was glad she was dead, she was. She had been a bad woman all along, wicked, nasty, vile. And now George would swear that he had seen her at the window. She looked at him again and asked, 'Was it only the once you saw her?'

'No ... no.' He shook his head and each movement had a definite emphasis to it. 'I had to prove to meself that I wasn't just seein' things, or goin' round the bend; and so I got up the next night, and there she was again. But the third night it was raining whole water and although I stood under the arch I couldn't see her. But I've seen her twice since, and it was both on moonlight nights. The moon wasn't bright like it was that first time, it was on the wane, but nevertheless it was light enough for me to see her standing there, and also to see her turn about and move away from the window.'

'Why didn't you come and tell the master this afore?'

'Well'—he now half hung his head—'I was in a bit of a stew; I didn't know what to do for he was supposed not to know that she could move from the bed. I thought this was a bit odd—he was her husband, he could go in and out of the room when he liked.'

'No, he couldn't, George. She had a way of locking the door; she could push a bar across it from where she was sitting in the bed. The head of her bed was next to the door.'

'Well, I never! But, you see, I thought there was something fishy an' I kept tellin' meself to keep me mouth closed because I wanted to stay on here—it's the best job I've had in many a long day an' I'm sick of the road—so you see how I was placed.'

'Aye, yes, George; I see how you are placed. But now, you go in there and tell him exactly what you've told me; it'll make all the difference, I'm sure. But mind, you'll likely have to go to court to speak, you know.'

'Oh, I don't mind that. The only thing is they might say I was just makin' it up 'cos it'll only be my word, for nobody else, I don't suppose, has ever seen her walk. You haven't?'

'No, not me, George. No'—her voice held a deep note of bitterness—'No, I certainly never saw her walk.' She now rose from the chair, saying, 'Come along, I'll take you in.'

It was an hour later when Larry, having changed into his working clothes, came through the kitchen. He stopped by the table and, without any preamble, said, 'It was good of him to come forward, but I doubt if they'll take any notice of him on his own.'

'There is somebody, if he had a mind, I'm sure could bear out what he said.'

'Abbie?'

'Yes, Abbie.'

He gave a short laugh and half turned towards the door, saying, 'And do you think that if one word could save me neck he would speak it? No; Abbie would see me swing first. He's enjoying the situation at this moment. Do you know something?' He turned his head towards her again. 'I saw him standing in the arch when we rode in. He looked a disappointed man for he was hoping they'd stick me behind bars straightaway.'

'Oh no!'

'Oh yes, Emily; you know I'm speaking the truth.' He thrust out his lips, nodded, then went out.

From the window, she watched him crossing the yard. There was a stoop to his shoulders and her heart ached at the sight, for he had always held himself so straight, too straight for naturalness she had sometimes thought, and as he disappeared through the arch she whispered to herself, 'What'll I do if they send him along the line?' And the answer came: 'Wait until he comes out.'

It was the following morning at eleven o'clock when the knock came on the back door. There was a high wind

blowing and Emily didn't take any notice of the first
knock, thinking it was the sneck rattling, but when the
knocking became louder she went to the door, opened it,
and then said, 'Oh! ... Why! hello!'

'Hello. Can I come in?'

'Oh aye, yes, come on in.' Emily pulled the door wide,
then banged it closed on the girl who was walking before
her into the kitchen, into the kitchen in which she had
worked for three years.

'Sit down. Sit down, won't you? I'll get you a cup of tea;
it's an awful wind, it chews you, doesn't it? Would you
like something to eat? Have you come far?' She was gab-
bling and she didn't exactly know why except she'd got a
gliff to see the girl standing there.

Chrissey sat down, and she looked around the kitchen
before making any answer. 'Aye, I could do with a cup of
tea,' she said.

As she thrust the kettle into the heart of the fire Emily
said, 'Have ... have you come after a job?'

'A job? *No! No!* Why, I wouldn't work in this house
again if I was paid with gold dust.'

Emily straightened her back and turned about and
stared at the girl, and her expression was demanding,
'Well then, why have you come?'

'Is he around?'

'You mean the master?'

'Aye, who else?'

'He's over at the farm.'

'Well, tell him I'm here and I've got somethin' to say to
him, somethin' to tell him.'

'Yes, yes, all right.' Emily turned about and only just
managed to stop herself from flying from the kitchen. She
must show a little dignity in front of this girl whose place
she had taken, and not act like a brainless numskull, as
she felt inclined to do with the excitement in her, because she knew there could be only one reason for the girl

coming here this morning, and that was to help him in some way.

But having passed through the arch she did run. Lifting her skirt and petticoats, she jumped the gutter that ran down the middle of the yard, looked in the byres, then the barn, where Abbie turned to her and said, 'What is it?' Ignoring him, she ran on and into the harness room. And there he was, and she grabbed at his arm as she spluttered, 'It's Chrissey ... you know, Chrissey who worked here. She's come; she wants to see you about something.'

'Chrissey?'

'Aye, yes, you know, Chrissey. She hasn't come lookin' for work. She said she wouldn't work. . . . Well . . . I mean, I think she's come to tell you something, I feel it. Come on. Come on.' She tugged at his arm as she would have done if he had been George, and then they were both hurrying side by side across the yard and through the arch.

When they arrived in the kitchen Chrissey got to her feet, and Larry, walking to the table, looked across at her and said pleasantly, 'Hello, Chrissey.'

'Hello ... sir.'

'Have you had a drink?'

Chrissey turned her head and looked towards the stove, saying, 'I'm about to.' Then wetting her lips, she went on, 'I ... I saw the papers last night, and me ma and da thought I should come an' see you an' tell you somethin'.'

'Yes, Chrissey?' He pointed to the chair again. 'Sit down. Sit down.'

When she had seated herself he, too, sat down and, putting his forearms on the table, leaned towards her, saying, 'Go on.'

'Well, it's like this.' Chrissey didn't look at him but her eyes moved about the room as she began to talk. 'You know how feared I was an' upset about things towards

the last? Well ... well there was a reason for it. The first
time it happened, 'twas ... 'twas a long time ago. It was
during the time you were heavy on the booze an' ... an' I
was sleepin' in, an' me ma was sleepin' out. Remember?
Well, I had the toothache and I came downstairs. I could
hear you snorin' afore I reached the foot, I was in me
stockinged feet and I made no noise. I hadn't brought the
candle because I knew there'd be a glimmer, as there
always was from the lamp at the top of the stairhead.
Well, I'd just reached the bottom step when I saw it. It
was a ghost, a tall ghost. It was bent forward as if leanin'
on something, an' it walked right through the mistress's
door, at least that's what I thought. I ... I must have
passed out with fright because when I came to I was
sittin' with me back propped against the foot of the stairs
an' me head leaning sideways on me arm, just as if I'd
slid down. I ... I didn't tell anybody 'cos ... 'cos they'd
say I was makin' it up, not even me ma, but as you might
remember I was off sick with diarrhoea for a week.'

She now gulped in her throat and wet her lips.

Without taking her eyes from her, Emily turned to the
stove and, taking the boiling kettle, mashed the tea, and
when she brought it to the table Chrissey was talking
again.

'The next time was on Fellburn Fair Day. You had
been out all day and when you came back you had a load
on, and not being satisfied you had some more. Then you
came upstairs singin', and you went into the mistress's
room. You were bawling at the top of your voice bar
songs an' the like, and she screamed at you. Then she
shouted for me and told me to put you in your room and
to lock the door an' bring her the key. And I did. But I
didn't go upstairs to bed 'cos you were carryin' on so
much I knew I would never get to sleep.... I sat in the
kitchen here with me head on me arms an' I fell asleep;
an' when I woke up it was nigh on two o'clock in the

mornin', so I tiptoed out and up the stairs. Me eyes were still full of sleep. And then just as I was nearin' the landing I saw it again, the ghost as I thought. It was standin' outside your door.' She now nodded slowly at Larry, and as he looked at her his head moved slightly back on to his shoulders and his mouth fell open before he said, 'Go on.'

'Well, it was bent over two sticks; but it was the sticks that showed me it was no ghost 'cos one was longer than the other. One was the one with the rubber end an' the shepherd's crook handle that she used for banging on the floor when I didn't answer the bell quick enough; the other was a slat of ordinary wood. I didn't recognize then what this was in the dim light, but I recognized it the next mornin' all right; it was one of the slats from out of the back rest. You know, they slide in and out.... Well, I stood there petrified. I was more frightened then when I knew it wasn't a ghost an' ... an' it was her. I ... I saw her trying to support herself against the wall with one arm. I think she was aiming to open your door with the key but she couldn't do it, an' she turned round and came back towards her own door. She seemed to float. She was bent over to the side but still she seemed to float.'

'Drink your tea, Chrissey.' His voice was deep and soft as he put out his hand and pushed the cup towards her.

She drank the cupful without taking breath, and then he said, 'I'm not going to ask you why you didn't mention this a long time ago, because I know that if you had no one would have believed you.'

'No ... that's it, you're right, nobody would've believed me; in fact, 'cos of the way I acted me ma thought I was goin' wrong in the head. You see, you know yourself, sir, she couldn't move in bed, at least so she made out. An' then there was the doctor givin' me instructions what to do and what not to do to make her comfortable.'

'Was that the last time you saw her up?'

'No, no. That last time was the night afore I walked out, or ran out. You know, she had the keyhole bunged up so you couldn't look in; and now I knew why she barred her door. To keep her privacy or some such, she used to say. But this day when it was barred, I heard a shuffling noise just beyond the door and so I got flat on the floor and lay on the side of me face. I knew I wouldn't be able to see far into the room but I was sure there was a pair of feet moving close to that door, an' sure enough I saw the side of her foot. I wouldn't have been able to make it out if it hadn't moved an' in its place came a bit more light; but then, with lying so near the floor, the dust must have got up me nose 'cos I sneezed.'

She now looked from Larry to Emily, and it was to Emily she said, 'I was petrified to go in with her meal that night, but when I did, do you know what she said?' She now turned her eyes towards Larry. 'She just looked at me straight in the face, sir, and she said, "They lock up mad people." Aye, she did; that's what she said. And I knew she was tellin' me that if I opened me mouth people would say I'd lost me mind. It was as plain as if she had put it into words. I couldn't stand any more. Even me ma, when I told her, would hardly believe me. An' then me da said to keep me mouth shut because people like her could have you up, and if you weren't put away you could go along the line for defaming them.'

'Oh! Chrissey.' He put out his hand and took hers and shook it up and down. 'Thank you for coming. Thank you, thank you. Now will you be prepared to repeat all you've said in court? And listen'—he wagged her hand again within his—'you're not the only one who saw her. George did, the new hand. He saw her up at the window two or three times, but like you he thought it wiser to say nothing. It's funny'—he now glanced up at Emily—'it was a thing I never even dreamed of. She looked so helpless and she acted so helpless, except with her tongue.

Oo ... h!' He rose abruptly to his feet and walked round the table and then towards the fireplace, where, turning and standing with his back to it, he raised his arms upwards and exclaimed, 'I'll never again know relief like I do at this moment.' Then as if realizing what he must do, he took three strides towards Chrissey, grabbed her arm and said, 'Come on; I'll get Archer and we'll go in right away and tell the authorities.'

'But I've got to go back to me job.'

'Never mind about that, I'll make it up to you, doubly, trebly. Come on.'

Emily was again standing at the window, laughing now as she watched them running across the courtyard hand in hand. They looked funny. The laughter welled in her, she laughed out loud; she laughed as she hadn't done for months. Swinging round from the window, she picked up the sides of her wide serge skirt and whirled round the kitchen table, until she collapsed on to the settle, still laughing. It was over. It was over. Everything from now on would be marvellous. The house would become happy. She would open all the windows and let great draughts of air blow out the stench of that woman, the evil stench of her, then with the help of Mrs Riley she would spring-clean from top to bottom. Yes, autumn or no autumn she would spring-clean.

And what about the situation?

What situation? She was no longer laughing as she asked herself the question. Aw. She got to her feet now and, lifting up the teapot from the hob again, she carried it to the table and as she poured herself out a cup of tea she told herself to stop beating about the bush. He liked her, he more than liked her. She could see it in his eyes. And she ... well, she had grown fond of him, more than fond.

As much as she had liked Sep the thought of marriage to him had been distasteful to her; but not this time; not to this man. No; this time the thought of marriage was filling her brain and body with a whirlwind of excitement.

Don't be daft.

She was standing now with her hands flat on the table, her arms stiff and her body bent over them.

He won't marry you.

It was as if her sensible grown-up self was admonishing the romantic girl who still resided somewhere within her. You can argue as much as you like that he's not a gentleman born, but he's master now of a gentleman's house, and the land and farm. And people have short memories; they'll now recognize that he's the boss, whereas all the while she was alive they looked upon him as a hired man. But now he'll get out and about, an' the women, who have the shortest memories of all, they'll be after him.

What about Mrs Rowan's daughter?

Aye, what about her? She'd likely come running now. And what if he were to meet her half-way?

She straightened her back. What would she do if that happened? She'd go. Oh aye, she'd pack up her bags and walk out, for such was the feeling within her that she couldn't stay in this house now with him if he took another woman to be its mistress.

FOUR

He was acting like a man who had suddenly and surprisingly come into his inheritance; he was young again; he looked handsome and full of vital life. Last night, in this very kitchen, he had taken her by the shoulders and there was a suspicion of moisture in his eyes as he had cried, 'Emily! Emily! I'm free. Do you understand that? I'm a free man. I can roam the world, jump over the moon if I like, or just stay here ... here, which is now home, and enjoy it all. Oh! Emily.' He had shaken her vigorously twice, and when her cap bobbed on the back of her head she had put up her hands to it and laughed with him as she said, 'Well, you can leave me cap, I'll be needing it.'

She hadn't intended the remark as a cue, but she saw immediately that it could be such. And his answer to it could have been to rip it off her head and say, 'You'll never need that again in your life, Emily, not as long as I'm alive....' Sep would have done just that, but her master didn't. What he did was to turn from her and walk up and down the kitchen, all the while speaking of his plans.

Abbie was to go. Well, she knew he would do this but she was sure he wouldn't send him out empty-handed. Then he was going to negotiate for the spare land that ran down to Wilber's Brook, and that was almost a third of a mile away. He was going to extend the byres and enlarge the herd with Galloways which sounded more like pit ponies to her than cows, because that's what they called the horses down the pit. And he wasn't going to forget about inside the house. He had overruled her idea of spring-cleaning by declaring he was going to have the whole place redecorated right from the top to the bottom. And lastly, he was going to get her a modern kitchen range with dampers, and ash box an' all.

At eleven o'clock last night she had left him here in the kitchen still planning what he was going to do.

Having said, 'Well, I'm off to bed, else I'll fall asleep on me feet,' she had stood for a moment longer by the dresser looking at him; and he had risen from the table and come towards her and, touching her cheek with his fingers and smiling softly at her, had said, 'Good-night, Emily. A new day 'll begin tomorrow ... or the next day.'

She had blinked at him, nodded and turned away. It had sounded a sort of promise, for tomorrow was to be the day of the funeral, and the following day they would really start a new life. But would they? She was still uncertain in her mind of what that life might hold for her.

And now she was waiting for them to return from the funeral. The table in the dining-room was laden with food. 'Make a good spread, Emily,' he had said. 'There'll be only six of us, but make a good spread.' Besides himself, there were Mr and Mrs Rowan and their daughter, and the solicitor and his clerk.

She glanced at the wall clock. If she reckoned the time right she had about fifteen minutes in which to change her frock and apron and make herself decent.

Today was the day of the funeral, and as he had said yet again this morning, tomorrow would be the beginning of the new life. Standing before her in his handsome new black suit, he had looked deep into her eyes as he said quietly, 'I'm not going to be a hypocrite, Emily; I'm

so full of joy at this moment I could sing. You understand, don't you? Yes, of course, you do.' He had cupped
her cheek with his hand and it was then he had said
again, 'Tomorrow begins a new life for all of us.'

As she ran up the stairs she had a desire to burst into
song, but she checked it. In her room, she took off her
thick serge skirt and striped blouse and got into a print
dress. It wasn't very warm but it looked smart. She pulled
the straps of her wide-bibbed apron over her shoulders,
crossed them at the back and buttoned them to the
waistband, then she picked up her mob-cap and looked at
it. She wished she hadn't to put it on again, it covered
most of her hair; and anyway, mob-caps were old-fashioned. Her hair looked bonny this morning. She had
washed it last night and the deep waves had bright
brown lights in them which the mirror reflected back to
her. It seemed to heighten the colour of her skin, and to
make her lips look redder and her eyes darker, almost
like the colour of the hair itself; but the white mob-cap,
she considered, caused her skin to appear pasty.

Reluctantly, she pulled the cap on to her head, peered
at herself once more in the mirror, opened her lips wide
to see that there were no pieces of food adhering to her
teeth, for since scrubbing them with soot and salt as she
did every morning, she had eaten her breakfast. Then she
went from the room and almost skipped down the attic
stairs, across the landing, and down the main staircase.

Coming to the foot of the stairs, she paused for a
moment and looked around the hall. It was a beautiful
place, she'd never before really looked at it like this; but
then she'd never had time to breathe before, had she?

As the big black kettle spluttered in the heart of the
fire she heard the carriages rolling on to the drive and she
pulled it quickly on to the hob, smoothed down her
apron, adjusted the two truant strands of hair behind her
ears, then ran from the kitchen to the front door.

When she opened the door Mrs Rowan and her daughter were just stepping from the first carriage; Mr Rowan followed; the master was already on the gravel holding the carriage door ajar.

From the other carriage two men alighted. One was a stocky man in his fifties, the other a younger man, thin, with slightly stooped shoulders.

The two women were the first to enter the house; and she noted that Mrs Rowan's daughter was now taking stock of her, staring into her face as if she were weighing her up.

Emily, in turn, merely glanced at the woman, but even so she could tell she was her father's daughter.

When Larry went to help her off with her coat and she said, 'I'll keep it on, we won't be able to stay long,' her voice sounded ordinary, even coarse. Then turning about, she looked at Emily yet again before leading the way towards the dining-room as if she were already in charge, already the mistress.

Larry came into the kitchen. The cold air had whipped colour into his cheeks; his eyes were bright. He looked excited, but under the circumstances was doing his best to subdue it, at least for the moment; but she could imagine that once the house was clear and the will business over, he'd whoop round the place like a dray horse let loose in a field.

'They won't want tea,' he said, looking towards the spluttering kettle and the teapot; 'just serve the soup. The men are having spirits, the ladies wine.'

She said nothing but she thought it a funny arrangement. They could have spirits and wine at a funeral in Shields too, but it was always accompanied by tea.

'You did make soup, didn't you?'

'Aye, yes; it's on the side hob.' She nodded to the big black pan. 'I can bring it to the boil in a minute.'

'Good.'

Once again he put out his hand and touched her cheek and they smiled at each other. But even as they did so she was still seeing Miss Lizzie Rowan marching towards the dining-room ahead of the others.

The meal was over, the Rowans were just going. George had brought their trap from the stables to the front door; Emily had handed Mr Rowan his hat and coat, and the man had not even said 'Thank you'. But what he did do before going out of the door was to turn and look slowly around the hall before his head made two almost imperceptible nodding motions as if he were giving himself a satisfactory answer to something. Mrs Rowan had smiled at her and said, 'It was a good meal, girl.' And it seemed to Emily that the little woman had laid emphasis on the word girl, conveying not the idea of youth, but of maid or servant.

Then Larry emerged from the dining-room accompanied by Miss Lizzie Rowan. He was smiling at her, and taking her arm at the door, he guided her across the gravel to the trap. Perhaps it was because the wind was still blowing ... and perhaps it wasn't. Then when she was seated he looked up at her and said something. But it was lost on Emily, as also was her answer. But when Mrs Rowan cried, 'We'll be expecting you,' her words were loud and clear; and as the trap moved off he raised his hand and nodded as if in acceptance.

The solicitor and his clerk now came out of the dining-room and she turned to them and said, 'Will you come this way, please?' and as they entered the drawing-room Larry banged the front door closed behind him and hurried across the hall. At the drawing-room door he stopped to allow Emily to pass out of the room, but he didn't look at her; and when he shut the door behind her he banged this one too.

She stood and looked at the door for a moment. If he

didn't give rein in some way to his excitement he would burst. He looked as if he was about to take off into the air. It wasn't, she thought, quite seemly, not gentlemanly like. Granted the missis had been a wicked woman, but a gentleman, a real gentleman, would have hidden his feelings; at least until tomorrow. Oh! why did she keep yarping on about him not being a gentleman? Her way of reasoning was stupid, for the one thing she should be thankful for at this moment was that he could lay no claim to being a gentleman because, if he was, her chances of staying on here would be slim, wouldn't they?

She was about to pass the front door when she stopped and she saw beyond it the picture of him looking up at Miss Lizzie Rowan; but more vividly did she see the picture of Miss Lizzie Rowan looking down at him. Slowly, she walked on into the kitchen. And now her mind dwelt on the fact that it was strange but only once had he mentioned Miss Lizzie Rowan's name to her, and that was last night here in the kitchen when he was telling her how many to lay for the funeral tea. She remembered now that he was looking into her face as he said, 'She's a fine woman, you would like her, Emily. And she can run a farm as good as any man, and better than some.' But she hadn't read anything into the words then, for he had immediately touched her chin gently with his fingers....

She had just finished clearing the dining-room table. She had the last tray of dishes in her hands and was thrusting her buttocks out against the kitchen door when the drawing-room door opened and the thin clerk came hurrying towards her. He put out his hand and pushed the kitchen door wide to allow her to pass through before saying hurriedly, 'Would you go and tell the farm hand, Mr Abel Reading, to come please?'

'Abbie?' She put the tray on the table and turned to him.

'Yes.'

She did not go immediately to do his bidding, for she was wondering why the master himself hadn't called her to tell her to fetch Abbie, but she supposed it was all right, clerks were for doing this kind of thing.

'All right.' She turned from him, grabbed a shawl from the back of the door, put it round her shoulders, and ran out.

She found Abbie in the harness room. He was sitting on an upturned tub before the boiler. He was looking a picture of dejection until she said to him, 'You're wanted over at the house; the solicitor's man said you're to come. They're in the drawing-room.'

'Me?' He was on his feet as if he had just been injected with life. 'The solicitor's man said I had to come?'

'Aye.'

He picked up his cap from the saddle rack, buttoned his coat, dusted down his trousers, made an effort to straighten his back, then marched out into the yard.

He went into the kitchen without wiping his feet, and she wanted to shout at him, 'Look at my floor!' but she stood watching him until he disappeared into the hall, and as she slowly pulled the shawl from her shoulders and hung it up again she thought to herself, She's left him something. . . .

It seemed that Abbie had hardly got into the room before she heard the shout. But when she glanced at the clock she knew ten minutes had passed, and during that time she had got all the dishes into the sink. She hurried up the kitchen now and opened the door and looked across the hall. There was someone shouting and she hadn't to ask who it was; it was as if he was up in the room above the kitchen again yelling at the mistress.

She sprang back and closed the door as she heard the drawing-room door burst open, and she was busying herself at the sink when Abbie entered the room again. As

305

she turned she looked at him and her hands became still in the water. As with the master, the years seemed to have dropped from him, but in a different way; his face was full of merriment, glee, like that of an imp. He came to her with a step that had a spring in it, and with his doubled-up fist he punched her on the shoulder as he cried at her, 'God's slow but He's sure! Always remember that, girl. God's slow but He's sure. How are the mighty fallen!' he said, and he meant it. 'This is the happiest day of me life, girl. This is the happiest day of me life.'

Slowly, she pulled up the hem of her coarse apron and dried her hands on it and, taking a step back from him, she said, 'What's happened?'

'He's got his deserts, that's what's happened. I've always told you, haven't I, one day he'd get his deserts? An' by God! it's come about this day. Aye, aye, it has that.'

'What's happened?'

The tone of her voice took the smile from his face, and he thrust his wrinkled countenance towards her as he cried, 'This is what's happened, lass. The missis has left me two hundred pounds. Do you hear that? Two hundred pounds! An' she's left me in charge of the whole lot. The whole lot!' He threw his arms wide.

'Left you in ... ch ... charge?' She couldn't get her words out straight. 'What do you mean? What's happened? The farm's the master's, like the rest of the place.'

'You think so? Huh! You think so? Well, I've got a surprise for you, girl. You've always been on his side, haven't you? He's had you on a string, he's used you. I've seen it all the time. If things had gone as he thought you'd have been out on your arse and Miss Lizzie Rowan would have been installed here, an' her father wouldn't have raised any objections now. Oh no, not now, not with a farm and property like this he wouldn't. When his lordship was merely a drover old Rowan kicked his backside off his place more than once, but now. . . .'

306

'Tell me what's happened.' She had him by the shoulders now and she had the desire to throw him against the wall, him and his spewing vindictiveness.

With a heave he pushed her away, and none too gently, and as she staggered backwards he said, 'Aye, I'll tell you what's happened. The mistress left everything to her husband.'

Emily was standing with her side pressed against the stone sink; one arm was gripping her waist, her other hand was across her mouth. She said nothing but she screwed up her eyes and peered at the old man and watched him toss his head from side to side, his glee evident again as he spluttered, 'Did you hear what I said? I said, left it to her husband. She was married afore. What do you think of that? It turned out that on that trip to America she married a young bloke who got himself jailed for ten years for killin' another fellow. He would have got life but it came out he was defending his wife. It's all there signed and sealed, marriage certificate, newspapers about the case an' all, the lot. And I'll tell you something else, lass.' He was now stabbing his finger at her. 'Those headlines in those papers 'll mean nothing to the headlines here when this gets about.' He paused and stared into 'mily's gaping face, then went on, 'By! how she must have hated him all these years, practically from the start. An' she was clever ... cute. Aye, she was that, for what does she do but go to another solicitor an' get a will made, an' gives her name as Mrs Stuart, as it legally was, an' then seals it an' delivers it to her own family solicitor with the instructions that it's not to be opened till she dies. That was thinking ahead, wasn't it? By! they'll have a bonfire in the village when they get wind of this. Aye, they will that. An' I'll be the first to put a light to it.'

'You're a vindictive swine! That's what you are, Abbie Reading; you're as cruel as she was. And ... and I don't

307

believe a word you say. It couldn't happen.'

'What you mean to say, lass, is, you wish it couldn't 'cos you had your eye on him, hadn't you? But let me tell you, you hadn't a chance in hell, hinny. You hadn't a chance in hell. Warm his bed ... oh aye, aye, he would have used you for that, but make you mistress of this place? Huh! huh! you couldn't have really thought he would have been as daft as that, or as decent.' His eyes narrowed and his lip stuck out as he repeated, 'Or as decent. No, not him, because, lass, at rock bottom he's a swine. All right, you can say it as well as look it, I'm a swine an' all, but I'm out in the open an' I keep me place, I've never aimed to be above meself. But him. My God when I think of how he came here beggin' for work, just like Georgie back there'—he thumbed over his shoulder —'and how he toadied and sucked up to her, how he worked her up, tempted her with his manhood. Aw, the things I saw. She would have been happy to have had him up in the loft, but no, he made her pay the price for her satisfaction. An' the price, as he saw it, was this house and farm.... But oh, isn't God just, eh, lass? Isn't He just? ... Aye, I would sit down.' He nodded at her now. 'It caused him to sit down, too, after he had almost throttled the solicitor man. The way he got up from the chair and bounced at the fellow, a spring-heel Jack couldn't have been quicker. A week she's given him to get out of the place, a week. An' what else? As much as he can get on a flat cart. Ha! ha! God! that I should live to see this day.'

When the old man's head went back she jumped to her feet and screamed at him, 'Get out! And I hope a flat cart goes over you, an' not a small one. Go on!' She advanced on him, and such was her attitude that he backed from her, but slowly, his face grim now, and when he was standing in the open doorway he jerked his head sharply towards her, saying, 'And you ... you want to mind your place, 'cos I'm in charge now, don't forget, until the rightful owner comes. I can put you out on the road.'

'You won't put me out on any road; I wouldn't stay here and work under you, not for a pound a day I wouldn't, you wicked old swine you.' When she banged the door in his face she heard him stumble back and gasp, and the last words he yelled at her were a mouthful of obscenities.

She now leant against the back door and stared down the kitchen. It wasn't possible; she couldn't have been that bad. *'I'll have the last laugh on you.'* She could hear her voice. How many times had she heard her say that to him, I'll have the last laugh on you? And now she could actually hear her laughing. She put her hands over her ears and ran towards the fire and sat down on the settle. What would he do? What would become of him? It was enough to drive him mad.

When the kitchen door opened she jerked her head around. It was the clerk again. He came down the room towards her, saying, 'We're leaving now but ... but we'll be back tomorrow.' His voice was low, his words slow as if he were talking to someone just bereaved.

She looked up at him and said, 'It can't be true.... Is it?'

'The old man told you?'

'Yes.'

'I'm ... I'm afraid it is.'

'And ... and he can't claim anything?'

'Nothing; only what was left to him in the will. His wife, or the deceased, said he'll be allowed to take as much as he could get on to a dray to furnish his home.... Has he another house?'

'A little two-roomed cottage up in the hills.'

'Dear, dear. It's a most strange case. I don't think I've ever come across a stranger.'

'How ... how's he taken it?'

'He's very distraught. That's what I came to say to you. I think someone should be with him until he recovers.'

'Yes'—she pulled herself to her feet—'Yes, I understand. Hasn't ... hasn't she left him any money at all?'

'A small wage that she would have paid a farm boy. The rest, everything goes to her legal husband.'

'Could ... could he protest, I mean take it to court?'

'He could, but it would take time and cost a great deal of money should he lose the case, and if he hasn't any money'—He spread out his hands and his coat sleeves slid up his arms, and she saw that his white cuffs were false and attached to a blue striped shirt like a working man's and the front of his shirt was covered by a white dicky. 'It's very sad,' he finished. 'And I'm sorry for him.'

'When ... when will the other man be coming?'

'We're not quite sure, we have to go into it.' He smiled weakly at her. 'If the man has been of good conduct he may have been allowed out before he has served his full term of imprisonment. There's a lot to go into.'

She nodded mutely at him and he said kindly, 'Good-day to you,' and she answered, 'Good-day.'

He had turned and was walking up the kitchen again when he stopped and said, 'I was on my way to tell the groom we're ready,' and at this she pointed to the back door, saying slowly, 'Straight through the arch.'

She didn't move from the kitchen until she heard the wheels of the carriage going across the gravel drive, and then in actual fear of what she would find she went out of the kitchen, across the hall and towards the drawing-room.

After tapping gently on the door and receiving no answer, she pushed it slowly open. He was sitting in the chair hunched forward, his joined hands extended towards the fire; he didn't move, even when she was standing by his side.

She became as still as him in the silence that pervaded the room. So motionless were they, they could both have been frozen in death. But they weren't dead, they were alive, and she knew she would scream if she didn't break this awe-filled quiet.

Her mouth was opening to speak when he turned to her and there was only one word to describe his look and that was ferocious, and it was intensified when he spoke because his words were growled out through clenched teeth. 'Don't smile,' he said; 'don't say you're sorry; and don't ... don't for Christ's sake come out with any of your pet wisdoms such as never say die.' He now tore his locked hands apart and his fists, doubled up until the knuckles showed like bare bones through the skin, banged down violently on to the arms of the chair.

She was staggered by his attitude which was in the nature of an attack. When she entered the room she had seen herself putting her arms about him and drawing his head to her breast and telling him that he wasn't alone, that she would stay with him, go wherever he went, look after him, help him, and that if he put a brave face on things he would come out on top. In short, she would have said the words that he had dared her to repeat.

In actual fear now, she stared into his face. It was unrecognizable. She had seen him in all kinds of moods. She had seen him come raging down the stairs from the room above the kitchen; she had seen him surly; she had seen him brought low with weeping; and as excited as a schoolboy; but never had she seen him look like this. He looked mad. And she was now made to think he had gone clean mad for, suddenly springing up from the chair, he dashed around the room kicking at one piece of furniture after the other, chairs, settee, little tables. When he reached the end of the room he picked up a porcelain vase that was standing on top of a narrow china cabinet placed between the two tall windows and, lifting it above his head, he turned and hurled it against the wall. As the pieces splayed across the room she cried out, 'Don't! Don't do that! That won't get you anywhere. If you start breaking things up they might even make you pay for them.'

She stood, her mouth agape, fearing again what his reaction might be. She watched him become still, then turn slowly and look at her and now say grimly, 'Yes, they might even do that an' all, they might make me pay for it out of me wages. Do you know what she left me for wages, eh? What she would have paid a boy, six shillings a week. Why, before I married her she paid me fifteen shillings a week.... Married, did I say?' He kicked the base of the broken vase towards the fireplace, yelling as he did so, 'She committed suicide. She planned it. She did it on purpose just to bring me down. I hope she rots in hell for ever and a day. The bitch! The dirty, stinking bitch!'

'Don't say that 'cos curses come home to roost.' Her voice was merely a protesting whisper, but it seemed to infuriate him further.

'What do you know about it? In fact, what do you know about anything?' He came at her now as if he were about to strike her, but she didn't back from him. For some reason, perhaps because of his last denigrating words, the fear had gone from her; in fact she was feeling defiant, even aggressive. Although she realized he had experienced a great shock, his reaction to it had diminished her pity. What she couldn't explain to herself was the fact that her own reactions were caused mainly by witnessing his reverting to type, for at this moment she was seeing him as a farm labourer, a drover, not the man who had acted as master of this place for eight years.

She glared back into his face as she cried at him, 'What you goin' on about anyway? It isn't the end of the world;

you've still got a pair of hands on you. You can use them; other's have had to. . . .'

His face looked aflame, even his eyes appeared red, and the saliva ran out of the side of his mouth as he cried, 'Who do you think you're talking to? Get out! Get out!' He thrust his finger towards the door. 'By God! it hasn't taken you long to sum things up. Jack's as good as his master now, is he? And look here, me lady, if you think I'll marry you because I'm finished, you've got another think coming. I'll never marry you or anyone else as long as I live. So get out afore I say something I shouldn't.'

'You've already done that.' Bitterly she held his glance for a moment longer, then turned from him and marched from the room. She didn't run, nor did she make for the kitchen now, but she went upstairs, across the landing and up into the attic room. Nor did she fling herself on to the bed and burst into tears; she was too angry, tears were for later.

She stood at the small window, her arms folded tightly under her breasts. The night was spreading over the land, and in the far distance she could still see the spire of the village church. She pictured the village street to-morrow morning, or even tonight if Abbie should get that far; they'd all be dancing jigs in The Running Fox. And when she came to think of it, could she blame them? They knew him for what he was, an upstart who had married the mistress of this house for her possessions; and when he had been lifted from the gutter as it were to the level of the gentry he must have played the great I am for them to hate him as they did. And now she herself hated him.

Shivering, she turned from the window and went to the cupboard, took down her coat and put it on, then went and sat on the edge of the bed. What was she going to do? She could walk out, she wasn't penniless, she had more than twenty pounds altogether saved up. She could, if she liked, go all the way down to the place where Lucy was and look for a position there. Yes, she could do that, and she would, and before Abbie got the chance to give her her marching orders.

FIVE

For two days and two nights he had drunk himself silly and now he was lying in a stupor on the couch in the library.

She had seen her father drunk, but he was a different kind of drinker. He would get blind drunk at night and sleep it off the next day, but him, as in her mind she now thought of Larry, had kept at it hour after hour, dozing off, waking up, and starting all over again. That was, until dinner-time today, when he had fallen into a deep sleep. Twice she had approached close to him because she thought he had stopped breathing. Mr Tooton told her not to worry, he knew men who drank like that. After a long sleep they would wake up and then not touch it again for some weeks. But he had no need to say that to her, she told him, because she wasn't worrying.

Mr Tooton had been in the house since yesterday. Mr Sutton had brought him back and explained the situation to her, for Mr Birch was past understanding. He said Mr Tooton would be in charge until Mr Birch left the premises, and afterwards would act as a sort of temporary bailiff until the rightful owner took over. He did not know how long this would be but he guessed from the papers available that it would be only a matter of a few months.

She had meant to be away by now; in fact she didn't know why she was still here. Last night she had cried herself to sleep, telling herself she had grown up more during the last two days than she had in the past two years, and never again would she have any girlish fancies about marrying the master of any house, gentleman or otherwise. Anyway, she must have been stupid, daft even to dream of it. Well, her head was firmly on her shoulders now, and by the end of the week her feet would be planted in the direction of that place called St Leonards. She had already written to Lucy to tell her what had happened and what the future might hold.

She liked Mr Tooton; she found him a pleasant man and, although he must be of considerable education to be a clerk to a solicitor, he was easy to talk to. She was surprised to learn that he was married and had six children; from the looks of him she had at first imagined he'd be a man who lived alone. She also observed that his clothes weren't very good; his overcoat was almost threadbare and the bottoms of his trousers were frayed.

She learned that he didn't live in Fellburn but in Newcastle, and she gleaned from his conversation that he wasn't missing his family life but was very pleased with his present situation. He enjoyed his food, always taking a second helping when she offered it; and he wasn't uppish about the company at the table for he sat side by side with Mrs Riley, and they talked together as if they'd known each other for years.

Mrs Riley's verdict about the clerk was that he was a canny man, not like some of them that worked in offices who had no tails to their shirts because they had been used for patching; these were the ones who walked over your wet floor and called you woman. Snots they were. Oh, she knew them, for there was a time when she had cleaned their offices.

Mr Tooton and Mrs Riley had finished their evening meal but over their cups of tea were still carrying on a conversation about the glaring headlines in the paper which George had brought in only an hour ago.

'Nine days' wonder.' Mrs Riley inclined her head towards Mr Tooton. 'That's what they say. An' that's what it'll be. It'll float away on the wind an' like all other nine days' wonders it'll be forgotten.'

'Perhaps you're right, Mrs Riley. Perhaps you're right. But coming on top of the extraordinary circumstances of his ... the lady's death, I don't know, I really don't know.'

Emily, carrying into the pantry a dish, with the remains of a leg of lamb on it, repeated to herself 'Float away on the wind'. Aye, but the wind would blow this nine day wonder no farther than the village and Fellburn, and it would swirl around there for years, especially if he went back to the cottage.... Where else would he go? ... to Rowan's Farm? Yes, yes, he could go there, she supposed. Anyway, she didn't much mind where he went, for as soon as he sobered up she'd tell him she was going and she wouldn't have to say, 'Thank you very much for all you've done for me', or even for what he'd done for Lucy in getting her into that hospital and paying her train fare down, for she had worked morning, noon and night in this house for the past year, and for what? She had been cook, housekeeper, maid of all work ... and nurse. Oh aye, she had done the work of a nurse; the stench of it was still in her nose. No, she had nothing to thank him for. But she'd wait until he came out of his deep sleep and get at him before he started on the bottle again. It was odd but she hadn't known he was given to drink until Chrissey mentioned it; and then she could hardly believe it because he was very sober in his drinking, if she could put it that way. But during the past two days he had given proof that Chrissey was right.

She was placing the meat dish on the marble slab when she heard the kitchen door open and then the chair legs scraping on the stone floor.

Within seconds she was back in the room and looking

to where the figure came stumbling down the room towards the table, his hand shielding his eyes.

She watched him grope for the edge of the table, steady himself, then reach out and grip the back of the chair that Mr Tooton had vacated, and with the clerk's help lower himself down, then sit silently staring at his hands lying flat and limp on his knees.

'Make some coffee, strong, black,' Mr Tooton was whispering to her. But she didn't move for she couldn't drag her eyes away from the dejected figure of the man who had once strutted like a peacock around this house and farm. Not matter what his mood, he had strutted. Nine days ago she had seen him change from the sombre, worried, always part angry master, to an individual so gay as to be unrecognizable with his former self. Then two days ago his personality had been swamped under anger so blinding as to touch almost on madness. But the man she was looking at now was a complete stranger. It wasn't that he was dishevelled, unshaven, and looked overall as if he had just awakened in a hay loft, but that he looked utterly pathetic. She sensed that he was fully awake inside himself, fully aware that he had lost everything, and there was no strength left in him. This man was incapable of fighting.

Not a word was spoken by anyone until, the coffee made, she took it to the table and silently handed it to him. She had almost to push it into his face before he raised his head, but he kept his eyes cast down as he took the cup from her.

She watched him drink the coffee, in fact they all watched him drink the coffee, and when he silently handed her back the cup she went and refilled it. He again drained it, but he didn't utter a word.

He did not hand her the cup back this time but pushed it along the table and sat looking at it. It wasn't until Mr Tooton said in a small voice, 'Well, I'll be away to my bed,' that he showed any sign of interest. And now he turned his head slowly and looked at the man; and Mr Tooton looked gently back at him and explained in the same small voice, 'I'm staying for the present on behalf of my employers.... Good-night, sir.'

When he turned away and walked up the length of the kitchen Larry's eyes followed him until the door closed behind him, then he turned his head towards the table again, but now looked at Mrs Riley who was silently gesticulating towards Emily that she, too, was on her way to bed, and what was unusual for Mrs Riley she took her departure out of the back door in silence.

Alone with him now, Emily found she couldn't bear to look at him for the sight of his dejection was so painful that it was bringing the tears to her eyes. His anger she could stand up to, his silences she had learned over the past year to ignore, but this surrender, this giving in, was as if she were witnessing him dying rapidly from a distance, for life, real life seemed to have gone from him.

She busied herself about the kitchen. She washed up the odd crockery, she laid one corner of the table for the breakfast; and in between the clatter of the dishes the clock's ticking grew louder and louder.

She was ready for bed, the fire was banked down, the kettle was pulled to the side of the hob. She had taken the tea towels from the brass rod and folded them neatly up. She had done everything she had to do, but she could not walk out of the kitchen and leave him like this.

When finally he said, 'Emily', she did not immediately turn to him but stood still. She was at the dresser, the candlestick in her hand, her back to him.

'Emily.' His voice was low and hoarse.

She turned towards him now and they stared at each other.

'I'm sorry.' He did not say for what he was sorry but she knew he was remembering clearly the incident in the

319

drawing-room. The seconds ticked away before he spoke again. 'What am I going to do, Emily?' he said.

Oh dear God! She put her hand under her breast and pressed it tightly against her ribs. How could anybody stand straight and unbending and keep remembering two nights ago when a man such as he had been was now going to pieces before her eyes.

She stretched out her hand backwards and placed the candlestick on the dresser again, but as yet she didn't move towards him, for she couldn't help remembering the look on his face when he had bawled at her, 'And look here, me lady, if you think I'll marry you because I'm finished, you've got another think coming. I'll never marry you or anyone else as long as I live.'

But would the man he now was think along the same lines? If she went with him up to that stone cottage on the windy hill, would she go as his wife or his woman?

What did it matter? She would go anyway.

She went towards him and put her arms about him and as she had done before she pressed his head into her breasts, and neither of them spoke. Her future was set.

SIX

Mr Tooton, George Archer, and Emily stood looking at the long, old dray cart, its wheels half-buried in grass where it lay in the field behind the barn, and George, glancing at Mr Tooton, said again, 'The will stated as much as he could get on the dray, you said?'

'That's right. That's right.'

'But it didn't specify like what dray?'

'No, no, it didn't. But from what I've seen of the farm implements I'm sure she meant the small dray that you use for carrying things to the market.'

'Oh aye, I won't argue with you there, she meant it to be that one all right, but she just said a dray and ... well look at that, that's a dray.'

Mr Tooton looked at the old cart, but it was Emily who asked, 'Would one horse be able to pull it if it was laden?'

'Aye, out of the gates and along the flat road. I walked along as far as the turnpike yesterday, you could get all your stuff as far as that; then it would have to be humped over the hill and along the valley and up the other side, but that won't be too much of a problem, for as soon as you got the cart outside on the road you could let the livestock off and that would make it easier for the horse.'

'The livestock?' Mr Tooton's countenance showed surprise.

George now bent towards him and his voice low, he

said, 'Aye, Mr Tooton, livestock. There was no mention of what kind of stuff had to go on the dray, was there? And they've got to survive up there; they've got to have something to start with; an' by God! he deserves that if nothin' else. Bloody crying out shame, that's my opinion of the whole affair. And I've said it afore, haven't I, Mr Tooton?'

'You have, you have indeed, you have.' Mr Tooton nodded emphatically; then he added, 'But the old man?'

'Oh, I've thought of that,' said George. 'One of your lot sent him a letter an' I had to read it to him. On Monday he has to go into Newcastle to sign some paper or other, so he'll be out of the way and the cart will be gone afore he gets back. An' if he should say anything ... well, I have me own way of dealing with the old boy. Never hit a man when he's down I told him yesterday, 'cos the tables could turn on you, an' human nature being what it is, the sympathy could go to the loser.... But'—he shook his head—'I've me doubts about it in this case.'

'Yes, and so have I, George.'

Turning to Emily, George said briskly, 'I'd get busy, Emily. Make out a list of all the things you want to set up with. There's plenty to pick from, and so if I was you I wouldn't be mean with meself. What do you say, Mr Tooton?'

Mr Tooton smiled primly and replied, 'I'm sure Emily will take nothing but what is required, and, speaking from experience, there's a great deal required when setting up house.' His smile widened and as he turned away George remarked. 'He's a bit of all right is Mr Tooton. Surprisin', when you think of it, to find somebody in his position with understandin' of a situation like this.... Well now'—he poked his head towards her—'what do you think of that idea?' He was pointing to the old dray cart, and she nodded and said, 'I think it's a grand idea, George. An' thanks, I'd never have thought of it meself.'

'Aw aye, you would; you think of most things, Emily.'
He was staring at her now, and his face took on a sombre
look as he went on, 'I'm going to miss you, the place
won't be the same without you. Do you know something,
and I'm not jokin' when I'm sayin' it, but I'd give anything to be in his shoes.'

As her eyes widened slightly he moved his head slowly
up and down, then cast his gaze to the side as he con-
fessed, 'I cottoned on to you from the start. But there it is,
you've made your choice, an' you'd made it long afore I
put in an appearance. I know that now, but I'll say this,
if ever you're in need of a friend, Emily, and I'm anywhere about, all you have to do is to shout.'

She swallowed deep in her throat and lowered her
head slightly. 'Thanks, George, I won't forget,' she said.

As she was about to turn away he said, 'Can I ask you
something?'

'Yes, anything George.'

'Is ... is he going to wed you?'

Her head did not droop now but she looked past him
as she said, 'I shouldn't think so, now or ever.'

For the next three days they walked silently side by side
up on to the hill, down into the valley and up the further
rise to the cottage. The first day she lit a fire inside and
got the thick of the dirt out of the place, then brushed
the inner walls down ready for whitewashing, while he
cleared the shippons and hung the doors back on.

It wasn't until she watched him taking a scythe to the
long grass that was reaching up to the front door that she
saw return a flicker of the man who had raged. Changing
from the slow, steady rhythm, he suddenly began to slash
at the grass as if each clump were part of a mob which he
was aiming to exterminate.

She stood to the side of the small window and watched
his progress towards the broken gate, and when he

reached it he threw down the scythe, tore up the gate from the tangle of matted bracken and flung it aside, the rotten wood, as it hit the ground, falling away quietly like so much mush. Then, as if exhausted, she watched him lean against the low stone wall, and, allowing his head to fall back between his shoulders, stand gazing up into the sky.

She could imagine him as a boy standing like that, dreaming of his future, asking the stars at night what they held for him, willing them to guide his destiny away from the restrictions that threaded his life in this two-roomed cottage, away on to a plane even beyond that of his grandfather, the small farmer; on to a plane where he could be looked up to.

This is what she had always sensed he had needed most, to be looked up to. He must have seen himself as a pattern for other men, and he must have thought that he had reached his goal when he became master of Croft Dene House and farm. It was true he had turned the farm into a pattern for other farms, but as a pattern for a man he had failed, for his own would not recognize him as master, and those to whose level he aspired would not recognize him as friend. And now he was back where he had started, or even further back to where his father and mother had started, for they, too, must have cleared this ground, mucked out the shippons and tried to make these two rooms habitable.

Her heart was full of pity for him.

... And love? The question sidled into her mind.

Yes, and love, for how otherwise could she do what she was about to do? She had always sworn inside herself she would never become a man's kept woman, and that she knew would be the tag they'd put on her in the village. Well, damn them in the village!

She moved from the window and, taking up a narrow branch of wood, snapped it over her knee into three pieces and threw them on to the fire.... There was one thing she would do, she'd show that lot down there that she wasn't frightened of them; she wasn't going to hide away as if she'd committed a crime. No, she'd show them. She didn't know yet how but she'd think of something to let them see that they hadn't got her so scared she daren't put her foot in the village.

On the Sunday, which was the third day, he carried the bag of lime, two wooden buckets and brushes, and she carried a basket of food, a clean pail, and a kettle, for she was determined there wasn't going to be a repeat of the last two days when they hadn't had a bite or sup from the time they left the house until they returned; and even then he had hardly touched the food Mrs Riley put before him.

There was a thin rain falling and it was driven on a wind that could have foretold snow, so biting was it, and when finally she pushed open the door and they entered the bare, mouldy smelling room she looked at the grate and said as lightly as she could, 'Oh, look! the ashes are still warm; we'll soon have a fire goin' and the kettle boiling. Will you get some water?'

She turned towards him. He had just straightened his back after depositing the buckets and sack on the floor, and he didn't give her any answer as she handed him the pail but he looked hard at her, and she couldn't define the expression on his face. There was no surliness in it, nor aggressiveness. Yet there was something. The explanation she gave herself was that he looked like a dumb man, a frustrated dumb man.

It was half an hour later when, she sitting on a low log at one side of the fireplace, and he on the upturned wooden bucket at the other, sipping at the hot tea, that he spoke. Putting his mug down on to the uneven stone hearth, he looked into her face and said, 'You haven't got to do this, Emily; I can look after meself. I'll get by.'

She took a long drink from the mug; then picking up a spoon from the food basket and putting it into the mug, she scraped up the unmelted sugar from the bottom of it, and she licked the spoon for the last time before she said, 'I know I haven't got to do it, but I'm goin' to.'

He was still looking into her face as he said softly, 'You haven't experienced the winter up here; it can be terrible.'

'No worse than the river front at Shields with the snow up to the window sills many a time.'

'There's no comparison. You can be snowed up for weeks. And the wind, it never seems to lessen. You feel you're going mad.'

'Well, I'd say you're more likely to go mad on your own than if you have company.'

'It's different for a man.'

'Look.' She put the mug down on the hearth and gazed back into his face as she said, 'I've made up me mind, I'm stayin'. And tell me'—her voice was rough edged now—'tell me the truth. What would you feel like if I walked out on you an' all? Because I haven't seen many friends rallying round you. Where's that Mrs Rowan? She's never shown her face. Now that to my mind is very odd, 'cos when they thought you had come into a house and a fortune they all turned up. My, didn't they! But not any more....'

She watched him rise to his feet, turn his back on her and go towards the door, and she didn't say to herself now, 'Eeh! you shouldn't talk like that to him,' because, as she saw it, she was to be his wife and was, therefore, entitled to speak plainly.

As if he had heard her thinking, he said, 'You know I won't marry you. What I said the other night in anger I say it now quite calmly: I won't marry you, Emily. And for more reasons than one. But one is, that if I did I'd be tying you, and some day you'll want to walk out. Oh yes, you will.'

He turned slowly about and looked at her, and as she gazed up at him she wanted to jump up and fall on his neck and cry, 'No, no! Not me. I'll never walk out on you. It could be the other way about, but I'll never leave you, not as long as you need me.' But what she said was, 'Well, you've had your say, so let's leave it at that an' get on with some work, eh?' for she had discovered he wasn't a demonstrative man except when emotionally upset. It was a disappointing discovery, but there it was. And if you knew what to expect you wouldn't be disappointed, would you?

As she rose to her feet she had a silly thought, for she said to herself, and wistfully, 'I'm only seventeen.'

SEVEN

They were all ready to go. The big dray was packed high at the front with a conglomeration of household goods, and each side was buffered by two large trunks which held Larry's clothes and personal effects—Emily's filled her bass hamper and two bundles. A space had been left up the middle of the dray into which they hoped to marshal the cow and the three sheep, and the crate of hens. If the situation had not had its tragic side Emily would have laughed long and loud at the sight the dray presented.

They were almost ready to go but there was one thing she must see to before leaving. She had earlier unpinned the watch from her shift, and now she must ask Mr Tooton to do her a service concerning it.

She had just stopped Mrs Riley from putting another tub of butter on to the already laden dray, saying, 'It'll only go rancid, it won't keep.'

'You can boil it up, girl, an' it'll be as good as new.'

She sighed as she said kindly, 'No, we've got plenty already; you've put enough food on there to last us for the next six months.' Then, she exclaimed pointing towards the drive, 'There's Mr Tooton. I ... I want a word with him,' and she now ran through the kitchen, into the hall, to meet Mr Tooton as he entered by the front door.

Panting, she asked, 'Can I have a word with you, Mr Tooton, please?'

'Of course, Emily.' The clerk's voice was grave. Then, as if he had lived in the house all his life, he led the way to the drawing-room, standing aside to allow her to pass before him he closed the door and walked towards the fire, saying, 'Now, I'm at your service, Emily.'

'Well, it's this way, Mr Tooton, I ... I fear we're goin' to need all the money we can get. I know in a little while he'll get the lump sum of his wages, but in the meantime we've got to live and ... and get things going. And I don't know how much he's got on him. But I have this.' She pulled the watch from her pocket, laid it on her palm, then extended her hand towards him, and Mr Tooton stood gazing down on it. Then he looked up at her and said briefly, 'This belongs to you?'

'Oh yes, yes. It isn't the mistress's! Her voice was rising. 'Don't think that.'

'Oh, I wasn't, I wasn't. Don't mistake me, Emily. But it's a very beautiful piece.'

'Yes, it is; and it was given to me by the man I was goin' to marry afore I came here.'

'Really! ... He must have been a very wealthy man.'

She saw immediately that he didn't believe her, and so she protested firmly: 'This watch is mine, Mr Tooton. An' Mr McGillby wasn't a wealthy man, not like the master ... I mean like he was. Mr McGillby was a gaffer in the docks, and his wife died and I looked after the house. I'd been there two years afore she died, an' we were going to be married when I was seventeen. He was a very honourable man ... Mr McGillby. Well'—she now moved her hand with the watch in it—'he met a lot of sailors—you see it was in Shields on the river front we lived—and these sailors were often hard up and they had brought things home with them, what they had bought abroad, trinkets an' things, and Mr McGillby sometimes bought a piece off them. Well, he had a number of pieces, but when he saw this he had to sell all his other pieces to get it, so that makes me think it's worth something.'

'Yes, indeed, indeed, Emily, I should say it's worth something ... may I?'

'Yes, yes.' She handed it to him, and then she watched him move his finger gently along the row of stones on the strap from the pin down to the winder on the watch; then around the edge of the gold strap, and lastly around the face of the watch itself.

'Do ... do you think it's valuable?'

'Well'—Mr Tooton pursed his lips—'there are a great many stones in it. Of course, I'm no authority on jewellery, but yes, I would say off-hand it is worth a good few pounds. I presume you want to sell it, Emily?'

'Yes, yes, I want to sell it; but ... but I thought if I went into Fellburn or Newcastle and tried to get money on it, even in a pawnshop, they might think I'd stole it. An' I'd have to explain about Mr McGillby, an' then they might think he'd stole it. But he didn't. Oh, he didn't! Mr McGillby would never steal anything; his wife had brought him up Chapel.'

She now nodded her head slowly, and Mr Tooton nodded as slowly back at her as he said, 'Chapel are mostly honest people.'

'Mr McGillby was honest.'

Mr Tooton made no comment on this but, looking at her, he said, 'How much do you think it is worth in your own mind?'

'Aw, I don't rightly know, but all of thirty pounds ... or ... or more, I should say.'

'Thirty pounds ... or more.'

'Do you think I'm overstepping the mark?'

'No, no, Emily, no. But, of course, as I said, I'm no authority. But if you wish me to dispose of it ... and that is what you do wish, isn't it?'

330

'Oh yes, Mr Tooton, yes. I'd like you to ... to dispose of it.'

'Well, I'll do my very best for you. I may be able to sell it outright, or on the other hand I may only be able to pawn it.'

'Either way it wouldn't matter, Mr Tooton, because you see I've never been able to wear it, an' I've less chance now than ever, haven't I?'

'That's true, Emily. That's true. Well now'—Mr Tooton looked up towards the ceiling—'today is Monday. I'll be going into town to report on Wednesday. I should be back here on Thursday. If I have managed to sell it, I'll come up to your cottage....'

'No, no, don't do that. I wouldn't want him ... Mr Birch to think I had to sell anything of mine to ... to ... Well, you know what I mean.'

'Yes, yes, of course, Emily. But where shall I contact you?'

'Well, the only place is me Aunt Mary's. Her name is Southern, Mrs Southern; and she lives at number forty-seven Billow Street, Gateshead.' Mr Tooton now took from his pocket a notebook and wrote down the address; then said, 'I'll write to you there as soon as I've concluded the business.'

'Thanks, Mr Tooton. Thanks very much. You've been very kind. All along, you've been very kind. I used to think clerks and people like you were too uppish to speak to ... well, ordinary folk, but I've found me mistake out.'

'Oh, Emily, Emily.' He was smiling sadly at her now. 'How little you know of life or people. I'm afraid you are the kind of girl, Emily, who'll get hurt. Time and again you'll get hurt; and I'm sorry that this is so.'

'Oh, don't worry about me, Mr Tooton; I have me head screwed on the right way, and I never see any harm in trusting people. Speak as you find, do to others as

you'd have them do to you, that's what Sep ... Mr Mc-
Gillby used to say.'

Why did she keep mentioning Sep at this time? It was
the watch, she supposed.

Mr Tooton now took hold of her hand, and he shook it
warmly as he said, 'I wish you the best of luck, Emily, in
... in your future life.'

'Thanks. Thanks, Mr Tooton. An' don't you worry
about me, or him. We'll get by somehow.... Never say
die.'

Eeh! there she went again, talking brave talk ... never
say die, when at this very moment her heart was in her
boots; and it wasn't only because of the hard life that was
stretching ahead of her, and she had no illusions about
that, but tonight would be her wedding night, today was
a kind of wedding day, and she was all worked up inside,
not exactly frightened, but not exactly looking forward
to it either.

Well, she had burnt her boats. He had given her the
chance to take up her bag and go her own way, but she
had chosen to go his road; so she'd have to face tonight,
wouldn't she, like many another afore her. Tomorrow
she'd know all about it.

It was almost dark when Larry and George carried the
last trunk between them up the slope towards the cottage,
with Emily following some way behind leading the horse.

The horse wasn't young, but Larry had chosen him
because he was used to the plough. This, Emily thought,
was a bit short-sighted because if they ever managed to
get a small cart, Bonny would be too cumbersome to
pull it; he was more suited to a beer dray.

After settling the horse in the stable, she heaved a great
sigh and now slowly, because she felt so tired, she walked
the few steps towards the cottage.

Standing in the doorway, she viewed the room. It was cluttered with pieces of furniture, some looking as out of place as it was possible to imagine. And she herself had picked it all, including the pretty French table, and the clock, and the bureau from the drawing-room.... And all to grace these two small rooms and a scullery!

She smiled weakly at George, who was standing in the middle of the pile shaking his head, and she said, 'What won't go round the walls we'll furnish the shippon with,' and at this he laughed and said, 'Aye. Aye. You could.' Then he added, 'Well, I'll ... I'll leave you now to get settled in.'

As he turned towards the door, Larry, edging his way out of the bedroom, said, 'Thanks, George,' and Emily put in, 'I'll ... I'll never forget your kindness, George. We ... we couldn't have done it without you. I'll always remember that ... an' the big dray!'

'Aw, you'd have thought of somethin'. Being you, Emily, you'd have thought of somethin'.' He jerked his head towards her; then on an embarrassed laugh he went out, and Larry followed him, closing the door behind him.

With a soft plop now she sat down on the top of a trunk and looked towards the lamp that was set on the stone mantelpiece and was spreading its soft light over the odd assortment of furniture and kitchen utensils. Well, she had arrived.... They had arrived. From now on this was to be her home; in these two rooms she'd likely spend the remainder of her life. She was seventeen years and four months old and at this moment her life ahead seemed to cover a long, long time ... never ending ... eternity.

When the door opened she went to rise from the trunk, but when Larry said quietly, 'Sit where you are, I'll make a drink,' she obeyed him without murmur. And when presently he handed her a mug of tea she reminded herself the last time he had handed her anything to drink had been on New Year's Eve when they'd had that bit of jollification.... Would she ever know a bit of jollification again? She doubted it.

'You're tired.'

'What? ... Oh aye. Yes.' She smiled up at him where he was now standing over her, looking down into her face.

'You must get to bed; we won't do any more moving or lifting tonight.'

'No. No, I don't think I could.'

'Would you like something to eat?'

'No, no, thanks. I'm not hungry. But ... but I'd like a wash.'

'A wash?'

'Aye, I feel filthy.' She held out her hands. 'An' me face, it feels full of grime.' She now moved her fingers around her cheeks. 'I don't know what I look like.'

'You look beautiful, Emily; you always look beautiful.'

She bowed her head and told herself she mustn't cry. All he had said was she looked beautiful, but he had said it in the same way as he had said you're tired, in a kindly fashion. But at this moment she couldn't even stand kindness.

She slid off the lid of the trunk, saying, 'There's no water in; I'll have to get it from the rain butt.'

'I'll get it,' he said.

She lit a candle, which she took into the bedroom; and when he returned with the bucket of water, she emptied most of it into the black kale pot, and as she swung it up on to the fire, she muttered, 'I just want the chill off it.'

She now searched among a high heap of utensils piled in the corner until she found the small tin bath and, emptying its contents on to the floor, she took it to the fireplace. After a few minutes she tested the water in the kale pot. It had barely got the chill off it, but she poured it into the bath. Then, having pulled a towel from a bundle, she lifted the bath and went into the other room, and with her buttocks she pushed the door closed behind her, aware all the time that he was sitting on the other trunk watching her.

She placed the bath on a small clear space at the side of the wooden bed, then with a shiver she began to undress. Stripped to her waist, her shift hanging over her outer clothes, she washed the top half of herself; then put on her blouse again, took off her skirt, petticoats and drawers, and her shift, and, standing in the little bath, finished the rest of her toilet. By the time she pulled her shift and clothes on again her teeth were chattering in her head.

She now told herself she should have got into her nightgown, but she had left it in one of the bundles back in the room. Anyway, she felt a bit fresher now and she didn't want to go to bed yet; it was too early, she'd make a meal.

As she buttoned up her blouse a wave of panic assailed her, and from shivering with the cold she now began to sweat. She didn't want to go to bed at all; it seemed funny, but she didn't.

She lay staring upwards into the deep, thick blackness. It was over. It had been over for some two hours now but she was still in it, terrified, repulsed, sickened, exhilarated. Up to a short while ago she had known three sides of him, now she knew four, and the fourth she liked least of all. For the past hour or so Alice Broughton's sayings had punctuated her thinking: Some men eat you alive. ... Some men are never satisfied; breakfast, dinner and tea wouldn't satisfy some of them.... She had to go to the priest about him, and a lot of damn good that did her....

Do your duty; keep at it; if you don't somebody else will. That's what they told her.

Then there was the faint memory, but distinct now, of her mother crying out, making strange sounds as if she were being tortured, but in the morning looking happy and smiling and cooking her da a big breakfast, especially if it was a Sunday morning.

She was cold, although there were four blankets and a hap on the bed. The air in the room was like nothing she had ever breathed before, not even when the snow was lying feet deep in Shields, and the noise of the freezing spray lashing the pier walls was like thunder over their part of the town. This was a different cold, a damp penetrating, deadening cold. She wanted to turn to him and snuggle against his body, as she would have against Lucy's for comfort, but she daren't move in case she roused him. So she lay still and stiff; her body couldn't stand another attack, she told herself; for that is what it had been like. And yet, she had to admit if she remembered rightly, there were moments when she had responded to him. . . .

Would she always feel like this about it? Would it be like this every night? She hadn't bargained for this. No, she hadn't bargained for anything like this. She had thought, in a way, she had known what it was all about, but she hadn't.

He moved, snorted slightly, heaved himself round in the bed, and his arms sought her again, but they did not clutch at her; instead his head snuggled into her breasts, his lips touched her flesh lightly, and he sighed and breathed her name, 'Emily,' he said. 'Oh, Emily.' His breathing fell into rhythmic flow. He was asleep.

Slowly, slowly, her body relaxed against his. Then her hand moved up under the bedclothes and lay on the back of his head. She felt warm now. She was warm, drowsy. As

336

she drifted into sleep she thought she heard her Aunt Mary laughing and shouting at her: 'You've got a lot to learn, lass. You've got a lot to learn. An' you've only started. But you'll come through, never fear ... never say die.'

PART FOUR

THE HILL
THE FIRST YEAR

ONE

For three full weeks, except to gather wood, they did not move from the precincts of the land attached to the cottage. They worked from dawn till dusk through wind, rain, and early sleet showers. Larry had made all the outhouses dry; he had cleared the back and front yards of grass and weeds and young hawthorn, and laid a path of broken slabs across the back yard. He had repaired, here and there, the rough wall that bordered his three acres of ground. But after the evening meal he would sit before the fire, his hands idle; and not once did his face lose its stiff, sombre, bitter expression.

As for Emily, she had first of all arranged the furniture inside the cottage. What couldn't stand around the walls she placed on top of other pieces, such as the glass-fronted cupboard which she put on top of the chest of drawers, and the whatnot she placed on the lid of one of the trunks. Why, she asked herself, she had brought a whatnot when there were no bits and pieces to put on it, she didn't know. The bureau she set in the corner near the fireplace, and the French clock she placed on the mantelpiece in between the two brass jugs, and also the tea caddy. The little French table she put at the side of the bed. Her pans she hung on the iron hooks in the wall down the side of the fireplace. At one side of the hearth she placed the settle, at the other, the big leather chair she had taken from the study. One step from the chair was the narrow kitchen table, which had acted as a side table down in the house, and two straight-backed wooden chairs. On the floor was a carpet and she had known this to be a mistake from the beginning for within the doorway it was already caked with mud. Yet, in spite of its cluttered look, the kitchen had taken on a homely air.

But she did not waste much time inside the cottage. She cleared the front garden, and side by side with Larry she dug it up, not to be arranged into flower beds but for vegetables that would have to be their mainstay in the time to come. The carrying of the water from the burn was a task in itself, as was the gathering of wood. And as the days went on she found that she had to go further and further from the cottage in her search for wood in order to keep the fire going, because, as she had remarked to Larry, it ate the blooming stuff, the chimney had too much draught.

Her hands had been rough before, but now the backs of them were marked with keens; and her nails were worn down to the quick. She had worked hard down there in the house, long, tedious hours, but she realized now that that work had been light compared with her present tasks. This was navvy's work.

And now at the end of three weeks they were faced with a problem. The horse needed fodder, the chickens needed mash and corn. Nearly all that George had stacked on the cart had gone.

No one had been near them. She hadn't seen a soul since she came up here, not even George. But in a way she could understand George not coming up: it was sort of delicate, courtesy like. So she explained it to herself. But she would have been so pleased to see him ... to see anybody for that matter.

The longing had come on her last night to see the town again, to mix with people, just for a short while, an hour or so. If she could look forward to that every week it would get her by, so she told herself.

And so strong was the urge still on her that it helped her to speak out on this Tuesday morning when the sun was shining and the wind for once was light but still biting, and the sky was high, and the light all about them a silvery white. 'We'll have to go down,' she said.

'What!' He was scooping up the last spoonful of porridge from the bowl and he hesitated before putting it to his mouth. Then he placed the spoon back in the bowl and pushed them away across the table before saying, slowly and heavily, 'I'm not going down there.'

'Well, you can't expect to stay up here all your life.'

'Why not?' He was looking straight at her.

'Why not?' She moved her head from side to side. 'We've not tasted meat for a week; the hens want crowdie; there's not one of them laying now and they never will if they don't have their hot mash at this time of the year. You know that well enough.'

He got up from the table, swung round and took the one step it needed to reach the mantelpiece. Taking from it a briar pipe, he knocked the noddle against the rough stone, then with a penknife scraped the bowl until her teeth were on edge, forcing her to cry at him, 'Well, if you won't go I'll have to. And George's likely left stuff down there for us; do you expect me to lump it up?'

She stopped abruptly for he had turned and was staring at her, and the look he was levelling at her was one she had often seen on his face when he was acting the master; and in this moment she knew he was seeing her again as the servant who was stepping out of her place. But he was wrong, wasn't he? She wasn't stepping out of her place, not any more she wasn't. She knew what her place was. But even now, when he had lost his, he didn't know where he stood, and so she cried at him, 'Don't look at me like that. We're no longer down there, and don't you forget it.'

When she saw his face twitch and his head move downwards with that slow painful movement as if it were being forced from behind, she ran round the table and put her arms about him, saying contritely, 'Oh, I'm sorry. Larry ... Larry, I'm sorry. I didn't mean it. It's my mouth; I should keep it shut. I know, I know. But look at me. Look at me.' She pushed her doubled-up fist under his chin bringing his eyes level with hers. 'This thing has got to be faced, we've got to live. An' the animals have got to live. We all need food. The only thing we've got at present is milk. I can make butter of a sort, and a bit of cheese, but we want bread. And for that I need flour and yeast. And we want a bit of meat. You, most of all, want a bit of meat.'

'I can't go down there, Emily.'

'Not just to the bottom of the far hill to carry up the stuff?'

He blinked and seemed to consider; then said, 'Aye, well, perhaps that; but I've sworn inside meself never to go on that road again.'

'But there are other roads.' She pointed in the direction of the bedroom, saying, 'Across that way you could get to Birtley an' Chester-le-Street.' She stopped herself from adding, 'An' the Rowans' farm is that way an' all.'

He never spoke of his friends to her, of either the father, the mother, or the daughter. She had pondered on this, thinking that the reason might be he was hurt by their desertion of him. If it wasn't that, then there was another reason that was too delicate to broach. Her thinking on the subject stopped here.

She swung round from him now and hastily began to gather up the dishes from the table; and he looked at her enquiringly as he asked, 'What are you going to do?'

'I'm goin' into the town, I'm goin' by the carrier cart an I'm goin' to get on it in the village.'

'No, no, Emily. No, you're not!'

'Yes, yes, I am.' Her hands became still on the table. 'But first of all I'm goin' down into that village this mornin', because there'll come a time when we'll be snowed up here and we'll be lucky if we can reach even there, for it'll be impossible to get into Fellburn. So I'm going to put in an appearance, when the goin's good.'

'They'll hound you.'

'Huh!' She wagged her head. 'Just let them try. That's all, just let them try.'

'Do you remember what happened to Con?'

She became still and her lip trembled slightly as she replied, 'Aye, yes, I remember what happened to Con. Only too well I remember what happened to Con. But you can take it it won't happen to me. There's a piece in me little book. I was lookin' at it just last night and I thought how right it is. It says: "Fear is the enemy, fear is the foe, if you run before it down you'll go. But if you stand and look it in the face, God will pour into you the bravery of grace".'

He still did not smile as he said, 'Oh Emily, you and that book.'

'It's got a lot of sense in it that book.' Her tone was now defensive.

'It all depends on what you call sense. Your bravery could lead you into trouble; I've no need to tell you what they're like down there.'

'People change. Anyway, they're not all alike.'

'Aw-w, Emily!' He closed his eyes and turned his head away and his lips moved back from his teeth as if he were smelling something stinking, and, his head still turned from her, he said, 'They're still worrying me alive down there. Don't you know that? They're still licking their chops, the lot of them. An' not only them, but for miles around. I'm the man who stepped out of his class and I've been put back in me place. From all sides they're seeing it

344

that way, and they're laughing as they've never laughed for years.'

'Well, we'll only have to try to wipe the laugh off their faces, won't we? Anyway'—she jerked her chin upwards—'I'm going down 'cos we can't remain buried alive here for evermore. And the first time's always the worst ... with everything,' she added, 'an' I'll never feel more like tacklin' them than I do at this minute. So you can't stop me. The only thing I ask of you is for you to come to the bridge near the beck in about a couple of hours' time. I'll leave the stuff I get in the village there afore I catch the cart into Fellburn.'

'Why do you want to go into Fellburn if you mean to get the stuff in the village?'

She gathered up the dishes now and went to the corner of the room and put them into the tin dish which was standing on a little table, and as she poured the water on them from an enamelled jug, she said, 'I've got a hankering to see me Aunt Mary.'

'A hankering?'

'Aye, a hankering.'

'... You're lonely?'

'No, I'm not lonely.' She turned her head sharply over her shoulder and looked at him. 'But I just want to see me Aunt Mary and——' Only just in time she stopped herself from adding 'And have a bit of a natter an' a laugh.' She hadn't laughed since coming into this cottage; she had never even smiled, and she needed to smile, to have something to smile about ... something to laugh about. And, of course, she was anxious to know if Mr Tooton had sold the watch.

'She'll tell you not to come back.'

'What!' She again looked over her shoulder. 'Me Aunt Mary? You don't know what you're talkin' about. You should see her, an' hear her. The last time we chatted she told me if she had her time over again she'd start up a

345

house for fallen women, not to redeem them like, those were her own words, but to let them get on with the job.'

She turned her face towards the wall again. A house for fallen women, not to redeem them, but to let them get on with the job. Was it laughter that was bubbling up in her? Whatever it was was choking her, but when it burst through her lips it surprised her, for it was high and uncontrolled, and when her face was pressed against his shoulder it turned into sobs, and the more he murmured, 'Oh, Emily, Emily,' the louder these became.

She didn't go down to the village that day because her eyes were too red and swollen, but she went down the next morning; and he stood and watched her go from the doorway. When she reached the bottom of the slope she could still feel his eyes on her back, and so she turned and, cupping her mouth with her hand, she yelled, 'Don't forget, around three o'clock.' And she waited until he raised his hand before going on her way again.

The sun was shining again today, again the world was bright. Once upon a time on a day like this she would have felt glad.

She entered the village street by the top end, as she would have done had she been driving into it in the trap. As she passed the forge she turned her head fully and looked in. There was a new man at the anvil. He raised his head and glanced at her, that was all; but when she passed the two women standing outside the house-window haberdashery shop they actually turned their bodies fully round and gaped at her.

A little way farther on down the street she stepped off the cobbled pavement on to the dried mud road so as not to disturb some children playing there; then she was passing The Running Fox, and again she turned her head fully and looked towards it before walking on. And now she was outside the butcher's shop with its high window headed by the words: DAVID COLE. PRIME BEEF.

There were three women in the shop, and the reactions of two of them were as if they were seeing an apparition, for, like the women in the street, they too turned fully about and their mouths fell agape.

Mr Cole was at his block, a chopper in his hand, chining a neck of mutton. He held the chopper poised for a moment while he stared at Emily, and his look became a glare before he turned to his lady customers again. Addressing one of them, he said, 'About ... about two pounds you said, Mrs Robinson?'

Mrs Robinson gulped, then repeated, 'Aye, two pounds, Mr Cole.'

Emily remained standing to the side while Mr Cole served his three customers. In the meantime, two more came into the shop, and the only sound between question and answer was Mr Cole's knife sliding softly through steak or his chopper going through bone.

Two of the very surprised ladies left the shop together, one of them remarking to the other as she kicked at the sawdust on the floor, ''Tis a wonder it doesn't catch fire.'

'Well'—Mr Cole was addressing himself solely to Emily now—'What ... what can I do for you, *madam* ... *Mrs* ...'

'Miss.'

'Oh aye'—He nodded at her, gave a slight leering smile, and repeated, 'Miss.'

'I'll take a pound of hoff meat, a pound of sausages, and that brisket point there.' She extended her finger towards a slab on which were some pieces of beef.

Silently Mr Cole weighed out the sausages, the hoff meat, and when he came to weighing the brisket he said, 'It's big, weighs just over eight and a half pounds. It'll cost you'—he started to reckon in his head—'half a crown.'

347

'Thank you; I'll take it.' She had adopted a slightly high-falutin tone, and he, following her pattern, now bent slightly towards her and said, 'Will I send it ... miss?'

She did not turn her head in the direction of the titter behind her but, looking straight back into the butcher's eyes, she said, 'Yes, you can do that, *Mr ... Mr ... Cole.* You know the cottage, Rill Cottage on Bailey's Rise?'

She watched the colour flooding up over his already ruddy countenance and his lips formed a thin line before he replied, 'The ... the lad doesn't get that far.'

'Oh. Well, in that case I'll take it with me.'

She watched him parcel the meat up roughly, and when he thrust it at her she offered him a full sovereign, which he stared at for a moment before putting it in the till and giving her the change.

'Good day, Mr Cole.'

The only response to her farewell was a telling silence.

It was odd, but as she walked out of the shop she imagined that her manner had been similar to that which Rona Birch would have used towards the butcher, and the thought made her feel slightly elated.

She knew that Mr Cole's eyes and those of his customers were watching her progress across the street to the baker's shop, which was also part corn chandler's, and so she held her head high, and lightly pulled up the edge of her skirt so that her walk across the rough road should be unimpeded.

Mr Waite was behind the counter, as was Mrs Waite. They both stopped what they were doing and gazed at their new customer; then Mrs Waite, after taking a deep breath, swung a small paper bag between her two hands until its ends formed corkscrew points before handing it across the counter to a small boy, who after proffering her a penny, was about to disappear through the door when she brought her attention quickly to him as she cried at him, 'Don't you eat that yeast mind, Eddie! You take it

348

straight home.' The boy made no reply, he just grinned at her and went out.

And now Mrs Waite was about to turn her attention to this brazen piece when her husband forestalled her. His voice quite civil sounding, he said, 'And what can I do for you, miss?'

His manner and tone was almost Emily's undoing for it threatened to take the stiffness out of her back, the tilt from her chin, and the self-confidence from her manner.

'Could I have a half stone of flour, please?'

'Aye, you could.' He bounced his head at her. Then turning and looking straight at his wife, he said, 'Weigh up half a stone of flour, Sarah.'

His Sarah glared back at him for a moment, but only for a moment; then she went into the back shop and there was a sound of a heavy weight being banged on to a scale.

'Is there anything more I can get you?'

She wanted to say, 'Yes, I'll take a stone of boxings and some corn. And could you drop a bale of hay near the bridge?' for she had realized before entering the village that you couldn't walk with much dignity if you were laden down with bags, and she wanted to walk out of this village with dignity, at least today, and so she said, 'I'll have a quarter of yeast, please, and half a dozen of your nice tea-cakes.' She nodded towards a tray of freshly baked tea-cakes.

'And that you shall have ... a quarter of yeast and half a dozen tea-cakes.'

The tea-cakes had been put in the bag and placed on the counter before her, and the clicking of the scale told her that the flour had been weighed, and so, quickly now, she leant slightly towards Mr Waite and said below her breath, 'Thank you, thank you, Mr Waite, for receiving me in this way.'

For a moment he looked surprised, then he said, 'Aw,

349

hinny'—he shook his head slowly—'I'm sorry for you. And him an' all. Is there anything I can do for you?'

She did not pause a moment before she whispered, 'Oh, if only you'd drop a stone of corn and one of boxings, an' a bale of hay near the bridge. I'd ... I'd be ever so obliged.'

'All right, lass; I'll do that.' His voice had been just above a whisper, but it rose sharply when his wife, her skirts flouncing, came into the shop again and he said, 'Now, let's see. Half a stone of flour, six tea-cakes and a quarter of yeast, you're takin' with you, and you want delivered one bale of hay, one stone of boxings, and one stone of wheat.' He paused, and his smile widening, he said, 'What about some sausage rolls and meat pasties, made fresh this mornin'?' He pointed towards a wooden tray.

Her voice now had a slight break in it as she answered, 'Thank you. Yes, I'll take some. Four ... four of each.'

'Four of each. Wrap them up, missis.' He turned his head and looked at his wife, then added up the purchases on the back of a paper bag, and when he turned it towards her he said, 'All right, miss?' and after barely glancing at the total, she answered, 'Yes, Mr Waite. Quite all right.'

A few moments later, as she was leaving the shop, she said, 'Good-day, Mr Waite. And thank you. Good-day, Mrs Waite.' She nodded to the silent, prim-faced woman, who made no reply, but her husband called loudly, 'Good-day, miss. Good-day. Call again.'

Carrying the half stone of flour on the crook of one arm and the rest of her purchases in the bass bag, she walked smartly on down the village street that had quite suddenly become alive with people, people in their gardens, people cleaning their windows, people standing talking together. And no one spoke to her; and no one seemed to look at her; and only one remark came to her ears. It was from a woman who was picking up a child from the middle of the road where it was sitting playing in the dust, and as if she were talking to the child, she said, 'Pity the stocks are not in use no more.'

But what did it matter? The baker had been nice to her, more than nice, most kind. When she got back to the cottage she'd say to Larry triumphantly, 'I was right; people are not all alike.'

Having reached the broken-down bridge and placed the bags under cover of some old wood and stones, she sat for a moment on what remained of the parapet, for of a sudden she felt tired, drained. And she wanted to cry again, as she had done yesterday, but she checked herself, muttering aloud, 'No more of that. No more of that. Get yourself up and on your way, else you'll miss the cart.'

Mary Southern greeted her with open arms. She hugged her to her flabby breasts and she kissed her and she cried over her, 'Eeh! lass!' she said, 'I thought you'd never come. From what our Pat read out of your letter I thought, the silly little bitch, she'll keep away, thinkin' she should be ashamed to show her face.'

'I'm not ashamed of what I've done, Aunt Mary.' Emily released herself from the hefty arms and, looking into the kindly face, she said, 'It's me own life.'

'Aye, lass, you're right, it's your own life. Come on and sit down. Get your things off first. The tea's on the hob, I'll get you somethin' to eat.'

'I can't stay long. And Aunt Mary. Was there a letter come for me?'

'Oh aye, a letter.' Mary tossed her head from side to side; then grabbing up the tea caddy from the mantelpiece, she lifted the lid and said, 'I stuck it down here 'cos it's the only place me squad don't put their fingers into 'cos if I caught them I'd cut 'em off.' She now knocked the tea dust off the letter against the side of the tin canister, then handed it to Emily; and she watched her open it and take out two pieces of paper. One was a sheet of ordinary writing paper, the other was a narrow slip of paper. It was at this slip that Emily looked first. Then she looked at her aunt, and Mary said, 'Bad news?'

'No, no, Aunt Mary, but ... but I'm just a little disappointed. You see.... Oh, it's a long story. I never told you, I've never told anybody, it's only Lucy knows, but ... but Sep gave me a watch.'

'A watch! A good one?'

'Oh aye, a bonny one.' She now went to the table and sat down, the two pieces of paper still in her hand, and briefly she described to Mary how she had come into possession of the watch and how she had asked Mr Tooton to sell it for her. But she finished up wagging the slip of paper between her finger and thumb, saying, 'It wasn't as valuable as I thought. He said he could only get twenty pounds for it. This is a cheque, he says, but ... but what can I do with this? I haven't got any bankin' account.'

'Oh, you needn't trouble about gettin' it changed. Ma Harris 'll change it for you if it's genuine like. She's the one that runs all the clubs an' things. You know, the money clubs. I've told you about her: a shilling on a pound club and a bit of a backhander when you get your money, not forgettin' a penny in the shilling a week for borrowing. She does all right, that one; loaded up to the eyebrows I'd say. Oh, she'll change it, but she'll charge you a bit. Twenty pounds? Oh well, you'll likely have to stump up a pound, lass.'

'Oh, I'll do that, Aunt Mary.'

'Well, don't look so glum; you'll still have nineteen left, an' that's a small fortune.'

'I think we're going to need all the small fortunes we can come by afore we're finished up there, Aunt Mary.'

'Is it as bad as that, lass?'

'Well'—Emily lowered her head—' 'tisn't bad, at least for me, but for him it's ... it's awful.'

'Aye, I bet it is, even goin' by what was in the papers. An' to think you're living with him, lass. Eeh! life's funny, isn't it? ... Is he kind to you?'

'Oh yes, yes, he's kind enough.'

Mary, leaning across the table and her breasts hanging on her forearms, asked quietly, 'You didn't say that with much conviction, lass. Do ... do you care for him?'

'Yes, Aunt Mary; yes, I care for him.'

'Big enough, an' deep enough to spend the rest of your life up there with him?'

Emily considered for a moment, and then she chided herself inwardly that she had to consider; then she said, 'Aye ... aye, for the rest of me life with him.'

'He must be some man.'

'He's not....' Now why had she said that? But then she could talk from her heart to her Aunt Mary. 'Well, I didn't mean what that sounded like. In looks he's all right, I'd suppose you would call him handsome, at least when he smiles. But he doesn't often smile ... or laugh.'

'That's a pity. A face can lose something if it never stretches in a laugh; it sort of becomes wantin'.'

'Aye, I think so an' all, Aunt Mary. But it isn't so much in his looks that he's wantin', it's ... it's in something inside; he kind of lacks something that should make him fight back. Even the solicitor said ... well, the solicitor's clerk, Mr Tooton, the man who sold the watch for me, even he said that he had a case, and he could have taken it to court. At least he would have got some decent compensation for his years of work, not just what she would have paid the lowest lad on her farm. But you see he wouldn't, Aunt Mary, he wouldn't fight. He's kind of stubborn and fearful inside. He thinks of it as bein'

proud, but ... but I don't see it like that. There's nothin'
to be proud of in letting other people walk over you.
What do you think, Aunt Mary?'

'No, begod! there's nothing to be proud of in that, lass.
Once you let anybody wipe their feet on you, you begin
to think of yourself as a doormat. You've got to talk him
out of that state.'

'I doubt if I ever will.'

'Well, does he intend to remain up in that eagle's nest
for the rest of his life, because I know where that place is
an' Windy Nook isn't in it? The wind up there would
take the lugs off an elephant. You've got something afore
you this winter, lass.'

Emily didn't comment on this but she sighed, and
Mary said, 'Aw well, never say die. That's your motto,
isn't it, lass? So never fear, you'll pull through. If there
weren't any valleys there'd be no hills. I tell meself this
often. Oh yes'—she wagged her head now at Emily—
'there's days when I'm so down I couldn't get any lower
unless I went down the pit. But then I say to meself,
"Come on, climb up and look out of the window. Now
what's up there? ... The sky. An' who's in it? God. Well,
remember, God helps those who help themselves." Aye,
an' God helps those who are found helpin' themselves.
Six months. Stand down.'

Now her head went back and she gave one mighty
bellow of a laugh, and Emily, laying her hands flat on the
cheque and the letter, bent her head over them and her
shoulders shook until the tears ran down her face; and
when their laughter subsided she wiped her eyes and
said, 'Oh! Aunt Mary, I needed that. I've longed to see
you these past days just to get a laugh.'

'Best medicine in the world, lass, a laugh. God gave it
to the poor for compensation. You never see a rich man
laughin', now do you? Not that I know any rich men.

354

But the lot that launch ships and open bridges an' the like, you never see them laughin'. Smilin' stiffly, aye, but never laughin'. And there's Ma Harris, why if she laughed she'd need to have her face stitched, and that'd cost money.'

They were off again, and they laughed and they talked for the next hour. Then Mary put on her shawl, warned the youngest members of her family that she'd brain them one by one if they put their noses out of the door or went near the fire, then guided Emily to the female moneylender.

When, half an hour later, Emily emerged with nineteen sovereigns in her purse, she pressed one amid loud protests into Mary's hand. And they parted at the street corner, Emily promising to make the visit a weekly one in future.

In Fellburn she bought a quarter of a stone of oatmeal, two pounds of rough salt, half a dozen pigs' trotters, three pounds of spare ribs, and odds and ends that filled two bags; then she took the carrier cart home.

There were six people on the cart and she, being the last to arrive, had to sit on the tail end, her legs dangling over the edge.

After they had passed the side road that led to the quarry she called to the driver to stop near the stile. A few minutes later she was carrying her bags through the copse to where in the distance she could see the broken-down bridge and Larry standing waiting beside it. Hurrying towards him, she thrust the packages at him, then bent forward and kissed him on the lips, saying, 'Have you been waiting long?'

'I came an hour ago. I ... I thought I saw the cart pass.'

She looked at him in silence for a moment. He had thought he had seen the cart pass, and she not on it, which was the reason for the look on his face now. He did not look exactly happy but he certainly looked different from when she had left him this morning. Suddenly she felt gay, glad. She hadn't felt like this for ... oh, she couldn't tell the time. She laughed aloud now as she said, 'Well, I did it. You got the flour and the meat?'

'Yes, I got the flour and meat.'

'By! it was as good as a play. They were staggered.'

'Yes, I can imagine they were. But wait till next time they'll be ready for you.'

'Oh no, they won't'—she tossed her head—' 'cos we've got somebody on our side.'

'Somebody on our side! Who?' He turned to her.

'Mr Waite, the baker. He's delivering and he wanted to be remembered to you.'

He now stopped dead. 'Don't make up tales like that, Emily.'

'I'm not makin' them up. He was as kind as kind. He nearly had me crying again, that's how kind he was. And once she was out of the shop—his wife—he spoke to me, and ... and he sent you a message. He said'—she paused—'Give Mr Birch my best respects and tell him ... tell him I'm with him.' Well, she felt sure that if he'd had time he would have said something like that; it was in his face.

'Waite said that?'

'Yes, he did.'

'Well! Well!'

'So I was right. There are different people in the world, even in the village. Everybody isn't the same.... What have you been doin' when I've been away?'

He turned his head and looked at her. 'Thinking about you.' He smiled.

She looked ahead. Her chin wagged; the setting sun was bathing everything in a warm glow; the sky was beautiful. The dead bracken on the hills before her had turned them to pure gold; the wind had risen and carried on it the sting of a frosty night, and the smell of winter. The whole world was beautiful, and this was a lovely part of it. Everything was going to be all right. Oh aye, everything was going to be all right.

TWO

Christmas came and went, and New Year followed, and there was no season of good will, for it takes more than one to create a jollification. But it didn't seem to matter much; what did matter was keeping warm. One day towards the end of January when they had been snowed up for nine days, she came in from the byre and cried with pain as she thawed out her hands at the fire; and he growled at her, 'I told you what it would be like, and you've tasted nothing yet. Wait till it crucifies you.' That moment was the nearest she came to thinking of leaving him. If it had been possible to get down the hill she might have packed up there and then, but as she then told herself, the thought wouldn't have occurred to her if the hill had been clear, for then he himself wouldn't have been tested to the limit of his endurance.

As the weeks wore on what was testing them both too was the question of money. It wasn't until he had received the third letter from the solicitor concerning his wife's bounty that she persuaded him to take the trip into Newcastle in order to sign the papers which would enable him to receive the money.

Persuade was hardly the correct term for her attitude in spurring him to leave the hill. It was in desperation she had shouted at him, 'Will you tell me what we're goin' to live on until the land gets going?'

He knew nothing about the money she had received

from the sale of the watch, for after two days of carrying the eighteen sovereigns round, tied in a bag in her petticoat pocket, she decided that her best plan was to hide them outside the house, and some day they would come in handy, for in the nature of things there were bound to be very lean days ahead. So, in a corner where two walls met at the extreme end of their land, she scraped a shallow hole in the earth, placed the bag in it and moved a small pile of wall stones that were lying near on to the top of it.

At first she felt guilty at her deception, but as the weeks went on and he refused even to answer the solicitor's letters she thought the time would not be far off when she'd have to move those stones again.

This morning, when she had shouted at him, he had not retaliated except by glaring at her, then stamping out of the cottage, and it was with difficulty she had prevented herself from running after him and saying she was sorry; as she told herself, this was no time to apologize or act soft. Recently she had asked him why he hadn't brought more than a bare fourteen pounds from the house when he left it, and he had explained that he had been in the habit of going to the bank once a month to draw out a certain amount, most of the bills being paid by cheque. He had been due to go to the bank the very day of the funeral; but, of course, from then on the bank was closed to him.

This morning she had also wanted to cry at him, 'You don't want to help yourself, do you?' but that would have been untrue because he worked from morning till night clearing more land, tearing at the ground, uprooting bracken, and carting away boulders to make it possible for ploughing in the spring, and as most of the land was on a slope the work was even more hard.

He remained outside for half an hour. When he returned he walked straight past her, into the bedroom, and she heard him fling back the lid of the trunk that held his suits. Ten minutes later he came into the kitchen dressed as she hadn't seen him dressed since the day he left the farm. He was wearing a grey tweed suit and an overcoat to match.

He held his hat in his hand and he stood looking at her for a moment before he said, 'At bottom you're like the rest of them, you won't be satisfied until you see me grovelling.'

'Aw ... aw'—she moved her head slowly to the side—'that isn't fair ... to say a thing like that to me, that isn't fair.'

'Well how do you think I'll feel, going into that office and having them sniggering at me?'

'Well, if they're gentlemen they won't snigger....'

'Oh my God!' He swallowed a mouthful of spittle as he closed his eyes and screwed up his face. 'You're so ...'

'Don't say I'm ignorant'—her voice had risen now—'an' that I don't know people, or what I'm talkin' about, 'cos I'm going to say again, if they're gentlemen they won't snigger. Mr Tooton didn't snigger, and he was only a clerk; he was sorry for you and thought you'd been dealt a dirty deal.'

He gulped deeply as if his throat was dry; then, his manner softening, he asked her quietly, 'Is there anything you want bringing back?'

She thought for a moment. 'No,' she said, 'except that we need more fodder and meal and such; but if we can settle the bill Mr Waite 'll drop that down below for us.' Then smiling a little, she moved slowly towards him, saying, 'There's something you could bring back if you wouldn't mind carrying it. I'd love a leg of pork.'

'A leg of pork!' He was looking into her face now and his head was moving gently. 'Don't you want anything for yourself?'

'Only that you should come back.'

'Oh, Emily!' He leant forward and kissed her gently on the lips, and she put her arms around his neck and held him close for a moment; then she buttoned the high lapel of his overcoat, patted his chest, and exclaimed on a high note, 'You haven't got any gloves on.'

'I don't want gloves.'

'You're going to put gloves on; you're not going into the town dressed like that without gloves.' She dashed into the other room, thrust open the lid of the trunk, put her hand down the side of it and brought up a pair of lined kid gloves; then running back into the kitchen again, she handed them to him, saying, 'Now, you'll have to hurry; you've got a good mile and a half to tramp if you're going t'other way to catch the carrier cart. And mind'—she now admonished him with her finger—'you take the cart, don't you attempt to walk into Birtley and catch the train. Now mind, 'cos you'll not get back the day if you do.'

He made no answer, but opened the door and went out, and she stood on the step and watched him as he strode down the path and through the gate and into the frosted field. Then stepping back into the room for a second, she snatched up a shawl, put it over her head, and ran down to the gate, and from there she shouted, 'Take care.'

He did not turn round but he lifted his hand in recognition that he had heard her. . . .

The day passed slowly. She spent the rest of the morning cleaning out the shippon and the stable, seeing to the animals' needs, milking the cow, and sawing and chopping wood into sizable lengths for the fire.

At noon the light suddenly changed and when the thin wind that sounded like a mournful song came threading from the far trees and swirled round the house, she looked anxiously up into the sky. There was snow coming again, the smell of it was on the wind. Oh! ... snow. She hated snow. She hoped it didn't start before he got back, for it would turn the hill into a skating rink. She'd thought they'd seen the last of it. If it did come they'd want more wood than there was already stacked against the end of the house. She'd better get herself away down to the stream to see if there was any bits washed up on to the bank. She'd have a cup of tea first and then she'd set off.

As she sat in the kitchen drinking her tea the wind died completely away; she felt she could hear the stillness. She looked about her. The room, though crowded, looked cosy enough; everything was clean and tidy, and the wood fire glowing in the blackleaded stove gave a homely appearance to it all. Yet without him, the place was like a graveyard. She'd go mad if she had to live up here on her own. She wished they had a cat or a dog. Why was it you could talk to a cat or dog more than you could to a cow or hens, or even a horse? Because they were kitchen animals, she supposed. She'd ask him when he came back about them having a kitten ... and a dog. Funny, but he wasn't partial to dogs, and him being a drover once. There had been two dogs down on the farm, nice sheepdogs, but she had never seen him walk with them, likely because they looked on old Abbie as their master....

What would he be doing now? She looked at the clock. He'd likely have got the money and was going round shopping. If he left Newcastle around two he should be back about four or thereabouts, depending on which way he came, of course. If he came through Fellburn or the village he could do the journey in an hour, at least to the bottom road; but then he'd never come that way.

It was a strange life living up here in the cottage. Sometimes it almost became unbearable, but when this feeling came on her she would look at him and think how much worse it was for him. If only she could see her Aunt

362

Mary more often, or somebody from Shields. Her da. Yes, if she could see her da, and their Lucy.

She hadn't heard a word from her da; but, of course, she wouldn't, would she? If he sent any letters Alice Broughton would put them straight in the fire, after reading them of course. But then it wasn't likely her da would send her any letters; he wasn't much hand at writing; what her da did was to turn up, just walk into the house as if he had been gone but half an hour or so.

She felt lonely. Oh, she did feel lonely the day, lost somehow.

Come on, get yourself out of this.

In answer to her own command she got up hastily from the table, took her mug and rinsed it in the bowl of cold water, hung it on a hook, put on her old coat, then her shawl over her head, and laced it under her breasts and tied it in a knot at the back of her waist. Then having donned a pair of home-made mittens she went out to the shed and, picking up a rope attached to a board, which was itself attached to two sets of small wheels, she pulled it behind her over the rough ground and down to the stream bank, and for the rest of the afternoon until the light almost faded, she made dragging journeys with the trolley up the hillside.

She was almost exhausted when at last she went into the cottage. After pulling off her outer clothes she sat down and looked at the clock. It was ten minutes past four. The time had flown as she had intended it to, but she told herself she shouldn't have stayed out so long; he'd expect a hot meal when he came in, and he should be here at any minute, and so, tired or not, she'd better stir herself.

An hour later the light had almost gone and so she put on the old coat and shawl again, lit a lantern, and went out and down the slope.

On reaching the bottom she called, 'Larry! ... Larry!'
Receiving no reply, she went at a stumbling run up the
far hill, and from the top she made out the very erratic
swinging of another lantern.

Her heart seemed to stop beating for a moment. He
hadn't taken a lantern down with him. Something had
happened to him. He had gone through the village and
they had attacked him.... It was Con all over again.
They were bringing him home.

She almost measured her length on the ground as she
took a leap forward and only just in time managed to
save herself.

As she approached the other light it stopped its swinging and the glow became steady, which meant it was on
the ground, and when she came panting within range of
its beam she stopped dead and looked through the light
into George's face, then down at the huddled figure on
the ground by the side of his feet.

'Hello, Emily.'

She didn't answer but walked slowly forward. She
didn't ask what had happened, she knew he was dead
drunk. She looked up at George when he said, 'He came
by cab from somewhere. The cabbie dumped him at the
side of the road. I wouldn't have known anything about
it but one of the village lads told me the cab passed
through the village an hour or more ago and he was singing at the top of his voice. I ... I don't know what made
me take a dander along here, but it's just as well I did,
because he would have been stiff by the mornin'.' He
paused, then ended, 'There were quite a number of
packages scattered around him; I brought them over the
stile in a sort of relay.' He made a sound in his throat
that wasn't a laugh. 'I left them by the old bridge; I
thought I'd better get him up first.'

Still she didn't speak, but when he bent down and
hooked his arm under that of the heavy limp body she

went to the other side and did the same. But when the body made no response and they were having to drag him along she realized the impossibility of getting him up the hill in this condition, so she took her arm from his and let him slump against George's side again. Then gripping him by the ears and part of his hair, she wagged his head on his shoulder—as she had seen her mother do to her father many a time in order to get him to mount the stairs—until he spluttered, then began to curse. 'What the hell! I'll knock ya bloody head off! I'll ... I'll....'

'Get on your feet and move!' Her voice was harsh, loud. It could have been that of Alice Broughton, or any woman in Creador Street, and in answer to it he actually stumbled to his feet and when, after a fashion, he moved, they all moved.

Following his drunken route, they swayed from side to side. Once George dropped the lantern and the candle went out and they were left in total blackness until, exclaiming aloud and groping for matches, he lit it again. ...

When at last they entered the cottage, not only did Larry slump to the floor but both George and Emily reached out towards the settle and dropped on to it, and for some minutes the only sound in the kitchen was their combined gasping.

Drawing in a long shuddering breath, Emily now rose to her feet and asked quietly, 'Will you help me off with his clothes, George?'

'Aye, Emily. Aye.'

Again they hoisted him up and, his legs trailing behind him, they dragged him into the bedroom and dumped him on the bed. When presently he lay in his small clothes, Emily said, 'Thanks, George,' and drew the blankets over the prostrate body. Then picking up the lamp, she led the way back into the kitchen, and after placing it on the table she looked at it as she spoke, saying again simply, 'Thanks, George.'

For answer George said, 'There's those packages and parcels down there, they should be brought up.'

'They can wait until daylight.'

'Well, I doubt if some of them will be there by daylight; there was pork sticking out of one, and a duck's head dangling from another; and ... and there's a small case of the hard stuff.'

She lifted her head now sharply and looked at him; but he did not meet her gaze as he went on, 'The meat stuff won't last long, the foxes 'll have a field day.'

'I'll go down and get it.'

'You'll do no such thing. I'll bring it up.'

She stared at him as she said, 'It's too much to ask.'

'What is?' He gave a small laugh. 'To take a dander in the dark? Anyway'—His chin drooped forward as he ended, 'It's good to see you again, Emily; we miss you down there.'

She looked at the lamp again. 'How are things going?' she asked.

'Oh, as usual. Old Abbie trying to rule the roost. But the new one, I think, will put a spoke in his wheel.'

She jerked her head round towards him. 'He's come then!'

'Oh aye, about a fortnight ago, a fortnight the morrow to be exact. A Mr Davies came from the solicitors and told us to expect him.... Mr Tooton's not there any more. He left, you know, and went down to some place in the West Country so I was told.'

'What's he like?' she asked quietly.

'Hard to say as yet; quiet but misses nothing. When old Abbie gets yapping he just looks at him, then turns away without saying a word, leaving the old fellow up in the air. His name's Stuart, Nicholas Stuart. It's a Scottish name but he's no Scot, not from the looks of him, he's got a foreign appearance somehow.'

'Have ... have you taken to him?'

George nodded slowly as he said, 'Aye, in an odd sort of way; aye I have, Emily, I've taken to him. He's no fool. He's not throwin' his weight about either, he's biding his time and weighing things up. But ... but somehow I feel he's going to have a very lonely life of it unless he gets himself married. But who is there to take him on around here, he's got the prison stamp on him? Why, they tell me when he went into The Running Fox it was as if they had all been struck dumb, they just sat looking at him, and when he finished his pint they say he looked back at them, one after the other he looked at them, and then went out without a word. And he hasn't been back since. Ma Riley says he's easy to please about his food; she hasn't had any complaints so far.' Now George grinned as he ended, 'And that's sayin' something for she wouldn't get a prize for her cookin'. I think Jenny would make a better hand at it if she'd let her have a try. She's the new lass,' he explained; 'she's quite nice, pleasant. I've often thought you would have got on well with her; I could have seen you laughing together.... You happy, Emily?'

She now looked fully at him, and it was a moment before she answered, 'I would be, George, if he was.'

'That's askin' something.'

'Aye, yes, it is.'

'What sent him on the day's benders?'

'He went to collect the money she left him. I had to make him go—I wish I hadn't now.'

'He was a fool; he should have stood and fought it. There's even those in the village now who say he's had a rotten deal.'

'I wish they would tell him to his face then, it might bring him some comfort. But he believes everybody's against him, from the top, middle and bottom, everybody. Even his so-called friends haven't shown their faces ... the Rowans.'

'Ah well!' George now hung his head, then looked to the side, and she waited for an explanation of the implication that had been in the two words, but without venturing one he turned away towards the door, saying, 'Well, if I'm to beat the foxes I'd better get down there, Emily,' and she answered, 'Thanks, George. It's good of you, so very good of you.'

She stood looking at the closed door for a moment before turning towards the bedroom. There was a reason why the Rowans hadn't shown their faces. George knew it, likely everybody knew it but herself. Was she closing her eyes to something? No. No. Give him his due, he wasn't a man like that. What had been between him and Miss Lizzie Rowan was in the past long before she herself had come on the scene. She mustn't get things like that into her mind. No, she mustn't; she had enough to put up with.

But it wasn't long before she found out the reason why the Rowans' hand of friendship hadn't been extended in Larry's hour of need.

George had made two journeys back to the house. On the first he deposited the pork, the duck and a parcel which held a thick lined winter coat for her, together with other small packages of fruit and chocolates, two tins of toffee, and a decorated cake which was all broken up.

The second journey George made was to carry up the two small crates, one holding six bottles of whisky, the other the same number of quart bottles of beer.

When Emily bid him good-bye she took his hand and shook it slowly as she said, 'I don't know what I would have done without you, George'; and to make light of it he replied, 'Much worse with me, Emily.' And she let him go at that.

She was utterly weary and sick of heart when at last she

took her place in the bed, lying pressed close against the wall because at the moment she couldn't bear contact with him. It was some time before she fell into a deep sleep. At some time in it she dreamt that she was back in the house and it was another New Year's Eve and they were in the library again having a bit of jollification. She heard Larry singing, his face was bright with happiness, his head was back and he was singing that old touching song, 'Oft, In The Stilly Night'. She heard every word:

> Oft, in the stilly night,
> Ere Slumber's chain has bound me,
> Fond Memory brings the light
> Of other days around me;
> The smiles, the tears,
> Of boyhood's years.
> The words of love then spoken,
> The eyes that shone
> Now dimmed and gone,
> The cheerful hearts now broken!

That song always had the power to make her cry.

When she listened to the chorus being sung again she blinked her eyes and realized that she wasn't dreaming. She put out her hand. His side of the bed was empty. She sat up but didn't get out of bed. Drawing up her knees, she put her arms around them and drooped her head on to them. She shouldn't have left that crate there. How long had he been drinking? It was a repeat performance of a few months' ago.

He had stopped singing now and was talking. She raised her head slightly as his voice came in a growl, saying, 'You're a mean bugger, Dave Rowan, a mean minded bastard! Oh aye; all was forgiven when I was to come into the house and farm. You would have let her come to me then, wouldn't you, you rotten swine you? You were willing to forget the times when you were goin' to kick me arse over head if I came within smelling distance of your gate, and her. Then you almost had a seizure when I got a place of me own, a farm of me own, a place that made yours look like a dung heap. You couldn't forgive me, could you? It ate you up. The envy ate you up. But then, it all changed, Dave, didn't it, it all changed, when Rona died. You didn't mind Liz coming to show her condolences then, oh no, it was all cut and dried, an' I like a bloody fool was willing to let bygones be bygones, for who better than Liz to run the house and be a farmer's wife . . . an' be a farmer's wife, eh? And such a house. And such a farm. But me world blew up, didn't it, blew sky high? An' where am I now?'

There was the sound of a bottle crashing against the stone hearth, and as it splintered he yelled, 'I'm back where I started from! But you won't down me, not you, Dave Rowan. I mightn't beat the rest of them, but begod I'll beat you. I was like a bad smell in your nose you once said, but afore I'm finished, I'll choke you with that smell. An' I've got a way of doin' it an' all. Oh aye, I have that.'

His voice faded away. The only sound now was his grunts and his snorts. He'd be asleep with his head on the table.

So that was it. *That was it. My God!* he would have married that Lizzie Rowan. Yes, he would. What had he said about her? She could run a farm as good as any man. He had married the first one for what she could give him, and he had been prepared to marry the second one an' all for the same reason, so as she could come and help him run the farm. Likely that is why he'd gone after her all those years ago in order to get his foot in a farm, any farm that would take him away from here.

She had been barmy, daft, romantic, like some of those lasses she had read about in the *Ladies' Weekly*; how from them being servants they had married their masters, lords and such, and had been trained to be ladies. Eeh! she had been blind, and gullible. Well, it was finished. Once he sobered up she'd let him have it, and then she'd get away from this frozen hilltop, away from this backbreaking, heartbreaking piece of land and this little stone box of a house.

It was some long time later when she rose from the bed and got into her clothes.

The clock on the kitchen mantelpiece said fifteen minutes past six. He was lying half sprawled over the table. She had to step warily as she went towards the hearth for broken glass was everywhere. She put some wood on to the pale embers of the fire, put the kettle on the top of them, then set about sweeping up the glass from the hearth and picking it out of the carpet. When this was done she went to the table and stood looking down at him.

Near his outstretched fingers was a bottle threequarters full of whisky. There were still four left in the crate, which meant that he had swilled more than a bottle of the stuff from the time he had got up, and that on top of what he had already taken would, she surmised, keep him in a state of stupor for a few hours more. The new coat was lying across the wooden settle. She didn't even glance at it. What she did now was to light a lantern and place it on the doorstep; then taking the bottle with the remaining whisky from the table, she put it into the crate with the other four, carried them outside down the path and to the garden wall, and there one after the other she smashed them on top of the stones.

She did not do the same with the beer. Beer, she considered, never had the same effect as spirits on people; and, anyway, he'd need something to get over his sore head when he came round.

As she returned up the path towards the door the first

large flakes of snow began to fall and she thought, Let it come thick and fast, 'cos I won't be here to clear it away....

He came to quicker than she had expected. It was about nine o'clock when with groans and grunts he raised his head painfully upwards and glared through blinking lids around him; then his hand went groping for the bottle.

She had just come in from milking the cow. The snow was coming down so thickly now it blotted out everything within a yard or so. She stood within the closed door and watched his hand groping round the table. She watched him stagger to his feet, turn and face her, then splutter, 'The bottle ... where's the bottle?'

She didn't answer but went back to the door, flung it wide open, pointed and said, 'It's with the other four.'

He screwed up his eyes at her trying to understand.

'You'll have a job picking the broken glass up, it's splayed over the patch you dug a while back.'

'*You! You!*' He choked on the second word and his dry tongue came out searching for moisture round his lips; and now he roared at her, 'You! you smashed them?'

'Yes, every one of them.'

'You young bitch you!'

Before she knew what was happening his fist had come out and she was knocked backwards on to the crate of beer. There was a searing pain going through her eye and coming out of the back of her head, and a smaller pain attacking her hip; both were unbearable. She let herself sink away through the dark layers that were enfolding her; she thought she was going into death and she made no fight against it....

When she came round she was on the bed and he was kneeling by her side. The pain was still with her but mostly in her head. She saw him through a haze. He looked sober and he sounded sober and she heard him say, 'Oh my God! Emily; I'm sorry. I'm sorry. Oh, I . . . I thought you were gone. Oh Emily! Emily, I didn't mean it; I wouldn't hurt you for the world, I wouldn't, I wouldn't. . . . Oh Emily! Emily.' When his head drooped on to her breast she did not put her arms about him as she lay thinking, I wouldn't hurt you for the world; no, but I'd go and marry me old sweetheart after I'd led you on to believe that I had a feeling for you. He was crying again, he always cried in a crisis.

'Forgive me, Emily. Say you'll forgive me. God! I wouldn't have done that to you if I'd been meself, not to you. Say you forgive me. Oh Emily! Emily.'

She didn't say it; but when she patted his shoulder it conveyed her unspoken words and she knew that she'd still be here to clear the snow away after the big fall.

PART FIVE

THE SECOND YEAR

ONE

She couldn't believe she had been living in the cottage for only a year; nor could she believe that she was but eighteen years old, because she felt a woman, a fully grown woman, one who was used to shouldering responsibility, one who was used to ... carrying a man. From the day he had struck her and she had succumbed to his genuine sorrow she knew that the pattern of her life was set inasmuch as it would be she who must lead, but covertly, for she must never let him imagine that even on his own small plot he had failed.

They had harvested their crop of potatoes and vegetables in season. They still had a good supply of milk, butter, cheese and eggs, and they did an exchange with Mr Waite for fodder and oddments, and the sheep had doubled to six. He had considered doing away with the horse for it didn't earn its keep, but she had been against this for she had grown fond of the animal. But meat, oil and candles had still to be bought, and as yet there was no return in cash for their labours.

They were seriously thinking of taking up pigs; but then so many people kept pigs, almost every cottage round about had its sty. What was evident to her, however, was that they must take up the keeping of some livestock that would bring in a steady, if small return, and quickly. A pig could issue ten to a litter whereas a sheep gave one, or two if you were lucky. And anyway, before you could make money on sheep you wanted a good sized herd, and a wide range to run them on; they had neither the herd nor the range.

These thoughts were very much to the fore in Emily's mind as she sat on the carrier cart, not on the tail now but up front with Alf Morgan. She was a regular customer of his and so he afforded her the courtesy of the front seat. And he didn't hide the fact that he considered her a handsome lass, and a pleasure to look at for she had a skin on her face like a peach. More than once he had thought it was a bit of a shame that her hands were as rough looking as a navvy's; but then she needed them to be hard and strong, for by all accounts she had a tough life of it up on Bailey's Rise.

After stopping the cart he swung her bags from under the seat and down to her, saying, 'See you next week then, lass,' and she replied, 'Yes, Mr Morgan, see you next week.' And that was another thing he liked about her: she didn't take liberties, she always gave a man his title. There was a divided opinion about her on the road. Some said she was a loose piece living up there with a man who had once been her master; others that she was only a bit of a lass who had been led astray by a fellow who was no more than a nowt. He placed himself among the last group for from what he remembered of that fellow Birch his head had been too big for his hat.

There was a light breeze blowing, but the sun was bright and still warm although it was the middle of October.

She swung up the hessian bag, which she had made into the shape of a long knapsack, for ease in carrying it up the hills, and after putting her arms through the straps she hitched it on to her shoulders; then picking up the two smaller bags, one in each hand, she started along the road towards the stile.

She'd had her head slightly bent so she wasn't aware

377

until she lifted her foot on to the first step of the stile that a man was approaching from the other side. As he came nearer and she stared at him her throat went dry. She had seen him a number of times before; even if she hadn't realized who he was she would have recognized the trap which he was driving when it had passed the carrier cart on the coach road. But on these occasions when she merely glanced at him she'd had no idea of what manner of man he was except that she endorsed George's description of him looking like a foreigner.

But now she was seeing him close up, face to face. They stood, one on each side of the stile, and they both knew who the other was. She saw that he wasn't very tall and he was thin with it, but it was a hard thinness. She couldn't describe it to herself except to think that he appeared like some of the men in the steel works in Jarrow who'd had all their flesh melted off them with the intensive heat. His face, too, was thin, but it held no resemblance to that of any steel worker, for the skin was brown, a sort of pale brown, like a tan. But it was his eyes that were different; they were dark, all dark, seemingly no whites to them, and their shape was not like that of any Englishman she knew. Was he Chinese? No, he didn't look like a Chinaman, and she'd seen numbers of Chinamen in Shields, Arabs an' all, and he certainly didn't look like an Arab, yet he didn't look English.

'Can I help you?'

When he held out his hand towards her she lifted her foot quickly back from the stile step and shook her head.

'Then let me lift your parcels over.'

Again she shook her head while all the time feeling stupid. Her thoughts were racing madly back and forwards in her head. Why had he come over to this side of the road? Surely he knew who lived on this side. Was he looking for trouble? But his voice didn't sound like that of a man who was out for trouble. It had a lazy sound, slow, quiet; nice, she thought, if it had belonged to anyone but him.

He was smiling at her now, a half amused, half pitying smile; then he said, 'I am not going to eat you.'

Now she did speak; she didn't like to be treated as if she were a frightened lass. 'I don't imagine you are,' she said.

'Then why be so afraid?'

She stared straight into his face now and her head lifted and her voice sounded harsh as she replied, 'You know right well, you know who I am and I know who you are, an' I'm surprised to see you this side of the road.... Don't you think there's been enough trouble?'

His face was unsmiling now as he replied, 'I had walked round the quarry; I took a side path, I didn't know where it led but I suppose if I'd stopped to think it would have told me. Anyway, I'm glad now that I didn't because I've wanted to speak to you for a long time.'

She drew her chin in, her eyebrows moved upwards and she went as if to step further back from the stile as he rested one arm along the top bar of it and said, 'I don't see why this situation should continue. I apparently have inadvertently done Mr Birch out of his livelihood and his home, to my mind his rightful home, and I feel that it is time that we got together with regard to me making some reparation.'

She wanted to protest immediately at the madness of his suggestion; she wanted to say there'll be another murder if you ever come face to face with him; whether he's drunk or sober he'll go for you. And she believed firmly that he would. But she said nothing, she just stared at him as she thought in amazement, he talks like the gentry do. She had never heard Larry talk this way; he wouldn't know how. It was sad when she thought of it that Larry's one aim had been to appear like a gentleman, whereas this man who had stepped into his shoes, the man who had been in prison all these years, talked like a natural one, which belied his looks, for she had half expected him to speak in broken English.

'Do you think you could arrange that we should meet?'

'No! no!' She was shaking her head wildly now. 'Oh no, please, don't you ever go up there.'

'But why not?'

'Well——' She now dropped her two bags by the side of her feet and, still moving her head, she said, 'I shouldn't have to explain to you, you know yourself you walked into his shoes; everything he had went to you. You came out of the blue as it were. It was like him sort of handing everything to a ghost who he wasn't able to fight.'

'He should have fought, he should have taken the case to court. Even if he hadn't won completely he would have had some decent reparation, much more than she left him.'

She looked at him now through narrowed gaze. The way he had said she, it could have been Larry speaking of her.

'Do you really want to be of help?' she asked.

'Yes, sincerely I do.'

'Then please do as I ask, leave him alone. He would sooner die than take a penny off you, and he'd likely try to do you in if you suggested it to him.' And she knew this to be true; she knew that in many ways Larry was a weak man, but that on this one point, namely the hate of the man who had usurped his position, he was strong, and his hate, she felt, would keep him strong until he died.

They stared at each other for a long moment before he stood aside; and now when she lifted up the bags from the ground and put them on the top bar of the stile and he lifted them down, she made no protest, but when he offered her his hand she ignored it.

She did not give him any farewell but went on along the path, her back slightly stooped under the weight of the knapsack and she didn't stop until she was through the copse and had reached the broken-down bridge. There she leant against the wall and closed her eyes, and said to herself, 'If it isn't one thing it's another. I might have guessed things were running too smoothly.'

TWO

During the next two weeks or so she was afraid to go down to the road in case she bumped into 'him'. As she told herself she mustn't have any truck with him, for she had only to be seen talking to him and the village would be alight again. Yet she thought about him often. He seemed a nice man, quiet. She couldn't imagine him murdering anybody, but he had done, and served his time for it; yet somehow he didn't look any the worse for his long years in prison. There was a sort of—she searched in her mind for a word, and the only one she could think of was calmness. Yes, there was a sort of calmness about him which she considered odd after what he must have been through, and again and again she told herself how surprised she had been to hear him speak so well. Under other circumstances it would have been a pleasure to listen to him, but now she didn't wish for that pleasure, and if he ever tried to speak to her again she'd squash it in the bud quick and fast. She would that. She'd tell him straight.

She was coming out of the byre when she saw Larry going towards the gate in the stone walled compound that they had erected to house the sheep in the roughest of weather, and she called to him, 'Where you off to?'

He turned sharply and, pointing to the trolley, called back, 'What does it look like?'

'But I didn't know there was any wood over that way.'

'There's a rotten branch came down beyond the rise, I noticed it yesterday.'

'Oh, good.' She nodded at him.

Wood was becoming a problem and although they might have been able to afford a hundredweight or so of cheap slack coal each week it was the getting of it up here that posed the problem.

Last year when they had searched for wood they had done it together, but of late he had taken to going off on his own; and she was glad of this for it left her free to sit down for a time. Not that she couldn't sit when he was present, but she was never able to think quietly, or even to sit and read without a sense of unease. She had taken to reading in the evenings; sometimes it was the stories in *Ladies' Weekly* or *Red Letter* which she purchased on her weekly visit to the town and her Aunt Mary's, and sometimes, and more often of late, she looked through the little black book.

There were fifty-eight pages in the book, and on each was a piece of prose or poetry, some pieces consisting of only two lines. But it was with secret pride that she had memorized more than half of them, and often she quoted them to herself word for word whenever their meaning seemed applicable, as at the present moment when she was unpicking, of all things, the coat she had bought in the second-hand shop in Fellburn, the coat that had caused such a stir. It was good material and she had decided she could get a skirt from it besides a sleeved waistcoat. The line that came into her head now was one of the short ones, and it went: 'Language is the dress of thought'. It was said by somebody called Johnson. She mightn't be using it in the same way as the man meant it when he wrote it, but she always found that when she took a needle into her hand her thoughts became clearer, more wise like, and she considered it was a pity that she couldn't turn all her thoughts into language, but once she let them flow down from her head into her mouth, there they stuck, or if they did come out they were expressed in a very ordinary fashion, and not in the fine garments she had made for them in her mind.

There was another reason why she enjoyed her time alone, because then she could talk to the cat. She called him Tiddles. He was still a kitten but very affectionate and very often when she addressed him he mewed back at her and she swore that he understood every word she said.

She stooped down now and lifted the kitten from the hearth and on to the settle at her side, saying, 'There now, what will we talk about this afternoon, eh? There's a nice story started in *Red Letter* but I only hope it doesn't ramble on for ever and a day like the last one. Oh, the things that happened to that poor girl. And I never knew how she did end up because that was the week I missed. Remember, when I had that shocking toothache?' But besides her reasons for liking to have some time to herself she wanted at the moment time to dwell on the consequences of what might happen should the suspicion that kept niggling in her mind be correct. She stopped stroking the kitten as a slight sweat broke out on her.

The kitten mewed for more attention, then curled into a ball and purred. The wood on the fire spluttered and crackled. A crow called from the chimney-top and as if Daisy were answering it there came a loud moo from the shippon, and Emily, now picking up the scissors, went snip, snip down the gores of the coat.

When the knock came on the door her scissors froze in her hand. No one had knocked at that door during all the time they had been here. It couldn't.... No, no! it mustn't be him. Eeh! it would be murder. Thank God Larry was out. She took the coat from her knee and slowly laid it aside; then taking a deep breath, she went to the door and pulled it open, and on a great gasp and a loud cry she actually yelled, 'Da! Oh Da! Da!' The next minute she had her arms round the tubby red-faced man standing on the step, and he was holding her tight, not saying a word, just holding her tight.

Now she was pulling him into the room and closing the door behind him; they held each other at arm's length, then again they were enfolded; and now she was crying and laughing and spluttering all at the same time. 'Oh Da! Da! where have you sprung from? Oh, am I glad to see you. Oh Da!' She rubbed both sides of his stubbly cheeks with her hands and, her face awash with tears, she gulped as she muttered, 'Oh you're a sight for sore eyes. I ... I wouldn't change this moment for a thousand pounds. No, no, I wouldn't.'

'How are you, lass?'

'Oh, me? Oh, I'm all right, Da, I'm all right. Eeh! I was just thinking of you last night. I thought, Where's he got to, it's a trip and a half? It's well over two years. But sit down. Give me your coat. Let me get you a drink.' As she flung his coat and cap across the back of a chair, she turned to him laughing through her tears, the old Emily, as she cried, 'I said, get you a drink, it's only tea.'

'Tea 'll do fine, lass.'

But she didn't hurry to make the tea, she stood looking at him, and he at her; then once again she was rushing towards him, and now there was no laughter threading her tears and her crying was not that of a girl, or even that of a young lass, but of a woman; and her father recognized this as he held her tenderly.

When he had last seen her she still looked a child, in a way, but a child full of life and jollity; yet here she was, two and a half years later, so changed that he hardly recognized her. She had jumped girlhood, there was no remnant of the fledgling on her any more, and her but eighteen. She was still bonny though. Oh aye, she was bonny all right, more than bonny. He held her from him now and, his voice thick, he said, 'Give over, hinny, give over,' and with her head down she muttered, 'Aye, Da, aye....'

She made him a dinner of cold meat, pickled cabbage, new bread, and an apple pie, and she heard how he had reached home yesterday to find Alice Broughton and her brood gone and the house in a shambles. Alice had made a hasty retreat with another lodger after his boat was reported due in; and she heard how he had dashed round hoping to find her and Lucy at McGillbys', only to receive a garbled story of what had happened there from Mrs Gantry next door. Late last night he had landed up at her Aunt Mary's. And now here he was.

She, in turn, told him of Lucy's good fortune in getting into the hospital in St Leonards, and in making a friend of this lady called Miss Rice, whose people lived in Hastings and who were welcoming Lucy into their home and apparently making much of her. She brought out Lucy's letters and watched him read them, nodding as he did so, but making no comment until he was reading the last one; then, looking at her, he said, 'You shouldn't be separated.'

'It was for her good, Da; she was bad, real bad. Look'— she picked out a letter—'she says herself she hardly coughs at all now and she eats like a horse.'

'Aye, she does; but she also says she misses you and wishes you were there.' He pushed his empty plate away from him now, but kept his eyes on it as he said, 'Why don't you go, lass?'

She went to the fire, put on more wood and moved the kettle along the hob before she replied, 'What's done, is done, Da. Things happen in life, and you can't fight them. It all seems worked out for you somehow.'

John Kennedy stared at his daughter's back. Yes, indeed, the girl was gone for ever and it was a woman who was talking.

'Is he good to you?'

'Yes. Oh yes.' She straightened up and came back to the table.

'How has he taken the change from the big house to here?'

'Badly.'

'Aye, well, it's to be expected. Why aren't you married?'

'Well, it's understandable why I'm not, isn't it?'

'I don't see it.'

'Well, if Aunt Mary told you the whole story you would know that he thought he had been married for seven years and then found he wasn't, so it's natural he'd have a thing against marrying again, for who's to tell I wasn't married afore?'

'Don't be daft, lass.'

'I'm not daft, Da. Sep ... Mr McGillby, he wanted to marry me.'

'Sep McGillby? Him! Why, he was nearly as old as me.'

'Aye, I know he was, Da, but I liked him. I mean that was all, I realize now. I only liked him, I didn't love him or anything like that. But I didn't know it at the time. Anyway, I promised to marry him the minute I was seventeen.'

'Begod! you did.'

'Aye, I did. Well then, say I had, and say what I know now, I doubt if I could have stayed with him. I might have gone off and come here and ... well, I could have married Larry, and he'd have been done in the eye a second time.'

'Aw, that's damn nonsense. But to think that Sep Mc-. Gillby had the gall to expect you to marry him and his wife hardly cold. It's just as well he did die or I would have knocked his bloody head off when I got in.'

She did not say, 'The man I'm living with now is of the

same age,' but with a deep note of nostalgia in her voice she asked, 'What's it like down there, Da, the same?'

'Aye, I suppose. Well you've seen it since I saw it last.'

'Not number six Pilot Place. Eeh! I liked that house. And to think that Jessie Blackmore's got it now.'

'Oh no, she hasn't, lass. I learned that much an' all from Mrs Gantry. She never got as much as her foot in the door by what I can gather.'

'No?' Her face brightened. 'Then who did it go to?'

'The nephew. It so turned out that Mrs McGillby left the house to McGillby for his lifetime, but should he die it was to pass to her nephew. He's a fellow who lives up in Westoe and I think by all accounts he's pretty comfortable himself.'

'Well I never! Who's in the house then?'

'Oh, it's rented to somebody; she didn't say who.'

'Aye well, rather anybody but her for I've always felt so ... well so incensed like about that woman having the place.' She looked towards the window as she said musingly, 'I used to keep it lovely; you could eat your meat off the back yard. I used to scrub every flag separately on a Friday and bath-brick the back step. Yet nobody ever saw it, except Sep when he came in that way.'

She continued to stare towards the window but in silence now, until he said, 'You wish you were back here, lass?'

She turned her head slightly towards him, 'You mean in Shields, Da?'

'Aye, in Shields.'

'Oh yes.'

'Well, why don't you go? There's nothin' stopping you.'

She swung fully round now, her face straight as she looked at him. 'Don't let's talk about it any more, Da; I'm here an' I'm here for good. But I'll tell you something'—she now made a face at him—'I'm going to give meself a couple of days off afore the year's out and I'm going into Shields. I've thought about it many a time. But then I thought I could never go and look at Pilot Place, not with that woman in that house, but now I can. I'll go and I'll walk past the door, and I'll go down the pier, then I'll walk right back up Ocean Road and King Street and through the market, and up the Mill Dam Bank and have a look in the shops in Frederick Street. I always liked Frederick Street, better than King Street, although they weren't half as swanky. Yes'—she nodded at him—'I'll do that.... How long are you in for?'

'Well, if I go back on this one, three weeks I'd say.'

'Are you going back on her?'

'What is there to stay for, on shore I mean? You're not there: the house is empty.'

'Are you going to keep the house on?'

'Oh aye, yes.' He nodded emphatically. 'My bits an' pieces are there, and it's always some place to come back to. I was talkin' to your Aunt Mary about it and she, as usual, found an answer.' He smiled widely now. 'You know young Jimmy's getting married shortly and he's working in the yard at Hebburn, well, Shields is nearer to Hebburn than Gateshead, so she said what about letting him rent the place off me until I needed it, an' then they'd find a shanty of their own, an' I said, aye, well, that suited me.'

She now leant across the table towards him, her face bright and eager as she said, 'I'll tell you what, Da. I'll take those couple of days off next week and you and me 'll have a jaunt round, eh?'

'I'd like that, lass. Aye, I'd like that.'

'All right, how about next Wednesday, I'll meet you at me Aunt Mary's and we'll go down home ... I can think of it as home now, an' I'll stay there the night and we'll do Shields and Jarrow and right up the river to Newcastle.'

He cocked his head at her now, saying, 'Aye, we will if I haven't gone through the lot afore then.'

'Well, don't you go through the lot afore then. Now I'm tellin' you'—she wagged her finger at him—'you keep your hand out of your pocket. . . . Well, that's a date; next Wednesday at me Aunt Mary's.'

John Kennedy sat back in his chair and looked about the room and, as if the thought had just struck him, he asked, 'And where is he then?'

'He's out gatherin' wood. He shouldn't be long. It's a business keepin' the fire goin'. Do you want another cup of tea?'

He got up from his chair now, walked to the bedroom door and, pushing it open, glanced inside. Then looking at her again, he said, 'You're a bit crowded, aren't you?'

'Yes, we brought more than we should. It . . . it was my fault I suppose; I picked the stuff. I thought he was entitled to it. There's one or two nice bits.'

He walked back to the fireplace, grinning at her as he said, 'You should have built another couple of rooms on first to hold it, there's enough stuff here to furnish an up an' downer.'

'I thought about having another room on, a sort of lean-to,' she said. 'Now that the land's cleared and we've got quite a bit of it set, we might get down to it. It only means carting the stones, and a bit of plaster and a few beams.'

After a moment or so he looked at his watch and remarked quietly, 'He's a long time.'

Yes, she thought so too, he'd been gone over two hours. 'I'll see if he's come back,' she said; 'he might be at the wood block.'

She went through the scullery, out of the back door, ran down the path, through the gate and up a sharp incline. And then she saw him. He was pulling the wood trolley, but there didn't seem to be much on it. She waved to him whilst he was still quite some distance off, and then ran towards him.

'What's the matter?'

He had stopped and waited for her coming.

'Nothing. Well, nothing bad that is. We've got a visitor.'

She watched his face stiffen and so she hastened to add, 'It's ... it's me da; he's come back from sea. He just wanted to see me.'

'Your da?'

'Yes; I've got a da.' She laughed outright now. 'I've told you he was at sea. Did you think I was making it up? He's been on a longer trip than usual.'

'How did he find out where you were? ... Oh ... oh'—he closed his eyes and nodded his head—'your Aunt Mary.'

'Yes, me Aunt Mary.' Her face was straight as she repeated his words then said, 'Well, aren't you comin'?'

'Does he want to see me?'

'Of course he wants to see you.'

'What for, to knock me down?'

'Don't be silly.'

'I'm livin' with his daughter ... or his daughter's livin' with me.'

She drew in a sharp breath. 'Are you comin'?' she said; 'he's got to go soon.'

It seemed to her that he intended to remain standing where he was for he didn't make a move for at least a full minute; only when she was about to speak again did he tug at the rope and go forward.

In the yard he dusted down his clothes, saying, 'I can't go in like this.'

'Don't be silly, you're a workin' man. What I mean is, you can't work in best clothes.'

He had cast a sidelong sharp glance at her and now he nodded his head and said, 'Yes, you're right, you're always right, I'm a working man.'

As she led the way back into the house she prayed that he wouldn't take a high hand with her da because her da was quick to notice such things.

In the kitchen the two men looked at each other. It was John Kennedy who spoke first. He had surveyed his daughter's man, and even before that man opened his mouth he had settled in his own mind what he thought about him. What he said now was, 'Aye, well, I'm her da. As you perhaps know I've been away to sea these two years or more; if I hadn't she wouldn't be up here now. But that's life, I suppose.'

'She's free to go whenever she feels like it.' Larry's face and tone were stiff.

'Well, I would say that's easier said than done; there's feelings come into associations of all kinds. It doesn't take an educated man to know that feelings are stronger than chains to tie you to somebody. But there, she's made her bed, as she would say herself, an' she's willing to lie on it. But I'm going to say to you now, an' I don't think I'm speaking out of turn or too quickly as we haven't been lookin' at each other for more than seconds, but what I'm going to say is that if you're any kind of man you'll bury the past and you'll marry her, because she's worth marryin'. And I'm not sayin' that simply because she's my lass. Anyone with a pair of eyes in their head would recognize she's worth something more than the name of a kept woman.'

'Oh Da! Da! please; I've told you.'

'Aye, lass, aye'—he turned to her, nodding his head deeply now—'you told me, but I had to have me say. That's what I came for. Now hand me me coat and cap and I'll be on me way.'

'Oh Da! please.'

'Come on, lass, hand them over.'

Before picking up her father's things she glanced at

Larry. His face was almost purple, his eyes, through his narrowed lids, gleamed black. He was in a rage, just like the times when he used to stamp down from the bedroom above the kitchen, after *she* had gone for him.

She almost thrust the coat at her father now, but he was slow to don it and he buttoned each button carefully before taking his cap from her; then turning one last look on Larry, he said, 'As I see it, she's up here as an unpaid skivvy, temporary wife and farm hand combined. Afore this she got a wage. Afore this she had a chance of respectable home an' bairns. But what has she now? You could walk out on her the morrow, and what would she be then? A cast off woman. And what choice have such? They've got to pick from the dregs. I know ... I've travelled, I've seen life an' I know.... I think nowt on you, mister, an' that's straight.' And on this he turned about and walked out.

Emily closed her eyes tightly and her fingernails dug into her palms. She daren't look at Larry but, snatching up her shawl from the back of the settle, she followed her father outside; and she had to run to catch up with him for he was striding away down the hill.

'Da! Oh Da!' She caught his arm.

'It's no good, lass, I had to have me say. I meant to have it; that's why I came. And I'm going to tell you something, lass.' He stopped so abruptly that she fell against him, and he gripped her arm and brought his face close to hers as he said, 'I don't like him. He's no good, he's a snot ... a nowt. Oh aye, you can shake your head like that but I know men. I've had experience of men from the top to the bottom and I say it again, he's a nowt.'

'You didn't give him a chance, Da; you didn't allow him to open his mouth or say a word.'

'I didn't need to, it's in his face, something about him. I've met his like afore, comrades when things are going smooth, but once the fight's on, God! how they run. And from what I've already heard of him, he'll run. Why didn't he stay and fight his claim? Any man worth his salt would.'

'You don't understand, Da. You don't understand.' She was crying now.

'I understand well enough, lass.' His voice had lost its harshness. 'I said it back there, feelings are stronger than chains, you'll never see him as he really is because of your feeling for him, and if you've made up your mind to spend the rest of your days with him ... well it's just as well you're blind. But don't expect me, or others, to be blind.... Aw lass.' He bowed his head now and screwed up his eyes tightly, and she put her arms around him as she murmured, 'I'm sorry, Da. I'm sorry.'

'You're not the one who should be sorry, lass, it's me. I should have had a shore job and looked after you. Your mother begged and prayed me for years to get a shore job, but the bloody sea's in me blood, I get land sick as others get seasick. I'm never happy unless I feel the swell under the soles of me feet. Ah well, there it is.' He rubbed his hand round his face; then walked on again. And she kept by his side until they came to the road, where she said, 'It'll be another hour afore the carrier cart comes along.'

'There's a village back there,' he said, 'I'll walk along to it and get meself a drink; then I'll make for Mary's.'

They stood looking at each other until he asked, 'Is next Wednesday off then?'

'Oh no, Da, no. I'll look forward to it.'

'Good.' He bent and kissed her gently, and once again she flung her arms around his neck; but after a moment he pushed her from him and walked briskly away in the direction of the village.

She watched him until he was out of sight; then turning about, she ran through the copse, past the bridge and up the hill, not stopping until she reached the top. And there she stood gasping for breath. Then she was off again, down the other side of the hill, across the valley and up the slope to the cottage.

Panting, she entered the kitchen, but stopped just within the door for there he was waiting.

It seemed to her that he had not moved from the spot where he was standing when her father had gone for him. She pulled the shawl from her shoulders, closed the door and hung the shawl up on the hook, before turning to him and saying, 'I'm sorry.'

'Why didn't you go with him?'

'Don't be silly.' She slowly drew her gaze from him and was walking towards the fire when he bawled at her, 'Don't say to me, don't be silly! Who do you think you're talking to, anyway?'

She stared at him now, waiting for him to add, 'You forget yourself.' But what he said was, 'You treat me like a sick man. The only things you can come out with are, don't be silly, forget about it, or some such claptrap out of your book. Now your father turns up and looks at me as if he hated my guts, and that's afore I have a chance to open my mouth, and you say, don't be silly.'

'Well, he had a right to.' Now she was yelling back. 'You came in an' stood there an' looked at him as if ... well as if you were still lord of the manor an' him an inferior. And you're not lord of the manor any more. And aye ... aye you are sick; in some ways you are sick, and I'm tellin' you, an' that's straight. You're sick with fear, fear of what people 'll say about you. You're frightened of your own shadow. You can't forget you missed trying to be somebody....'

As the last words passed her lips his hand came up, but she screamed at him, 'Don't you dare! Not a second time.' She drew her head up and back and her chin became knobbly as she compressed her lips for a moment. 'You attempt that just once more and you will be on your own, really on your own. I forgave you the last lot, 'cos you were drunk, but never no more. No man's ever going to strike me again. I swore on it then, and I swear double on it now. You aim to strike me again and I'll take up the first thing to hand and let you have it. I'll do what you told me to do to her up in the bedroom, but there won't be any make believe this time. So I'm warning you, I'm givin' you fair notice.' She looked about her as if in search of a weapon, only for the sound of his breath hissing through his teeth to bring her eyes to him again, and she watched him fighting for control. She saw his rib cage stretch, almost forcing his waistcoat buttons apart; then he flung round from her and went out, and she was left standing, her head drooping now on her chest as she asked herself why she stayed with him. Why? Why?

The fight suddenly going out of her, she became limp and groped for a chair. After sitting for a minute or so, she said to herself, 'You shouldn't have said he couldn't forget he missed trying to be somebody; he knows it well enough himself.' And with this reaction she gave herself the answer to why she stayed.

THREE

'By! isn't this grand havin' you both together like this.' Mary flung her arms wide as she looked to where her brother and Emily were sitting at the far side of the table, and she cried at them, 'Don't you think this calls for something stronger than tea? What about you slippin' out and gettin' a bottle, our John?'

'No, no, Da.' Emily stopped her father from rising. 'Look'—she now wagged her finger at her Aunt Mary—'we're goin' down to Shields, an' there's a long day afore us; if he starts this early, well....' She now slanted her gaze at her father, and he laughed and said, 'Perhaps you're right, lass, perhaps you're right, but me tongue's hangin' out just at the thought of it.... Go on, Mary, pour your stewed tea out.'

'Me tea's never stewed, our John, you know that; boiled, aye'—straight-faced, she nodded at him—'but never stewed.'

When the gales of laughter died down Mary poured out the mugs of tea, then seating herself at the table, she looked closely at Emily, saying, 'I know the wind's enough to wipe the lugs off you up there, but it doesn't seem strong enough to put any colour into your cheeks. What's the matter with you? Sickenin' for somethin'? You look as pale as a lady in decline.'

'I've had a cold, Aunt Mary.'

'What! Why only last time you were here you told me

it was impossible to catch cold up there. You said yourself the wind acted like that thing that I said they were trying to do to the bairns, which I would have none of, no begod! knock-u-lation. That was it, wasn't it? Well, I was tellin' you about that doctor wantin' to do the bairns 'cos of smallpox, remember? You said the wind up there acted in the same way against cold.' She now turned to her brother and, her expression as pugnacious as only her expression could be, she declared, 'Doctor or no doctor, I almost kicked his arse out of the door. He wasn't stickin' manure an' stuff into my bairns, smallpox or no small-pox. I told him I had one cure for everything from diphtheria to skites, an' that was a steam kettle; it had brought all mine through so far ... *Knock-u-lation!* I wonder what next they'll think up. Leave us alone, I said, an' we'll pull through all right ... waggin' our tails behind us.' She sang the last words, and again they were all laughing.

And so it went on for the next hour until they bade her a great laughing farewell and took the train for Shields.

It was as they passed Jarrow that Emily, looking out of the window towards where, in the distance, the three streets and two terraces formed the hamlet of East Jarrow which was situated on the banks of the Jarrow slacks, and nearer still the little stone bridge and the church of Simonside, experienced such an overwhelming feeling of homesickness that she turned to her father and said, 'Da, let's get off at Tyne Dock.'

'Oh aye, yes, if you like. But why? Do you want to walk through the arches again?' He laughed at her.

'Not so much the arches but along Thornton Avenue and on to Pilot Place. I'd like to see it again.'

'Well, that wish is easily granted, lass. Here we are coming into the tunnel.'

When they came out of the station and into the top of Hudson Street, Emily paused for a moment and looked about her. It was as if she had been away for years in a foreign country and was only now stepping on to home soil.

They went down the Dock Bank, past the familiar sight of men standing in groups against the railings and the walls of the dock offices, waiting for a man such as Sep had been to set them to work on one of the boats, and she felt a lump in her throat as she crossed the open space between the line of bars and the dock gates themselves; then they were going down Thornton Avenue, and in a short while they could see the river proper.

It was a dull day. The sky looked low as it often did in this part of the country at this time of the year. The water in the river appeared like molten steel; only when the bows of a ship sliced it apart did it rise and change its colour and become white tipped; but then, when the stern had passed through it, it would fall back into place and, heaving gently now, assume again its leaden look.

They continued to walk on the river side of the road until they came to Pilot Place. Opposite No. 6 Emily stopped. The house looked the same except cloth curtains were now hanging at the windows, not Nottingham lace ones like when she was there; and she was quick to note that the step hadn't been bath-bricked that morning; in fact, it looked as if it hadn't been touched for a week.

'Come on, lass.' John tugged at her arm; then looking at her closely, he urged, 'Ah, come on now. Come on. Don't cry over spilt milk. The time you spent in there has gone, lass, never to come back.'

Slowly she turned about and walked by his side in the direction of The Lawe. It was some time before she spoke, and then, more to herself than to him, she said, 'It doesn't seem fair you're not able to realize when you're happy; those were the best days I'll ever have in me life.'

'Don't talk nonsense, lass. Come on, snap out of it; you've got a long way to go. An' let me tell you something.' In a slightly embarrassed fashion he now linked her arm and pulled her close to him as he went on, 'You'll not end up your days on that blasted hill, oh no! I can see further than me nose. Moreover, I can smell when there's something rotten in a cargo. Instinct I suppose it is, I've always had it. When I was just a flamin' stoker I had it. But these past few years when I've been up on deck an' coming into contact with men for long spells at a time, that, you know, Emily'—he jerked her arm into his side—'that's when you know men, when you're with them for long spells an' there's nowhere to go to get rid of them, that's when you get to know men. And I know men. And I know what I'm talkin' about. And I say again you'll not end your days up on that hill.'

'Oh Da! Da, don't keep on.'

'I'm not keepin' on, lass, I'm just trying to comfort you. And another thing I've been thinkin'. I made a mistake in lettin' Mary's Jimmy have the house. If I'd known then as much as I know now you could have come back and lived there, and brought Lucy home.'

'No, no, Da. Thank you all the same, but I would have never lived there. And I certainly wouldn't bring Lucy home, because she, at least, seems to have fallen on her feet. She's better in health than she's ever been in her life by the sound of it. No, Da'—she smiled at him now—'things have a way of working out. And look'—she pulled him round now to face her—'stop worrying about me, I'm old enough to take care of meself, and as me Aunt Mary would say, I'm not as daft as I'm cabbage lookin'.'

'Eeh! your Aunt Mary. She's a one. She'd bring a guffaw from a corpse, wouldn't she?' And now he asked, 'Where do you want to go first, back home? ... I've tidied it up as much as I can. They've nearly battered the furniture to bits but it's all clean. Or shall we go to that place just off the market and treat ourselves to brown bread an' mussels, an' a drop of brown ale?'

'Oh yes, Da, yes I'd like that. I used to pass it often but I've never been inside.... Oh, I'd like that.'

'Then come on, lass, let's enjoy oursels.'

The following morning their plans for the day were brought to an abrupt end when, at eight o'clock, John, roused from a deep and sober sleep by a knock on the door, opened it to one of his shipmates who gave him the news that they were signing on again that morning because the boat was being moved to the London docks to pick up its next cargo.

When John came back up the stairs Emily was waiting for him, and when he told her his news, the disappointment showing on his face, she said, 'Well, don't worry, Da, at least about me. You'd be happier aboard, now wouldn't you?'

'Aye, lass, I suppose I would in a way. Aye I would.'

'Well then, let's get some breakfast and off you go.'

'What about you?'

'Me?' She considered for a moment. 'I think I'll do what I've promised meself for years, I'll go and have a look round Newcastle. Me Aunt Mary's always talking about the fine shops there. And I'll buy everything I set me eyes on.'

'Aye, do that. Do that. And I'll give you somethin' to help you do it.'

'You won't.'

'But I will.'

'Oh you! Da.'

'Oh you! Emily.'

They both laughed; then, her laughter ending abruptly she threw herself against him and he hugged her tightly to him.

Having said good-bye to her father at half-past nine, she didn't linger in the house; for more reasons than one.

Not only did she imagine she could still smell Alice Broughton there, but, although her father had done his best to tidy up the place, to her eyes it still looked dirty. And then there were the neighbours. She knew that by now the whole street would know she had come back; that she would be a thing of curiosity. Hadn't she been in the papers? Moreover, it wouldn't surprise her in the least if they were aware that she was living with a man who had thought himself married and found he wasn't. And so, by half-past ten she was sitting in the train bound for Newcastle.

Today the weather was kind; the sun was shining and there was hardly any wind. She found it a pleasure in itself to be able to walk without being buffeted by the wind. And then there were the wonders of Newcastle: the buildings, the churches, the monuments. She had never seen anything like them. In an odd way she felt a bit put out that Newcastle should look so much finer than Shields. But then Shields was home, and it was a canny place, and this town hadn't that feeling about it. Grand yes, almost overpoweringly grand. Look at that statue on top of that pillar. Earl Grey, it said. And then there was the Theatre Royal, and Grey Street. And the markets, covered in! They were amazing.

By one o'clock she was slightly footsore, and more than slightly bemused by the size and grandeur of the imposing shops. So she took to the side streets, looking for some place, not swanky, where she could get a meal.

Going up one such side street, where the shops were smaller, but mostly jewellers and clothiers, there right in the middle of the street over a very unimposing window was the word RESTAURANT. The window had a sort of lace curtain across it so she couldn't see into the place, but it was a restaurant and some place where she could eat, so she went in, and immediately she had closed the door behind her and a 'gentleman' in a black suit came towards her she realized she had made a mistake.

The 'gentleman' looked at her for a moment while she dumbly returned his stare, then he said, 'Will you come this way, madam?' And he now bowed to her as if she were somebody, and she managed to keep her head up and her back straight as she followed him in and out of a number of small tables at which mostly gentlemen were seated.

The waiter, for such he was she now recognized, pulled out a chair in front of a small table set in the corner of the room and invited her to sit down; and then he spread a napkin over her knees and offered her a large folded card.

She looked at the card. It merely described the meals that were being offered. Heading the list was roast sirloin; but she pretended to peruse the whole list of dishes, thinking that this was the kind of place he would have come to, even if he didn't feel at home. But his wife would have felt at home here. She gulped slightly in her throat before looking up at the waiter and saying, 'I would like the roast beef please.'

'Would madam like a soup to begin with? And the fillet of sole is very good today.'

She looked straight into his eyes as she said, 'I'll have the soup, but no fish, thank you.'

'Very good, madam. Would ... would madam care for a little wine?'

Her mouth opened to repeat the word wine, but she closed it, shook her head slightly and said, 'No, thank you....'

As she ate the courses brought to her she kept her eyes concentrated mostly on the food. She was aware that her nails worn down to the quicks and the roughness of her hands could not have escaped the notice of the waiter, yet he continued to treat her as if she were a lady.

She was glad she was wearing the coat Larry had

bought her. It was the first time she had put it on, and her hat was plain but decent.

Twice when she raised her eyes from her food it was to meet the gaze of gentlemen sitting at nearby tables. Two smiled faintly; one of them, when for the second time she happened to look in his direction, inclined his head just the slightest towards her, and this brought her colour flushing up so fiercely that she imagined her face to be aflame.

The lunch over, the waiter brought her bill. She almost gasped aloud as she looked at it. Seven shillings and six-pence. *Seven shillings and sixpence!* Her mother hadn't had much more than that to feed them all for the week. Eeh! she had been a fool to walk into a place like this.... No, she hadn't. Why shouldn't she walk into a place like this, eh? Why shouldn't she? She knew how to pass her-self; she knew how to use table cutlery, she had laid it often enough; the only thing she didn't know was how to talk properly, but if she once put her mind to it she could do that an' all—she was quick to pick things up; and so she wasn't going to tell herself she had been a fool to come in here, and although she would never again pay seven and six for a meal she was doing it now, and she was going to do it properly.

She took the half sovereign that her father had given her from her bag and placed it on the salver with the bill. The waiter took it, came back and handed her the salver with the change on it, two single shillings and a sixpence.

He would expect a shilling by way of a tip; somebody mean might give him the sixpence. She looked up into his face, smiled at him and, pushing the salver gently away with her hand, said, 'Please to keep it.'

The warm glow she experienced when she saw the man's eyebrows move slightly upwards was compensation enough for her extravagance, and when his face moved slowly into a broad beam and he said softly but deeply,

'Thank you ... thank you, madam,' she experienced a feeling almost of elation.

When she had buttoned the front of her coat and gathered up her bag his hand came on to her elbow and he assisted her from the chair, then weaving his way through the tables he preceded her to the door, and there, bowing deeply towards her, he said, 'Good-day, madam. I hope we may see you again.'

She moved her head slightly towards him, and went out into the street. Her head was high, but her knees were trembling. She had just been treated like a duchess. For the first time in her life she had been deferred to. Oh, of course, there had been Sep, but this was different. This is what money did for you, it made people respect you. Not always. Not always. The voice was loud in her head as she remembered that all the money Larry had once had, or thought he had, hadn't brought him respect. Well, she wouldn't delve into that now, but back there in that restaurant she had been treated as she had never been treated in her life before. Moreover, she felt glad inside, and that was a feeling she hadn't experienced for a long, long time.

She had the urge to skip, she felt a lass again—No, not a lass, she laughingly chided herself inside, a young woman ... a lady. Madam ... fancy being called madam.

She let out a long breath, her head came down from its high position; she wished, oh she wished she had someone to talk to, to go over the whole scene again from the minute she had stepped over the threshold ... in boots mind. She looked down at her boots. Had he noticed her boots? He must certainly have noticed her hands. And those men, they had kept smiling at her, *They* had noticed her.

Not for a long time had she felt so bonny. Once or twice Larry had said she was beautiful, but somehow it had meant nothing for what she had wanted to hear at those times was that he loved her. But now she was feeling bonny.

She stopped in front of a shop window towards the end of the street. It was a jeweller's. She could see her reflection against a large square of black velvet reposing on a tilted shelf in the middle of the window and it told her that from the way she was looking at this moment she was indeed bonny.

But as she stared into the black velvet the smile slowly left her face; her eyes crinkled. She now leant forward until her nose was pressed against the plate glass window. *It couldn't be. It couldn't be.* But it was; there couldn't be two like it. There was her watch, her watch that Mr Tooton had sold for her. There it was. But was she going daft? She must be, or the light was mixing up the figures. She moved to the side, her nostril now almost flat against the window.... *Four hundred and twenty-five guineas.*

No, no, it couldn't be her watch. *But it was. It was.* There was the red stone in the top near the pin and the white stones all down each side of the gold strap and the row of blue ones down the middle, and the little watch hanging from the end with the smaller stones around it. She had looked at that watch every night and every morning since Sep had given it to her. It was her watch.

She stood straight and turned her head from side to side now; she felt faint. What should she do? What could she do? If she went into the shop and told them the story, what would they say to her? They would ask how she had come into possession of a watch such as this, worth four hundred and twenty-five guineas; and then she would have to tell them about Sep and how he got it, and they would say he had stolen it.

Oh, Mr Tooton. Mr Tooton.

She felt sick inside. She had trusted Mr Tooton; she had thought he was a nice man, a good man. She could see now why he had left the firm and gone away. Oh yes, yes. Were there any honest people in the world? Were there any good people in the world? Oh. She turned to the window, putting her two hands flat against it as she whispered to herself, 'That's my watch, my watch.'

She heard a bell tinkle to the side of her as the jeweller's door opened and she turned her head quickly, then stared at the man who was staring at her. It was him from the house.

Now, as if she had been waiting for him, as if he had just left her to go into the shop, she spoke to him, or rather gabbled at him as she pointed through the window to the square of black velvet and the object lying on it. '*You see that!*' she said. 'You see that! four hundred and twenty-five guineas. That's my watch. That's my watch!' Her voice was rising.

He was standing close by her side now, staring at the watch. Then he looked at her and said, 'Are you feeling all right?'

'Yes, yes, I'm all right, but that's my watch.'

He took her arm in an effort to draw her away from the window but she tugged it from him, and turning to face him, she said, 'I'm not daft or anything. I'm not out of me mind. That's my watch. I gave it to Mr Tooton to sell for me. He was the clerk to the solicitors who did your business and Larry's. He came and took over, like the bums, you know, until Larry got out of the house. He was a nice man.' Slowly now she moved her head from side to side, uttering no word as she did so; then she drew in a deep breath and went on, 'At least ... at least I thought he was. I knew it was valuable an' I asked him to sell it for me because, you see, if I went to sell it.... Oh'—she shook her head again quickly now—'it's a long story. But he sent the money to me Aunt Mary's. Twenty pounds he sent me; he said that's all he got for it. And ... and then he left the firm and ran off, or went off....' Her voice trailed away.

He was looking at her differently now, and when he turned his head and stared at the watch lying in its nest of black velvet she gripped his arm and said, 'You believe me?'

'Yes, yes.' His tone was sharp, his face serious, as he answered, 'Yes, yes, I believe you. But come ... come, let's find some place to sit down and talk. There's a restaurant farther along the street.'

When he went to take her arm she shrugged his hand away, saying, 'No, no, I've just been there, I've had something to eat.'

'Oh!' His face showed slight surprise. 'Then there's a churchyard just along here with seats at the back, let us go there.'

He had almost to drag her away from the window, and when they reached the back of the church and were seated on a wooden bench she leant forward and put her hands between her knees, pressing them tightly as she said, ' 'Tisn't only the watch, it's him. To do that to me! And I liked him; I thought he was such a good man.'

'Perhaps he was in great need himself, and you never know what you'll do when faced with a situation like that.'

'You're for him?' She was glaring at him now.

'No, no, I'm not for him, and if I had him here now I'd want to knock whatever money he got for the watch out of him, although'—he shook his head and smiled wryly—'I made a vow once never to lift my hand to a man again as long as I lived, yet as I said, when one is tempted....'

She turned and looked down at her hands again as she repeated, 'Four hundred and twenty-five guineas.'

'He wouldn't get that price for it; the jewellers expect a big profit, and especially when buying something as unusual as that, because it isn't everybody who can afford four hundred and twenty-five guineas. Although there are some very rich men in Newcastle, and no doubt their ladies dress magnificently, they wouldn't be in the habit of paying that price for a fob watch.'

'A what watch?'

'Fob watch; that's what it's called, a fob watch.'

'Oh.' Her head wagged a number of times.

'Would you like to tell me how you came by it?' His voice was quiet.

She didn't answer immediately but straightened up and lay back against the seat; then slowly and dully she related the story of Sep and the watch. And he listened until the end without interrupting, but when he did speak it wasn't about the watch. What he said was, 'The man Sep, he must have thought a great deal of you.'

Sep. She cast her glance towards him, then turned it back on to the grey stone buttress attached to the wall at the far end of the path from where they were sitting, and in a strange way she likened it to Sep, because Sep had been strong. He would always have supported her, and she would have liked that, felt safe in his keeping. Even after discovering what marriage was all about, she would still in a way have been happy, encircled by his strength. Now, she had only herself to rely on, and she had to gather enough strength to support two people.

'He was a good man,' she said, 'caring. You know what I mean?' She was looking at him again. 'He was much older than me, thirty-five.'

'Thirty-five. Dreadful age!'

She saw that he was smiling at her, and she gave a small smile in return as she said, lamely, 'Well, it was a good age.'

'You think so?'

'He could have been me father.'

'So could I.'

Her eyes widened slightly. 'You're not thirty-five!'

He laughed outright now, 'George has a saying which

409

is very explanatory. It's ... not a kick in the backside off; and I suppose you could say that about my age, I'm nearly thirty-five.'

'Well, you don't look it. And after what you went throu ...'

She bit on her lip and shook her head and looked apologetically at him, but as he looked back at her the expression on his face had a gentle touch to it.

It might have been a matter of thirty seconds before he said quietly, 'You're the first one who has attempted to make any reference to my time in prison....'

'I'm sorry.'

'Please ... please'—his hand came out and touched hers—'don't be. It's like opening the door of a room that has been closed for years, letting the breeze through. When people don't mention it except with their eyes, as in the village and thereabouts'—he nodded his head slowly—'I feel as if I'm still paying for what I did. It's even worse than being in prison, because that time wasn't all bad, at least not for me. I suppose I developed a way of looking at life and things that helped me through. It wasn't the same for everybody, oh no.' His head moved very slowly now as he repeated, 'Oh no, it wasn't the same for everybody.'

She realized that his hand was still lying on top of hers and that hers was resting on her knee. She knew she should withdraw it, because here they were in the open. Although this was a quiet corner of the churchyard they were still in the open, and there were people passing at the end of the path, But she didn't withdraw it. It was something in his face, in his eyes, that made her let her hand remain where it was.

He was still talking and she had missed part of what he was saying because her mind had been on the hand business, but now she gave him her full attention for he was speaking of Larry....

'Of the two of us, as I've said, he's had the worse deal because, by all accounts and what I can piece together, she must have led him the hell of a life ... and you, too.'

'She wasn't easy to live with, and ... and although she was your wife I must say this, I think she was a bad woman.'

'She was a bad woman, you're right; and bitterness made her worse. What happened to me reflected on her and she broke off all connection with me. Seeing me now, you could say she made it up to me at the end but you'd be wrong, for what she did she did to spite Birch. As for me, what she left me is a crippling legacy, nothing more.'

He paused for a moment, and she watched his thin lips press themselves into an even thinner line. He had a nice mouth, she considered, wide; and a good set of teeth. He had a nice face altogether; although it looked a bit foreign it had something about it. She thought that given the place and opportunity he would like a bit laugh too, and a joke. He was a pleasant kind of man, a man you could talk to. But now his expression was looking anything but pleasant as he said, 'There was a clause in her will, which stated that should I marry I forfeit all that she left me. As it is, all her money she left to her cousin's family in America. The house and farm she willed to me on certain conditions, which are that the farm must support the house and itself. Whatever profit is made, half of it must go back to replenish stock et cetera, the other half is mine, a sort of wage. So'—he pursed his lips—'it's up to me to see that the business is a success.' And now he gave a dry laugh. 'The funny thing about it is, when I stepped into that place I knew no more about farming than I suppose you did when you first went there. And you know something?' He now leant towards her. 'I know a little more now; it's George who carries the farm. He's a very good fellow, George. He's going to be married, did you know?'

'No, no, I didn't. Oh, I'm so glad, I like George; he was a good friend to me.'

'And he liked you too. He told me so.'

She turned her head away for the moment as a thin thread of regret spiralled through her. She could have married George and lived on the farm in comfort under this man.... Oh, shut up!

'Tell him I'm glad he's going to be married, will you? ... Eeh! no.' Her hand jerked away from his now. 'No, don't say anything; I'll tell him meself when we meet 'cos....'

As she blinked rapidly and her colour rose, he said quietly, 'It wouldn't do for him or anyone else to know that we had met and talked, that's what you mean to say, isn't it?'

She looked him straight in the eyes now and said, 'Yes, that's what I mean. And it's right. And I shouldn't be sittin' here.'

'No, I suppose you shouldn't. Being the person you are, you would see it as something disloyal. But I'm glad you are sitting here because, you know, this is the first real conversation I've had with anyone, and I mean just that, the first real conversation I've had with anyone since I came back to this country. I had much more companion-ship in prison.'

She wetted her lips and her head drooped slightly as she continued to look at him, and he went on, 'I had killed someone, I had killed a man; I was classed as a murderer and I was put among criminals. I had to live with them, and do you know most of them were just ordinary men. There were exceptions. Oh yes.' He nod-ded his head quickly now. 'There are men who are born bad and are never happy unless they're looting or killing. But the majority of the prisoners were ordinary fellows, men who had given away to temptation of one kind or another. And there were one or two even like myself who

412

had killed in defending a woman; not knowing then that she wasn't worth defending. You know I've never looked upon myself as a murderer because what happened, happened so quickly, and the blow I struck didn't kill the man.'

'No?'

'No, it didn't. You see'—he looked away from her towards his feet, swallowed deeply, and rubbed one hand tightly across his mouth before looking at her again and saying, 'I was on a paddle boat, a river steamer, and I met this girl. She was on a holiday from England, and I was on a holiday from England, or you might say I had escaped from England. It was like this. My father was born in London. His father was a tailor, and my father didn't like tailoring, so he travelled for a tea company. During his travels he met a Polynesian girl. I was the result. I can't remember my mother or anything about her. He brought me back to England when I was three years old, and for some reason he lost his taste for travel and took over the tailor's shop. I took after him in many ways, because I didn't care much for tailoring either. He was a very thoughtful and considerate man; he sent me to a good school until I was sixteen. But from then I had to go into the business. He died when I was nineteen, and the business became mine. It was a good little business— we made clothes for those termed toffs—but what little interest I had in it I soon lost. As I said, I was like my father, I wanted travel. And so when I was twenty-four I sold up and off I went. I was going to see the world. I was going to educate myself further by travel, as my father had done.

He smiled a deprecating smile, and then went on, 'So a few months later I was on this paddle steamer going up the Mississippi River, and as I said, there was this young lady, English also, although as I remember I had to make my nationality evident to her, she took me straightaway for a foreigner.' He put his head on one side now as if he were looking back down the years as he said, 'Paddle steamers are very gay places, bands playing, gambling, singing, dancing, and eating. I was twenty-four, the young lady was the same age, we were both ready, even pining, for love. Within a month we were married, secretly by the way, for her cousin and her family, to whom Rona introduced me, also looked upon me as a foreigner and ... not quite a gentleman, for I made no bones about my upbringing or the business that I had inherited and sold. But in that family trade was looked upon in the same way as leprosy. Anyway, Rona was supposed to be going off alone to visit another branch of the family, and that gave us the chance to get away on another paddle steamer to begin our honeymoon.

'She was an attractive girl in those days.' He nodded at Emily now, as if to prevent her contradicting him, then went on, 'And very vivacious. Men buzzed round her like bees round a honey pot. There was one in particular who buzzed too close for my liking. He was a gambler; his name was known up and down the river and in a number of states. He had the kind of status that a popular actor would have in this country. I came on deck in the moonlight to see him with his arms around her. I've often wondered since if her arms weren't around him. But the sight raised a blind fury in me. I sprang at him. I must have taken him by surprise because my first blow to the jaw knocked him backwards. If he hadn't staggered he would have regained his balance and likely killed me because he was a big-made fellow, and I was, in those days, even thinner than I am now. Anyway, he fell against the capstan. His head jerked to the side and he never moved again.'

Once more he wiped his hand tightly against his mouth, and it was some seconds before he continued, 'I couldn't believe it. Nobody on the boat could believe it, yet I was quick to take in that there were more than a few who were relieved to see him gone, for he was known to be a bully. But he was a wealthy bully, and he had made powerful friends. And it was these friends who saw to it that the verdict wasn't accidental death. I look back now and realize I was lucky not to be lynched. Anyway, my wife of such short duration disappeared quickly from the scene, and I don't know to this day if the cousins in America knew that she married again when she returned to England, but I do know that they were aware she had a husband in prison for certain things happened during the latter part of my term, acts of provocation, orders given which had I disobeyed even by as much as a look would have lengthened my sentence. And I'm sure the powers behind the scenes would have succeeded in keeping me there if the particular governor hadn't died two years before I was due for release. The man who took his place, although his rule was iron hard, was apparently someone who couldn't be bought, and because of this he didn't reign long. He was due for transfer shortly after I was discharged.... And so, Miss ... Kennedy'—he now bent towards her, smiling—'that's my life story.'

'And it's a sad one.'

'Let's say it all adds up to experience. But you know something? I feel better at this moment than I've done for years. I've been able to talk about it. Confession, they say, is good for the soul. You're easy to talk to, you know.... May I call you by your name?'

'You just did.'

'I want to say Emily.'

She shook her head now as she rose abruptly to her feet, saying sharply, 'No, no! An' ... an' what's more'— she now turned to him where he was standing facing her—'you know what they're like back in the village, and I've got enough to put up with as things are, and although if it were possible I wouldn't mind ... well, I

415

wouldn't mind talking to you.... Well, you know what I mean. As it is it'll save me a lot of trouble if you just pass me by, kind of ignore me.'

'Oh! Oh!' His smile was gentle, his voice soft, but there was a touch of merriment in it as he said, 'That's an impossibility; no one could ignore you, at least no man.'

She was hot all over. She recalled the looks of the diners in the restaurant.

She said to him now, 'Please ... please, don't come along with me. I ... I've enjoyed our talk though. Yes, yes, I have.' She nodded her confirmation at him and smiled. 'You say you feel better for talking to me, well, I can say the same because if I'd had to keep it bottled up, I mean what I felt about Mr Tooton, I think I would have exploded. Eeh!'—she now shook her head slowly from side to side—'I'll never get over him: I thought he was the nicest man on earth. But you live and learn, don't you?'

'Yes, you live and learn, Emily. And as this is the only time I'm to be allowed to talk to you, won't you let me accompany you to the train?'

'No. No, I'm sorry. Anyway, I'm not going by train, I'm going to call at my aunt's. She lives just over the bridge in Gateshead.'

'Is she the friend that Mrs Riley talks about?'

'Oh yes, yes, I suppose so. Well, good-bye, Mr....'

'Stuart, Nicholas Stuart. I used to be known to my friends as Nick.' He held out his hand, and she took it, and her face was warm again with embarrassment as she said, 'Well, good-bye, Mr Stuart.'

'Good-bye ... Emily.'

She withdrew her hand from his and walked away up the path. Her handbag felt like lead on her arm; she didn't seem to be able to walk straight.

When she reached the main street and became lost in the crowd she felt a little easier. But eeh! the things that happened to her. She seemed to walk into hot water no matter what she did. And if anybody had seen her talking to him and in Newcastle, and not only talking to him but sitting with him and his hand on hers, by! what would they have made of that? It would have set the village alight again. Why did these things happen to her?

The quicker she got back up that hill and into the cottage and stayed there, the better for her and all concerned; for there was this other thing niggling at her mind, and if it were true, even Mr Tooton and the watch would fade into insignificance. By yes! if that happened she'd be right in the cart.

FOUR

It was almost dark when she got down from the carrier cart near the stile. But if it had been pitch black she would still have found her way over the hills, for as she was wont to tell herself, she knew the path like the back of her hand.

From a distance she could see that the cottage door was open and she felt both a warm glow and a feeling of guilt as she saw the lantern come swinging towards her; and both these feelings were intensified further by Larry's concern when he came up with her. There was no reprimand in his voice when he said, 'Why did you leave it so late?'

'I missed the other cart.'

He took hold of her arm, and she looked at him in the swinging light and saw that he was pleased, more than pleased about something, and it couldn't be entirely due to her return because he had never greeted her like this before. But then she hadn't stayed away for a night before. He hadn't asked her how she had enjoyed herself, but of course, she didn't expect him to; she had been with her father and there would never be any love lost between them, that was sure.

When they entered the kitchen, and even before taking her things off, she stood for a moment looking at him. She had never seen him like this, well not since the night of the jollification.

'You seem very pleased with yourself,' she said. 'Have you discovered a gold mine?'

She actually started as his head went back and he let out a deep laugh, and it was the first time she had heard him laugh since they had come here. And when he said, 'Just that. Just that. A little one, but a gold mine, nevertheless,' her mouth fell open.

He now grabbed up a small bag from the mantelpiece, saying excitedly, 'I was looking for some stones, decent ones. I found a small pile in the far corner, and a rabbit or some animal had made a way underneath them, and there to the side of the run this little bag was lying.'

She watched him tossing it up in his hand. 'Look, the top's chewed off. I couldn't believe my eyes. Eighteen sovereigns. My dad must have buried them there. He was a careful one, a bit near where money was concerned. I never did believe he got as little as he said for the stuff he sold. Well, I was right, wasn't I?'

As he spilled the sovereigns on to the table she screwed up her eyes tightly against a storm that was brewing inside her. It was too much, it wasn't fair: finding out about Mr Tooton, and now even the money he had given her for the watch to be taken from her. She would, in the first place, have given it to Larry, every penny of it if it hadn't been that she would have had to explain where it came from. But giving, and having it taken away like this were two different things. And he was so pleased with himself. His father's savings ... my God! He had once admitted they had lived from hand to mouth.

She was going to choke. If she didn't let the torrent inside her loose she would choke. She stumbled forward and, grasping at a chair, dropped on to it and buried her head on her arms, while he stood looking down on her in amazement, listening to the noise she was making, which couldn't be described as weeping, or even crying, for the choking sobs that were coming from her sounded as if she

419

were in anguish from intense pain.

'What is it? What's the matter?' He took her by the shoulders and pulled her to her feet; then shook her and brought her round to face him as he demanded again, 'What is it? What's happened? Tell me, something's happened?'

Yes, something had happened. A number of things had happened today. She had found out you couldn't trust anyone; she had found out that men liked to look at her; she found her watch; she had found that murderers could be just ordinary men; and that strange things happened to your senses, things over which you had no control, for she had found that this particular murderer was kind and gentle in his ways, he was someone you could talk to ... and she had liked talking to him, and she had liked listening to him talking ... she had liked him altogether.

There was a space between each sob now, her head hung slack on her shoulders. She drew in a shuddering breath and groped for the chair again, but she had hardly sat down when he was again holding her by the shoulders, demanding now, 'What's happened? You've never been like this before.'

As she looked back into his face, which at one time she had thought so handsome and attractive, she knew that her outburst would have to have some explanation, and so she gave it.

'I think I'm going to have a baby,' she said.

If a bee had stung him he couldn't have recoiled more quickly. 'No! No!' His pleasantness had completely vanished. 'Not that!'

His tone and attitude had the same effect on her as her news had had on him; and now she bridled. Wiping the tears from her face with the back of her hand, she demanded, 'Why not? It's natural, isn't it? And how do you think one can stop such a thing happening? You tell me.'

'Yes, I could tell you.' His voice came from a growl

deep in his throat now. 'Oh, my God!' He was holding his head as he turned away from her. Then as quickly he was facing her again, and his next words cut into her heart more surely than if he had taken up the bread gully from the table and driven it into her, for what he said was, 'Don't think that this will make me marry you, because it won't.'

He stood glaring at her, waiting for some response, and when none came he flung round from her again and went to the fireplace. Gripping the mantelpiece, he growled, 'I told you before you came up here I wouldn't marry you. I warned you, but you would come.'

His head turned slowly over his shoulder as he watched her rise from the table, saying as she did so in a quiet odd tone, 'Aye, you did. You are right there; and so was everybody else in the things they said about you.'

For a long moment they stared at each other; then she walked into the bedroom and closed the door.

A month ago she could have walked out, any minute of the day she could have walked out, but she hadn't wanted to then, not really, because she was still sorry for him; and aye, yes, still had a feeling for him. Now the feeling was gone; it had been stabbed to death back there in the kitchen. But she couldn't leave now because where would she go with a bairn inside her? To her Aunt Mary's? To one room in her da's house that was now let to Jimmy Southern? And she'd have to work until her time came because she had no money of her own now, she had spent it on him, and the needs of their life. Perhaps if she'd had those eighteen sovereigns to pick up she might even at this moment have gone down the hill. But now if she were to go down the hill it would be to beg someone for shelter. But who? The only place she could go to without feeling beholden to them was the workhouse, because as everybody knew their payment for housing a mother and child was fourteen years of work until the child could be put out to work for itself. But in her case, her da would take her out when he came back. If he came back. Ships sank.

No. What she had inside her now was his child and whether he gave it his name or not it would have to be born in this cottage and reared here.

That piece in the book: 'Life is the time it takes for the shingle to be wet.' Aye, life might be as quick as that for some, but for others it was long, for each pebble was a pain.

FIVE

The following morning when she put his breakfast before him, he took hold of her hand and said, 'I'm sorry, but ... but it's as I said right from the beginning, you knew when you came.'

Her hand remained limp within his and she looked straight into his eyes as she replied, 'Yes, I knew when I came; there's no one to blame but meself.'

'Don't talk of blame. What you did, you did out of the goodness of your heart, I know that. You're too much that way.' He smiled faintly at her. 'You act first and think after.'

'Aye, I suppose I do. Well, I'm payin' for it, aren't I?'

He let go of her hand, and she turned from him, while he, slowly picking up his knife and fork, went on with his breakfast....

From then on his manner towards her was gentle; that is, up to the Sunday when he came back from a stroll.

Of late, he had formed the practice of donning a good suit on a Sunday afternoon and going out for a walk. She had asked him where he went, and he had told her he generally got as far as Chester-le-Street, going by the fields where he could. He had never asked her to accompany him, and this she hadn't minded, for more and more she was cherishing the time she was left alone in the house.

When he returned from his weekly walk she always had his tea ready, and it being a Sunday she aimed to give him something special. Today was no exception. But when he entered the cottage, she saw at once that his manner had changed considerably during the time he had been away from it. To her statement, 'The wind's high again,' he made no response whatever but passed her and went into the bedroom, where he took off his overcoat and hat. But he was back in the kitchen within seconds.

Nor did he look at the table and make some remark such as 'That looks good' or 'I'm ready for it', but resting his hand on the back of the tall chair, he looked at her where she was pouring the boiling water into the teapot on the hob and said, 'I never asked you what you did the other day when you were with your father.'

She now glanced at him over her shoulder, placed the kettle by the side of the teapot, straightened her back, and replied, 'I went round Shields and looked at all the old places.'

'Is that all?'

She narrowed her eyes at him, and it was a moment or so before she said, 'No; we were going to go up to Newcastle to have a look round on the Thursday, but he was called away to his boat in the mornin', so I went up meself.'

'You went to Newcastle yourself?' His words were slow.

'Aye, that's what I said, I went into Newcastle meself. And ... and I went into a restaurant, a good class one, where there were men waiters dressed in black, and I had a dinner and I was charged seven and six for it....'

'You went to a place ... to a restaurant on your own, the kind where you pay seven and six for a dinner?' His eyes were like slits.

'Aye, I did. I didn't think it was that kind of place when I went in, but anyway I stayed. An' everybody was very nice to me, more than nice.'

'Aye, I bet they were.' He nodded his head slowly now.

'And you went in there by yourself?'

'I've told you, aye, I did.'

She knew what was coming but, strangely, she found that she wasn't trembling, she wasn't in fear of him. In some way, God only knew how, he had found out she had been talking to Mr Stuart. She could see that he was raging inside, there was a white line all round his mouth. Still, it didn't make her feel afraid and she showed it when she said, 'What more do you want to know?'

'Who took you into that restaurant, that's what I want to know?'

'I told you, I went in by meself.'

'You're a liar!'

'Thank you; I'm in good company then.'

She saw the white line disappear from his face under the dark red glow that was now flushing his skin.

'You're very brave all of a sudden, aren't you?'

'I've got nothin' to be afeared of, I hope.'

'Then speak the truth, tell me who took you into that restaurant.'

'I was tellin' you the truth when I said I went in alone. But I'll tell you what you want to know, everything, when you tell me how you came to know about it.'

She now watched the colour deepen in his face; she watched him blink rapidly as if to wash dust from his eyes, then move one lip hard over the other saying, 'I called in a pub for a drink along the Chester-le-Street road, and I ... I met a fellow there who knew me and you, and all about everything. He told me he saw you and that——' His lips pursed as if to spit before he went on, 'That individual down there. You were sitting to-gether in a cosy nook in a churchyard. Deny it. Go on, deny it.'

'I'm not going to deny it.' Some of her calmness had gone now. 'Aye, it's true; I told you I would tell you the truth. I was sittin' with him on a seat in a churchyard but

I'd just met him by chance. I was looking in a shop window and he came out and ... and he spoke to me.'

'Not for the first time then?'

'No, not for the first time. I've talked to him once afore in the fields here when he was taking a stroll and when I told him he shouldn't be on this side of the road. He said as much as the land wasn't yours, and neither it is.'

'Get back to the point.' His teeth now were grating against each other, his lips squared away from them. 'It was all arranged, wasn't it, you and visiting your da? What do you take me for, a bloody fool? And what were you talking about when you sat there hand in hand on a church bench, eh? Hand in hand!' His voice was almost at the pitch of a scream. 'Were you making arrangements to go down and run his house for him and supply his needs? Because you're the only one he could get around here; it takes some stomach to go to bed with a murderer.'

She was strangely still inside now, and empty; it was as if all the blood had drained from her body. The other night she had decided that she could never leave here because of the child that was within her, but in this moment she knew that the workhouse would be preferable to living with him any longer, and she told him so. But first of all she stung him to the quick by saying, 'He has never asked me to share his bed, and I'm sure he never would because he happens to be a gentleman. He hasn't to pretend, it's there for anyone to see. An' now I'll get me things together and I'll go.'

Before the last word had passed her lips he was bawling again. 'Oh no! Oh no, you don't!'

She stared at him in surprise as he thrust his arm out and jabbed her shoulder with his finger. Emphasizing each word, he now slowly brought out, 'You'll stay here for as long as I want because if you go down that hill and don't come back, I'll take a gun and, before God, I'll blow his bloody brains out. I'm not going to be made a laughing stock for a second time. Oh no, not again. You go to him and that'll be the finish of him.'

Up till now there had been no fear of him in her, but as she looked into his contorted face she saw that he meant every word he was saying, she could actually see him doing it. She had known for a long time that he was a weak man, a vain man, and in the present case it would be his vanity that would give him courage to carry out his threat.

They stared at each other while the French clock on the mantelpiece ticked its silver sounding seconds away; it was as if they had become frozen in time.

It was she who moved first. Her shoulders slumped, she drew the air into her chest, swallowed deeply, then went past him into the scullery and there, closing the door behind her, she went to the stone sink and vomited.

SIX

The atmosphere in the cottage had completely changed. He had never been talkative; not once during the time they had been together had they discussed any subject but that which concerned the few livestock, the land, and the weather, and although often at night she had wished he would have chatted a bit she felt she understood his reticence, it even intensified the feeling of care she had for him. Time and again she had wanted to put her arms round him and say, 'Come on, cheer up, there's another day the morrow.' But he wasn't the type to respond to such homely philosophy, and increasingly she had become aware of this. So the silences between them had lengthened. However, they had been quiet silences, kindly silences, understanding silences. But no longer. She now cooked his meals and placed them before him without a word, and he ate them without a word. She rubbed shoulders with him in the shippon; she carried the kindling that he was now cutting from the far wood, and piled it on the trolley and dragged it to the cottage gable end; side by side with him she clamped the last of the potatoes, and also the swedes; and they didn't exchange a word.

But the nights were the worst. She had contemplated sleeping on the wooden settle in the kitchen, but it was too short; and anyway there was no kind of a pad or mattress to put on it, and so she lay by his side, but as far from him as she could get, which meant lying close against the wall. He, on his part, lay on the edge of the bed until he fell into sleep, when he would turn on his back and snore.

The lack of contact was nothing new, for during these past months he had taken her less and less, in fact she reckoned the unloving act that had created her conception and which he had woken from sleep to perform, was by way of a mistake, for previously two whole months had gone by and he hadn't touched her.

She didn't know how long she could continue to go on living like this, yet she was frightened, even terrified to break away because such was his state of mind she knew he firmly believed that she would go down into that house and live with its present owner. And that, he had said, he wouldn't let happen.

On the Wednesday morning she got ready as usual for her weekly visit to Gateshead. It was then that he spoke to her for the first time in days. Looking at her coldly, he said, 'If you don't come back you know what'll happen. I'll keep me promise if it's the last thing I do.'

She made no reply, she just stared back at him as she tied a scarf round her hat so that the wind, which was blowing high, wouldn't take it from her head; and she went out and down the hill and caught the carrier cart.

Her Aunt Mary's greeting was as warm as ever, but this time there was something added to it. Wagging her finger in Emily's face, her head to the side, her eyes slanted, she demanded, 'Now, tell me, me lass, what you up to? What game are you playin'? Come on now, come clean with your Aunt Mary.'

'I don't know what you mean, Aunt Mary.'

'Well, you should do. Here, give me your coat. You look as white as a sheet. Are you in trouble?'

Emily slowly sat down and, holding her hands out to

the blaze, said, 'Yes, Aunt Mary, you could say I'm in trouble, and in more ways than one.'

'Well, if you will play fast and loose, what do you expect?'

Emily's head jerked round. She was on her feet again, demanding, 'What do you mean, fast and loose? I'm not playin' any fast and loose. What d'you mean?'

'Now, now! don't get agitated. You tell me your side of it first and put me in the picture. I'll listen quietly, aye, I'll listen quietly.'

'Well, my side is, I'm going to have a bairn.'

'Oh my God!'

'Yes, that's what I said when I knew.'

'He'll have to marry you.'

'He won't.'

'He's a swine then.'

'Yes. Yes, I agree with you, Aunt Mary, he's a swine.'

'Ah, lass, what's happened to you? Sit yourself down.' She put her hand on Emily's shoulder and pushed her gently back into the chair; then bending towards her, she said, 'It it this other fellow?'

'What other fellow, Aunt Mary?' Emily now screwed up her face. 'What on earth do you mean?'

'Well, lass, now I'll tell you what I mean. Yesterday afternoon, about two o'clock, there was a knock on the door an' when I opened it there stood a man, a gentleman. Dressed up to the nines he was; signet ring, gold albert, top coat with an astrakhan collar, the lot. An' what d'you think he says to me? Well, he says, "Are you Miss Kennedy's aunt?"

' "Aye, I am," I says back at him.

' "Well, can I have a word with you?" he says.

'Well, I take a breath, and I looks at his face. He didn't look quite English although he spoke it all right, quite fancy I'd say, an' so I said, "Come in", and I didn't apologize for the state of the house, nor the bairns'—she waved her hand around the floor where two of her brood were sitting on the corner of the mat and another was playing with a clouty doll under the table—'I didn't say "You can take me as you find me", I hadn't asked him to come, but what I said to him was, "You can be seated if you wish." And he sat himself down by the table there.' She stabbed her finger now towards the table, then went on, 'Then he said to me, "When your niece visits you next would you be kind enough to give her this parcel?" and at this he takes a packet from his coat pocket and hands it to me. And ... here it is.'

Emily watched her Aunt Mary lift her arm to the mantelpiece and take from a Coronation mug a small, narrow parcel; and when she placed it in her hand she said, 'There it is. And I might as well tell you me fingers have been itching like mad to open it. I don't think I could have lasted out another day.' She gave a high laugh. 'So go on; don't keep me in agony any longer; let's see what's in it.'

As if she were performing in a dream, Emily slowly tore the two layers of paper, one brown and one white from the parcel, and she ignored the envelope attached to the white paper as she gazed at the red leather case. But she didn't open it, she just sat staring at it. She knew what was inside, and she could find no words at all in her mind, nothing, to explain her feelings at the moment. It was only Mary bawling now, 'If you don't open it, be-god! I will,' that made her lift the lid, to disclose the watch lying on a red velvet bed.

'Eeh! beloved Jesus! Did you ever see anything like that in your life? Eeh! what is it, a bangle? No!' Mary's grubby fingers lifted the watch from its bed and she dangled it in front of her face. For a moment she too was lost for words, and not until she had replaced it in the case did she speak. Then, pulling a chair forward, her knees touching those of Emily's, she said quietly, and firmly, 'I'm not one to take kindly to stuffin' so now don't tell me, lass, that you know nowt about this man who's given you this.'

'Aunt Mary.'

'Aye, lass?'

Emily swallowed. 'It's a long, long story.'

'Well, I've all the time in the world, lass, and nothin' to fill it, so go on, start at the beginnin'.'

And so Emily started at the beginning; and her story held Mary speechless until she finished, saying, 'And that's the whole story, Aunt Mary, from beginning to end. And it's true as God's in heaven, there's nothin' atween him and me. As I told you, there I was lookin' at it in the window and he came out of the shop, and I was so upset about Mr Tooton that he found a place for me to sit. Somebody must have seen me there with him, and, of course, it got back to Larry; and as I said an' all, it's been hell ever since. I'm frightened, Aunt Mary. I was never frightened afore, not really, not of anybody, but I know that if he's shamed again, as he says, he'll not stand it. But, Aunt Mary'—she shook her head—'it's so fantastic ... well, I haven't got words to describe it, I can only say I would never go into that house again, even to work, it wouldn't be decent.'

'No, you're right there, lass. Either way it wouldn't be decent. Aye, by!' Mary bit hard down on her lip. 'Nobody'd believe it. But you know what they say, truth's stranger than fiction. But ... but all this apart, that fellow should marry you and give your bairn a name.'

'Aunt Mary'—Emily's voice now was hard, as was her expression—'Aunt Mary, I wouldn't marry him if he went on his knees to me, not now. And if it wasn't that I'm scared of what he'd do to Mr Stuart I'd be out of that cottage an' down that hill afore you could say Jack Robinson. I'd sooner have the bairn in the workhouse than have it up there now if I'd any choice.'

'Well, you'll have no bairn in any workhouse, lass.' Mary got to her feet. 'An' don't talk such rubbish. As long as I've a roof over me head you'll have shelter. As they say in those fancy stories our Annie reads to me, "Her home left a lot to be desired"—well, that applies here. But what we have you're welcome to, lass. An' your Uncle Frank would say the same.'

'Thanks, Aunt Mary.'

Now Mary, pointing to the wrapping that lay on the floor beside Emily's feet, said, 'Don't you want to know what he says?'

Emily looked down towards the paper and the envelope attached to it, and stooping she picked it up and opened it.

It read quaintly, for it was headed:

'Dear Emily—dear friend,

I want you to accept this gift and not question the whys or the wherefores, just look upon it as doing me a favour, for I have no one to be kind to, no one to give presents to, and so you will do me a great kindness by keeping what is, after all, really your own property?

May I say that the time we spent together in Newcastle was the happiest I have experienced since returning to this country, and although I must respect your wishes I hope that when we do meet, accidentally, you will give me a few minutes of your time, for there is no one I would rather talk to than yourself.'

She turned the page over now and continued to read:

'I have explained to the jeweller that it may happen you would want to sell the watch back to him. I have given him your name and description. He will, of course, bargain with you, that is to be expected; but I think he is a fair man and will not try to cheat you over and above the profit his trade demands.

Do not attempt to return this to me because if you do, I, being of a persistent nature, will only deliver it back again to your aunt.'

She bit tightly on her lip as she read the last lines:

'Please remain yourself, Emily; do not let anything change you.

May I end by calling myself your friend,

Nicholas Stuart.'

She had never received many letters in her life, an odd illiterate scrawl from her father, and something along the same lines from Lucy, yet she knew that this was an unusual letter. Somehow it reminded her of his face, the foreign look on his face. It wasn't, she imagined, an ordinary Englishman's type of letter. She didn't know how she was aware of this for she had no other letters with which to make a comparison, yet she was deeply aware of it.

'What did he say, lass?'

She didn't want her Aunt Mary to know what was in the letter, yet under the circumstances she couldn't but read it to her.

When she had finished she gently folded the letter up, and Mary, her head bobbing now, smiled and said, 'Begod! that fellow could write books. Now to my mind, lass, just going on what he said there'—she tapped the letter in Emily's hand—'and if I'd never clapped eyes on him, I'd says there's a man for you. Smallish he was, he had no bulk about him, as thin as a lat you'd say, but it was a good thinness, a strong thinness, and it comes over in what he says.' She again indicated the letter, then asked, 'What you goin' to do with it ... the watch?'

'I don't know, Aunt Mary, I can't keep it on me. Eeh!'

434

—she moved her head very slowly—'I'm flabbergasted. I wouldn't have believed anybody could be so kind, ever. But anyway, as I said, I can't keep it on me. Would ... would you keep it for me here, Aunt Mary?'

'Aw, lass'—Mary now spread her arms wide—'I'd never know a minute's peace with a thing like that in the house. Those are jewels on that strap. An' he's had to pay a small fortune for it. Eeh! lass, no, I'd be on tenter-hooks every minute of the twenty-four hours. And if our Kathy clapped her eyes on it she'd have it pinned on those twin pontoons of hers an' out that door afore I could nail her. No, lass, you'll have to think of some place to put it other than here.'

She had thought up some place to put the eighteen sovereigns but he had found them. Yet there were a thousand and one places in the crannies on the hill in which she could hide it. She could dig a deepish hole, and it would have to be deep enough so that nobody, unless they were starting quarrying, would come across it. She said to Mary, 'I'll bury it on the hill some place.'

'Well, if you can think of no place better, then bury it there, lass. But mark it well in your memory so you can pick it up when you want it, 'cos to my mind there lies your future. Why, if I were you, hinny, you wouldn't see me for dust, I'd be over that bridge an' into Newcastle to that jeweller's an' sell the damn thing an' be off an' start up a new life.... So why don't you?'

'And what would happen to Mr Stuart, because Larry 'll carry out his threat once I don't show up. It would be like biting the hand that fed you.'

'Aye, I suppose you're right; there's always two sides to everything. But it's a damn shame that such a load of responsibility has been put on your shoulders, especially at this time when you've enough weight to carry with what's inside you. Still'—she grinned at Emily now—'let's have a cup of tea to drink to your fortune, eh? Come on, lass, cheer up, never say die. And who'd need to with a windfall like that? As the gipsies say, you have a lucky face. An' that's what one said to me once. She said I'd marry a rich man and travel across water on a ship. An' what other way would you travel across water? I ask you. She said I'd have three children, an' I'd been born with a lucky streak; in fact, she said, if I fell on me backside down the midden I'd come up smelling of honeysuckle, an' I believed her. Eeh! my God, how gullible you are when you're young.'

Yes, how gullible you were when you were young.

Emily didn't join in her Aunt Mary's laughter.

PART SIX

THE BONFIRE

ONE

She was in her eighth month of pregnancy. She was carrying the child high; her breasts, especially when she was
lying down, seemed to be resting on her stomach. After
the first three months, physically she had felt remarkably
well and had continued to work, and was still doing so.

But when she looked back over the past months she
wondered how she had endured them. She had learned
that the silence of the open spaces was companionable
but that the silence of an aggrieved person was hell to
bear. Yet over the last few weeks his manner had softened
slightly. She could pin-point the day and even the hour
when it began to change. It was a Sunday in late April.
Spring was tempering the wind; the sun that came out
between showers was warm. She'd had a longing to walk,
to see some place different from the cottage and the hills
about her. She realized, this particular Sunday, that apart
from the path down to the main road in one direction
and to the river in another direction, she hadn't been
further afield than half a mile from the land that surrounded her cottage.

So on this bright day she put on her coat and a scarf
over her head and went for a walk. Larry had been gone
more than two hours and she purposely didn't take the
road that would eventually come out at Chester-le-Street
and which led to Durham, but she went, as she thought,
further inland, and after walking through field paths,

over stiles, and panting for breath climbing two hills, she came out on top of a flattish piece of ground. There she sat looking before her.

The hill wasn't very high but it showed a good view of the surrounding countryside. There weren't many houses she noted, and most of the land was tilled. In the far distance she picked out a black building standing solitary in a field, which told her it was a barn and that there would likely be a farm somewhere tucked away in one of the valleys beyond.

The land, even on the slopes, looked well tilled; the whole scene below her was one of farm order. But she hadn't seen a soul for more than half an hour: no families out for a Sunday walk, no pit lads strolling in two's and three's; no courting couples; this part of the world seemed as isolated as the hill-top on which the cottage stood. Then of a sudden two people appeared. She saw them walking from the direction of the barn. The farmer and his wife, she thought, taking a Sunday stroll round their domain. Farmers did that kind of thing. When Larry was master of the house, he used to put on fresh-polished leggings and his best tweeds and walk round the whole place on a Sunday afternoon. At one time the thought would have aroused deep pity in her for what he had lost, but not any more. The man she was living with now was more like a gaoler who had been given power, and through it had turned into a petty tyrant.

To be treated as if she weren't there, never to be spoken to, she just didn't know how she was standing it. Sometimes she thought she would go down and tell Mr Stuart the whole business and let him deal with it. But then the thought would come that if he did deal with it, he might, in order to prevent himself from being killed, kill again. What would happen then? She wouldn't be able to bear that; she would do something desperate to herself. Oh yes, she wouldn't be able to bear that. Why was it, she asked, as she watched the two minute figures crossing the field, that one never came to know one's own mind until it was too late. Youth was a time of false values. You laid stock on all the wrong things because something inside of you urges you to believe they were right. And later, when you had your eyes opened, the urge was just as strong telling you that you had been wrong about that particular feeling, but the new feeling you were experiencing was right. This business of youth was very complicated. She had tried to sort it out in her mind but had come to the conclusion you couldn't really give yourself the answers, you just had to live to get the answers. Life itself gave you the answers by making you go through things, experience them. You had to suffer in all kinds of ways before you got the answers.

When the child inside her began to kick she put her hand gently on the place. There should have been joy in the action; the gladness that was once hers should be flooding her now; but all she felt was pity for the life inside her and what lay before it.

It was some time later when she rose to her feet and went from the hill-top. The shadows were stretched out now; she hadn't realized how long she had been sitting there.

Some little distance further on she had reached a stile and was cautiously lifting her leg over the top bar when she looked along the path to her right and saw Larry approaching in the distance. She saw him stop; and he continued to stand still even after she had got down on the other side of the stile.

When he did come up he spoke to her for the first time in months. 'What you doin' here?' he asked gruffly.

'I was just takin' a walk.' Her reply was quiet and ordinary; and after staring into her face she saw his body relax, and he spoke his first kind words to her since she had told him she was going to have the child. 'You shouldn't have come this far,' he said; 'it won't do you any good.'

'I'm all right.' It was silly but she felt grateful to him in this moment for speaking to her. If he spoke a word now and then life would be livable; it was the silences that were killing.

They had covered some distance before he asked, 'Do you often get this far?'

'No; I've never been this way afore. It's nice; I didn't realize that there was so much flat land about. I thought every place must be like ours, all hills.' She smiled weakly; then she asked, 'Have ... have you been to Chester-le-Street?'

'No.' He shook his head quickly. 'No, I didn't get that far.'

'It's a nice day for walkin'.' Even as she spoke she was despising herself for being so easy, making herself cheap as she thought, just because he was civil to her.

And from this time he had continued to be civil to her, not talkative, but civil, giving her such words as, 'Those three old hens are eating their heads off; you'd better put them down for the pot.' And once he had actually said to her, 'When is it due?' Moreover, he had become quite concerned about her walking. 'You could slip on the scree banks,' he said, 'and you could lie there for hours, or, if a mist were to come up for days, and no one would find you.'

Such concern made her life tolerable.

During the past months she had seen Nicholas Stuart only twice, once recently, when she was sitting in the carrier cart and he in the dog cart, when he had raised his hat to her and the other passengers had stared at her. The first time had been in Fellburn, while she was waiting for the carrier cart. It was three weeks after she had received his gift and she was still full of fear at the consequences of what might happen should he and Larry meet, and so her thanks had been hasty and stammered, yet at the same time she had managed to convey to him the deep gratitude that she felt for his kindness. And she had further said to him, haltingly, 'After what you told me, Mr ... Mr Stuart, about the profits an' that from the farm, are ... are you sure you did the right thing, because it's a small fortune you spent?'

And he had answered, 'I spend as I go, because if I decided to leave, to get married say, which I just might, I could take very little with me. Do you follow me?'

She followed him. In a way he was getting his own back on his wife. And who was to blame him? People like her would make a fiddler of any honest man. She said to him, 'I was going to write you when I got the chance, but ... but....' And he had finished for her, 'I understand,' and to her embarrassment he had stayed with her until she had mounted the cart; then he had raised his hat to her and walked away.

She had only come across George once since his marriage; and the meeting had been little more than a greeting and a good-bye, for he seemed embarrassed. All she learned was that he had married Jenny, the new maid, and that she was 'a canny lass', and she had said that if he liked her she was bound to be a canny lass.

Today was the last Thursday in June. She had been into Gateshead for her weekly visit. For months past, she had changed the days on which she visited her Aunt Mary so that there'd be less chance of running into Mr Stuart.

On the second of the month she'd had her nineteenth birthday, and within herself she was surprised that she was only nineteen, because she felt old, thirty at least; and her distended body helped to emphasize this impression. Over the past three days she had been feeling odd; she couldn't explain to herself just why she felt this way.

She wasn't sick, she had no pain, she just felt—odd. There was no reason at all why she should feel like this because she had another month to go before her time came on her.

Alf Morgan drew up his cart near the stile, and after she had descended from it, he admonished her gently as he handed her the four bulky bags from under the seat. 'Go careful now,' he said, 'you shouldn't be carryin' all that lumber. And mind yer feet, it's still slippery from the downpour we had.'

'I'll go careful. Thanks, Mr Morgan. Good-night.'

'Good-night, lass. Hoy-up there!' He whipped up the horses, and the cart rumbled on, leaving her standing on the grass verge with the four bags of groceries at her feet.

Since her stomach had risen she hadn't been into the village. There was a standing order for hay, flour, boxings and corn with Mr Waite, which he dumped by the stile on a Thursday; but the rest of the household necessities she carried in from Fellburn.

Most weeks their needs filled only two bags, but during today's shopping she had bought some soft lawn, enough to make a robe and a gown for the child. She had also bought some yards of cheap holland, which she intended to bleach and cut into napkins and binders. She had also treated herself to a box of Fuller's Earth powder. She had Fuller's Earth back in the cottage, but it was the rock kind which you made into a paste and which, when applied to the tender parts of your body, was very soothing. Two pennorth would last you for weeks; but this small box had cost her fourpence ha'penny.

She was pleased with her purchases, and the bags although bulky had seemed light in Fellburn, but now when she lifted them, two in each hand, it was as if their contents had suddenly been turned to coal, for she found them so heavy that in the short distance she had to walk to the stile, they dragged her body sideways.

When she reached the stile she set them on the ground again; then leaning on the top bar she looked to where Mr Waite had stacked the weekly delivery, and she gave an impatient jerk of her head as she thought, He hasn't come down for them yet. What's he been up to all day?

Lifting one bag in her hand, she now swung it over the top bar and dropped it on the other side; the second one followed. It was as she was stooping down to lift the third one that the pain gripped her and her mouth stretched wide in a sort of surprised scream; but she made no sound, for the scream, like the pain, seemed trapped inside her.

As quickly as it had begun it passed, and she leant over the top bar gasping while the sweat dripped from her chin.

Had she strained herself while lifting the bags over? No, no; she had been lifting things for weeks. Only this morning, before it was really light, she had forked the muck from the shippon.

Slowly now, she bent and picked up the bag that had dropped back against her feet and, gently, put it on the far side of the stile.

She had picked up the fourth bag and was lifting her foot on to the first step of the stile when the terrible pain gripped her again; and now she was bent over the step, clutching the bars of the stile and moaning aloud. The pain seemed to be tearing her bowels from their casing. What was the matter with her? Was she in labour? Had she started? But it wasn't due. And according to her Aunt Mary you started with a griping pain, and it might be hours before you had another. You always got plenty of warning, so her Aunt Mary said.

Oh God! she couldn't bear this. Somebody ... somebody come. She was going to have the child here on the edge of the road. But it couldn't be; no child came as quick as this. She remembered the women in Creador

444

Street, Mrs Oliver, Mrs Smith, Mrs Garrick, and so many more; their bairns had taken a long time to be born, some two days in fact. She couldn't stand this for two days. Oh no! no! She would die.

The pain eased a little, until she attempted to straighten her body, and then it started again, even worse, if this were possible.

She was lying on the grass now, her knees up to her stomach. She was crying aloud, 'Larry! Oh Larry! please ... please. Oh! somebody, help me.'

A blackness swamped her and the pain was lost in it, but when she opened her eyes to the light again there it was, somebody was cutting her open all the way down her right side. She pressed herself into the ground, and again she was crying aloud. She was crying so loudly that she didn't hear the sound of the horse or of the wheels of the trap on the road; nor was she actually aware when the arms went around her and attempted to straighten her; but she heard a familiar voice saying, 'She's going to have the bairn, sir.'

She recognized the voice. It was George's voice. Had she married George? No, no; don't be silly. Oh my God! Please ... please, God, ease it. Ease it.

'It's all right. It's all right.'

She opened her eyes and looked up into the foreign face ... Mr Stuart. She didn't want to see Mr Stuart because Larry would be down in a minute, he would be down for the fodder. 'Go away!' she said. 'Go away!' And when she tried to push him away he held her all the tighter, saying, 'It's all right. It's all right.'

What were they doing? They were taking her to the trap. Oh no! She knew where the trap would go, back to the house. Oh my God! No! No! They mustn't take her to the house. She actually fought them now. Then grasping George's arm, she looked up at him pleadingly and groaned, 'George! George! get me ... get me up the hill.

445

Please ... please get me up the hill.'

'All right, Emily. All right.'

'She's not fit to walk up the hill; she'll never make it. Get her into the trap and we'll take her home.'

Again she was struggling; and now she was crying, screaming, 'No! no! He'll shoot you. He said he would an' he will, he'll shoot you!'

Her head was down now pressing into her swollen breasts; her knees were up to her stomach; she was half lying, half crouching on the grass verge at the edge of the road; she had her eyes closed and she imagined for a wild moment that they had both gone and left her. Then she heard Mr Stuart saying, 'How far can the trap get up the hill?' and George reply, 'With her alone in it, to the top of the first one and down the other side and across the valley bottom. But he wouldn't be able to manage the rest of the way, 'cos the slope's very rough, except for a narrow footpath.'

He was bending over her now, saying softly, 'Listen, Emily, listen. We're goin' to take you up to the cottage. It's all right now. It's all right. But you must ride in the trap as far as you can. Come on. That's a girl, come on.'

She could make no resistance now because the pain was using up her breath, but when she found herself lying on the floor of the trap she gasped out to the face hanging over her, 'Let George take me, not you ... not you.'

'All right, all right. Here's George now.'

'You're all right, Emily; I'll see to you. I've put your bags with the other stuff. You're all right. Just lie still; you'll soon be there.'

As the trap jolted forward it was as if she were being rocked, and the pain eased slightly, but only slightly. The child was coming, she knew it was coming, but oh dear God! if this was giving birth she never wanted to go through it again; oh no! never, never again.

She wanted someone's hand to cling to. If only she had

someone's hand to hold. Her mother's. No, no; her mother was long gone. Her Aunt Mary's. Yes, her Aunt Mary's. Oh, she wanted her Aunt Mary's hand to hold.

The pain was easier. Had she been asleep? She seemed to have just woken up; but she was still in the trap. She opened her eyes wider and looked over the mound of her stomach. A man was walking by her feet; he was holding them.... Oh no, no! he mustn't go up the hill.

When she went to protest she seemed to fall asleep again, until the pain shot her, startling her into wakefulness. She felt herself being lifted up and knew she was lying on two pairs of arms. She couldn't protest, for all her energies were twisted up in the pain....

When she heard the voice bawling, as if in her ear, 'Put her down!' she tried to raise herself from the cradle of the arms, but it was impossible for she was still being moved forward. Then George's voice seemed to bellow in her other ear, 'Don't be a fool, Mr Birch! She's bad, real bad; the bairn's on her.'

'*I said put her down.*'

'I'll put her down when there's a bed to put her on.' This voice wasn't bawling, it was even, almost cool.

She tried to struggle upwards again, but the words 'Steady! Steady!' almost fanned her face, and she lay back gasping. Her head was resting against a shoulder. Whose shoulder, she didn't know.

'I'll shoot you, as true as I'm standing here. If you don't put her down this minute, I'll shoot you!'

'You do that ... shoot.'

'You bloody foreign swine! You! ... you! ...'

There followed a mouthful of abuse, some of which she hadn't heard before, some of which she had. She felt sick at the sound of them; they became interwoven in the pain and in a way were hurting her as much as the child was doing. She felt disgusted, ashamed.

She knew they were going through the cottage door

447

now. When her body was lowered to the bed she immediately drew her knees up and put her head towards them and, gripping the bed tick, cried, 'Get somebody! A doctor ... somebody!'

'All right, all right. We'll get a doctor.'

'Get out of here! else before God I'll put a bullet through you.'

'Why don't you then?'

The voices were coming to her from the kitchen, both loud, both harsh and frightening now.

'For two bloody pins!'

'For two bloody pins, Mr Birch? You, let me tell you, haven't got the guts to shoot, for the simple reason you understand what the consequences would be. You, Mr Birch, have hidden behind a woman's skirts since you could toddle in this very cottage. When I first came here I was sorry for what my wife did to you, but now I see that she took your measure right away and in the end gave you your just deserts. In fact, there was a pair of you, you were well suited....'

There came now the sound of something heavy falling to the floor and Nicholas Stuart crying, 'You couldn't even use the butt end properly. You know what you are? You are what they say you are down in the village, a nowt, a miserable underhanded, two-faced nowt.... I'm going now, but I'm leaving you with a warning.' The voice dropped here. 'Stop playing your double game, or else.... Anderson's barn is not as isolated as you imagine. I should cut out your walks if I were you.'

There was silence all around her now; she didn't know whether she was alone in the cottage or not. The agony in her was subsiding a little. All her clothes were wet with sweat. She wanted a drink. If only there was somebody here, somebody to hold her hand. Was she going to die? She didn't mind now; it would solve all problems if she went. And the child too. But if it lived, it should have the watch, shouldn't it? The watch. The watch. In years to come someone digging would find the watch.

When the pain gripped her again she closed her eyes tight and prayed for death to come soon.

It was half past three in the morning when the doctor, who had come all the way from Birtley, dragged the un-resisting baby from her womb. It was quite dead, and as he looked at its mother his thoughts were that she would soon follow it. He told this to her husband, or at least to the man who had given her the child. But he received no response, one way or the other.

He said he would look in later in the day to see what had transpired, but he warned the man that he'd be sur-prised if she were still alive by noon, because he'd had to do a lot of cutting and she was now in a very weak state....

It was early evening when he returned. She was still alive, and the cowman's wife from Croft Dene House was with her, and what she said was, 'I thought she was gone more than once, but she keeps holdin' on to me hand and won't let it go. But she can't last, can she?' and he re-plied, 'I'd say no, but then I'm not God, and she's in His hands.'

TWO

She got out of bed for the first time at the end of the third week, and for the next two weeks she sat either in the kitchen or on a chair set outside against the cottage wall. She didn't talk and she scarcely moved.

George's wife had come up the hill every day to attend to her needs. She liked George's wife; she was a canny lass. She wanted to talk to her and tell her how grateful she was for all she had done, but the words just wouldn't come. At times she thought she had lost the use of her speech. But yesterday when Jenny had come up the hill for the last time—Larry had now told her that he could manage—she had held her hand tightly and looked into her homely face as she murmured, 'If I hadn't had you to cling on to I wouldn't have pulled through. Thank you, Jenny.' Yet even as she thanked her she thought it was a great pity that she had pulled through. Had it been left to Larry she certainly wouldn't have, for he had hoped she would die. More than once, as she lay too weak to move, she had felt that he was willing her to die.

From the middle of August she slowly took up her duties again, and soon life in the cottage appeared to have resumed its normal pattern. And yet Emily knew that nothing about their life together up here was normal. She had a strange feeling on her. She seemed to be marking time awaiting the outcome of something; what, she didn't rightly know. Pieces of conversation floated about in her mind, going right back to the time when Mr Stuart and George found her on the road. She would hear his kindly tone, saying, 'It's all right. It's all right,' only for it to be shot through with words from the vile tirade that Larry had levelled at him; and then something about Larry taking a walk, or not taking a walk, to Anderson's barn. She didn't know of any farmer around here called Anderson; perhaps she had dreamt that part because Mr Stuart wasn't likely to tell Larry to stop taking walks. Yet, no, she hadn't dreamt it; she could recollect her mind grasping at it; but for what reason now she couldn't recall.

She wished she felt strong enough to take the cart into Gateshead to see her Aunt Mary. Just to sit in that kitchen amid all the clutter and muck would be such a comfort. Not to have a laugh; no, she didn't want to laugh.

Three weeks ago her Aunt Mary had trekked all the way up here, bringing the two youngest with her, to see how she was; and she had sat by her side and cried like a child. But she hadn't stayed long because Larry had barely been civil to her.

'So that slattern is your aunt,' he had said. 'Well, with all your talk about her you must be seeing her through different eyes from anyone else.'

It seemed to be this remark that had given her the urge to get back into the life-stream, because she wanted the strength to tell him that if he lived to be a thousand he wouldn't be fit to wipe her Aunt Mary's boots.

It happened all of a sudden, Larry's complete change of front towards her. He stopped her carrying the wood in; he even beat up a raw egg in milk and made her drink it, telling her she must have this twice a day. He went down the hill on a Thursday morning and humped up all the fodder; he even went as far as Chester-le-Street for what provisions they needed.

She took his attentions silently but with a question in her eyes; and he answered it one day by saying, 'I must get you on your feet before the winter comes'; then he added, 'Anyway, I don't think you could stand another up here, the way you are.'

At nights she would lie thinking about the sudden change in his attitude towards her, and she would tell herself there was something behind it.

As she grew a little stronger she walked farther, and one day she strolled right down to the road. She found it pleasant just to be able to take her time meandering over the hills without having to carry any bags.

She was standing leaning on the stile looking first one way and then the other along the road when she heard the sound of horses' hoofs. She kept her head turned in the direction from where it came and saw coming towards her the first of a number of carriages. The drivers, dressed in black, held whips from which dangled black bows. As they passed her at a trot she noticed that the carriages were all empty, and behind the fourth one, at a more leisurely pace, came a farm cart. As she looked towards it she smiled and called, 'Hello, George.'

'Oh, hello there, Emily.' He drew the horse and cart to the side of the road and, quickly dismounting, came towards her, saying, 'By! it's good to see you down the hill again. I might have passed you, I never thought to see you there. How you feelin'?'

'Oh, much better, George, thank you.'

'You look better, but still very peaky. You've got to take care.'

'George.'

'Aye, Emily?'

'I'll never be able to thank you or Jenny for what you did for me; I know that without you both I wouldn't be here.'

'Nonsense. Nonsense.'

'No, no.' She looked down to where the step divided them and said slowly, 'No, it isn't nonsense. Without you both I'd have been heading those coaches.' She made a motion with her hand to the left of her. 'By the way, has somebody died round here?'

'Aye, Farmer Rowan.'

'Farmer Rowan! Had he been bad long?'

'No, about a week I think. He had a heart attack they say.'

She stared at George now for some little time. Then folding her shawl further over her breast, she asked, quietly, 'Where's Anderson's barn, George?'

'Anderson's barn? Oh, it's on the border of the Rowans' land...' He stopped suddenly, blinked hard, turned his head to the side, then asked, but without looking at her, 'Why do you want to know where Anderson's barn is, Emily?'

'You know as well as I do, George.'

He was looking at her again. 'How long have you known?'

'Only since you told me who'd been buried.'

'Oh my God! my mouth.'

'Don't blame yourself, George; things have been gatherin' in me mind for a long time, and now they're all of a piece. He treated me like dirt when he knew I was going to have the bairn, then just a few days ago his manner suddenly changed. He started feeding me up, strengthening me I suppose to enable me to take the blow.' She nodded her head and looked away, and she kept nodding it as she mused, 'I know where Anderson's barn is; I've actually seen them both coming out of there. He didn't open his mouth to me in weeks and then he comes across me suddenly on the hill near the barn. I can see him now. He was struck dumb, but when he realized I hadn't been spying on him his manner changed and he treated me

453

civilly for a time.'

She turned towards George again, saying, 'I suppose everybody knew? It's always the way isn't it, the one that should know is always the last to hear.'

'Aye, Emily, that's always the way of it. But as far as I can gather it's been going on for years. The mistress knew of it. That's what made her mad and act the way she did, old Abbie said. But they say old Rowan hated his guts and threatened more than once to do him in if he caught them together. Of course'—he pursed his lips now—'that was afore he thought your Larry Birch had come into the farm an' property. He was known to be a hypocrite that Dave Rowan; there's nobody in the village had a good word for him; in fact it was a toss up who they disliked more, Birch or him. Skin a louse for its hide they said he would.... What you going to do, Emily?'

She kept her eyes fixed on his for a moment before she said, 'I don't know yet, George, I don't know. I'll have to get meself gathered together.'

'Will you tackle him with it?'

She tilted her head to the side as if listening; then she gave a sad little laugh as she said, 'Not till the time is ripe. It's funny, George, but I was always the one to chatter, remember? But of late I've learned to hold me tongue. In that way, you're able to think more, to weigh things up better. And that's what I'll do, I'll bide me time and weigh things up. But you can be sure, George'— she put her hand out and patted his arm—'I'll let you know exactly what happens.'

'You're always welcome above the stables, Emily.'

'I know that, George.'

'And you know something more, Emily?'

'What, George?'

'I'm no reader of minds but I know that you'd be very welcome in the house an' all.... No offence meant, Emily.'

454

'And none taken, George.... Good-bye.'

'Good-bye, Emily.'

She turned from him and walked slowly through the copse and along the field path, and more slowly up the hill and down it again, then across the valley and up the last incline to the cottage; and all the way she kept repeating, 'I must get you on your feet afore the winter comes.'

His next move was made evident to her the following day. Sitting across the table from her, he looked at her with a gentle expression on his face, and if she hadn't known what she did know the concern in his voice would have touched her heart again as he said, 'Emily, I'm going to say this to you, and I mean it, you're free to go; I'll not stop you by word or action.'

She had the sudden almost uncontrollable desire to spit in his face. Lowering her eyes and keeping her voice soft, she said, 'I'm content to stay where I am.'

'But it's too much for you up here.'

'What ... what would you do if I went?' She still kept her gaze lowered.

'Oh, I'd fend for meself, don't worry about me. I've done it afore, I can do it again.'

At this she rose from the table and went about her duties in the kitchen, knowing that he was still sitting there looking at her. But she didn't look at him, nor did she speak again.

Every day during the following week he took his long walk, and each time he returned and she looked at him she longed for her old strength, for the time when she had been so full of life that she wouldn't have tolerated him or his carrying on for one minute more. Yet, somehow, her very weakness seemed to have a strength of its own; it was, as it were, making her bide her time, as if preparing for the climax.

She thought the climax had come when, on Sunday night as they were sitting at tea, he said, 'I'm worried about you, Emily, this business of the baby and all that. I know what I said about me not marrying, but I think you should marry, and I know I'm spoiling your chances keeping you up here. You're the kind of woman that ... well, could do well for herself just by the looks of you.... You could sort of pick and choose, if you see what I mean.'

As he stared at her and she at him, a voice was crying loudly in her head, 'Yes, yes, Larry, I see what you mean. You would even condone me going down the hill and across the road now, wouldn't you? You would put no obstacle in me way now about taking up with the foreign bastard. You're not naming anybody, are you, but that's who you mean. You don't want to shoot him now, do you? For two pins I'd ... No, no!' she cautioned herself; 'don't be stupid; bide your time.'

He was still talking; between mouthfuls of food he said, 'Even if you didn't decide to take up with anybody I wouldn't see you short; and if you got a place of your own you could have some of this furniture.'

When she looked at him and said quietly, 'Thanks,' he became silent while continuing to stare at her; then he rose abruptly from the table and went out.

A few days later she didn't know why she opened the trunk where he kept his clothes, because he had always seen to his clothes himself, folding them and laying them away, but when she did she saw it was almost empty.

Then came the morning when she woke up to an unusual silence about the place. There was no mooing from the shippon, nor any sound from Bonny in his stall at the other side of the wall. After lying still for a few minutes, she got out of bed and into her clothes. The kitchen fire was bright, the kettle was on the hob, the sun

456

was coming up, it was a fine morning. She went straight out and into the shippon; the cow wasn't there. She went into the stable, and the horse wasn't there. The chickens were still about scratching for an early morning meal, but there were no sheep in the fold. She looked about her, over the wide landscape, down into the valley, up to the further hills. Then she went back into the cottage and, looking at the mantelpiece, she saw the letter. The envelope wasn't sealed or even addressed. She took out the two sheets of paper and read:

'Dear Emily,

I have given you the chance to go time and again but you wouldn't take it. You would have had to know sooner or later about Lizzie and me. I would have married her in the first place if it hadn't been for her father, but now he's gone ... well, I'm going to the farm. As I said, I won't leave you stranded. I've left five pounds in the jar on the mantelpiece, and you can stay in the cottage as long as you like. But as I've already told you, if you go and want to set up for yourself you can take the furniture, with the exception of the clock, the French table and the bureau. I have taken the animals as I didn't feel I could go over there with nothing. However, I won't see you short of milk; I'll leave a can every other day at the old turnpike gate for you and a bit of butter and cheese to keep you going.

I'm sorry things have happened this way, but as I indicated the other night you'll not be alone long, you'll soon be picked up. Good luck, and thanks for all your kindness.

Yours,
Larry.'

She sat down and put the letter on her knee and, looking straight in front of her, she said aloud, 'You'll soon be

457

picked up. Whores are picked up, dock women are picked up.'

'You'll soon be picked up!'

And he'd leave her a can of milk over by the tollgate. Would he now! That was kind of him to leave her a can of milk. Up till she had taken to her bed it was she who had tended the animals: milked the cow and mucked her out and saw to the horse, even groomed him.

And he had kindly left her five pounds. How long could she live up here on five pounds? To his knowledge she hadn't a penny of her own.

And the furniture. She could take it except the clock, the French table, and the bureau. They were the three best pieces, the only pieces of any real value. It was she who had brought them from the drawing-room; with the help of Mrs Riley she had dragged the bureau into the hall and also the French table with its thin legs and gallery top. She had chosen that because it was pretty; and also the clock. The clock, she knew, was of value; he had told her that; also that the colonel had brought it from abroad. For the rest of the furniture, there was the chest of drawers with the little china cabinet on top of it, the settle, the table and chairs, and, of course, the two big trunks that had held his clothes and which now held only a few old shirts and small clothes.

You will soon be picked up!

You can have the furniture except....

I have taken the animals because I couldn't go over there with nothing.

No, he couldn't go over there with nothing, but he had left her here with nothing. Five pounds, and a few sticks of furniture, and free milk if she walked a mile each way to get it.

What did he take her for?

She had bounced up so quickly from the chair that it fell backwards. She walked into the bedroom and gazed about her. She went from there to the scullery and came back to the kitchen. It seemed in this moment that she had spent her entire life in this cottage. All she'd had to give out she had given out here; she had worked from dawn till dusk six days in every week all the year round; even on the day she went into the town she had risen never later than five o'clock in the morning in order to get her chores done. She had sat through sullen silences night after night, she had loved him, pitied him, cared for him, suffered him, and his moods, while all the time he was paying his visits to Anderson's barn. And while doing that he had dared to threaten what would happen if she spoke to Mr Stuart! He wasn't going to be made a fool of a second time. Yet as soon as the way was clear for him to step into a dead man's shoes and become master again of a farm he had been willing, aye, that was the humiliating part about this whole affair, he had been willing that she should go down the hill to Mr Stuart.

She knew now for a certainty that all this time together he had still looked upon her as a servant, at best a kept woman, one that could be turfed out or passed on. This is what the gentlemen did with their mistresses. But gentlemen left them provided for. They didn't say, 'I've taken the cow and the horse and the sheep, and I want the clock, and the bureau, and the French table.' No, a gentleman would have said, 'You can have all these things and more, Emily. And here's the deeds of the cottage and a sum that will keep you for the rest of your life.'

It paid to be a prostitute; it paid to be a mistress. But love, compassion, tenderness, and grinding daily work didn't pay.

She ran outside now and down to the gate and, gripping its top, she moved her head slowly, taking in the expanse of land. When she faced in the direction of the river her head became still. She had a desire to run towards it; but not to drown herself; no, but to take off all her clothes and lie in it and let it wash over her, wash away the dirt on her body, wash away the fact that his hands had ever touched her; wash away the memory of the agony that she had gone through in giving birth to his child.

Once she had been a girl who felt glad inside, whose password had been, Never say die, whose one aim in life seemed to be to cheer people up; but that had been at the beginning of her life, when she was a young girl of fifteen and sixteen; yes, and even seventeen. But over the last two years she had spanned a whole lifetime; she had grown from a girl into a young woman. And now she was a woman fully grown, old inside herself, aged as only tens of years can age. Yet in this moment it seemed but a flash in time since she was a small child sitting with her bare bottom on the warm flags outside their front door in Creador Street. Again she thought of the line in the little book: Existence is the time it takes for the shingle to be wet. Aye, but don't let them forget the countless pebbles in the shingle and that each one represented a pain of some sort or other.

Her life was over, finished, in that she would never care or feel for anyone again; nor trust anybody again. No, by God! that she wouldn't, ever again.

She turned from the gate and looked towards the cottage. What was she going to do? Pack up her few things and go down the hill to her Aunt Mary's?

There was the watch. Aye, there was the watch. She hadn't forgotten about the watch. The watch would be her lifeline. Sep had thrown her that line in the first place but she had lost it. Then Mr Stuart had put it into her hand again, and in this moment she thanked him for it; from the bottom of her heart she thanked him for it. And she would cling to it and haul herself up on to some place high and dry by it.

Before she did that, however, there was something else she was going to do; but she would have to wait until the day ended for it to have the proper effect. Yes, she nodded down at the cat, which was rubbing against her legs. It wouldn't take effect until it was dark.

She walked slowly up to the cottage and brewed herself a pot of tea. Then, taking her time, she carried the wood, piece by piece, from the gable end towards the gate where the ground rose slightly, and, laying it carefully, she made a platform of most of it. It was heavy work and it took her almost till dinnertime to complete.

Now she went into the cottage again and she cut herself two shives of bread and placed some cheese on them; then sitting by the table and her actions still slow, she ate, and after she had finished she brewed herself another pot of tea. Later, she went into the bedroom and lay down on the bed and rested, for as she had often experienced of late, a weakness had overtaken her.

It was about three o'clock in the afternoon when she started removing the furniture from the cottage. First, she took her belongings and laid them to one side; then she dragged piece after piece down to the platform, and those pieces that she couldn't place on top of it she set around the sides. The kitchen table and the china cabinet posed problems, until she chopped the legs from the table and unscrewed the glass doors from the china cabinet.

The trunks posed another problem, but this she got over by using the hatchet on them....

By seven o'clock in the evening there was only the bedding left, and this she flung, one bit after another, up on to the top of the pile where some caught on the edges of the furniture, spreading out in the light wind like banners. She didn't even feel any emotion when she saw the huckaback hand towels flying. She had been proud of the huckaback towels. She had been introduced to them down in the house, and she had brought half a dozen

461

with her. She felt somehow they were good class, they had a quality about them.

She was feeling very tired now, exhausted in fact, yet in an odd way triumphant. She looked up at the gigantic heap. The legs of the French table were sticking out from the side like four golden rods and the pendulum of the clock was hanging out like a tongue begging water.

She turned and looked in the direction of the sun. It would be some time yet before it would be right down, but she could wait. She had all the time in the world. It would be black dark, perhaps midnight, when she would go down the hill, because she would stay here until the embers died down. Oh yes, she would stay until the embers died down because not until the fire went down would she feel clean again. It was an odd feeling, this wanting to be cleansed in some way. And on the way down she'd pick up her watch, she could find the place in the dark. And then she would walk, she'd walk all the way to Fellburn, then on to her Aunt Mary's. And there she would rest for a time.

It was nine o'clock when she brought a can of paraffin from the shed and sprinkled it over the base of the pile. She set light to it, and the initial flame licked in and out of the wood like a live snake, refusing at first to take hold of the base but fastening on to the pieces of furniture that were dry with age; then it shot up to where the bedding was, and now it was away.

The pile was fully ablaze before the long twilight fell into night. She stood against the wall of the cottage with her old coat and hat on—the coat that Larry had bought her was on the pile—and she watched it burn. It was a bonny sight. The sparks were flying up into the darkening sky like sprays from fireworks. Yes, that's what it looked like, a firework display. She had seen a firework display once, when they were celebrating something in

462

Shields. She had forgotten what.

She felt a quiet sense of satisfaction as she watched the payment for two, no three years of her life go up in smoke, and when a tiny thread of guilt touched her thinking and she said to herself, 'I shouldn't have burned his pieces I should have kept them aside,' she brought herself from the support of the wall and answered the thought aloud, crying at herself, 'Don't be so bloody soft, Emily Kennedy! You'll regret nothing. No, by God! you'll regret nothing of this night.'

She was still standing straight when she heard the voices calling from the valley bottom. She couldn't make out what they were saying, but when she saw dim figures approaching the wall she knew she had been expecting them. They were the villagers come to see the upstart's cottage burning. And now she looked towards them as they formed a lengthening row against the wall, and she said to herself, 'Well, they've turned out in force.'

And now there were voices coming from behind the cottage. These would be the miners from the colliers' rows outside the village; they had likely rushed over the hills to come and give a hand.

The miners didn't stop by the back wall, they leapt it and came towards her. She could see their faces clearly in the firelight. There were some women amongst them, and they all looked at her open-mouthed, and one called, 'What's up, lass? What's up? You celebratin'?'

It was a moment before she called back, 'Yes. Yes, you could say I'm celebratin'.'

'What you celebratin', missis?' Another man came towards her.

'Oh'—she looked at him now where he was standing within an arm's length of her—'just a piece of me life that's over.'

'You all right, lass?' He came even closer, and his quickened breath came on her face; he was still panting

463

from his running.

'Yes, I'm all right, thank you.'

The man turned now and looked towards the fire. 'Where did you get all that lot, I mean to make that pile? You can see it for miles.'

'It's me furniture.'

'Your what?'

'Me furniture.'

She looked now at the gathering faces about her. The villagers too had come over the wall, not so close as the pitmen but close enough to hear what she had to say, and it was to them she spoke. 'The furniture was in payment for three years of me life. I had no use for it, so I burned it.'

No one spoke, but they were all looking at her, and so she said, 'It's a pity I didn't give you warnin' of it, you could have brought the bairns. Bairns like bonfires. You could have made a night of it.'

Still no one spoke, but they continued to gape at her. Suddenly a section of the pile fell inwards and the sparks sprayed into the night, weirdly illuminating the whole scene and showing up a running figure that didn't stop when it came to the edge of the crowd, but thrust its way forward. Then she was staring at him, giving him her full attention. Funny, but she knew now that this was what she had really been waiting for, hoping for, unknowingly praying for, willing that he should come and face her.

'What's happened?' He looked from her to the blazing pile; then without further words he ran to the cottage door and peered in. And now the crowd watched him walk slowly back to her where she stood with her bundles at her feet, and although his voice was a low growl they heard distinctly what he said. 'You gone clean mad?'

'No; I've never felt more sane, in fact I think I've just come to meself; 'cos I realized the day I'd lost me wits when I came up this hill with you.'

'What had you to do that for?' He thrust his arm back towards the flaming pile.

'I can do what I like with me own; that's what you gave me. You said I could take the furniture, except of course the best bits which were the French table, the bureau, and the clock. Well, I didn't like the stuff to be parted, it had rubbed shoulders for so long with the rubbishy pieces; the rubbishy pieces that were so necessary, like meself, you know.' She bounced her head at him. 'And by the way, when you took the livestock you forgot to take the hens with you. An' thank you very much for offering to leave me a can of milk every other day down by the turnpike. It would have been a nice walk in the depth of winter with snow up to me chin.'

'Shut up!' His voice came in a low growl from between his tightened lips and his eyes flicked from her to each side where the crowd had now thickened; then, like them, he started as she screamed at him, 'Don't you tell me to shut up, not again, you two-faced, double dealing hypocrite! An' you can have that back.' She now flung at him the bag with the five sovereigns in it, and as it hit his chest he grabbed it and she cried, 'That's it, it'll help towards the dowry you're takin' to her. You couldn't go to her empty-handed, you said, well, tell her that five pounds is from me. And one last thing I'll say to you. I've only seen her but twice in me life, but I got her measure, and if I'm any judge she'll give you as much hell as your supposed wife gave you. And when that time comes, remember me.'

A shower of sparks sprayed the sky again, the flames lighting up all their faces. Every eye was on them; no one spoke. She now stooped and picked up the bundles at her feet, and, her shoulders straight and her head up, she turned her back on his livid countenance and walked towards the throng. They parted for her, and she took the path past the bonfire to the gate, where George and

Jenny were standing. They turned and, one on each side, they walked with her down the hill.

It was as they crossed the valley floor that they heard the jeering and loud cat-calls, and at this she paused in her walk and looked back, and there came into her mind the words, I'll never be sorry for the day I picked you up in Fellburn Market Square. When she moved forward again her head was down. They reached the road and she said brokenly, 'Thanks, George. Thanks, Jenny,' and George said, 'Where do you think you're goin' the night?'

'I'm goin' to walk to me Aunt Mary's.'

'Not the night you're not.'

'Tomorrow,' said Jenny, gently taking her arm.

'Oh no! No!' She stiffened. 'I'm not going back to the house. Oh no!'

'Nobody's askin' you to go back to the house.' George spoke sharply now. 'Anyway, Mr Stuart's away. He went on holiday the day afore yesterday, gone to France he has, for a bit of life I think. And who's to blame him. Anyway, you're comin' back with us, an' the morrow morning I'll drive you in to wherever you want to go.'

She stood, her head deep on her chest now. What should she do? One thing she couldn't do was to dig up the watch the night, not with all those folk on the hills.

She went with them, docilely now, along the road; but before they entered the gate she stopped and said, 'What about old Abbie?'

'Oh, he's gone. The boss pensioned him off some weeks ago. We've got a new lad now.'

As she walked over the courtyard towards the arch, she glanced, not at the kitchen door, but at the window above it, and she thought, As bad as you were you weren't all wrong. No, you weren't all wrong....

The rooms above the stables were comfortable and homely. There wasn't a bed for her but they made her a shake-down in the kitchen, and although she hadn't had a proper meal since yesterday she still couldn't eat. But when George gave her a good measure of hot whisky and water, and black sugar, she drank it gratefully.

A short while later she lay staring up into the blackness. Her mind seemed empty. Her whole being seemed empty. She didn't know at what time she fell asleep.

She woke the next morning with George shaking her gently by the shoulder and saying, 'Would you like a cup of tea, Emily?'

'Oh! Oh. Aye. Yes. Yes, please.' She pulled herself into a sitting position and her hands shook as she took the mug from him.

'How you feelin'?' he asked.

She thought a moment. The picture of what had happened last night was as clear in her mind now as if she were still on the hillside standing in the light of the fire, and every action of hers that had preceded the fire was clear in her mind too. She looked at George now and she said, 'I shouldn't have done it. I don't mean burning the bits and pieces, but sayin' what I did to him. They jeered him; they'll give him hell now. I shouldn't have done it.'

'Devil's cure to him, I say. He's asked for all he's got. I was for him when I first came, but when I found out things an' the game he was playin' with you, oh, I quickly went off him. He's no good, Emily. You told him the truth, and so you have no regrets about it, oh no. They would give him hell in any case, for Farmer Rowan's boots haven't got the sweat out of them yet, and he couldn't jump into them quick enough. That alone has got their backs up. An' you were right, Miss Lizzie Rowan 'll wear the pants. Her mother's not a bad sort, but she's a tough piece. Aw, don't you worry your head, Emily; have no regrets. But you did something last night that'll be remembered for many a year to come. Now just you take it easy this mornin'. What time do you want to go in?'

'As soon as you're ready, George. But there's one thing I'd like to do afore I go.'

'What's that, Emily?'

'I'd like to walk up the hill once more by meself. And another thing, George. Me cat. It must 've got frightened with the fire and ran off. I was going to bring it with me. If I can't see it, would you have a look out for it?'

'Aye, yes. Don't worry your head about it. I'll bring it down here; one more won't make any difference. An' by the way, Jenny's over at the house but she'll have the breakfast ready in about half an hour or so.'

'Thank you, George.'

When he had gone, she rose stiffly from the couch, put on her skirt and blouse, washed herself in the scullery; then donning her hat and coat, she went quietly out.

She saw no one as she crossed the farmyard, nor as she crossed the courtyard. She stood for a moment and gazed at the front of the house. She hoped Mr Stuart would find happiness here, even if he had to live alone. Yet he didn't seem a man who should be alone. She was glad he was away. What would have happened if he had come up the hill last night, she didn't know; perhaps he would have got her down before Larry came, because he was that kind of a persuading man. And then she wouldn't have spilled her mouth open in front of everybody. She was sorry for that, yes, she was.

She walked slowly along the road towards the stile. She felt very tired. Her limbs were heavy, almost as heavy as her heart. She crossed the stile, went through the copse and towards the old bridge; then picking up a piece of wood that was somewhat pointed, she walked along by the bank of the narrow burn until she came to the haw-thorn tree to the left of her. From it she took three steps parallel to the burn. Here was a small mound of shaly earth, and at the front of it she started raking.

Her heart began to beat rapidly when after uncovering

about six inches of the shale she couldn't see the parcel; but when her now frantic efforts reached a depth of twelve inches or more and the point of the wood unearthed the piece of brown hessian she had wrapped the box in, she sat back on her heels and closed her eyes and let out a long drawn breath. She hadn't realized she had buried it so deep.

Tenderly now, she unwrapped the hessian and gazed down at the red leather box. It was slightly stained where the water had soaked through the outer cover. Then she pressed the little spring, and there it was, bright and beautiful ... and delicate. Yes, that was the word for it, delicately beautiful. She touched it where it lay on the folded letter she had inserted at the bottom of the box. She wished she could keep it.

Don't be silly. The admonition brought her to her feet, and she roughly scraped some of the shale back into the hole with her foot. Then putting the box inside her blouse, she walked back to the old bridge. But she didn't go up the hill towards the cottage for that, she told herself, she never wanted to see again as long as she lived; nor the hills. And the cat would be all right, George would see to it....

She said good-bye to Jenny at ten o'clock; she thanked her warmly and told her that some day she might be able to repay her and George for their kindness to her; and Jenny wept a little and spontaneously they kissed and parted.

Sitting beside George in the front of the trap, they drove through the village. The few people who were about turned and looked at her; but there was a different expression on their faces now; she imagined that one or two might have even smiled at her had she glanced directly their way. But she didn't, for she didn't want their smiles now, they had come too late.

When the trap stopped in Fellburn market she repeated her thanks to George. He held her hand and, looking into her eyes said, 'I'll always have a feeling for you, Emily, you know that. And what I also know is that you'll pull through. You know what you said to me the first day when I came to the farm footsore and weary? You planted the first square meal afore me that I'd seen in weeks, an' you said, "Get that into you, and you'll find your feet here." Well, you'll find your feet an' all, Emily. Good-bye, lass.'

'Good-bye, George.' She was too full to say any more. She turned about and walked away from the life that had begun in this market place three years ago and was now ending here.

PART SEVEN

FULL CIRCLE

ONE

'And you mean to say you set fire to the lot of it?'

'Aye, Aunt Mary; yes, I set fire to the lot of it.'

'My God! lass, what a thing to do! You should have carted it down here; it was worth a bit that stuff. Even I knew that.'

'Not really, Aunt Mary; only the three bits that he wanted.'

'You think so?'

'Yes, I'm sure of it.'

'And you say they swarmed up from the village and thereabouts?'

'Yes. Yes, they swarmed up from the village and thereabouts. It was like Mafeking night.'

'And you say he came?'

'Yes, he came.'

'And what did you say to him?'

Emily paused for a moment and turned her head to the side before she replied, 'Things best left unsaid, but nothing I could say to meself when I saw him made any difference, I had to hit him with something, and I had only me tongue to do it with, so I told him what I thought about him, an' I didn't mince me words.'

'Good for you, lass. I only wish I'd been along o' you, for he was an upstart swine if ever I saw one. I know what he thought of me'—Mary wagged her finger at Emily now—'blowsy, dirty old faggot. I could see it in his eyes.

An' he never asked me if I had a mouth on me. I wasn't expectin' a drop of the hard stuff, but me tongue was hangin' out for a cup of tea. Well, lass, all I can say is you're well rid of him. Did you manage to bring the watch with you?'

'Yes, yes, I did, Aunt Mary.' Emily patted her chest.

'And what did Mr Stuart say about all this?'

'Nothing; he wasn't there I'm glad to say, he was away on holiday.'

'Well, there's one thing I do know, if he had been there you wouldn't be here now.'

'Oh yes, I would, Aunt Mary.' Emily shook her head slowly but with emphasis. 'I want no truck in that direction, in fact any direction. All I want is some way to make a living. And I've got the means here.' She again patted her chest.

'Aye, lass, you have that. Will you set up house on your own?'

'Yes; I mean to go back to Shields an' have a look round.'

'Will you bring Lucy home again?'

'I've been thinkin' about that, Aunt Mary, but ... but somehow I don't think it would be fair, she's very happy where she is. In her last letter she said this Miss Rice was being discharged and was going home and she wanted to take her along of her, and what did I think about it. I wrote back and said I thought it was a good thing.... No, I don't think Lucy would want to come back now. She's tasted a different kind of life; I can read atween the lines.'

'Aye, it's often the way. When they leave home and see how the other half lives they take to it. And who's to blame them. Well, lass, drink up your tea and let me say here and now, this house is your home as long as you care to make it so. I won't ask you to sleep in it, though, be-

473

cause there's no comfort sleeping on a shake-down, but Mrs Pritchard across the way 'll put you up.'

'Thanks, Aunt Mary, it'll just be for a night or two. I'm ... I'm going into Newcastle now to see the jeweller about the watch; I'm taking Mr Stuart's letter with me to prove it's all above board.'

'Aye, I'd do that, I'd get it out of me hands as quick as possible if I was you. It's a lovely piece of jewellery, I've never seen a bonnier, but it'll bake no bread for you ... aw lass, don't cry. Don't cry.'

'No, I'm not, Aunt Mary; no, I'm not going to cry.'

No, she wasn't going to cry, but she wished she could, for then she might get rid of this great lump that was blocking her chest. But tears, like laughter, had gone from her. Her eyes seemed filled with sand, and her heart with lead.

Mr Goldberg said almost the same words as her Aunt Mary had: 'It's a beautiful piece, miss, but you'd rather have the money?'

'Yes, if you don't mind.'

Emily was sitting in a room at the back of the jeweller's shop. It was a very comfortable room. It had a deep red carpet on the floor and was furnished with two leather chairs and a leather-topped desk, and the walls were lined with bookcases. Mr Goldberg was a small man with a thin face, but he had a pleasant expression.

When she had entered the shop she had said to the young man behind the counter, 'Are you the owner?' and after surveying her for a moment he had answered primly, 'I am Mr Goldberg's assistant; what can I do for you?' and she had replied, 'I would like to see Mr Goldberg himself, please.'

When Mr Goldberg stood before her at the opposite side of the glass-topped counter and said, 'Yes, madam, how can I assist you?' she said, 'Mr Nicholas Stuart

474

bought a watch here some time ago on a certain understanding.'

'A watch, madam?'

'Yes, yes, a fob watch, a jewelled fob watch.' She now
opened her bag and held out the case towards him and
watched his face lighten as he said, 'Oh yes, yes; that
watch. Yes, yes; of course. Would you please?' He now
lifted his hand and indicated the end of the counter, and
she walked round it and through the door he held open
for her, and he seated her in one of the leather chairs
before he went behind the desk and sat himself down.
Then he leaned towards her, saying quietly, 'Mr Stuart,
yes, he indicated that you might at some time want to sell
the article again.'

'And you said you would buy it?'

'Yes, yes, I did, madam; and I'll be only too pleased to
purchase it from you when we come to an arrangement
. . . an amicable arrangement.' His smile broadened and
he held out his hand, and she placed the case in it.

She watched him lift the watch out and lay it across his
palm. He did it gently, she thought, as someone would
who was handling a rare flower, or a new born child. Her
mind shied away, she didn't like to think of new born
children—It was then he made the remark about it being
a beautiful piece. His voice was soft now as he went on,
'I have never seen a finer. It would be very interesting to
know its complete history.'

'Yes, yes, it would be,' she said.

'From what little I gathered from Mr Stuart I understand it was left to you as a gift by . . . by a gentleman.'

'Yes, that's right.' Her face was unsmiling.

'And when you were in dire straits you asked a certain
person to sell it for you?'

'Yes, yes, I did.'

'And that person misled you as to what he had got for
it?'

475

Now she merely nodded her head.

'Twenty pounds, I understand?'

'Twenty pounds,' she repeated.

His face was grave as he said, 'It's a pity you didn't decide to prosecute. And I made my views known to Mr Stuart. But I can assure you'—now he smiled—'I can assure you you'll get much more than twenty pounds this time.'

'Thank you.'

'I can offer you, say, two hundred and fifty pounds. How is that?'

She stared back at him. The price on the watch in the window had been four hundred and twenty-five guineas; which she had already calculated as four hundred and forty-six pounds five shillings. That meant he was giving her little over half. Two hundred and fifty pounds was still a fortune and she was about to say, 'Thank you very much,' when he laughed and said, 'I don't know if your silence means you're going to bargain with me or not.'

She had not thought about bargaining with him; it had never entered her head until he had mentioned it. Mr Stuart had said he was a fair man and so she supposed that in the course of business two hundred and fifty pounds was a fair offer, but she heard herself saying, 'The price on it in the window was four hundred and twenty-five guineas.'

'It was, it was indeed, madam, four hundred and twenty-five guineas.' He pursed his lips and wagged his head at her. 'So shall we not beat about the bush? I am in business, I have to make a fair profit. Now, now'—he wagged his finger jokingly at her—'don't say that I have already sold it once and made a fair profit, I know, I know.'

She found herself smiling back at him now, and when he said, 'All right, I'll take a straight hundred, three hundred and forty-six pounds ... and five shillings,' he laughed.

She opened her mouth to speak, closed it again, and swallowed before she could say, 'That is quite, quite acceptable.' She thought her reply sounded sort of good, educated like.

'The bargain is sealed then?'

'Yes, it is sealed.'

'How would you like the money? Have you a banking account?'

'No——' She paused before adding, 'Not as yet.'

He looked at her straight for a moment before saying, 'Then may I suggest you open an account with a bank?'

'Would ... would you be kind enough to recommend one?'

'Yes, yes, of course.'

'And ... and would it be possible to have the forty-six pounds in cash please?'

'Again of course.' He was nodding his head at her.

'Thank you.'

He was in the middle of writing out the cheque when, his eyebrows moving upwards, he looked at her from under his lids as he said, 'How is Mr Stuart these days?'

She stared back at him as she read behind the question, and she kept her voice level and her face straight as she answered, 'Very well; he ... he's on holiday in Paris at the moment.'

'Oh, in Paris. Good, good.' He was writing again. Then as he blotted the cheque he said, 'Very nice gentleman, very nice indeed. And he has an eye for good pieces.' He now opened a drawer, took out a handful of sovereigns, counted them, then placing them in a chamois bag, he stood up and came round the desk, and when she got to her feet he handed her the cheque and the bag saying, 'You'll find those correct I think, and I hope, madam'—he was bending towards her—'as your fortunes change, as

477

I am sure they are about to do, you will honour us with your custom, whether it is buying or'—he waved his forefinger in a flowing motion back to the desk and the watch—'selling.'

She found herself smiling at him again as she said, 'Yes, if I should want anything in the jewellery line I shall certainly come to you, Mr Goldberg. And ... and thank you for your fairness towards me.'

'It has been a pleasure, madam.'

She was about to go towards the door when she stopped and took one last look at the watch lying across a piece of velvet set at the side of the writing pad, and she felt an urge to go and touch it and bid it a personal farewell. She turned and looked at Mr Goldberg and he said quietly, 'Who knows, madam, but at some future date it may be in your possession again.'

She said nothing to this but went on through the shop and to the door, and it was Mr Goldberg who opened it for her, with the parting words, 'Good-day, madam, and good fortune go with you.'

Good fortune go with her. What he meant was, I hope you become a mistress to a rich man. He imagined that's what she had been to Mr Stuart, but that it was now over. Yet such was the way he had put it she hadn't felt insulted. And anyway, who was she to feel insulted by anyone suggesting she should be a mistress to a man, for hadn't she been that for the last two years? But the name they had given her roundabout hadn't been as fancy as mistress, she had been known by such names as, Birch's piece, or his fancy woman. Well, there was one thing she was sure of, never in her life again would she earn that title....

An hour later she came out of a bank. The manager himself hadn't shown her to the door but, nevertheless, he had been very civil when he understood that she wanted to deposit a cheque for three hundred pounds with him. Open an account, was the way he put it. At the same time, he hadn't been as civil as Mr Goldberg in that he had taken stock of the way she was dressed and had tempered his courtesy accordingly. She thought that it shouldn't have mattered to him if she had come in a sack as long as she was putting money into his business.

But the visit to the bank told her one thing, she needed clothes and badly. And she was going to have them, for at this moment she was greatly in need of something, anything to help alleviate the feeling that she was of no account. But, she told herself, she wasn't going to pay the price they were asking in the fancy shops in Newcastle. No, she'd go back to that second-hand shop in Fellburn. This time she knew what she wanted and she wouldn't come out dressed like a comedy actress. Moreover, the buying of clothes would take her mind off things and the strong desire in her now to give way to a paroxysm of grief, for she had the desire to cry as she had done when a child, with her body bent and her arms hugging her waist, and like that just cry and cry and cry.

It was half-past six when she returned to her Aunt Mary's and she was taken aback when she entered the kitchen. It had seemed crowded when she had left it, with the small children on the floor, but now the whole family was gathered, with eight of them sitting round the table.

Her cousin Pat, who worked with his father in the steelworks, was a big, hefty lump of a lad, almost a man, and at first he gaped at her, then grinned and said cheekily, 'Well! well! By! you look a spanker.'

Embarrassed, Emily passed her glance over them all, and they nodded at her shyly in greeting. Except her Uncle Frank who, getting to his feet, said, 'Well, I'll be damned! I haven't clapped eyes on you for years, lass, an' I've still been thinkin' of you as a bit of a girl. But by! I was bloody well wrong, wasn't I?' He held out his hand

and she took it, but almost instantly he was pushed aside by Mary who, standing in front of Emily, looked her up and down a number of times before exclaiming, 'Aye, lass, now that's something like it! By! talk about steppin' out of a band box. Where did you get that lot?'

'At the old firm.' Emily now made a slight face at her Aunt, and Mary cried, 'Fellburn, the second-hand shop? Aye; my! she's done you proud.'

And so thought Emily; but more so that she'd done herself proud, for on having asked to see something of good quality and quiet, and then been shown a mauve-coloured costume, she knew instantly that this was the kind of thing she wanted. The coat was slightly flared and of three-quarter length and was trimmed with narrow fur, not only on the collar but round the cuffs too, and the skirt hem had a thick silk dust fringe attached to it. It buttoned right up to the neck; and the buttons themselves were imposing, being made of fine black plaited cord.

Then the hat, a green velour, with one single small feather lying on the right side of the brim. And that was not all; for on her feet she was wearing a pair of shoes buttoned at the side by five pearl-studded buttons, and as Mary exclaimed about them, she lifted her foot and said, 'And you'd think they were made for me, they fit like a glove.'

'And what's that?' Mary was now pointing to a large brown case.

'Oh, it's ... it's a travelling case,' Emily said; 'it isn't real leather but it looks like it. I'd bought a few other things, an' then there were me own clothes, and so ... well, I bought it.'

Mary now stood gazing at Emily, as did her entire family; and then she said quietly, 'How did it go?'

'Very well, Aunt Mary.'

'Good, good, lass. ... Well, now, come on. Here, you

move your backside out of that!' She thrust one of her offspring off the end of the form that flanked the table. 'You've stuffed your kite long enough.' Then turning to Emily, she said, 'Sit yourself down there, lass, and have a bite.'

Before Emily sat down she took off her coat and hat, and Mary, taking them from her, said, 'Give them me here afore this squad gets their fingers on them an' clags them up.'

After she was seated at the table and Mary had put before her a plate of broth with mutton bones sticking out of it like the skeleton ribs of a ship, her Uncle Frank, sucking at a similar bone that he was holding in his hands, said, 'Hear you've been in the wars, lass.'

She gulped on a spoonful of broth before she said quietly, 'Yes, you could say that, Uncle Frank.'

'Well, you're welcome to stay here as long as you like, you know that. It's a pity though, as Mary just said afore you came in, that we couldn't sleep you, but you'll be all right across the road in Mrs Pritchard's.'

... 'Aye, the bugs 'll keep you company.' Pat was leaning towards her across the table now with an impish grin on his face.

'She has no bugs.' Mary's hand came out and gave her big son a clip across the ear, and he cried back at her, laughing, 'Well, has she got rid of them then?'

> 'I chased a bug around a hill,
> I'll have his blood 'e knows I will,'

chanted one of the children who was sitting on a cracket near the fire, and Mary cried at him, 'I'll have your bloody nose right off by its socket if you don't watch out.'

Pat was again leaning across towards Emily and in what was supposed to be a whisper, he now said, 'You might have the privilege of meetin' Polly.'

481

'Our Pat!'

'All right, Ma, all right; I'm just tellin' her, preparin' her like. You see'—he pulled a mock-solemn face at Emily—'Polly Pritchard's very special, well, everybody in the street knows she is, 'cos she's a fully paid up member of the Provident Society for the Protection of Practising Prostitutes.'

As his father spluttered into his soup and almost choked, Mary cried, 'I've warned you, our Pat! Mind, I'll bring me hand across your lug so hard a steel hammer 'll be nothin' to it.'

'Oh! Ma, I'm only tellin' Emily what to expect.'

'And I'm tellin' you what to expect, me lad.'

There were titters all round the table now. Frank kept his head down and attended to another bone, while Pat, still solemn-faced and still giving his attention to Emily, who was finding it impossible not to be amused by him, although she wondered if he wasn't getting a sly dig at her through this Polly Pritchard, went on, 'She's really a good girl, Emily, that's what I'm tryin' to tell you. She goes to confession every Saturday night—she's often there afore me—but sometimes mind she's in so long I'm half sorry for young Father Clapham, 'cos listenin' to what she has to tell him must make the young fellow sweat as if he were sittin' bare arsed on a fire lighter.'

The explosion at the table resounded round the kitchen. Some were bent double, some had their heads back. Even the very young ones who didn't know what the laughter was all about joined in.

Emily had her head down and her hand across her mouth. She had never thought to laugh again, but she warned herself not to let it have rein, for just as it had done once before her mirth could change to bitter anguish on the catch of a breath.

When Mary's hand, in a resounding crack, came across the side of her son's face, almost sending him to the floor, the laughter increased. Frank turned from the table choking as if the bone he had been sucking were stuck in his gullet.

'Get yersel up out of that an' away to your wash.'

Still laughing, but now holding the side of his face, Pat said, 'Ma, you want to let up on that, you'll knock me deaf one of these days ... or daft.'

'That would be impossible, you're already as daft as a brush. Get yersel away.'

A few minutes later, when the kitchen had sobered down, Pat's voice could be heard singing from the scullery the chorus of a bawdy song that Emily had heard often in Creador Street.

'I'll be up your flue next week,
I'll be up your flue next week,
Aye, Mrs Flanagan, I'll be up your flue next week.'

During the rest of the meal and for the rest of the evening Emily pondered the happiness and good humour that pervaded this family. The lads were coarse, especially Pat; but then, weren't all working men coarse? Didn't they all come out with things like that? ... But Sep hadn't.... Yet in this house it was like God bless you. In this house where there wasn't a stick of decent furniture, where there was no privacy, no books to read, and where even the crockery wasn't very clean, that there should be this feeling of warmth and closeness, and all threaded with laughter and good cheer, always amazed her. But even as she appreciated it she knew that she wouldn't be able to live long in such an atmosphere, she knew the kind of life she wanted from now on. She wanted something to keep her busy, but she also wanted time to read and think, but most of all she wanted some place to call her own, a house to call her own, some place where she could lay her head down and cry her heart out. Oh! this need to cry that was on her now....

She slept at Mrs Pritchard's, and she left her Aunt Mary's early the next morning and made her way to Shields. She was going to rent a house and she wanted it to face the sea. She had decided to go to The Lawe, even while she knew there was little chance of renting one of the houses there because they were mostly occupied by sea captains and well-to-do people and such. And although she knew too it would be like opening an old sore she meant to approach The Lawe, going by the water-front. So she got off the train again at Tyne Dock and went down the bank, past the dock gates, then along Thornton Avenue until she came to Pilot Place.

She had to move off the pavement when she passed the warehouse for men, there, were loading up a dray. She walked round the horse and cart, then on to the pavement again; and a few steps farther on she stopped. There it was, number six.

She saw immediately that the step was filthy and the sight made her sad. When she came up abreast with the front door she stopped. The paint had all peeled off. Now her eyes moved to the window of the front room. The curtains on it looked filthy too. But what caught her attention next made her take a few quick steps to Mrs Gantry's window where there was a notice which read: 'This house for sale. Apply Barratt and Flynn, 8 Bright Street.'

She turned quickly about and looked towards the wall that bordered the river; then she actually ran across the road and, straining her neck to see over it, she looked at the boats, big and small, moored against the bank, and a tramp steamer making its way towards the docks. And straining further still, she saw the men working in the repair yards, and the sight filled her with excitement.

Swinging round again, she stood with her back to the wall and gazed across the road to what had been Mrs

Gantry's house. She could buy it! She could buy that house. What would it cost? She had no idea. . . . 8 Bright Street. She knew where Bright Street was.

Ten minutes later, she entered the office of Barratt and Flynn.

Could they help her?

'Yes,' she said; 'she wanted particulars about number eight Pilot Place.'

'Oh'—the agent nodded at her—'Eight Pilot Place,' he said. 'Yes, it's for sale, but it goes with the other one.'

She narrowed her eyes towards him questioningly. 'The house next door is for sale an' all? Is it empty?'

'Yes, and has been for some time.'

'Did Mrs McGillby's nephew not come and live there? . . . You see I knew the people who once owned the house.'

'Oh . . . well, no; he never lived there, he's got a nice place in Westoe. And when he sold it, the buyer bought the old lady's place next door an' all, because he thought she wasn't long for the top. And she wasn't, and when she died he had the idea of knocking them into one to make a sort of small boarding establishment. Then he himself goes and dies about three months ago and it's his wife who now wants to sell them.'

Forcing herself to suppress her excitement, she thought, Eeh! it's odd, strange. I had to come down that way, I had to come back.

'How much does the owner want for them?'

'Well, she's asking a hundred and twenty pounds each if they're sold separately, but I think she would come down to two hundred if they were sold both together. I might as well admit they've been hanging a bit because she wanted to get them off her hands together. And what's more, there's a number empty round that quarter; it's no use closing one's eyes to it.'

She pressed her knuckles against the front of her coat between her breasts, and as she swallowed deeply her

head moved slightly to the side before she said, 'Tell ...
tell her I'll give her two hundred for them.'

'Don't you want to see inside them? I'm ... I'm bound
to tell you they're both in a bit of a mess; not a thing's
been done to them for years.'

'That's all right; I know the houses. When will I know
if she accepts?' There was a touch of authority in her
voice. She felt she was talking like a woman of means. At
another time she might have been amused by it.

'Well, I'm off round that quarter shortly; I could call
and see her. I'll be back by two.'

'Very well. I'll call again at two....'

The agent showed her out, and very respectfully.

She called again at two o'clock and was told that the
owner would accept two hundred and ten pounds for the
two houses. At this she made herself ponder for a moment, then as if coming to a decision, she said, 'Very well.'
She would pay what was asked.

Her hand was shaking as if with ague, she had written
out her first cheque for a ten per cent deposit on the
purchase. And now, here she was, standing in the kitchen
of the house where she had known such happiness, un-
aware happiness, for in those days she hadn't been aware
of what unhappiness meant.

The house, as the agent had said, was in a very bad
state. The wallpaper was dirty and hanging off the walls;
the stove that she had blackleaded religiously every Friday until it shone was rusty; the back window was broken
and someone had taken the scullery tap and its lead pipe.

But all this didn't matter. Here she was, not only back
in the house but soon to be the owner of it ... not forgetting the one next door. It seemed quite unbelievable,
and it all stemmed from Sep. Dear Sep.... Dear, dear Sep,
what she owed him ... and dear Mr Stuart.... No; she
shouldn't think of Mr Stuart as dear; kind, nice, but ...
but not dear. Yet why not? Because, despite Sep's kind-

ness, if it wasn't for Mr Stuart she wouldn't be here now.

It seemed odd that a man about whom she knew so little, and who knew so little about her, had been willing to spend four hundred and twenty-five guineas on her and ask nothing in return. He had made her the gift knowing full well at the time that she had nothing to give him, and could never repay him, for she'd never be in a position to do so. Neither he nor herself had foreseen the bonfire.

She looked back to the bonfire now as two years gone up in smoke, two long years, two long years during which she had been painfully forged into a woman. Every sixteen hours of the twenty-four that made a day had been long up on that hill. Was it just on forty-eight hours since she had burnt those years, and were they really burnt? Wouldn't the ashes of them be like grit in her teeth for the rest of her life?

All of a sudden she wanted to sit down. She felt weak and slightly sick. But there wasn't a stick of furniture of any kind in the place.

Hastily, she went towards the door that enclosed the stairs and, pulling it open, she sat down on the second step and the emotion that she had banked down on since walking from the hill two nights ago erupted. It began slowly, the tears just welling into her eyes and dropping from her lashes on to her cheeks; then like a swollen river, it became a torrent, and she turned and, leaning her elbows on the dirty stairs, she buried her face in her hands and sobbed aloud. . . .

When the paroxysm was finally over she pulled herself to her feet, adjusted her hat that had slipped to the back of her head, dusted her skirt and the elbows of her jacket, then, unlocking the back door, she went into the yard and to the rain barrel that stood next to the wash-house wall. Wetting her handkerchief in it, she sponged her face, and as she did so she remembered the day she threw the back door key away. It was the day she put her bundles on the cart to go up the hill.

When, some little time later, she went next door she found it to be in an even worse state than Sep's house—she would always think of it as Sep's house—but she didn't actually see the dirt and grime, for in her mind's eye now she was imagining what they would both look like when she had finished scrubbing, painting and papering them and making them into a home, a real home, her home, a place where she hadn't to wear a mob-cap, nor bow and scrape to anyone, but what was more a place wherein if she had no one to love she would certainly have no one to scorn her, or at best treat her like an obliging whore.

TWO

The agent had said she could go ahead with the painting and redecorating but she couldn't live in the house until the deeds were actually signed, which would happen in about a month's time. So every day she came down from Gateshead. During the first week all she managed to do was to strip the walls and scrub and rub down the woodwork ready for painting. She had engaged a man to paint the outside of both houses, back and front, but she was going to paint the inside herself . . . white.

When she told the painter this he had simply gaped at her before saying, 'Oh, miss, that'll be a mistake; you could never keep anything white for five minutes around here; a nice light brown now with a grain to it, a combed grain, that would look fine and you wouldn't need to touch it for a couple of years or more. But white; oh no; you'd have to have a pail in your hand washin' down every week.'

'I want it white.'

'Aw well'—he had shaken his head sadly—'you'll live and learn, miss. You'll live and learn.'

The painter finished his work in a week, and afterwards she found she missed him—there was no one to pass a word with—so she told herself the quicker she got the place ready for what she meant to do the better.

It was the agent saying that the previous owner had been about to turn the two places into a boarding-house that had given her the idea: why shouldn't she run a boarding-house for respectable gentlemen? Well, she wouldn't get many gentlemen around here, she knew that, not as one thought of gentlemen, but she decided firmly she would take only respectable men, not riff-raff. But she could see herself working for the next two months papering and painting these eight rooms; then there would be the business of going round the second-hand shops seeking furniture to fill them. The furniture would have to be second-hand because new stuff would make too big an inroad into what money she had left.

She reckoned that after furnishing the place she could live for a year without worrying even if she didn't get a boarder; but then, she was bound to get someone in that time. The best thing to do was to put an advert in the *Shields Gazette*....

She had been working on the house by herself now for ten days. Up till yesterday she'd had to go out for her meals, but only this morning the pipes had been replaced in the scullery and the water turned on, and so she was sitting now on an upturned box and drinking the tea she had brewed and eating the sandwiches her Aunt Mary had put up for her.

She had almost finished her meal and was about to rise and start work again when there came a knock on the front door.

That, she thought, would be the painter because she had sent him a note asking if he would come and give her a hand with the inside, because at the rate she was going she couldn't see herself finishing in three months, let alone two.

When she opened the door she was about to say, 'Hello there; you've been quick,' but her mouth remained open and it was the man on the step who spoke, 'Hello, Emily,' he said.

'Hello ... hello, Mr Stuart.'

'Well, aren't you going to ask me in?'

'Oh, of course, of course.' She stepped back, and he walked past her and into the front room. And then she was bustling forward, saying, 'Come this way; it's all in a bit of a muddle.'

In the kitchen, she stood near the box and looked down at the remains of her meal before removing it hastily, while she gabbled, 'This is all I can offer you.'

'I don't need to sit, I'm used to standing.'

'How ... how did you find? ... O ... oh! Aunt Mary.'

'Yes.' He nodded back at her as he smiled and repeated, 'Aunt Mary.' He looked about him now, 'You've been very busy.'

'Yes; but ... but there's a lot to do yet. Can ... can I offer you a cup of tea?'

'Yes. Yes, please.'

She hurried into the scullery, and rinsed her cup out under the tap, but before making a move back to the kitchen she held tightly on to the side of the sink and looked down into it and bit hard on her lip for a moment. She felt embarrassed, slightly afraid, all at sixes and sevens.

In the kitchen again, she poured him out a cup of tea; then asked, 'Do you take sugar?'

'No.'

'Not at all?' That was a silly thing to say.

'No, not at all.' He took the cup from her, sipped at the hot tea; then looking at her again, he said, 'How are you, Emily?'

'Oh, I'm all right, Mr Stuart, and I'll soon be settled in. And ... and I must say it'—her voice sank to a soft note—'it's thanks to you.'

'No! No!' He shook his head slowly. 'I'm not going to take any credit for this; what you've done, you've done yourself.'

She looked into his face. It was no use contradicting him, but she too shook her head. He now pointed to one

491

of the boxes, saying, 'Won't you sit down?' and when she was seated he sat opposite her on the box she had used as a table.

Her hands were joined on her lap, but not palm on palm, her fingers, linked together, were gripping each other.

She wetted her lips before she asked, 'Did you enjoy your holiday?'

'Not very much. Paris is for the very young and the not so young, and the not so old. I didn't seem to fit in.' He smiled, a self-deprecating smile. 'You are working very hard,' he said now.

'Yes'—she nodded—'it was very dirty. I ... I'm in a bit of a mess.' She moved her joined hands up and down indicating as it were the fact that this was why she was wearing a coarse hessian apron.

'You look pale, you've lost your roses.' His words brought the roses back into her cheeks for a moment as she said, 'I'll soon get me colour back; the wind along the river front is noted for making you either red or blue.' She gave a small embarrassed laugh.

They became silent while looking at each other; then as if with an effort, she unlaced her fingers and, putting her hands behind her back, she undid the strings of the apron, rose slightly from the box and pulled it from beneath her, then sat rolling it up waiting for him to speak again, for at the moment, although she was choked full with feeling she was empty of words.

Her hands became still when he said quietly, 'I was sorry I was away when it happened; George told me everything, at least as much as he knew. You must have been very hurt indeed to do what you did.'

Her chin was deep on her chest now, and her voice was scarcely above a whisper as she said, 'I shouldn't have done it, I know now I shouldn't have done it.'

'Can you bear to tell me what happened?'

It was a full minute before she spoke. 'He went off without a word. He was gone before I got up. He took the cow, the horse, and the sheep. He left me a letter with ... with not a line of regret in it, and five pounds. I ... I think it was the meanness that sort of unbalanced me. He said I could have the furniture ex ... except three pieces, a French table, a clock, and a bureau. They were the only pieces of any value. He implied that he couldn't go to her empty-handed. That somehow ... well, it did something to me.' She now raised her head and looked at him as she ended, 'If I could have cried then I might have washed the madness away but I was past crying, an' all that day I went about dragging the stuff out and piling it up. I didn't light it until it was near dark. An' then they all came up the hill, the villagers, and the people from the pit rows, and ... and then he came. I knew I was waiting for him comin' because he would think I'd burned his cottage down.'

She paused now and dropped her gaze from him as she said, 'It wouldn't have hurt him to give me the cottage, would it, although I'd never have stayed there on me own? But it was, as I said, the meanness that got me. Yet if I'd left it at that, I mean just burned the stuff, I would have had nothin' to regret, but ... but when I saw him face to face I spat out my bitterness in front of them all. That's what I'm sorry for now, because they'll take it out of him, not because they thought anything about me being thrown off, but because I've given them another stick to bray his back with. What I said aroused all the old bad feeling against him, and I think it had almost died away over the years. . . .'

He held up his hand now to check her going on, and his tone was harsh as he said, 'No, it hadn't, Emily. No, it hadn't. I know that much, and what I didn't find out for myself George filled in for me. He tells me there's been talk in the village for the past year or more to the effect

493

that someone should put you wise to the situation. I think they were only deterred by the thought that you couldn't be blind to it, that you must have known what was going on. Anyway, if nothing else would have aroused the old feeling, the fact that Farmer Rowan had scarcely settled in his box before he went and took over, that alone would have done it. His hurry was indecent. So you have no need to let him bother your conscience for one moment; in fact, as George says, you have the sympathy of the whole village.'

She got abruptly to her feet now. 'I don't want the sympathy of the whole village. Except for Mr Waite, the baker, they would have had me in the stocks at one time, if that were possible. And I'll never forget it was them who killed Con . . . I suppose you know about Con?'

'Yes, I heard about him.'

She walked to the kitchen window and looked out before turning slowly to him again and saying, 'There's one thing in his favour. He liked Con, he was good to him. He looked after him, and he nearly went mad when he died . . . and about the way he died.'

'There's some good in every man, Emily; there's no-body really black or really white, but some have more black in them than others. And as I see it, Birch's black-ness was merely weakness, and his strength greed, which in his own mind he would have termed ambition.' He paused and shook his head before he said thoughtfully, 'He must have coveted that farm a great deal to get Rona to do what she did because even from the short time she and I were together I realized I'd taken on a mettlesome horse; he couldn't have got her to the church, and to commit bigamy into the bargain, without some hard work on his part. But with regard to the bigamy, she would doubtless have felt safe here for she would know I'd never want to see her again.'

She was sitting on the box again and she looked

494

straight at him as she said, 'He also sent my sister to this home in St Leonards to be cured of consumption.'

'Yes, I heard that also, but I wouldn't give him too much credit for his motives there. He wanted the child out of the house, I think; she was standing in his path towards you.... Emily——' With a quick movement that was characteristic of him he had caught hold of her hands and he shook them gently as he said, 'Don't try to find excuses for him in your mind, excuses that will make you feel guilty about telling him the truth, for as I see it, it was time that somebody told him exactly what he really is, a nowt, as they say around these quarters.' His hands stopped their movement; he looked deep into her eyes and asked now, 'Do you still love him?'

Her fingers jerked within his grasp but he did not release them, only held them more firmly and waited. She did not bow her head, but she looked first to one side of the room and then to the other before she answered, and enigmatically now, 'What does anybody mean by love?'

'You're not answering my question, Emily.' He gave her hands a little shake. 'Do you still love him?'

Now she was looking back at him and she answered plainly, 'If you mean, have I got the feeling for him that I had two years ago, no; but looking back, I don't know now if that feeling was love or not. I was sorry for him, I wanted to comfort him, I wanted to give, I wanted to make him happy. It's a failing of mine, a sort of conceit I suppose you would call it that I want to make people happy, at least I used to. I've learned more sense now; you can't make people happy unless they want to be happy.'

'You're very wise you know, Emily. And there's some failings I think one should hold on to, even indulge in; so don't give up wanting to make people happy. There's one emotion I noticed that you didn't say you had for him, and that was liking.'

When she raised her eyebrows slightly he nodded and

495

went on, 'To my mind it's the most important emotion of all because without it love never lasts. You know you can love somebody and hate them at the same time, but you can't like somebody and hate them at the same time. I'd rather be liked, well liked, than loved.... Do you like me, Emily?'

She made a movement with her lips as if they were gummed together and were having difficulty in separating them, but when she did she said, 'Yes, yes, of course, I like you. It would be impossible not to like somebody who has been so kind to me. If you hadn't given me the watch....'

'Now, now!' He rose abruptly to his feet. 'We'll speak about the watch for the last time. Let me put it like this. If Birch had taken a different attitude towards me I would have shared everything in that place with him, because this much I've got in his favour, he put a lot of work into the farm, so I look upon the money spent in retrieving your watch as some form of recompense which, had it been given to him, he should in kindness have passed it on to you for all you did for him. But as things have turned out, I know now he would never have given you the watch, or its equivalent in money. So let's say the farm paid its debt in a small way, not me.... Now'—he bent down to her—'I want a straight answer to my question, do you like me for myself?'

She gulped in her throat and blinked before saying, 'That's a difficult question.'

'Why difficult? You must know inside yourself whether you like me or not.'

'Well——' As she went to turn her head to the side her neck jerked upwards, for he had taken her by the shoulders and, sitting down on the box, his knees touching hers, he commanded, 'Look at me, Emily!' And when she looked at him he went on, 'I'm not asking, do you love me? because that would indeed be a very difficult ques-

496

tion to answer, what I'm asking you is, do you like me ... like me sufficiently to marry me?'

She swung herself away from his hands and to her feet, and she backed a step towards the fireplace now while crying, 'Don't be silly! Don't be silly! Mr Stuart. You know what you told me yourself, if you marry you lose the farm.'

He hadn't risen from the box and he looked up at her as he answered, 'I know what I said, and yes, I'd have to leave the farm; but let me tell you now, Emily, that would be no loss to me. What do you think my life has been like during the past eighteen months or more? Do you know the only company I've had is George and Jenny and Mrs Riley? And they all have their own lives to lead. Where does that leave me? Night after night sitting in that frenchified drawing-room, or walking from room to room, or going round the farm pretending to inspect my domain, and not caring a tinker's cuss for any part of it, because let's face it, Emily, I'm no farmer. I don't run that place, it's George who's the farmer, George who runs it. Like you I wouldn't trust anyone of those villagers as far as I could toss them, but there was a time when I'd have been glad of a kind word from them. As for the farmers around, and those higher up, well, the men look through me and the women lower their glances, only the children stare because I'm the parents' picture of a bad man, a murderer, a man who served a long term in prison. Emily'—he now rose to his feet and came towards her—'I could walk out of there tomorrow and sing if I had any place to walk to, anyone to walk to.'

'No!' Again she swung away from him; and now she put the distance of the whole room between them and her voice sounded harsh in her ears as she cried, 'No! No! I'm not going to have that on me conscience an' all. And anyway, it couldn't be right living with two men who have owned the place.'

'I'm not asking you to live with me, Emily, I'm asking

497

you to marry me.'

'And I say no! No! Mr Stuart. What you must do'—she nodded at him now—'is take someone there to live with you; there are plenty of nice girls, women, lonely women. . . .'

'*Shut up!* please.'

Her eyes widened. She stared at him. He hadn't shouted at her, but his words carried more weight than if he had. His face had lost its smooth pallor, he looked angry and he sounded angry as he said, 'The only woman I would take to live with me would be you; and I wouldn't ask that of you. You're the only one I want to live with. I've known it from our first meeting. You are the kind of woman I dreamt of at night when I lay awake and sweated and tried to get the smell of human bodies out of my nostrils, tried to forget the sound of steel doors clanging, and worse still, the jingle of manacles. When I saw you first sitting on the back of the carrier cart, I didn't know who you were but your face was as familiar to me as my own, more so because for years I hadn't seen myself very often.' . . .

In the silence that fell between them they stared at each other, and she only just stopped herself in time from thrusting her hands out to him and saying, 'Oh, I'm sorry, I'm sorry.'

She walked back to the fireplace. Her head was down, her hands joined at her waist, and he came and stood beside her and, looking at her bent head, he said, 'I've rushed at it like a bull at a gap. I didn't mean to. I should have given you time.'

She now turned to him and shook her head, and her voice had a deep note of sadness in it as she said, 'I . . . I could never marry you because I would never know a moment's peace thinkin' about how I deprived you of what was rightly yours.'

'Rightly mine!' He laughed softly and repeated,

'Rightly mine! Do you know something, Emily? If she hadn't wanted to get her own back on Birch she would just as soon have given that place to the devil. And what is more, should she have been alive, and on her own, and I had turned up after my release, she would have shown me the door, likely with a gun at my head from what I can gather now. No, I have no more right to that place than you have. I say than you have, for you earned some part of it by nursing her as you did, whereas I came into it as a means of spiting the man she had come to hate.... One last question, Emily.' He paused and smiled gently at her now, 'Had we met each other under different circumstances would you have liked me enough to marry me then?'

She had no need to consider her answer. In deep confusion she looked away from him and put her hand up and pressed it on the thick coils of her hair circling the back of her head, and standing like that she muttered, 'I ... I don't know.'

It was almost a full minute before he said, 'I don't believe you, Emily. But enough, enough for the time being.... Can we be friends?'

Now she turned and smiled quietly at him as she answered, 'Yes, yes, of course.'

'And my name is Nick, remember?'

Her smile widened as she said, 'I'll, I'll try an' remember.'

'Now, now!' As if he had settled an important issue he swung round from her and, spreading his arms wide, said, 'And what do you intend to do here?'

'Didn't Aunt Mary give you all the news?'

'Yes, she did.' He laughed at her over his shoulder. 'But I didn't believe her. You couldn't possibly run a boarding-house.'

'Why not?' There was an indignant note in her voice now.

'Because you'd be eaten alive.'

'Eaten alive?' She screwed up her eyes at him.

He nodded at her. 'That's what I said, eaten alive. How many men do you intend to board ... because you won't get women?'

'Why not?'

'Because women don't usually seek lodgings on a river front, at least I shouldn't think so, unless they're of a certain type.' His eyes twinkled as the colour in her face deepened. 'You are much too young, Emily'—he shook his head slowly—'and too beautiful to be a boarding-house keeper on a seafront.'

'Nonsense!' Her head wagged. 'There's a number of women boarding-house keepers along Thornton Avenue and thereabouts.'

'There may be ... have you seen them?'

'... No. But do you have to be an old hag before you can open a boarding-house?'

'Yes.' He was laughing openly at her now. 'Yes, I would say you would have to be an old hag before you could safely open a boarding-house along here.'

Their gaze held for a moment; then she looked away from him. She had never thought about this side of it; and anyway, she felt that after her experience over the past years she was quite capable of handling any man who got out of place. Looking at him again, she said just that: 'I'll be able to handle them.'

'Well'—he sighed—'I won't say you know best, all I can say is go ahead and have a try. When do you propose to open your boarding-house?'

'As soon as I get the place ready.'

'And how long is that going to take?'

She gave a small laugh now as she said, 'On my own, much longer than I thought; but I've written to Mr Nesbit—he's the man who painted the outside—an' asked him to come and give me a hand.'

'Oh well, if it's a hand you want.' He had taken off his coat before she could protest. 'If it's just a hand you want I've two of them lying idle at the moment. Where do we start?'

'Don't be silly.' She was laughing at him now. 'You in your good clothes, they'd be all over paint afore you knew where you were.'

'Oh, I can easily get over that. I passed a shop along the way with dungarees hanging outside, all sizes I noticed. They'll soon fit me up.'

'No.' Her hand was out towards him now, and he stopped in the act of putting on his coat, and again she said, 'No, please, don't ... don't make it more awkward for me. Go back to the farm. Come ... come and see me some time when I'm settled.'

He finished buttoning his coat, his face was straight, and now he nodded slowly at her, saying, 'All right, all right, Emily.' He held out his hand and she placed hers in it, and when he covered it they stood staring into each other's eyes for a moment; and then quite abruptly he turned from her and went out through the front room.

When she heard the door bang she looked in its direction but didn't move. She felt an overwhelming urge now to cry just as she had done the first day she had come back into the house.

Do you like me? he had asked. You can love someone and hate them but you can't like them and hate them.

She liked him. Oh yes, yes, indeed, she liked him. But it could go no further, for as she had said she wouldn't be able to live with her conscience knowing she was the means of him losing the house and the farm. And it was all eye-wash him saying he was no farmer, all eye-wash.

Grabbing up her coarse apron now, she put it on and continued with her work; but, as she put it to herself, there was a damper on the day.

THREE

Nothing ever turned out as planned. Here she was back in the house of her dreams, all the decorating was done, the place was furnished comfortably, she had even had the wall broken down between the two yards and a gate put in for easy access to next door. She had been sleeping in the house for the past two weeks and was now admitting openly to herself that she was lonely. She was tired of reading, even the little black book had lost its interest. She had to keep stopping herself from locking up, getting on the train and going up yet again to her Aunt Mary's.

And there was now something puzzling her about her Aunt Mary. She had the idea that her Aunt Mary's welcome was a little cool these days; and yet she hadn't troubled her, not all that much.

She kept remembering what her Aunt Mary had said to her three weeks ago. 'It's about time you settled in there, isn't it? If you're goin' to run a business you've got to be on the spot. If you don't get down there until eleven o'clock in the day you could be missing people knockin' on the door.'

Well, apart from going out and doing a bit of shopping she had been in the house twenty-four hours of every day for the past two weeks and she'd had only two inquiries to her advert in the *Shields Gazette*. And she remembered them both with slight shudders. The first had been a small thin man in a greasy coat. He had a drop on the end of his nose which he kept wiping off on the back of his hand. He said he was a storekeeper in one of the big shops in King Street. She hadn't even shown him a room. She had kept him standing just within the front door, for when he asked, 'What's your charge?' and she answered 'Twelve and six,' he had exclaimed, 'Bloody hell! missis, you must be jokin'. I'm not askin' to take over the house, I just want a room an' a meal.'

At this she had barked at him, 'Well, go and find it elsewhere,' and almost pushed him into the street. Then going into the kitchen, she had stood biting hard down on her lip to hold back the tears.

Her second applicant hadn't quibbled about her charge. He said he was second mate on a short trip boat, and he'd be in every other week, and he was willing to pay for a room to be kept permanently for him.

Oh yes, he had been very eager to take up residence with her. He had pushed past her into the front room, then walked through into the kitchen, saying as he went, 'Oh, aye! all very nice and comfortable an' white paint! You're new around here, aren't you?'

She hadn't answered, but kept her distance from him; even so, the smell of drink on his breath wafted to her. When he took a seat and, having thrust his hand into his pocket, slapped down twelve and six on to the table, saying, 'There, that's me good faith in advance; I'll bring me kit along later. And we sail the morrow, so you won't see me for a week. Now, isn't that fair?' She turned about and, hurrying to the front door, yelled from there in no small voice, 'Get yourself out! I'm full up.'

It was some minutes before he came walking through the front room towards her, and such was the look on his face that she stepped out into the street. But he did not immediately follow; he stood in the doorway leering at her as he said, 'You're new to the game, lass; you've got a lot to learn.' Then after a moment he stepped on to the pavement, but before he had time to say anything more she sprang over the step, banged the door, then stood with her back to it.

That had happened the day before yesterday, and she hadn't seen anyone since, and not a soul to speak to. Last week she had gone round to Creador Street to see Jimmy and his wife, but the visit wasn't a success. In a way she felt she was embarrassing them. The house was anything but clean, and Jimmy's wife already looked a slattern, and Emily had thought, If they have a big family it certainly won't be a merry one like his mother's.

She sat in the kitchen now, her feet on the fender, staring into the fire. She had made a mistake; she had thought that all she wanted from life was to be back in this little house. And in a way that was true, but not to live alone like this. Nobody should live alone. For the past twenty-four hours she had been debating if she should send for Lucy, but had told herself again and again that would be selfish. It was this boarding-house idea that was all wrong. She should have just bought Sep's house and gone out to work somewhere as a daily, then everything would have been all right. As it was she was now saddled with two houses to look after, and rates to pay on them. What was more, the buying of the furniture, although second-hand, and all the new bedding had made a bigger hole in the money than she had anticipated and what she now had left of the total after paying for the houses and the solicitor's fees would only last out for another six months at the most, and then what?

In answer to the question in her mind she said, 'Oh, I'll have to talk to somebody; I'll go to me Aunt Mary's.'

'Well, I wasn't for it from the start.' Mary was wagging her finger at her.

'But ... but you said it was a good idea, Aunt Mary.'

'Aye, a boarding-house is a good idea, but not for

young women like you on her own; an' lookin' like you do an' all. A married couple, aye; or a mother and daughter, aye. Now if you'd thought of takin' some such place in Newcastle where there's gentlemen who want residences an' to be looked after, you would 've had no trouble with snotty-nosed individuals or second mates who would 've had me boot up their backsides if I'd been there. But, of course'—she now waved her hand and laughed—'if I'd been there things would have been different, wouldn't they?'

'Yes, Aunt Mary.' Emily's voice was dull. Was it, she asked herself, imagination or had her Aunt Mary changed towards her? She seemed to have lost interest in her affairs, merely putting up with her visits. And this time was no exception. Well, she wasn't one to stay where she wasn't wanted. She'd go back home because, lonely or not, it was her home, and she'd rethink things out. She could likely sell next door now that it had been done up. Yes, perhaps that would solve part of the problem, she would sell next door. But she wouldn't discuss her affairs any further with Aunt Mary; not at the present anyway. She rose from the chair, side-stepped the latest infant sitting on the mat, and said, 'I'll be getting away down, Aunt Mary.'

'But you've hardly got in, lass. Sit yourself down and have a cup of tea and something to eat. What's the matter with you?'

'Nothing ... nothing, Aunt Mary.'

'Well then, try and look as if nothin's the matter. Only to my eyes, you're makin' a poor show of it at present. You're not regrettin' leaving that hill, are you?'

'Oh no, Aunt Mary. Oh no!' Her answer was quick and emphatic.

' 'Cos if you were I'll give you somethin' to think on, he was married last week.'

'Married!'

505

'Aye, that's what I said, married.'

'Oh well, that's what I expected.'

Yes, she had expected it, but nevertheless it hurt. 'I'll never marry you or anyone else,' he had said; 'I'll never put me name to paper again as long as I live.' Well, he had put his name to paper, and got a farm at last, a farm of his own. Or would it be his own? She looked sharply at Mary now and said, 'How did you get to know that?'

'Oh, I get around here and there; at least, people get around to me. There's more comes in on a carrier cart than parcels and piglets.'

'I'll be away, Aunt Mary.'

'Well, just as you please, lass. Just as you please.' Mary walked with her to the door and there, her manner resuming its old friendliness, she said, 'Come on, lass, cheer up; there's always something around the corner. It's surprisin' what's just around the corner. Come on, never say die.'

It was almost too much. She bent forward and kissed Mary's cheek, then hurried away down the street.

When she awoke the next morning there was a rime of thick frost on all the windows, and she shivered as she went downstairs.

She pulled the damper out of the fire and it was soon blazing around the kettle, and as she made herself the first of the endless cups of tea she drank during the day, she told herself it would soon be Christmas.

During the morning she dusted the rooms and prepared herself a meal, and in the afternoon she cleaned the insides of all the windows.

It was as she was finishing the front bedroom window of Gantry's house, as she still thought of the adjoining property, that she saw the cab coming along the street, and when it stopped opposite her door she pressed her face to the pane and looked downwards. She watched the cab driver pull down a trunk from the driving seat, then go to the open door of the cab and take from someone's hand a case, a large suitcase; then another and another; and when the luggage was all on the pavement a man stepped out of the cab.

At the sight of him she jumped back from the window and pressed her hand holding the duster tightly over her mouth. Not until the knocker on the front door was banged for the third time did she turn round and hurry out of the room, down the stairs, through the back door and the gate in the dividing wall and so into her own scullery, then through the kitchen and the front room, and to the front door. But she didn't open it immediately; not until the knocker banged yet once again did she pull back the sneck. Then, drawing the door slowly open, she stared at him.

'You've been some time; I thought you were out.'

She looked from him to where the horse was turning the cab round in the middle of the road, and he looked at his luggage and said, 'Well, I'd better get these inside, hadn't I?'

She didn't offer to assist him, she just stepped back and watched him almost throw the cases into the front room; but the trunk he dragged carefully over the step; and when they were all inside he closed the door and stood looking at her for a second before he moved forward and, taking her by the elbow, turned her about and walked her into the kitchen. There, facing her, he said, 'Well, what have you got to say to your new lodger?'

For an answer she groped backwards, caught hold of a chair and sat down; and as she had done many years ago when she had faced Sep, she laid her hands palm on top of palm on her lap.

He did not come any nearer to her but laughed as he said, 'I can pay in advance, twelve and six a week, but the only thing is I'll want to occupy my room all the time.'

She closed her eyes. Her Aunt Mary. Her Aunt Mary had been in on this. That was why she had appeared funny. They had worked together. Everything she had told her Aunt Mary, her Aunt Mary had told him; and he had taken it from there. She said quietly now, 'You haven't, have you? You haven't given up the farm?'

Now all amusement slipping from his countenance, he answered, 'As from three o'clock yesterday. And the relief is great. I feel for the second time in my life that I've been let out of prison.'

As she stared into his face she couldn't help but believe that he spoke the truth; yet if it wasn't for her he would still be there, owner of a fine house and a marvellous farm, a rich man. She said in a whisper now, 'But you're left with nothing?'

'Oh, I wouldn't say that. Yet according to the will, I could touch no money, only my share of the profits in the past six months. But I suppose I'm a wily person, Emily. If it isn't a natural characteristic I must have picked it up in prison. One learns to look after oneself there. So during the period I have been supposedly owner of the farm, I haven't neglected myself. I often paid visits to Mr Goldberg when I had a fancy for a gold albert or gold cuff links or studs to match, and similar things like that, and put them down to expenses, under different headings of course....' He looked to the side before adding, 'I must have known that day would come when I'd have to go. And at the same time I suppose, being a normal man, I was hitting back at Rona for her subtle cruelty. I also spent money on pieces of good porcelain and silver. I hadn't realized I had an eye for those kind of things until recent years, and so I have a few possessions in the trunk that will see me through until I start my business.'

'Your business?'

'Yes, I intend to start a business, Emily. Oh no'—he raised his hand and smiled again—'I don't propose to be

508

a boarding-house keeper. No; I'm going to take up tailoring again, set up a tailoring establishment.'

'But you said you didn't like tailoring. That's ... that's why you sold the shop.'

'Yes, I did, Emily. But I've discovered of late that I like tailoring better than farming. And also I've looked around this district recently and there's not a decent tailor's shop within a mile. The demand here may not be for fancy clothes but I've yet to find the man who doesn't prefer a hand-made, well cut suit to a shop bought one, and will go out of his way to buy one. I was looking at next door the other day.' He motioned with his thumb towards the wall. 'If the front room window was enlarged would do very well for a showcase.'

Her hands unfolded themselves in her lap and one moved up to her throat, and then up to her lips, and lastly it covered her eyes and, bowing her head she let out a long, deep moan; and again she was crying as she had done the first day in the house....

He was kneeling by her side now, his arms about her holding her tightly, saying nothing.

He did not speak, even when the paroxysm passed. And she drew herself from his arms and lay back against the chair gasping. But taking his wallet from his inner pocket, he opened it and, withdrawing an envelope, he took from it a narrow folded strip of paper which he smoothed out and held before her face.

She moved her head to the side but her eyes still blinded with tears made it impossible for her to read what was on the paper; and seeing this, he said gently, 'It's a licence, Emily, for whenever you're ready. But not until; it can be arranged to suit you. There's no rush, no rush.'

Again the tears were flowing. And now she got to her feet and walked blindly backwards and forwards on the hearth rug; then stopping all of a sudden, she looked at him, and the next moment she was in his arms. But now she was holding him too, and when her mouth touched his he kissed her with such force that they almost overbalanced. Then they were leaning against the side of the table, their faces close, yet apart, looking into each other's eyes; and she said brokenly, 'I'll ... I'll never forget what you've done for me,' and in answer, he said, 'Emily. Oh Emily! My dearest, dearest Emily. My beautiful Emily, I'll never forget what you're doing for me.' Then closing his eyes tightly he held her to him again and buried his head in her neck. And it was as they stood enfolded in silence that, like the flickering of a picture in a magic lantern, she imagined she saw Sep sitting at the corner of the table and he was looking at her as he had sometime done when she had done something to please him. When Nick's lips reached her mouth again, and she answered the pressure of his embrace, she thought, Sep would have liked you; yes indeed, Sep would have liked you.

THE END

ABOUT THE AUTHOR

Catherine Cookson was born in East Jarrow and the place of her birth provides the background she so vividly creates in many of her novels. Although acclaimed as a regional writer—her novel THE ROUND TOWER won the Winifred Holtby Award for the best regional novel of 1968—her readership spreads throughout the world. Her work has been translated into twelve languages and Corgi alone has over 20,000,000 copies of her novels in print, including those written under the name of Catherine Marchant.

Mrs. Cookson was born the illegitimate daughter of a poverty-stricken woman, Kate, whom she believed to be her older sister. Catherine began work in service but eventually moved South to Hastings where she met and married a local grammar school master. At the age of forty she began writing with great success about the lives of the working class people of the North-East with whom she had grown up, including her intriguing autobiography, OUR KATE. More recently THE CINDER PATH has established her position as one of the most popular of contemporary women novelists.

Mrs. Cookson now lives in Northumberland, overlooking the Tyne.

CATHERINE COOKSON NOVELS
IN GORGI

ORDER FORM

All these books are available at your bookstore or newsagent; or can be ordered direct from the publisher. Just tick the titles you want and fill in the form below.

CORGI BOOKS, Cash Sales Department, P.O. Box 11, Falmouth, Cornwall.
Please send cheque or postal order, no currency.

U.K. Please allow 30p for the first book, 15p for the second book and 12p for each additional book ordered to a maximum charge of £1.29.

B.F.P.O. and Eire allow 30p for the first book, 15p for the second book plus 12p per copy for the next 7 books, thereafter 6p per book.

Overseas Customers. Please allow 50p for the first book and 15p per copy for each additional book.

NAME (Block Letters) ....

ADDRESS ....

....